FAREWELL KISS

Before he realized what she was doing, Neilly stood on tiptoe and kissed Damon's cheek. A sweet, shy kiss, but a bold gesture from a woman he had accused of being a liar. A generous kiss from an impostor who had refused to disclose her identity.

Before she could move away, Damon grasped her arms and pulled her to him. "We can do better than that."

He pressed his lips against hers with no concern for who might see them kissing on the front steps of Rosewood. He took her with his mouth, his hand on the back of her neck to prevent escape. He savored her lips, and teased her tongue, and delved into the corners of her mouth. Her warmth flooded through him. He pressed deeper and pulled her closer, cherishing the soft, round feel of her body against his.

He wanted her to remember forever that he was the man she'd allowed to touch her deepest secret places.

LINDA MADL
BAYOU ROSE

ZEBRA BOOKS
KENSINGTON PUBLISHING CORP.

ZEBRA BOOKS are published by

Kensington Publishing Corp.
850 Third Avenue
New York, NY 10022

First Printing: March, 1996
10 9 8 7 6 5 4 3 2 1

Printed in the United States of America

Acknowledgments

Thanks to all my family, my friends, and my agent for their support and help with this book: especially to Bobbi, Karyn, Libby, Judy, Gina, and Evan. Special appreciation to Sandy M. for serving as a medical resource.

He is a *Voyageur* in the lowlands of Louisiana.
. . . Then they would say.
"Are there not other youths as fair . . . ?
Here is Baptiste Leblanc, the notary's son, who has
loved thee . . .
come, give him thy hand and be happy!
Thou art too fair to be left to braid St. Catherine's tresses."
Then would Evangeline answer . . . "I cannot!
. . . Whither my heart has gone, there follows my hand,
and not elsewhere.
For when the heart goes before, like a lamp, and
illumines the pathway,
Many things are made clear . . ."

from *Evangeline*
—Henry Wadsworth Longfellow

Prologue

May 1850

Defeat swept over Miss Varina Stirling of Rosewood plantation, sapping her strength. With a heavy sigh she dropped the letter she was reading atop the others on the gallery table and slumped back in her chair. It was a hopeless task, absolutely absurd. In her fifty years on this earth she'd never been faced with a chore quite so taxing. It was definitely too much to deal with on a warm spring afternoon.

She glanced across at her sister. "Izzie, how can we possibly know from these letters which lady will bring Damon home to Rosewood for good?"

"We'll know," Isetta said, never taking her eyes from the missive she was reading.

The breeze fluttered her white lace cap and ruffled her gray curls. She waved at the pile of envelopes on the table. "Just look at the responses we received to our advertisement in *The Picayune*. We're bound to find the right girl among these."

She pursed her mouth as she returned to the letter; then she tossed it aside. "No, this one won't do at all. Damon's wife must be a lady of intellect and subtlety. We want someone who will appreciate Rosewood and do it honor."

"And pretty, she must be pretty," Varina insisted with a frown. She couldn't imagine intellect and beauty all wrapped up in one attractive package. Bluestockings were invariably plain. Besides that, they were frequently devoid of style and lacking in grace. And they never knew anything about roses.

"Not necessarily pretty, but alluring, of course," Isetta said, already squinting down her sharp nose and through her spectacles at another letter. "A handsome man like our Damon deserves an attractive lady at his side. That's why we requested a portrait in our advertisement."

Suddenly Isetta dropped the letter into her lap and skewered Varina with that forceful look that always made her uncomfortable—made her squirm as if she'd committed a sin. "You aren't having second thoughts, are you, Sister?"

"Well, yes," Varina said, stirring in her chair. "Damon specifically said that we were not to attempt to match him with any of the local girls. Remember, he said he's not the marryin' kind."

"Oh, we won't choose a local girl," Isetta said, brushing away the concern. "They're all empty-headed social butterflies or Jezebels . . . lightskirts interested in any man with money."

"Honestly, Izzie," Varina gasped. She'd never become accustomed to her sister's frankness. "What I'm trying to say is, Damon seems content as a bachelor."

"Oh, no, he's not," Isetta declared, reaching for yet another letter.

"How do you know?" Varina challenged, unable to dismiss a sense of guilt about meddling in her nephew's life, even if it was for a good cause. "When we see him, he always looks happy."

"Believe me, he's not happy." Conviction rang in Izzie's voice. "He just thinks he is. Men often make that mistake. Gallivanting across the ocean to gamble in England or to waltz in Paris—even fighting Indians in Texas—those are hardly the actions of a happy man. Trust me. Damon needs a loving wife and a home. He needs Rosewood."

"But he doesn't like Rosewood," Varina said, smoothing her rose-sprigged muslin gown over her plump thighs. "He even says so. Just ask him. He always sleeps in the guest house when he is here and only steps foot in the house to dine with us."

Isetta shrugged. "He has let old memories rule his emotions. He simply doesn't realize what Rosewood means to him."

Varina nodded. She wanted to believe that, but even she knew things were never that simple.

"Uncle Cato." She beckoned to the butler, who stood just inside the house in the shadow of the French doors. "Please bring us some more lemonade."

"Yeas, Miss Varina." The aging servant shuffled into the house.

"I know what you're going to say," Isetta said as soon as Cato was out of hearing and Varina opened her mouth. "You're still concerned about Papa's wishes."

"Well, yes," Varina admitted. She glanced through the gallery doors at Thomas Stirling's portrait, hanging inside over the drawing-room fireplace.

The lion-headed patriarch glared back at his daughters from the depths of the room, his steely blue gaze piercing the shadows. On the mantel below Papa's picture his silver flagon glowed in the afternoon light. Varina polished it herself, once a week; care of Papa's only drinking cup was far too important to be left to the servants.

Varina stirred in her chair again. She could hardly believe that Papa had been dead for nearly fifteen years. Sometimes late at night, when the house creaked and groaned, she thought she heard his spirit treading the cypress floorboards of his beloved Rosewood. No, he wouldn't like Isetta's plan at all.

"Papa didn't want Damon to inherit Rosewood."

"But the plantation is ours now to do with as we please,

Varina," Isetta said, still peering over her spectacles. "Papa's will no longer stands. Our attorneys have said so."

"I know."

"More importantly, Sister," Isetta continued, "Papa never knew what we know. Damon has more love for Rosewood in his little finger than Arthur Sitwell has in his entire body."

Varina nodded again. She knew that was true. If their other nephew inherited Rosewood, everything that Papa prized would be lost. Arthur would break up the precious art collection, sell off the land, and spend the money on his easy life in New Orleans. But Damon would hold on to it all out of pure stubborn spite, if nothing else. In his heart, their disinherited sister's son was more like his grandfather than he would ever admit.

"So you see, Sister, we must find a wife to hold Damon at Rosewood," Isetta said flipping through the letters on the table again. "It's the only way for the plantation to survive."

"What if Damon discovers what we are doing?" Varina asked. "He's no fool. We might drive him away."

"That's a chance we're going to have to take," Isetta said. "Let's hope the girl we choose will capture his heart, before he realizes what is happening. Besides being pretty, our choice must have knowledge and appreciation for good art. Rosewood deserves that."

"Yes, indeed it does," Varina agreed. No argument there.

"And she must be charming," Isetta continued. "Sweet and tempting. The flower to Damon's bee. You're the gardener, Varina. You understand that."

Varina stifled a gasp. Isetta's sly glance in her direction confirmed what Varina suspected; her sister took pleasure in shocking her.

"Damon is a passionate man," Isetta went on. "A legacy of his Creole blood. His wife must be a temptation, but—" Isetta thrust a gnarled finger into the air to punctuate her point, "but she must be passionate in return. We'll ensnare him however we can. Sometimes men mistake the arousal of one part of their body for stirrings in their heart."

"Isetta," Varina scolded, a blush rising in her cheeks. She preferred not to think about bodily functions, especially a man's.

"Here's an interesting face." Isetta held up a charcoal sketch that had fallen out of an envelope. The portrait of a young lady seated at a table was done in greater detail and on a better-quality paper than the common New Orleans street artist would use. "What do you think of her?"

Varina took the sketch and held it out at arm's length to better focus on the features of the young lady's face. Inconvenient though it was, Varina refused to spoil her looks by wearing spectacles, as Isetta did. She squinted at the oval face on the paper and noted the broad but beguiling smile. "Not exactly a beauty, but appealing. Why is she holding a pencil and leaning forward on the table like that?"

"I believe it's a self-portrait of Miss Cornelia Ashley Lind," Isetta said, reading the signature at the bottom of the sketch. "I like her looks. There's character in that face, and intelligence. Just what Damon needs in a woman. Let's see what Miss Cornelia has to say for herself?"

Isetta took up the accompanying letter. "She's well-traveled, an art lover and an artist, and—look at this—a graduate of Miss Charlotte Barrows' Academy for Ladies in Charleston. The best. Orphaned, poor dear. But her mother was an Ashley. The Carolinian Ashleys. Excellent! Good family connections without complications.

"Her father was a doctor. Too bad. But she has experience as a companion and a nurse. How perfect! This girl is ideal for our purposes. *Ideal*."

Isetta tossed the letter aside, thumped her hand against her breastbone, and groaned.

14 *Linda Madl*

The violent gesture startled Varina. "What is it, Sister?"

"Why, my heart condition," Isetta said. "I can almost feel the pain coming on right now. I think it's time for me to become ill, don't you? Very ill."

One

Hoofbeats thundered up the drive, annihilating the silence at Rosewood, a silence Neilly had gone to great lengths to establish for her patient.

Annoyed, she closed the copy of Dickens's *David Copperfield* that she'd been reading to Miss Isetta. The dear lady had just drifted off to sleep, and Neilly didn't want her disturbed. In fact, Dr. McGregor had warned against subjecting their patient to any loud scenes or undue surprises.

She heard Uncle Cato open the front door and listened to the clamor of surprised greetings from the servants. Who could it be? Uncle Cato knew to politely turn callers away. Dr. McGregor never arrived with so much furor.

The boom of a deep voice filled Rosewood's entry hall.

"Where is she?" the man demanded. "Is she all right?"

The slam of Rosewood's front door shook the house. The crystals of Miss Isetta's bedside lamp tinkled against each other. Neilly feared the noisy caller storming up the stairs was about to break every one of her rules about peace and quiet. She bolted from her chair to intercept the visitor.

"What was that noise?" murmured Isetta from the bed. Her eyes fluttered open.

"It's all right, dear. Just someone come to call." Neilly comforted the elderly lady with a pat on the shoulder and headed for the door.

Unfortunately, the door burst open just before she

reached it. The sudden draft tugged at her skirts and fluttered the ribbons in her hair. She stumbled backward.

A bear of a man in weather-stained buckskin and dusty fringed boots bore down on her. His force hurtled into the sickroom like a whirlwind. The smell of road dust and sweaty horse swirled in with him.

Neilly had only a moment to take in the breadth of his shoulders, the shock of black hair that fell across his brow, and the dark stubble that defined a stubborn jaw and outlined a sensuous mouth.

Neilly regained her balance in time to block his advance.

She knew of only two men who had the right to charge into the house like family—a nephew from New Orleans and a nephew from Texas. Since Neilly had arrived three weeks ago Miss Isetta and Miss Varina had said little of their New Orleans relative, but they had high praise for their other nephew. From the looks of his dress and manner, this had to be the man, Damon Durande, fresh from Texas.

"Sir, your aunt is very ill and must not be excited." She spoke firmly. "Doctor's orders."

He halted. His dark gaze raked over Neilly, dismissing her as he might a misplaced piece of furniture. Then his gaze came to rest on Isetta Stirling, ensconced in her fourposter bed.

"Aunt Isetta?" Hushed concern filled his deep voice, and the resonance of love in it touched Neilly.

He tried to brush past her, almost shoving her aside, but she wasn't going to have a travel-stained man blustering into the sickroom like the first gust of a hurricane. She had Miss Isetta's health to think of. Neilly planted her feet and resisted his advance.

"Please, sir, I can't have you disturbing Miss Isetta's rest or bringing dust in here."

He glared down at her as if taking note of the gnat blocking his path for the first time.

Neilly stiffened her back and lifted her chin to meet his gaze. "Miss Isetta is very ill."

"Out of my way, ma'am," he ordered, the softness gone from his tone, his dark eyes glinting bright and hard.

"Damon?" Isetta called from her bed. "Is that you? Cornelia, dear, it's all right. Let Damon in."

Neilly hesitated. Miss Isetta's condition was delicate, according to Dr. McGregor. The frail little woman in the white lace bed cap and the frilly lavender bed jacket struggled to sit up. "Damon would never do anything to upset this old lady's heart, would you, dear? Come kiss your ol' auntie."

"Pardon me," Damon said, with a derisive twist of his mouth. He seized Neilly by the arms. She felt her feet leave the floor as he set her aside, out of his path. Helpless, Neilly stared up into his face, but he only had eyes for Miss Isetta.

"Aunt Isetta? What's this Aunt Varina writes about a heart condition?"

"So you did receive the letter." Isetta held out welcoming arms and offered her cheek for Damon's kiss. "Such a long trip from Texas, Damon, but here you are."

To Neilly's wonder, the rugged frontiersman's scowl slowly dissolved into an attentive frown, and he strode softly to his aunt's bedside. With astonishing grace he pushed aside the snowy white mosquito netting and bent to bestow a loving kiss on his aunt's cheek. The ailing lady beamed up at him. For a moment Neilly marveled at the contrast of the huge man, dark and vital, hovering over her pale, tiny patient. Damon eased himself down onto one knee beside the bed and wrapped his strong, tan fingers around his aunt's gnarled hand.

"I saddled up my horse as soon as I received the news," he said.

Isetta shook her head. "Oh, well, leave it to Theo and Varina to dramatize things. It's not all as bad as that. I just feel a little weak now and then. Sometimes there's a fluttering in my chest. Theo calls it palpitations."

Drawn by the concern she saw in Damon Durande's face,
Neilly followed him across the room to be near her patient.
The love the two seemed to share captivated her, and she
lingered in the momentary warmth of its glow to arrange
the lace-trimmed eyelet pillows so Isetta could sit up more
comfortably.

"What else does McGregor say?" Damon suddenly
turned on Neilly. "Where is Doc, anyway? I want to talk
to him."

"Dr. McGregor is due to call this afternoon for tea,"
Neilly said, a little unnerved by the man's piercing regard.
Still bent on getting him and his dust out of the room, she
added, "I'll order a hot bath prepared for you so you can
join us."

Surprise and annoyance flickered in his lustrous brown
eyes. "Aunt Isetta, just who is this lady who seems so determined to be rid of me?"

"Oh, Damon. Do forgive me. Cornelia, my dear, let me
introduce you to our nephew, Damon Durande. Damon, this
is Miss Cornelia Ashley Lind from Charleston. She has consented to be my companion, haven't you, dear?"

"Mr. Durande." Neilly inclined her head. His gaze lingered on her this time in a way that made her finger the
button at the throat of her gray-striped bodice. It *was* fastened, wasn't it?

"Miss Lind," Damon greeted, his voice cold and dry.
"Uncle Cato?"

"Yeas, sah, Master Damon." The butler had followed
Damon into the room.

"Prepare a bath and put my things in the guest house as
usual."

"Yeas sah, right away." Uncle Cato left.

"Oh, Damon, I had so hoped you'd stay near me in Rosewood." Isetta suddenly looked disappointed. "Not in the
guest house."

Damon shook his head. "I'm fine in the guest house,

and I won't disrupt your household. Don't worry about anything, Aunt Isetta. I'll take care of whatever needs to be
done."

"Oh, I knew I could count on you, dear." Isetta beamed
a smile at her nephew, a brilliant, energetic smile that made
her look hardly ill at all.

"Where is he?" Varina cried from the hallway. "Where
is he?" She appeared in the doorway, carrying a basket full
of fresh-cut roses. Her straw gardening hat had been pushed
back on her head and a girlish flush brightened her round
face. "Oh, Damon, my dear, we are so glad to see you."

Damon rose from the bed and bent over his aunt's ex-
tended hand, kissing it in an amazingly genteel gesture.
Neilly couldn't resist admiring the incredibly refined move-
ment of such a large man dressed in buckskins and fringe.
"And how fares the loveliest belle in the South?"

"Oh, Damon." To Neilly's surprise Varina twittered, and
her blush deepened. "I've been counting the days until you
returned to entertain us with your adventures."

"And I have looked forward to telling them to the most
beautiful and attentive audience in all of Louisiana," Damon
said, still holding his aunt's hand.

A glance in Neilly's direction warned her that his unique
charm was about to be cast in her direction. "But you will
excuse me, won't you, Aunt Varina? Miss Lind's presence
continues to remind me that I must make myself presentable."

"Of course, dear," Varina said, turning to her sister. "Did
you hear that, Isetta? Damon has adventure stories to tell
us."

Damon Durande strode to the door, his warm Southern
charm evaporating with each step. "Miss Lind, I want to
see you in the hall."

Neilly followed him, her apprehension growing as he
closed the door behind her.

"How long has she been ill?" he asked without preamble.

"I'm not certain, about four or five weeks, I believe," Neilly said. "I'm certain Dr. McGregor can tell you more."

"How long have you been here?"

"Three weeks yesterday. I arrived from New Orleans on the packet."

"I suppose you replied to an advertisement in *The Picayune.*"

"Why, yes. How did you know?" Neilly said, wondering uneasily what she had done wrong. "I sent a letter in response to their advertisement. They were seeking a companion."

Damon turned away from her, shaking his head. A slight frisson of fear stirred in Neilly. The way Damon had suddenly burst into the quiet world of Rosewood plantation and taken charge could bode ill for her.

"My aunts are charming, generous ladies, Miss Lind," Damon said, his gaze becoming so uncomfortably intense that Neilly had to look away. "Unfortunately, they are prone to being taken advantage of."

Neilly sucked in her breath, wary of the near accusation. "I'm here at their request, Mr. Durande, and they have made me believe that they are quite satisfied with my services."

"I'm sure they are," Damon said, his eyes narrowing as he studied her. "But I'm not certain that someone from outside the parish is the best companion for them."

"Don't you think you should consult with your aunts about that?" Neilly asked, then bit her tongue a moment too late. She needed this position for reasons of her own. The last thing she wanted was to goad Damon Durande into dismissing her.

He eyed her for a nerve-wracking moment longer. She feared he would take in all the telltale details this time: her threadbare sleeves and the frayed lace of her collar. With great effort she resisted the urge to wring her hands.

"Mr. Damon, sah," Uncle Cato interrupted from the top

of the stairs, "Dr. McGregor is here. I showed him into the library. You said you wanted to talk with him."

"Yes, thank you, Uncle Cato." Damon turned back to Neilly. "For the time being, Miss Lind, carry on. But remember, in the future, no matter who is making the rules around here, those rules never apply to me."

"Yes, sir." Neilly gave him a small, cool curtsy. Only when he turned his back and started down the stairs did she allow a sigh of relief to escape her lips.

When Damon walked into the library Dr. Theophilus McGregor turned from the window. His red hair glittered with more frosty gray than Damon recalled from their last meeting two years earlier, but the warmth hadn't gone from the doctor's smile.

"Welcome home, Damon. I'm glad you're here, son. Your Aunt Varina and I have been praying for your arrival every day."

"McGregor." Damon closed the door softly and crossed the room to shake the doctor's hand. The Scotsman was more than the family physician; he was an old family friend. That made him loyal, if not always as objective as Damon would like. "Only just received your letter a few days ago. Why wasn't I informed of this heart condition before now?"

McGregor shook his head in bewilderment. "I swear, Damon, it just seemed to develop over the last month."

"What happened?"

The doctor sat down in a chair beside the library desk. "About four weeks ago Miss Varina sent Elijah for me. Isetta was complaining of pains in her chest. That was the first time I heard of it." He shook his head slowly. "I tell you, it was a shock to me. Your aunt has always been so— well, so vigorous."

Damon sat on the edge of the desk and watched McGregor stare thoughtfully at the Oriental carpet. He realized he wasn't the only one who cared for Isetta. Varina was warm and loving and always a dear, but Isetta was the life of the house, the backbone of the Stirling family. With a glint in her eye and an edge in her voice, she cut straight to the core of any matter. Disconcerting as it was, her frankness made her special to all of them.

"What's the treatment?" Damon asked.

"Rest is about the best thing," McGregor said, looking up at Damon again. "And special medication."

"For how long?"

"Until she gets her strength back," McGregor said. "Usually about eight weeks."

Alarmed, Damon was on his feet again. "It's as bad as that?"

"Not necessarily," McGregor said. "I'm just judging from the rate of her recovery until now. One day she is strong and the next she has no interest in leaving her bed. Spends the entire day with Miss Cornelia reading to her. But overall, I think she is doing well. I can hardly hear anything amiss with her heart, and I hope now that you're home her recovery rate will improve."

"I hope so, too." Damon released a long, deep breath. The weighty fear of losing his aunt eased from his shoulders. Reassured that she wasn't on her deathbed, he moved to the liquor cabinet.

He poured two brandies and handed one to McGregor. Just as he put the glass to his lips, the difference in the library struck him. He set his glass down. "What's been going on in here?"

"It's a nice change, isn't it," McGregor said, smiling at the room. "Miss Lind's doing. Have you met her? She had the heavy old draperies removed for cleaning and decided not to rehang them. Makes the place brighter, doesn't it? And the artwork is so much easier to see and appreciate."

Damon stared around at the light, airy library that he remembered as dark and cavernous. Books lined the walls from floor to ceiling, and the dark velvet draperies that had once hung at the long narrow windows giving the place a shadowy sobriety, were gone.

Now the gold lettering on the book spines glittered in the sunlight. The well-polished rosewood shelves gleamed rich and dark along the walls. Above the Italian marble fireplace the cattle in Constable's painting grazed in the afternoon light.

Such obvious evidence of Cornelia Lind's presence at Rosewood disturbed him somehow. "Just when did this Miss Lind start making changes around here?"

"Soon after she arrived," McGregor said. "I tell you, Damon, she's been a godsend. So efficient. Isetta and Varina took to her right away. Uncle Cato and Cleo jump to do her every request. She hovers over Isetta and runs the house without turning a hair."

"What do we know about her?" Damon asked, taking up his brandy again and sipping uneasily from it. Damon's relief at finding Isetta's condition better than expected drained away.

"Upon my recommendation, they ran an advertisement in one of the New Orleans papers for a companion experienced with heart ailments. Miss Lind applied. Her experience and references were outstanding."

"Wasn't that true about the French maid, too?" Damon demanded, hardly able to keep from glaring at the doctor. "Doc, you know my aunts' history almost as well as I do. Every time they bring someone to Rosewood through an advertisement there's trouble."

Damon saw the look of understanding on McGregor's face. Years ago Aunt Isetta and Aunt Varina had decided they needed a genuine French lady's maid to instruct them in the latest fashions, hair dressing, and such. They wanted to impress the younger ladies in the parish with their sophistication. The lady's maid they'd hired from the advertisement had taught them a few beauty tricks; then she'd made off with the family jewels.

In a dither, Isetta and Varina had sent for Damon, expecting him to rescue the jewels—and he had. For the better part of a week he had prowled the back streets of New Orleans until he'd found the jeweler who had bought the gems. Unfortunately, he'd never found the maid. But he'd managed to learn that she'd been a real maid, all right—but nothing more than an ambitious kitchen maid from a Creole household.

McGregor frowned and nodded. "Aye, I remember the French maid. And I seem to recall a gypsy soothsayer, too."

"Oh, the fortune-teller," Damon groaned. "He had Aunt Isetta and Aunt Varina convinced that he could foretell which years would be best for planting sugarcane and cotton. But the most foolish and costly fraud was the inventor who said he could build a machine to cool fruit for longer storage."

"Aye, now, hold it there," McGregor said, raising his hands in protest, clearly unwilling to hear words spoken against Isetta. "Have some respect for your aunt's ideas, son. The idea of a cooling machine has merit. Even though Isetta is sometimes high-handed and willful, she has some good ideas now and again."

"Well, that cooling machine idea cost her a lot of money," Damon persisted.

"You must understand, Damon, that your Aunt Isetta is something of a visionary," Theo said. "Take my word for it; she can see possibilities where others are blind."

Damon waved his hand toward the library door. "Then what does Aunt Isetta see in Miss Lind?"

"Now, Miss Lind is not to be cast in the same category as the French maid or the soothsayer, Damon." McGregor frowned into his brandy. "Excuse me for my frankness, but I'll be bloody damned if I'll allow Miss Cornelia to be considered as just another in a long line of charlatans at Rosewood. She presented herself to me without any feminine folderol, with good references and a surprising amount of knowledge about caring for heart patients. Cornelia has been exactly what your Aunt Isetta needs."

With that, McGregor drained the premium brandy from his glass.

"Now, Doc, don't take offense." Damon promptly poured a refill for the doctor and himself. He capped the decanter and sat down on the corner of the desk again. "Tell me more about what there is to recommend Miss Lind."

"She is cheerful, sensible, and energetic. She's not afraid of hard work. Look what she's done to this room. What's more, she's something of an art connoisseur, which pleases your aunts. I, for one, am pleased to have her at Rosewood."

"That's an amazing combination of talents." Damon sipped thoughtfully from his own brandy. "She obviously earned your respect. How nice that she is an art lover as well as a nurse. Rosewood is full of treasures; more than any one person knows, I suspect. Paradise for an art connoisseur."

"Meaning what, Damon?"

"Meaning a nearsighted, frog-faced nurse from the parish would put my mind *more* at ease."

"I assure you, there is no such thing," McGregor groused into his glass. "Certainly no one with Miss Lind's expertise."

"That's what concerns me," Damon said.

A knock on the door jolted him out of his speculation regarding Miss Lind. "Come in, Uncle Cato?"

"It's me, gentlemen." Miss Lind peered into the room, her starched muslin skirts rustling against the door. "Do you have everything you need? May I send in Uncle Cato with some food?"

Damon stood up and studied his aunt's nurse closely this time. He'd been too surprised by finding a stranger in the house to scrutinize her earlier.

Setting his brandy aside, he approached the lady ready to find fault but instead found himself gazing down into the bluest eyes—summer bayou blue. She met his gaze in a forthright manner.

As he stopped in front of her a stray tendril of hair fluttered at her temple, and he caught the scent of lilacs about her. Though her rich, coffee brown hair was neatly tied back, lustrous curls languished along a kissable neck. Unexpected desire stirred in his loins. He fancied that if he peeled away her prim-and-proper collar he'd find smooth white shoulders, a pair of delicate collarbones, and lower down—

"You wish for something, Mr. Durande?" She cocked her head and stared back at him.

Damon swallowed the lump of lust in his throat and scowled at the unexpected power of his reaction to her. He wasn't on the frontier any longer, he reminded himself. No gentleman allowed his appetites to become evident. What's more, she certainly didn't need to know that he found her damned attractive.

"Cornelia, my dear." To Damon's irritation, McGregor jumped to his feet, as if he was greeting a lady, not a servant. "How is Miss Isetta today? Any change?"

"Dr. McGregor, hello." Miss Lind shot Damon a look of cool disapproval. "Well, I'm afraid she's not going to get her nap this afternoon, not with the excitement of Mr. Durande's arrival. But seeing him has pleased her very much. She wants to join us in the dining room for dinner tonight."

"Well, now, that *is* a good sign," McGregor said, a cheery smile spreading across his ruddy face. "Your arrival obviously has been good for her, Damon. I hope you're going to stay for a long while."

"I'll stay until she's on the road to recovery," Damon said. He adored his aunts, but he never stayed at Rosewood one moment longer than necessary.

"Good," McGregor said, reaching for his black medical bag.

Miss Lind turned to Damon. "Uncle Cato says your bath is ready and fresh linen is laid out in the guest house whenever you're ready, Mr. Durande."

"Dr. McGregor, please inform Miss Lind that I'm not going to contaminate this house," Damon snapped, annoyed at her renewed determination to get him cleaned up. With a bit of a sneer to rattle her out of her virtuous composure, he added, "With all this talk of baths and fresh linen, if I weren't a gentleman, I might think Miss Lind is showing unladylike interest in my person."

McGregor appeared too aghast to reply.

Miss Lind's polite smile frosted over noticeably. "That's hardly the case, Mr. Durande."

Her eyebrows inched up skeptically as she regarded him from head to toe. "I apologize if I gave the wrong impression. I only thought to offer you the comforts of a hot bath and clean clothes after your long ride. There's no need to bathe on my account."

Her nose wrinkled in distaste. "Of course, if you wish, you may present yourself at dinner in your present state."

Before Damon could think of a suitably scathing response Cornelia Lind closed the door in his face.

McGregor chuckled. "I know what your problem is, son. You've been riding the Texas hills too long. You need to polish the rust off your Southern gallantry."

Damon reached for his brandy glass. "Nonsense, there's nothing wrong with me or my manners. It's Miss Lind who is the problem here."

"Well, I hope you change your mind about that," McGregor said, clapping Damon soundly on the back. "I'll look in on your aunt now. Glad to have you back."

As soon as the door closed on the doctor, Damon poured himself another brandy. He strolled around the room as he sipped the amber liquid, fascinated by the changes. It was almost like a different place: more spacious, no longer a dark, tome-filled chamber, but a bright place where one would want to sit and read. He stopped at the window to survey the room again, and he patted the bust of Plato on the head.

He had always preferred the library over the drawing room, where the portrait of Thomas Stirling glowered down on everyone. Fortunately, Damon's grandfather had left little of himself in the library. His books were silent. They did not glare. They took no sides and gave no allegiances. They never turned their backs when asked questions. They offered answers and demanded nothing.

Now, thanks to Miss Lind, the room was changed. As much as he resented her interference, he had to admit that the library was more inviting than he ever remembered any room of Rosewood being.

McGregor's glowing words about the lady echoed through Damon's head. An art connoisseur. Efficient. A godsend.

Damon shook his head. How dare she sail into Rosewood making changes no one had dared consider before. Rosewood had always been kept just the way his Grandfather Stirling had insisted it be. Grand. Solemn. Dark.

Resentment brought a frown to Damon's lips. But the memory of Cornelia Lind's blue eyes and luscious lips drifted through his head. His loins responded. Swiftly, he drained his brandy glass, taking perverse pleasure in the hot sting that burned down his throat. Truth was, what really bothered him about Miss Cornelia Lind had nothing to do with the changes in the library. He did not like finding her so damned desirable. If he wasn't careful, he'd be as addled over the little minx as his aunts and McGregor were.

To Damon's relief, the dining room was unchanged. Familiar summer-white dimity curtains hung at the windows and the cypress floorboards gleamed butternut brown. Overhead the crystal chandeliers shimmered rainbows across the ceiling and on the white tablecloth below. The mahogany punkah swung lazily, wafting the aroma of Mammy Lula's fresh bread throughout the room.

He had bathed and shaved and properly dressed himself as a gentleman, except for the soft Indian boots he'd refused to give up. He wasn't ready to forego that comfort yet. But he liked the feel of the clean shirt he'd donned, and the snug tailoring of his superfine coat suited him. He sat down at the table feeling like a new man, ready to take on the world and Miss Lind.

"So, Miss Lind, tell me more about yourself," Damon said, peering down the table to where the lady perched.

Her appearance had undergone quite a remarkable change from their meeting earlier in the day.

She had gathered her dark curls over her ears and dressed each cluster with white lace. Instead of the gray-striped muslin gown, she'd put on a pale blue lawn dress with a scooped neckline. Despite his determination to find fault with her, Damon liked the soft, feminine effect. She appeared fair, innocent and ethereal. It was nearly impossible to look upon her and think of any kind of villainy.

"Yes, Cornelia, tell Damon a little about yourself," Aunt Isetta urged from the chair to Damon's right. Aunt Varina sat to his left.

"There's not much to tell, Mr. Durande." Miss Cornelia glanced up at Damon for the first time since she had assisted him in sitting Aunt Isetta at the table. "I'm a doctor's daughter from Charleston."

Something about her clothes stirred Damon's persistent doubts. The quality of the stuff seemed good: He knew expensive lace and fine lawn when he saw it. But the fit was wrong, too snug in the bustline and a little too tight across the shoulders, as if she was about to outgrow the garment. He knew nothing about fashion, but the style of this dress was all wrong: too girlish, too fussy for a woman well beyond eighteen. It was almost as if her wardrobe belonged to another.

"Who employed you before you accepted this position, Miss Lind?" Damon asked bluntly, studying her face.

"An old New Orleans family," she replied without meeting his gaze. He wondered if her refusal stemmed from genuine modesty—or from guilt. "They hired me to nurse a case of lung fever," she added.

"Why did you leave their service?"

She looked up at him at last and smiled angelically. "Why, my patient recovered. Completely, of course. So I was free to come to Rosewood."

"They asked her to stay on to care for the children," Varina explained. "However, they always take the spring waters at Saratoga in the summer and Cornelia didn't want to go north. Isn't that right, my dear? They gave her a very fine reference."

"Yes, that's right." Miss Lind took sudden interest in the shrimp on her plate.

"I see," Damon said, certain something was wrong with her story. Nobody in their right mind spent the summer in New Orleans if they had an opportunity to go elsewhere— away from the heat and the disease. And what was to keep an educated woman from forging her own references? The jewel-thieving French maid had.

"Their loss is our gain, isn't it, Damon?" Varina chirped. "Now, don't be modest, Cornelia dear. Damon must hear all about you. She is an artist and a graduate of Charleston's finest ladies' academy. She's very talented. You should see her drawings."

"You flatter me, Miss Varina." Disarming embarrassment blossomed in Miss Lind's cheeks, and she bent over her plate once more to hide it.

Tantalized by her blush, Damon forgot about his misgivings as a rosy stain brightened her cheeks and spread down her graceful neck and along her delicate collarbones.

Her rosy bloom made a man wonder how much she would blossom and glow when he caressed her secret places. "I'm sure Miss Lind's drawings are delightful," he said.

"Oh, yes, and she's a fine reader with a pleasant voice, and Isetta says Cornelia's back rubs are divine." Varina paused only to catch her breath. "She makes an excellent cup of herbal tea, doesn't she, Izzie?"

"What's more, her mother was an Ashley," Isetta announced, her voice full of pride. "You remember, Damon, the Carolinian Ashleys of Bay Haven. A fine old family."

"Is that so," Damon said, still contemplating the paragon at the end of the table. Miss Lind certainly had connected herself well. The only thing that fascinated his aunt more than a fast-talking inventor was a member of an old, nearly extinct, aristocratic family. That also explained why his aunts insisted on treating Miss Lind like a poor relation rather than a hireling. "I'm impressed, Miss Lind. The list of your virtues seems endless."

"Miss Isetta is too kind, Mr. Durande," Miss Lind demurred, still refusing to meet Damon's gaze.

"Nonsense, Cornelia. And the servants like you—"

"Varina." Isetta's sharp voice halted her sister's babble. Isetta smiled politely. "Sister dear, weren't you going to serve your famous plum wine sauce to accompany the fine ham Mammy Lula has fixed for us?"

"My plum wine sauce?" Varina stared across the table at Isetta. Slowly, she drew her napkin from her lap. "Yes, of course. My plum sauce. It's a favorite of yours, isn't it, Damon?"

"Yes, but you needn't bother—"

"Oh, but I must," Varina protested, rising from the table. She cast Isetta a wary look. "I keep it locked in the kitchen pantry, you know. I'll be right back."

With uncharacteristic resolution, Varina marched from the room like a lady with a mission.

Isetta returned to Damon. "Tell us, dear, are plum sauce and ham served often in Texas?"

"Hardly." Damon chuckled. "More often it's bacon and prickly pear."

Glad to turn the conversation in a more neutral direction, he launched into a humorous commentary about food on the frontier. He spared the ladies the more indelicate aspects, making the most of the ludicrous ones.

Varina returned just as he was concluding the instructions for cooking armadillo.

"There you see, all done," she said, a false brightness in her quavering voice, her hands trembling. She sat down at the table and seemed to need to catch her breath. The two kitchen servants who had returned with her began serving fresh ham steaks with plum sauce ladled over it.

Conversation went on sporadically after that, consisting primarily of pleasantries and compliments about the food. Damon savored the fine fare, the best he had tasted in months. Being back in Rosewood's civilized company had its benefits.

The servants were just removing the last of the supper plates—and he was wondering if there was any fresh tobacco in the humidor in the library—when the plantation bell began to clang, its pealing frantic with urgency.

Varina's head came up instantly.

Isetta cocked an ear toward the sound. "I wonder what that's about. It's too late for the supper bell."

Uncle Cato burst into the room, his frock coat unbuttoned and his neckcloth askew. "Miss Isetta. Master Damon. Fire! Come quick! Fire! Big fire!"

Two

"Slow down, Cato," Damon said, rising from his chair, his fine meal forgotten. "Tell us slowly. Where's the fire?"

In his agitation, Cato wrung his hands and stammered. "It's the guest house, sah. There's smoke. It's boiling up to the sky 'nd big red flames. They is licking out the windas."

"Oh, no!" the ladies at the table cried at once.

"Stay here. I'll see what's going on," Damon ordered, concerned about exciting his aunt. "It's probably just an overheated lamp."

As he left the room he heard Miss Lind instructing Varina to tend to Isetta.

In the yard he found the servants running to and fro, some lugging buckets and others toting shovels.

Damon looked to the guest house, a story-and-a-half white clapboard structure with green shutters and a south-side gallery. Years ago it had been the original plantation house; then, later, it had been converted into an office and guest house when Grandfather Stirling had built Rosewood. Its old, dry timbers burned like dry kindling, sending gray smoke and orange sparks spewing out of the gables.

"Uncle Cato, is anyone in there?" Damon stripped off his coat and loosened his cravat. "Did Mr. Pugh get out of his office all right? He was working when I went in to supper."

"I think Agent Pugh was in the kitchen at supper with the overseer," Uncle Cato said.

"Then get a bucket brigade going," Damon ordered. "Put a good man on the water pump and have another ready to spell him as soon as he tires."

"Yeas, sah." The ancient butler disappeared, moving with surprising speed.

Cornelia Lind appeared at Damon's side as he rolled up his shirtsleeves. "How bad is it?"

"It doesn't look good," Damon answered. "We've got to keep the fire from spreading to any of the other buildings, and I need to get the plantation records out of there, especially the current ones."

"Can I help?"

Astonished, Damon looked down at her standing next to him, so fair, slender, and useless. "Not here, Miss Lind. This is no place for a woman. Just stay out of the way, and keep my aunts from becoming upset."

"But what about the clock in the guest room?"

"Clock? What clock?"

"The Lafayette Commemorative clock. The gold clock on the mantel. It's really quite valuable."

Damon couldn't imagine what she was talking about and turned away as the head groom sprinted past. He ordered the man to bring horse blankets from the stables; then Damon sent a gardener after more buckets.

Miss Lind trailed after him. "The clock is one of only a few made for General Lafayette before the end of the century."

Damon turned on her, resisting the urge to shove her toward the house. "Please go along and see to my aunts, Miss Lind. That's your job."

"Your aunts are fine. I want to help."

"Pugh. Over here." Damon ignored her and motioned to the man who came running from the direction of the kitchen. "I need some help in getting the plantation records out of there."

The agent looked at Damon as if he was speaking in a foreign tongue.

Damon swore silently. Of course he couldn't expect a hireling to risk his life for Rosewood's books, but the man could at least make himself useful. "Join the brigade. I'll go in myself. Where are the books, Pugh?"

Relief relaxed Pugh's strange pointed features. Something too fine and delicate about the man's features made Damon think of the drawback of inbreeding.

"You'll find the current ledger on top of my desk," Pugh said.

Damon grabbed a felt horse blanket from the head groom, soaked it with water carried by the gardener, and pulled the cover over his head.

Everyone started as something inside the guest house exploded and a window shattered. Smoke belched into the sky. Bystanders backed away. Damon swore aloud this time. He didn't exactly relish walking into a burning house.

"Master Damon, you ain't going in there, are you?"

Damon looked around at the huge black man who spoke to him. Elijah was a free man, a carpenter who had earned his freedom but had remained to earn his way at Rosewood.

"Afraid so, Elijah. We need those books."

"Here, you'll need these." The black carpenter shoved the thick leather work gloves into Damon's hand. "I'll go in there for you, sah."

"No, this is my job," Damon said, thrusting his hands into the gloves. "You say the ledger is on your desk, Pugh?"

"Yes, sir, the current record book is on top of my desk," Pugh offered. "Last year's is in the top left drawer."

"What about the clock?" Miss Lind worked her way in between Pugh and Damon. "You'll find it in the guest room on the mantel."

"That damned clock is the least of my worries," Damon snapped and turned away.

As he plunged into the burning office, a wall of heat hit

him. The blanket over his head grew unbearably hot. He could hear the hiss of the water turning to steam. Heat warmed the soles of his Indian boots. Smoke obscured his vision and stung his eyes, but he kept moving forward toward the far side of the room where he remembered Pugh's desk sat. He tripped over a burning piece of furniture. Sparks and flames flared up into his face. He winced and waved away the heat and cinders with the wet blanket, then stumbled on until he reached the desk.

Through the smoke he spotted the ledger, its cloth cover smoldering. Thank heavens he had Elijah's gloves. He wanted last year's accounts also, but the desk drawer refused to open. Heat had swollen it shut. Damon braced a booted foot against the desktop and hauled on it again. On the third try it yielded. He managed to get the drawer open enough to work the ledger out. With a book in each hand, Damon charged back toward the office door. Halfway across the room, the ceiling woomphed into flames, and Damon threw himself out the opening.

Elijah caught him and dragged him clear of the flames. Pugh took the books. Cursing and coughing, Damon threw the steaming hot blankets to the ground and gulped the cool evening air.

"Lord, Elijah," Damon swore. "If I never have to go into another burning building again in my life, it'll be too soon."

Elijah thumped him on the back. "Yeas, sah. I knows the feeling."

Uncle Cato appeared, dancing up and down in great agitation.

"She went in, Master Damon," the butler cried. "Went right in the other door with a blanket over her head. Just like you."

"Who?" Damon demanded, an uneasy feeling creeping over him. He'd never seen stately Cato so excited.

"The fire's worse now. She'll never get out, Master Damon. You've got to go after her."

"For God's sake, Cato, calm down and tell me who."

"Miss Cornelia! She done went in after that clock."

For a moment Damon stared at the blistering blaze in disbelief. The pretty girl in blue lawn and lace had dared to venture into that roaring inferno? For a clock? He glanced up at the flames licking treetop high now. Another upstairs window popped from the heat. Each bucket of water the brigade tossed onto the fire sizzled into vapor.

Damn Miss Cornelia Lind. He cursed in profanities he hadn't used for years. The little fool. Was she bent on committing suicide? Her skirts would be aflame the instant she stepped inside the door. Even with her willowy height, she wasn't big enough to push her way past burning furniture or blazing beams. He couldn't stand there and let her throw her life away for a cursed clock.

Damon grabbed the blanket and, without a word, Elijah soaked him with water again. There was no time to lose.

As Damon approached the guest house this time, the heat beat against his cheekbones and singed his brows, forcing him to duck low as he forged his way inside. Behind him something crashed to the floor. Smoke and flames billowed through the room. Sparks whirled around like a storm, leaving him momentarily disoriented.

Damon turned to get his bearings in spite of the searing heat and smoke. Where would she be? The mantel. She'd said the damned clock was on the mantel.

He shielded his eyes against the heat and peered in that direction. He'd only taken a few steps when he stumbled over a blanket-covered form kneeling on the floor.

"Cornelia?"

"I have it!" she shouted up at him over the roar of the blaze. "I have the clock."

"I don't care what the hell you have!" Damon shouted back. "We're getting out of here."

He grabbed under her arms from behind. "Leave it."

"No, not now!" she cried, struggling to her feet with an

object slightly smaller than a picnic basket clutched against her breasts. She lost her balance, stumbling against him as she fell. Live cinders swirled around them.

"I'm not leaving it after I got this far," she shouted over the crackling fire.

Damon pulled her to her feet again and turned toward the door. A burning beam blocked the way.

"We'll try for the window. Give me that thing."

"No, I'll carry it!" she said, clutching the timepiece as if it were the Holy Grail. "You lead the way."

Damon wasn't going to argue with her. The heat and smoke suffocated him, making it almost impossible to breathe. With a curse he bent down, hooked an arm under her knees and swung her—and the damn clock—into his arms.

As he started for the window on the far side of the room, another ceiling beam fell. It struck him against the shoulder, nearly throwing him and his burden to the floor. Pain shot through his arm and down his back. Damon groaned and staggered, but he managed to maintain his grip on the woman in his arms and to regain his balance. Cornelia clung to him, her arm tight around his neck.

Then the thumping began. Damon couldn't make out what the sound was. He suspected the main beams of the house were about burned through and the second story would come down on them anytime. But he knew that the opening ahead was their only chance for escape. As he neared it, he realized someone was hacking away at the window. From behind he heard the rending screech of another burning beam crashing to the floor. Damon plunged toward the window, throwing himself and Cornelia in the direction of daylight and fresh air.

Strong hands grabbed at them both, dragging them clear of the flames.

Damon sank to the ground beside Cornelia, gasping for the cool, clean air his lungs craved; then he coughed, chok-

ing on the ash in his throat. Gradually he became aware of
Elijah standing over them, staring up in dismay at the
flames. All that remained of the guest house was timbers,
black against the angry red flames. The heat had forced the
bucket brigade to retreat, each member gazing up at the
bright flames in defeat.

Cornelia lay beside Damon on the grass, coughing and
choking. "We saved it. We saved it," she mumbled in a
voice scratchy from the heat and smoke. She crawled to
her knees, with no concern for her tattered skirts or her
soot-smudged cheeks.

Tenderly, she unwrapped the bundle she had lugged from
the flames. As the blanket fell away, Damon stared at the
clock. For as long as he could remember, the gold-footed
timepiece with a toga-draped woman leaning against its face
had sat on the guest-house mantel, ticking away softly, col-
lecting dust.

Cornelia Lind proudly polished soot off the glass-covered
clock face and wiped the ash off the gold-wrought woman.

Cornelia sat back on her knees. "Aren't you pleased?"

Damon peered at the clock, trying to discover what was
so special about it that a young woman would risk her life
for it.

Cornelia gaped at him, obviously incredulous that he
didn't appear gratified. "Don't you know how valuable this
clock is? Only a few exist in the world. Your grandfather
must have been very proud to receive such a gift from General Lafayette."

"No doubt Grandfather was proud of it," Damon said,
with a shrug that didn't dispel his rising irritation. Grandfather Stirling was always overly attached to the pieces of
his collection. "But it's only a damned clock."

Cornelia's mouth dropped open. "Well, if that's how you
feel, why did you go in after it?"

"I went in after *you,* you little fool," he snapped, getting
to his feet and brushing the soot from his hands. Did she

really need to be told? "Only because I've gotten the distinct impression that I'd never hear the end of it from my aunts if I'd let you burn."

Varina clung to the white dimity curtains at the dining-room windows and peered out at the raging fire. She could hardly believe what a terrible monster the conflagration had become.

"Have they come out yet?" Isetta demanded from her invalid's place at the table. "What can you see, Varina?"

"Oh, Izzie, the roof is caving in and the flames are as tall as the trees." Varina bit her lip and fought the tears that threatened. "Mercy, why did I agree to your terrible plan? "I'll never forgive myself if . . . No, no. There they are. Damon with Cornelia in his arms." Varina took a great gulp of air to ease the terror gripping her heart. "Oh, thank God, they're both all right."

"You're certain they're all right?" Isetta asked, tapping her cane on the floor with impatience.

"Yes, Damon is setting Cornelia on her feet. Oh, Izzie, I'd never forgive myself if they'd been—"

"The accounts, I should have known Damon would go after them," Isetta muttered. "But who would have anticipated that Cornelia would dash into a burning building?"

Varina ignored her sister's grumbling as the last guest-house timbers collapsed in a spiraling storm of sparks.

"Of course, you realize they were never really in any danger," Isetta added with a sniff. "Damon is perfectly capable of handling the situation."

"I know, but Izzie, the guest house is completely gone. Burned to the ground," Varina wailed, her eyes brimming with tears again as the true measure of their loss took shape.

The fire had been so much fiercer than she'd envisioned, so much brighter, hotter, and angrier. When she had agreed to set the blaze she'd somehow imagined creating cheerful flames, like a bright Christmas bonfire. but tonight the inferno had licked up into the sky, roaring like an awful monster unleashed on all of them.

The monster had devoured the guest house: their childhood hideaway, a place for stashing treasures and for sneaking peeks at the forbidden picture books they had stolen from the library.

Still later Damon had lived in the guest house, growing from boyhood into youth, then into the tall young man who had ridden away from Rosewood—forever, they had feared. The little house that held so many memories, happy and sad, was gone.

Desolate, Varina sobbed. "Nothing's left but red-hot cinders and ash."

"I'll have no tears from you now, Sister." Isetta sternly rapped the silver handle of her cane on the table. "Indeed, sometimes we must build on ashes. We're only assisting fate. What are Cornelia and Damon doing now? He's taking care of her, isn't he?"

Varina pushed the curtains aside once more. "Damon is picking up something. It's a clock. Papa's memorial clock. He looks angry, Izzie. Oooh, very angry. I'm afraid your plan might not be working."

"Of course he's angry," Isetta said. "Despite his unfortunate parentage, Damon is a true Stirling, you know. He hates to lose at anything, even at fighting a fire. This plan will work. You'll see, Sister. I brought him home from Texas, didn't I?

"Now, Varina, go out on the gallery and call them in here." Izzie tapped her cane again. "Lord, I hate playing the shut-in."

Varina stepped through the dining-room doors, prepared to do Izzie's bidding. But when she saw Damon and Cornelia—clothing tattered, hair singed, and faces smudged—she forgot all about summoning them. A sob rose in her throat, and with a cry of relief, she threw her arms around these two dear people.

"My dears, are you all right?" Varina sobbed first against Cornelia's shoulder, then against Damon's broad chest. "Do we need to send for Dr. McGregor?"

"We're fine," Damon assured her, shifting the clock under one arm and supporting her with the other. Gratefully, she leaned against him.

"No reason to trouble Dr. McGregor," Cornelia said, "though I'm concerned about how Miss Isetta is taking the excitement." She hurried ahead. Claude Pugh followed, carrying two enormous ledgers, one tucked under each arm.

When Damon and Varina stepped into the dining room Cornelia, face smudged with soot, was already at Izzie's side. "How are you feeling, Miss Isetta? Any hint of palpitations? Do you need your medication?"

"No, I'm fine." Isetta dismissed Cornelia with a wave of her hand. "Sit down and rest yourselves. Cleo is bringing warm water and towels. How bad is the damage?"

Damon placed the clock on the dining-room table with a resounding thump.

"We've lost the guest house, but with Elijah's help I saved the plantation account books." With exasperation Damon added, "Of course, Miss Lind saved the clock."

Everyone turned to look down the table at Neilly, who stood at Isetta's side.

"Well, it's not just any clock," Neilly snapped. Dismissing the barbed tone in Durande's voice, she seized Miss Isetta's wrist to take the lady's pulse. She found it was strong and regular, if a little rapid. Nothing to be concerned about.

"I'd forgotten about the Lafayette clock," Isetta said. "I remember Father was very fond of that old timepiece. I think he put it in the guest house to impress visitors."

"You mean you didn't remember the Lafayette clock was in there?" Neilly asked in disbelief as she released Miss

Isetta's wrist. "You forgot about a clock especially made for General Lafayette to give to his hosts during his last trip to the United States? It must be one of only a dozen in the world. And it's a great honor to possess one."

"Yes, I know dear, but there are too many odd things like that around the house to keep account of all of them." Isetta gave an indifferent shrug. "We are grateful that you thought of the clock. Here's Cato with the brandy."

The clock was forgotten as Cato carried in a silver tray laden with the brandy decanter, the sherry carafe, and glasses. At his elbow Cleo stood, holding a washbasin and towels.

"Excellent suggestion." Damon took up the sherry carafe. "I think a bracing drink is just what the ladies and I need to settle our nerves. Don't you think that's wise, Miss Lind?"

"Yes, a wise idea," Neilly agreed, satisfied that Miss Isetta wasn't unduly upset.

When Damon had finished pouring sherry for the ladies he liberally splashed brandy into two snifters for himself and Mr. Pugh, who had settled into a chair next to Varina.

"I wonder what started the fire?" Neilly asked out of idle curiosity. She knew that plantation kitchens burned frequently. A guest house catching fire was a more unusual event.

"I'm sure I don't know." Pugh lurched to his feet, as if he thought he was being accused. "I hadn't lit the office lamp yet. And I haven't had a fire in the hearth for days."

"The fire could have started any number of ways," Damon said with easy calm.

"That's right." Pugh nodded and sat down again.

"Maybe a live cinder from the kitchen chimney," Isetta suggested. "Or a spark from the blacksmith's fire."

Varina jumped to her feet. "Oh, Damon, forgive me. I'd never be able to live with myself if anything had happened to you or Miss Lind. I really . . ."

Before Varina could say more, Neilly saw Isetta catch her sister's eye with a forbidding frown.

Varina ducked her head. "I mean . . . I can't imagine how the fire started." She sat down abruptly.

"It's no matter now," Isetta said, waving the issue away with her empty sherry glass. "But the loss of the guest house does present us with some problems. There is no office or bed for Mr. Pugh and, of course, no place for our Damon to sleep."

"I'll move into the rooms over the kitchen," Damon offered.

"Never, not with summer around the corner." Isetta spoke in her I-will-brook-no-argument voice, which Neilly was beginning to recognize. "What would the neighbors think? Damon Durande living above the kitchen like a hireling.

"Mr. Pugh, I think you can work in the library and sleep in one of the attic rooms," Isetta ordered. "The one on the north side of the house is quite pleasant. And, Damon, we will move you into the guest room on the east corner."

Varina's head came up slowly. The room grew silent and expectant.

Damon thumped the heavy cut-glass snifter down on the table. "You know I never sleep under Rosewood's roof."

His voice was so harsh, Neilly started, and she looked around to catch Varina and Isetta exchanging an uneasy glance once more.

"Cornelia, dear. Mr. Pugh. Would you excuse us please?" Isetta folded her hands in her lap and pursed her mouth. "We have certain family matters to discuss."

Neilly cleared her throat. "Miss Isetta, because of your condition I'm afraid I must insist on remaining in the room. I keep confidences just as a doctor does."

Isetta hesitated, and for a moment Neilly thought the older lady was going to order her from the room anyway.

"Very well. Perhaps you *should* remain." Isetta turned to

Damon again as Claude Pugh took his leave. "Damon, I think it's time to forget the past and let go of old attitudes."

Neilly watched Damon's face darken. His jaw hardened and his broad shoulders stiffened. He didn't need a face dark with stubble to once more look like the great bear of a man who had first charged into Isetta's sickroom. Warily, she clutched Isetta's cool dry hand.

"We're not merely talking about old attitudes, Aunt Isetta. My grandfather ordered me out of this house, if you remember? He told me and you and anyone else within hearing that day that I was never to sleep under Rosewood's roof."

"What a long memory an eight-year-old boy can have." Isetta sighed and stroked the white tablecloth with her free hand.

"Do you remember what I told him?" Damon asked.

"As I recall, it was something to the effect that it would be a cold day in Hades before you slept under Rosewood's roof again," Isetta said and sighed. "You always were an articulate child."

"I have always honored my grandfather's *request.*" Damon's dark eyes glittered. "It is the Creole way to respect the wishes of one's elders."

"Don't be impertinent, Damon." Isetta tapped her cane on the floor. "It's also the Stirling way to respect the wishes of one's elders. Your grandfather could never forgive his oldest daughter for marrying a Creole. We all knew his opinion of Creoles. Irresponsible, frivolous, idle. Every time he saw you, Damon, it reminded him of Rosalie's defiance."

"So he refused to ever look at me."

Neilly heard the anger and the challenge in Damon's words. Strangely, she could also imagine the wounded boy deep inside the angry man before her.

"But your grandfather has been dead for fifteen years," Isetta pointed out without taking her gaze from her nephew.

"Rosewood is our house now, Varina's and mine. You are welcome here."

Damon shook his head. "Dr. McGregor will put me up."

"Theo?" Surprise and outrage filled Isetta's voice. "Acorn Hill is nearly an hour's ride from here."

"That's nothing. I can ride it in less time if necessary."

"Well, it's something to me when my own flesh and blood refuses Rosewood hospitality," Isetta said, nearly rising from her chair.

"Miss Isetta, please don't excite yourself," Neilly urged, patting the older woman's hand to calm her. She shot Damon a warning look.

Damon turned his back on them all.

"Just suppose I have an attack." Isetta pressed the back of her hand to her chest. "Goodness, I can feel the palpitations coming on."

Fearful her patient might be about to swoon, Neilly put an arm around Miss Isetta.

Damon turned slowly, anxiety etching his features.

Isetta closed her eyes and continued, with her hand now pressed to her brow. "I hate to think that I might be racked with pain, struggling to breathe, needing you to be here *under the same roof* to see to things. But where will you be? Hours away because of some silly, stubborn grudge you've put ahead of your old aunt's welfare." She sighed heavily. "The thought is almost enough to make me give way to my failing body."

"Does my aunt truly need me close at hand?" Damon demanded of Neilly. He leaned across the table, his eyes alight with anger, suspicion, and touching concern that made Neilly go soft inside.

Puzzled by Isetta's conflicting symptoms, Neilly gulped and stammered. "Her pulse is very strong but rapid. I don't really expect anything to happen suddenly, but—"

When Neilly faced Isetta she found her patient glaring back with sharp disapproval. Even sweet Varina scowled at her from across the table. The uneasy realization dawned on Neilly that she was caught in some crossfire she didn't understand. She shifted in her chair, glanced up at Damon again, and chose the safe way out. "But it is difficult to anticipate developments in precarious cases like this."

"See there, Damon?" Isetta crowed, tapping her cane on the table. "Precarious. My case is *precarious*. Miss Cornelia says so, and I'm sure Theo agrees."

"Precarious?" Damon glared at Neilly for confirmation.

Isetta suddenly grasped Neilly's hand so tight she thought the older woman was going to wring it off.

"Yes, precarious," Neilly repeated. Isetta released her and blood flowed back into her fingers.

"All right." Damon threw up his hands. "I'll stay, but only if I can have the rooms over the kitchen."

"Oh." Varina gave a disappointed gasp.

Isetta slumped in her chair. "The kitchen rooms then. I have no more strength to argue with you, Damon. At least you'll be on the grounds. I'll be grateful for that. Cato, have Mammy Lula get the kitchen rooms ready for Master Damon."

"Yes um." Cato took up the silver tray and turned to go. "Hope you don't mind, Master Damon, but this is gonna take a while. We just laid in a big batch of food stuffs and we'll have to find a new place for them." The old servant sighed wearily. "Might take most of the night. But we don't mind, sah. Don't trouble yerself about it. We mighty glad to have you home."

"All night?" Damon shook his head and cursed under his breath. "All right. All right. Forget the rooms over the kitchen. I'll stay in the house."

Varina clapped her hands in pleasure. Damon shot her a quelling frown.

"Don't be too pleased about this, Aunt Varina," Damon drawled, a hint of Texas slipping into his speech. "This just might be enough to make Grandfather Stirling roll over in his grave."

The crystal goblets on Cato's tray began to rattle.

The blood drained from Varina's face.

"Oh, Damon, don't even joke about such things around Varina," Isetta scolded. "You know how superstitious she is. Personally, I like to think that Father has the good sense to leave managing worldly affairs to the living."

Three

After Isetta was settled in bed Neilly carried the Lafayette clock into the drawing room and placed it on the Italian marble mantel.

"Well, Thomas Stirling, here is your Lafayette clock," she said aloud, aware that the painting was her only audience.

She brushed a smudge of soot from the glass-covered face. Then, taking up her lighted candle, she stepped back to admire the arrangement. Next to Thomas Stirling's silver goblet and below the Andrew Jackson sword, the clock squatted on the mantel, steadily ticking away, as if fiery annihilation had never threatened it. Varina would polish all the mantel items tomorrow, Neilly knew, and the old time-piece would gleam once more in a place of honor.

"I suppose it was silly of me to go into the burning building," she said. Damon Durande's derisive words about saving the clock still smarted. "But saving the clock seemed the least I could do for your daughters. They've been so kind to me. I just didn't expect the thing to be so heavy."

By the time she'd realized how difficult the clock was to carry the flames were licking at her skirts and hissing at the edge of her wet blanket. There was nowhere to turn, no shelter from the heat. Confused and hopeless, she'd sunk to the floor, wondering in an oddly detached way if she would shrivel to a cinder in the heat or swell up and burst like a roasted chestnut. In either case, at least she'd never have to face Charles Ruffin and his vengeful family again.

Suddenly Durande stood over her, dragging her to her feet with a grip so strong that she knew he would never relinquish her to the fire.

The odd thing was, only minutes earlier at the dining table, he'd quizzed her as if she were some kind of criminal. Arrogant and elegant in his blue frock coat and snowy white cravat, he'd questioned her every answer. Then, amid the timbers crashing down around them, he'd risked his life to pull her from the fire.

She had never doubted for an instant that if Damon could find a way in, he would find a way out. Why he deserved such faith she didn't know. But now she owed him a word of thanks, if not more.

She held her candle a little higher to better inspect the portrait of Rosewood's patriarch over the fireplace. From the shadows Thomas Stirling stared back at her, his mouth set in a harsh line and his aristocratic nose sharp against the green willow backdrop.

"So you banished your oldest grandson from the house," Neilly said, scrutinizing the portrait a little closer, searching for a hint of softness in the angular face and the stone gray eyes. "That seems a harsh judgment against a boy who couldn't help what his parents did."

No answer came, of course. She was talking aloud to mere pigment on canvas. Yet she was disappointed to find no compassion in Thomas Stirling's face.

"Is it possible that a man who loved beautiful things carried no charity in his heart?" Neilly asked aloud. "You were Miss Isetta's and Miss Varina's father, and they are the sweetest pair of ladies I've ever met."

Thomas Stirling's portrait remained silent.

Neilly expected no answer, of course. The man was long dead. But she had taken such an instant liking to the Stirling sisters—and to Rosewood—that she wanted desperately to find something redeeming in the plantation's patriarch. The portrait offered none.

She shook off her disappointment. Her first feelings of recognition and affection for Rosewood had not worn off. The intensity of them still made her marvel when she recalled the first moment she'd seen the house from the river.

It had been early evening when she'd sighted the graceful white columns of the plantation house from the deck of the riverboat. That first glimpse of Rosewood, soaring templelike at the end of the green cathedral of trees, had been like discovering the home she'd been searching for all her life. She'd found her haven.

Her hands had itched to capture on paper Rosewood's familiar beauty. The overwhelming urge had nearly sent her digging through her luggage for her drawing materials. But fear kept her at the railing. Fear that if she looked away from the magic sanctuary, it would disappear and her new retreat would be lost forever. She scolded herself silently for such a silly notion but remained at the railing just the same, studying details and admiring lines.

Rosewood basked in the last of the day's light, its wide gallery shaded and peaceful. When she stepped through the front door she felt welcomed, almost as if the house had been awaiting the sound of her footsteps in the hall. At last she'd found the home she'd lost.

From that day nothing had changed the sense of recognition and warmth she'd known when she'd walked through the front door—not even the jungle she'd found inside.

She smiled at the memory of her first view of Rosewood's exotic entry hall, decorated with a hand-painted wallpaper jungle. Rosewood might be legendary for its collection of precious artifacts and art, but for Neilly nothing surpassed the jungle looming in the front hall and up the stairwell.

She'd had to tip her head back to see it all. Tall trees stretched to the ceiling, two stories above, with garishly striped boa constrictors wound around the slender trunks. Hissing snakes menaced from the cover of the foliage, while bright, exotic birds flew in a cloud-studded sky. Brilliant parrots and peacocks perched in the trees, almost hidden by the greenery. Between tree limbs brown monkeys swung over the heads of the solemn-faced orangutans below.

The best part, Neilly thought, was the lions. On either side of the library door a pride of lions—nearly shoulder high—crouched like ready guards, their hungry yellow eyes glued on any who dared to enter. Whether you approached the door from the left or the right, or even straight on, the beasts' eyes followed.

Varina, in a rare confidence, had admitted to Neilly that she'd been terrified of those lions all her life. But Isetta, always their father's favorite, had refused to have them removed, even after Thomas Stirling's death.

"The lions give you away, Thomas Stirling," Neilly said, shaking a finger at the patriarch's picture. "Shame on you. I have no doubt you loved the terror those lions inspired in the children and servants. You enjoyed the wide eyes and the hurried footsteps when the household passed your door."

Poor, gentle Varina, Neilly thought as she stood in the drawing room, staring up at the portrait. And Damon? Had the eight-year-old banished from the house been frightened of the lions? Not likely, she thought. She doubted little frightened the man from Texas.

Determined to find a glimmer of benevolence in Thomas Stirling's visage, Neilly peered closer. Perhaps the absence of humanity in the man's face was the fault of the artist, but somehow she didn't think so. The face in the portrait glowered back, the glint in his eyes scornful enough to convince her that he'd dismissed his orphaned grandson from the house.

Unfazed, Neilly drew back a step to better view the old man's whole countenance. "Unfair or unjust though it may be, I must admit, Thomas Stirling, you old tyrant, we agree on one thing: I, too, wish Damon Durande hadn't returned to sleep under Rosewood's roof. He asks far too many questions. Ones I dare not answer."

* * *

Cleo wrapped the thick towel around Neilly's head and dried her hair with a vigor that almost made Neilly dizzy.

"There now, Miss Neilly, you don't smell of smoke no more," Cleo said.

"Yes, thank you, that's much better," Neilly agreed, feeling refreshed yet exhausted after her hot bath.

Early in her work as a nurse and companion Neilly had discovered that her role in a household was sometimes difficult to reconcile. Servants often resented her, seeing her as an outsider who threatened their carefully balanced domestic hierarchy. Vexed servants could make life trying in a thousand little ways—cold food, misplaced laundry, disappearing button hooks. But that had never been a problem at Rosewood. From the first day she'd been accepted with a generosity and graciousness she found a blessing and a comfort. It made her feel at home.

"Has Mr. Durande been moved into his room?" she asked, still concerned about the things she needed to see to before she fell into bed.

"Now don't you fret none about that, Miss Neilly," Cleo said. "He's all settled in the room just down the hall. Him and all his clothes. Ain't it a stroke of good luck that his clothes and things was in the wash house. Mr. Pugh's things, too. Hardly nothing serious was burned up a'tal."

"Is that so?" Neilly said. What an interesting coincidence. "Is Miss Varina in bed?"

"Yes, ma'am, nothing to worry about there neither," Cleo said, helping Neilly into her wrapper. "Miss Varina took brandy in her warm milk this evening, too. More than you recommended. But that's to be expected, don't you think, with all the excitement?"

"Yes, it's to be expected." Neilly tied the sash of her wrapper and accepted her hairbrush from Cleo.

"It'll be different having Master Damon under this roof,"

Cleo continued as she went about tidying the room and turning down the bed. "But, lawdy, we're glad to have him back. He never lets his aunties down when they need him."

"Very admirable," Neilly said, wondering how she could gain Damon Durande's confidence so that he'd ride off to Texas again. "Thank you for your help, Cleo."

When the maid was gone Neilly strolled out onto the gallery, brushing her damp hair to dry it. Thoughts of Damon had ousted her exhaustion.

After the events of the day the evening seemed quiet, serene; even the crickets' chirps were subdued. An occasional bullfrog harrumphed in the night, counterpointed by the hoot of an owl. A few stars twinkled in the sky above, but on earth the night air carried the smoky scent of the recent fire.

Neilly sniffed it with regret. Odd, wasn't it, how she already felt as if Rosewood's loss was hers also? She was a part of the plantation now—or as close as she could hope to be— and she wasn't going to give up her place because the prodigal grandson, Damon Durande, had come home.

A heavy footfall made Neilly jump guiltily. Almost as if Damon Durande had been drawn by her thoughts, he came out onto the gallery at the other corner of the house. The candlelight from his room limned his white shirt, his dark trousers, and the soft buckskin of his Indian boots. His back was turned to her as he leaned over the railing to look down into the shadowy garden where the white marble statues posed like frozen ghosts.

As Neilly watched, he absently reached up to rub his shoulder. The blow he had taken as he had struggled to save them from the guest-house inferno must be paining him.

"Maybe you should let me have a look at that," Neilly said, her professional concern popping out before she thought about the consequences.

Startled, Damon turned. "What?"

Too late, Neilly realized that she wore only a nightgown

and an old wrapper. Her damp hair hung down her back in aggravatingly childish curls. She'd always avoided taking a position in households where men resided just to prevent awkward scenes like this one. Her state of dress was entirely improper, but she could not retreat without looking foolish. She was glad of the distance and darkness between them.

"Your shoulder seems to be bothering you, and I thought maybe I should look at it. Or perhaps in the morning Dr. McGregor . . ."

"It's nothing really," Damon said, rubbing his shoulder again. "Just aches a little."

"Is it a bruise or is the pain in the joint?"

"I think it's a bruise," he said, dismissing the injury.

"Well, I wanted to thank you for saving my life," Neilly said, aware of how awkward she sounded. "I wasn't very appreciative at the time, but I wanted you to know that I understand that you came after me at great personal peril."

He eyed her in silence for a moment. "I thank you for having such concern and interest in Rosewood and its treasures. Few others would have shown the care you did."

Neilly knew he was speaking of Pugh's lack of enthusiasm in helping to fight the fire. "It seemed the least I could do since your aunts have been so kind and generous to me. Rosewood holds so many things that would be a tragedy to lose."

"Yes, many things," Damon said, a vague cryptic tone to his voice.

"The cross-stitched fire screen worked by Martha Washington," Neilly began, always a little awed by what the Stirlings lived with and took for granted every day. "The Chickering piano. The rare Shakespeare portfolios. The Andrew Jackson sword. Is there an inventory of these things?"

Damon shook his head. "Not that I know of."

"I could do that," Neilly offered, intrigued by the possibility of discovering even more treasures in the house. "I mean, along with my other duties, of course, I could draft an inventory. Every house this size should have one."

"I suppose so," Damon said. "I never thought about it." He winced when he attempted to lift his arm again. Neilly could see from his frown that he was in a good deal of discomfort.

"Sometimes a good massage can ease sore muscles." This time she almost clamped her hand over her wayward mouth. Where was her seemliness? She'd given many massages to women. Except for her father, she'd never touched a male so intimately.

"What?" Damon's face was indistinct in the darkness, but the edge of pain in his deep voice gave her courage. "Why does a massage help?"

"I'm not sure. I think it's a matter of working the knots out of the muscles. My father had a bad shoulder—from an old buggy accident injury—and I used to rub it for him often."

"Come closer," Damon said, beckoning her toward him. "I don't like shouting down the gallery at you."

Neilly hesitated, sorry now that she'd offered the massage. She wasn't even certain that she'd be able to ease his discomfort, as she'd said. On the other hand, she owed him her life, and any relief she could offer him seemed the least she could do.

Tugging her wrapper closer about her throat, she started to close the distance between them.

"That's better," he said when Neilly reached the doorway to his room. In the lamp light pouring onto the gallery she glimpsed the hint of a smile on his lips for the first time—a charming lopsided grin. It unnerved her a little. "You look much better without soot smudged across your face. Now what's this about a massage?"

"Well, I was simply explaining how . . ." Under his scrutiny a foolish blush warmed Neilly's face, but she forged on, praying that the darkness hid her glowing cheeks.

". . . how doctors have discovered and midwives hav
known for some time that massage can be beneficial t
some injuries and muscle cramps."

"I see."

"I'm not certain what your injury might be." Neilly wer
on without taking a breath, "But I suppose that falling tim
ber might have bruised your shoulder and I must say . . .

"Yes?" He sat down on the balustrade so the light fron
his room fell on his face. He gingerly folded his arms acros.
his chest, his shoulders pulling the linen of his white shir
taut across his shoulders. The half-buttoned garment gaped
open at his throat, revealing dark curly hair and solid muscles underneath. Lazily, he stretched out his long legs toward her, the dark nankeen of his trousers clinging to his
well-shaped thighs.

Words deserted Neilly, leaving her mysteriously tongue-
tied. She tucked her hands into her wrapper sleeves for wan
of anything else to do with them. "About your shoulder?"

He faced her again. "Yes, do you want to examine my
shoulder?" He began to pull his shirttail out of his trousers,
as if he was going to undress right there. "Shall I take off
my shirt?"

"No, that's not necessary," Neilly stammered, holding up
her hands in protest. "Just turn around. I think I can feel
the extent of the injury through the fabric."

"How very intriguing." He stood, casting her that sar-
donic lopsided grin again, then turned as she asked. Female
patients were so much easier to deal with than men, Neilly
decided with irritation.

She reached for his shoulders but realized before she laid
her hands on him that she could not attain the pressure she
needed to properly diagnosis the problem, let alone to treat
it, with him so much taller than she.

"Please, sit on the balustrade with your back to me," she
ordered.

Damon obeyed.

Neilly let her hands glide over his shoulders, at first exploring only for the injury. She found the knot and the
welling in the right shoulder immediately.

"The timber struck you right there." She pressed gently
on the knot. The bruise went deep and had to be painful;
she regretted that she hadn't had the good sense to ask
about his injury before now. She wondered that he hadn't
complained about it sooner.

He groaned assent and winced from her exploring hand.

She let her hands rest on his shoulders until he relaxed
beneath her fingers again. Then she went to work finding
the other knots, the hard muscles and strong tendons. His
flesh warmed the linen as she investigated the landscape of
his well-muscled back. As she worked, she realized that she
liked the feel of his solid strength under her hands.

"You must be careful with the shoulder for the next
week," she advised, working her thumbs along the parallel
cords of his back. "No lifting. I wouldn't even recommend
horseback riding or carriage driving."

"Whatever you say, Doctor."

"Do you mock me, sir?" Neilly asked, letting her hands
drop away.

"Oh, never," he said, his voice thick with relief. "Don't
stop what you're doing, please."

Neilly smiled to herself. She knew he lied about teasing
her, but she'd found the hard knot that needed to be eased.
She went to work on it.

The strength in Cornelia's skilled hands startled Damon
into unwilling compliance. To his astonishment, the first
painful kneading brought relief to his strained muscles,
melting away the aching tightness that had troubled him.
Her hands moved sensuously back and forth, up and down
his spine, with surprising speed and accuracy, homing in
on exactly the right spots.

He'd only consented to the massage out of curiosity. But the results left him almost speechless with relief and wondering what more her strong, soft hands could do for other parts of him. If she had any passion at all, what a skilled mistress Miss Cornelia Lind could be. She'd already soothed nearly every tired muscle that needed soothing and was beginning to bring heat to parts of him that her hands hadn't come near.

"You're tense," she complained, her hands methodically kneading the resistance from his muscles.

Damon groaned as relief spread across his back and the ache swelled in his groin.

"Heavens, your lower back muscles are stiff."

"I know."

"Feel it? Right there. You're hard as a rock."

"It's not important," Damon said, gripping the balustrade he sat on.

"You're absolutely rigid with tension right there. Try to breathe deeply."

"Deep breathing isn't going to relieve what's troubling me," Damon muttered through gritted teeth. Lord, didn't this woman know what she was doing to him?

"Just try it," she insisted working lower on his back almost below his belt.

Abruptly, Damon jumped to his feet and grabbed Cornelia's wrists.

"Did I hurt you?" She looked up at him, innocent confusion written on her pretty oval face, her wrists warm and fragile in his grip.

"No, you didn't hurt me. I've just had enough," he said bravely resisting the foolish urge to kiss her deeply enough to show her what he really needed to relieve the tension.

Counting on the darkness to hide the bulge straining against his breeches, he released her. He almost shoved her hands away. "You'd best focus your nursing efforts on my aunt."

"Well, of course," she said, looking up at him with earnest blue eyes, large and dark, without guile or coyness. His heart skipped a beat. But his head warned him that it was dangerous to be too captivated by her.

"I can assure you I will do my utmost for your aunt's welfare," she added. "And I do advise that you ask Dr. McGregor to look at that bruise."

"Thank you for the massage," Damon said. "And one more thing . . ."

"Yes?"

"Please understand that in the past I have returned to Rosewood to find people here who weren't who or what they said they were," Damon said. "My aunts have been taken advantage of, and I won't tolerate it ever happening again."

"Just what are you saying, sir?" She blinked at him, and her shoulders squared perceptibly beneath her wrapper.

"It occurred to me that you were a little evasive about answering my questions tonight at the dinner table."

"I told you all you needed to know, Mr. Durande. Beyond that, my private life is my own affair." She gave him a cool, polite smile, touchingly righteous—almost virginal. Unaccountably, Damon found himself more aroused than before.

"I assure you, I care very much for your aunt's welfare," she added. "Just as you do."

"Good, I'm glad we understand each other," Damon said, aware that the evening and the company had grown chilly. "Shall I see you to your door?"

"How kind of you to offer, sir, but that's unnecessary, thank you."

Damon watched her march away down the gallery, her lacy crocheted slippers silent on the boards, her cotton wrapper clinging ever so slightly to her bottom and swaying seductively with each step.

He had to smile. If she was a fraud, some little baggage

out to take advantage of his aunts, he had to admit he liked her style.

When Neilly reached the door of her room, she turned to see that Damon was still watching her, just as she had suspected. His gaze had nearly burned into her back as she walked along the gallery. Raising her hand in a small wave to him, she escaped into the sanctuary of her bedroom.

In case he was still waiting out there for her to go to bed, she blew out the lamp. In the darkness she sank onto the edge of her bed, mulling over their unnerving encounter.

Her reaction to touching a man had been more intense than she had expected. With his strong back beneath her hands, a new, odd delight had surged through her, warming her deep inside. The thrill hinted at pleasures and power to be had that she'd never known before. Only with great discipline had she resisted the absurd urge to put her nose to the cloth of his shirt and breathe in the musky, male scent of him.

But she liked the feel of his defined muscles, hard with wondrous strength, moving under her hands as she'd worked, the same strength that had delivered her from the fire. She was glad now that she'd been able to help him with the pain.

Then he'd spoiled the mood with his remark about frauds. He'd struck so close to the truth that he'd chilled her heart. In fact, he'd struck close enough to make her more determined than ever to rid Rosewood of Damon Durande.

She could think of only two ways to make him leave. One was to convince him that Aunt Isetta was safe in her capable hands, which was true. The other was probably going to be more difficult—to annoy him into retreat.

Four

The next morning Varina found Isetta seated at the writing desk in the morning parlor. Feeling fine and fit, Varina swept into the room with her basket of freshly cut yellow roses and closed the door behind her.

Cornelia's prescription of warm milk and brandy certainly had done the trick. She'd slept like a kitten in a basket, then awakened refreshed and eager to clip the fresh flowers of the day and to review the events of the evening with Izzie.

"Well, Sister, aren't you up early for an invalid?" Varina asked, taking the faded purple iris from the crystal vase on the table. "Where's Cornelia?"

"Seeing to the airing of my room," Isetta said, without looking up from her *Harper's Weekly*. She was forever reading a newspaper—as if what happened in the world could ever change anything at Rosewood.

"And Damon—where is he?"

"In the library with Mr. Pugh." Isetta turned a page and adjusted her spectacles.

"In the library. That reminds me, have you seen my Empress Josephine snuffbox?" Varina asked, poised with a yellow rose in her hand. "I thought I left it in the library."

"No, I haven't seen it, Sister," Isetta replied, more intent on her reading than ever.

"I wonder where it's gotten to," Varina muttered, taking another yellow rose from her basket and slipping it into the vase. Sometimes she felt as if little things had a life of their own, just like the story their Aunt Abigail from Massachusetts had told them when they were little girls. How once a year comes a night when the witches gather in the great forest, magical forces ride the wind, and objects dance to life.

Isetta had sniffed at the story and called it Yankee tomfoolery. But Varina solemnly believed every word; she had to. Aunt Abigail's face had looked far too grave as she told the tale.

As she grew older, Varina even began to suspect things might come to life more often than once a year. Wasn't it possible that when a room was dark objects might scuttle about at will? How else could one explain why they turned up later on a shelf, even though they'd last been seen on a desk? Surely things had a life of their own.

"Oh, well, I'll find it." Unable to contain her delight over their success any longer, Varina shook a yellow rosebud at her sister. "We did it, Sister. Damon's living in Rosewood."

"I thought last night you said setting the fire was a mistake," Isetta remarked, still frowning over her newspaper.

"Well, last night it was such a shock, with Damon risking his life to save Cornelia and all, but this morning I can see how necessary setting it was." Varina was pleased with herself for being sensible and insightful, and she was disappointed that Isetta didn't notice.

"Did you see how Damon looked at Cornelia last night? He could hardly take his eyes off her." Varina pressed her hands together in an attitude of prayer and pleasure. "They looked perfect together, don't you think? She's just tall enough, and so fair next to his handsome, rugged good looks. Oh, Izzie, I think it's just a matter of time before they fall in love."

"Not necessarily," Isetta said, folding her newspaper and laying it aside.

"What?"

"If we're not careful, Damon will lock himself up with those account books, and he and Cornelia will exchange nary a word."

"I never thought of that." Confusion settled on Varina. "But you said the rest would take care of itself."

Isetta gazed knowingly at Varina over her spectacles. "Yes, well, I didn't mean that we wouldn't have to apply a nudge or two."

"Oooh." Varina considered her sister's words before she selected another rose for the arrangement. "You think Cornelia is a lady who wouldn't think of throwing herself at a man, even a handsome devil like Damon. And Damon is a gentleman who wouldn't dream of taking advantage of the living arrangements?"

"I'm not sure about that," Isetta said. "I think our Cornelia might be capable of very strong-willed passion. She is a pretty, healthy girl, after all. And Damon—he is a red-blooded male, and part Creole to boot. Why wouldn't he take advantage of the situation if it suited his purposes?"

More confused than ever, Varina waited for Izzie to explain.

Isetta removed her glasses, pulled a hanky from her sleeve, and proceeded to clean her spectacles. "But daily duties take them off in different directions, too. What we need is something to throw them together. Something that will help them see each other at their best."

"Oh, you mean like at a party? Yes, that's what Damon and Miss Cornelia need, a party." Varina loved social events, but she knew their nephew pretty well. She frowned. "But you know how Damon hates being paraded around in society."

"And we can't give a party, because I'm supposed to be ill," Isetta said, replacing her spectacles and taking up her teacup. "So this morning I sent a note off to Olivia Turnbull at The Laurels, informing her of Damon's return."

"Sister, you know how well Olivia thinks of herself. She

will insist on throwing a barbecue or a ball or something to show off The Laurels' lovely gardens."

"Precisely. I believe she is still showing off that sculptor—what's his name? The one all the planters want works from." Isetta frowned. "What's his name?"

"Oh, you mean Peter Hiram?"

"Yes, Peter Hiram. I think Damon needs to see just how appealing Cornelia will be to other Louisiana men and other artists. Damon will go if we put it to him right."

"Of course." Varina thought the idea absolutely inspired.

"And there's nothing quite like a waltz in each other's arms and perhaps a shared cup of punch spiced with spirits." Teacup still in hand, Isetta gazed off into the air above Varina's head, as if visualizing some far-off place and time that Varina suspected didn't include her.

"But will Dr. McGregor let you go?"

"I'll take care of Theo," Isetta said, suddenly clattering the cup down onto its saucer. "When the invitation comes you must say that you can hardly wait to go, in front of Damon. Say that it's the event of the year. It mustn't be missed by a soul in the parish. Do you think you can do that?"

"Of course." Varina stood a little taller. "I've done more daring things than that, haven't I? And I wouldn't miss one of Olivia Turnbull's parties if you promised me a new rose cutting."

"I'll insist on going for a short while, so as not to offend the Turnbulls, and Cornelia must come along, naturally. I can't be without my companion."

"That works out perfectly." Varina clapped her hands, delighting in the aptness of Isetta's plan. Trust Izzie to be so clever. Thoughts of a party brought up the question of clothes and jewelry. Varina frowned. "That means I *must* find my Empress Josephine snuffbox."

"Why? What do you keep in that fancy coffer anyway?"

Isetta asked. "I hope you haven't taken up the disgusting habit."

"Never." Insulted that Izzie would think her capable of such a repulsive thing, Varina turned her back to her sister and devoted herself to her roses. "I must wear my pearl-and-garnet earrings to Olivia's party. I keep them in that box."

"Oh, yes, the Tudor earrings Queen Elizabeth wore." Isetta took up another newspaper and began to leaf through it. "Well, boxes don't have legs, so it couldn't have gone far."

Like a felon, Damon slipped into the library and softly closed the paneled door behind him. He waited, listening to the familiar silence of Rosewood, slumbering, like its ladies, in the afternoon heat.

When the silence continued Damon smiled to himself. Alone at last in his refuge, he thought.

For the last three days he'd spent each morning with Claude Pugh, reviewing accounts. Over lunch he was assailed by questions and gossip from his aunts—today they'd pressed him to accept an invitation to the barbecue party at The Laurels. McGregor had approved of the outing, but Damon wasn't looking forward to it.

To add to the crowded inconveniences of life at Rosewood, the solicitous Miss Lind had become a damned nuisance, a literal menace of cleanliness and consideration.

Since the morning after he'd submitted to her massage she'd plied him with unrelenting thoughtfulness. With a soft knock on his door she'd inquired if he wanted breakfast coffee. He'd said yes before he remembered his habit of sleeping nude when afforded the luxury of clean sheets. For a groggy moment, while he groped for the twisted covers on the floor, he feared they were going to see more of each other than either had anticipated. Thank heaven she'd sent Cato in with the coffee tray.

Nevertheless, she was always on hand to see that his shaving water was hot, that his clothes and boots were brushed, that his laundry was satisfactory and his room in order. Her incessant attention was enough to drive a man out of the house.

He'd survive as long as he had a refuge. The library had always been that for him. Damon looked around the light and newly inviting room and relaxed slightly. In the silence of the books, guarded by the wallpaper lions at the door, all his irritation seeped away. The weight of the bothersome attentions lifted. He was alone with his thoughts for a while, as a man should be. He was invisible as he'd been as a boy in his grandfather's house. With invisibility came freedom, for when you were unseen no one required anything of you, and you required nothing of them. Damon liked things that way.

Damon had no regrets about his solitary childhood. Solitude had given him self-reliance, a useful strength in business and an essential skill on the frontier.

Only years later had he realized that Isetta, Varina, and Uncle Cato had purposely allowed him to go unnoticed. As Grandfather had soured, becoming reclusive, sometimes isolating himself in his room for days at a time, Damon's freedom in the house had grown. He'd defied the hallway lions to slip in and out of the library almost as he pleased.

In those boyhood years he'd come to his refuge to read about the world, to dream of real freedom in far-off places. But he always honored Grandfather's banishment. Even young boys have their pride.

Damon had never slept under Rosewood's roof—not until three nights ago. Though Aunt Isetta had made sense with her talk about time to put away old grudges, a secret part of him—a piece of the boy that remained in his heart—had expected to find Grandfather's ghost walking the halls that first night. At the very least he'd envisioned the old man's portrait flinging itself from the drawing-room wall in protest.

But the house remained quiet, cool and light by day and welcoming and cheerful by night. The only apparition he'd encountered had been Miss Lind, treading the creaky floorboards of the hallway.

Damon smiled to himself with satisfaction. Just last night he'd caught her off guard. He'd taken ungentlemanly pleasure in encountering her without the dignity of her crisp skirts, neat hair ribbons, and irritatingly efficient composure.

"I was only seeing to your aunt," she whispered when he'd confronted her in the upstairs hall well after midnight. In the candlelight she'd blinked up at him, her face still soft with sleep and her hair in dark disarray.

She wore her modest dressing gown over a gauzy nightdress—not seduction sheer, but well-laundered thin. Its transparency snagged Damon's interest, the worn fabric revealing the hint of a pretty pink-nippled breast. Before he could see more she clutched her wrapper closed at her throat.

"Miss Isetta seemed restless earlier and I wanted to be certain she was sleeping all right," she added unnecessarily.

Still smiling at the beguiling midnight memory of Cornelia, Damon went to the library desk for the ledger he wanted to examine. When he lifted the heavy book a shaft of pain lanced across his shoulders and down his right arm. He stifled a groan. He'd discovered that even the tug of the horse's mouth on the reins made riding uncomfortable. That's why he'd decided to tend to his book work now and ride out into the fields later, when the soreness was gone.

Damon grimaced. Grudgingly, he had to credit Miss Cornelia. She had been right about his shoulder.

Settling in the tall fireside chair with his back to the door, Damon opened the ledger and turned to the first of the year. He worked for some time, reviewing the account items and adding up numbers in his head. He could find nothing incorrect, yet he sensed something wrong with Pugh's work. He would be glad when the man was replaced. Claude Pugh was only a temporary accountant, recommended by a neighbor when the previous accountant had fallen ill.

Rosewood was a large operation, incorporating several sugar plantations and one of corn, four sugar houses, and a new mill. The accounting required the expertise of someone willing to learn the business and the holdings inside and out.

Just then, the sound of voices outside the door reached Damon, and he stopped work to listen. It was Miss Lind, talking rather rapidly to someone. When the doorknob rattled he cursed softly. He'd been found.

"There are a number of things in here that definitely should be on the inventory," Cornelia Lind was saying as she swept into the room, banishing Damon's precious solitude, evicting his cherished privacy.

He sat still, silently hoping this was only a brief visit. Maybe she'd leave quickly, without noticing him.

"Yeas, Miss Neilly," Uncle Cato replied. "I sure be glad to help you."

"Miss Isetta told me about the desk, but I know that you know about the other items as well."

Damon heard the rustle of her starched skirts as she crossed to the desk. He'd noticed that she seldom wore hoops when about the business of the household, but her skirts whispered briskly wherever she was at work.

"Well, Ol' Master Stirling was right proud of that inkstand on the desk," Uncle Cato said.

"This silver piece?"

"Yeas, ma'am. He said it was owned by Mr. Patrick Henry."

"Is that right? And it's here in Louisiana."

Damon could hear the sound of pencil on paper.

"I'm sure some patriotic Virginian would give his best racehorse to have that. What about this magnifying glass?"

"Well, that was supposed to have belonged to one of the first French governors of New Orleans, Miss Neilly, but I don't remember that Master Stirling ever said his name."

"French colonial governor's magnifying glass." Sound of pencil scratching across paper again.

"Master Stirling took mighty big pride in that painting over the fireplace, too. The one wid all the cows," Uncle Cato continued. Damon could tell the old servant was warming to the subject of the house. Sometimes he thought Rosewood's servants took as much pride in the house as his grandfather had. He'd heard them brag to servants from other plantations that Rosewood was a house of culture.

"Oh, yes, the Constable landscape," Miss Lind said, skirts swishing as she turned toward the fireplace. More pencil scratching. "I spotted that the day I arrived."

What on earth was she doing? Damon wondered. Then he heard her muffled footsteps on the Oriental carpet as she crossed the room, her skirt nearly brushing his hand as she approached the fireplace. She was so intent on the painting over the mantel that she never noticed him.

"This is a beauty, and I think Constables are going to become more and more valuable as the years go by," she said. "Master Stirling chose well, Uncle Cato."

"Yeas, Miss Neilly, he had an eye for pretty things," Uncle Cato said.

Miss Neilly? Damon wondered. Where had that name come from?

Slowly, Miss Neilly stepped back toward Damon, who remained seated in the chair. Her gaze never left the painting. From his position Damon admired the delicate line of her nose and the pensive fullness of her lips as she studied the masterpiece.

"It really is exquisitely done," she murmured, backing

another two steps. And another. "So effortless, so serene, and—oh!"

Before Damon could rise or warn her away, her slippered feet tripped on his soft Indian boots, her arms pinwheeled through the air, and her pencil and paper scattered on the carpet. Miss Cornelia toppled into Damon's lap, landing atop the ledger. An upheaval of petticoats rustled indignantly. Damon caught her around the waist before she tumbled to the floor.

"Oh! Who in the world? You!" She stared into Damon's face in astonishment. "I didn't think anyone was in here."

Miss Neilly struggled to rise, her efforts creating an intriguing sensation against Damon's thighs, even with the ledger between them. Lord, he wished she didn't have such an effect on him—the impact rendered him reluctant to let her go.

"I was working in peace and quiet until you interrupted me."

"Why didn't you say you were in here?" She struggled again, her cheeks growing pink. Damon held tight, his hands spread across her waist, his body warming to her struggle. Would she play indignant lady or giggling flirt? he wondered.

"I don't remember hearing you knock," Damon said. She struggled against his hold again, but he held tight, enjoying the narrowness of her waist in his hands.

"Didn't I knock?" she said. "How remiss of me. I apologize, sir."

She looked so cool, calm, and completely unrepentant that Damon knew she lied.

"You're not being very gentlemanly, sir," she whispered this time, glancing meaningfully in Uncle Cato's direction, her cheeks growing even brighter pink. "Holding me on your lap. Calling me by a familiar name."

"Miss Neilly? With all due respect, the name suits you better than that pompous Cornelia." Without releasing her,

Damon leaned closer to catch her scent—fresh starch and heady lilacs. "If you can rub my back, I think I'm entitled to hold you on my lap. Now, what is this you're making? An inventory?"

She frowned and braced herself, as if she was about to start fidgeting again. Then she seemed to think better of it and became very still.

A blush colored her cheeks and she folded her hands over his. "I mentioned it to you the other evening on the gallery. It came to my attention that your aunts have no list of what your grandfather has collected under Rosewood's roof."

"I'm not particularly surprised," Damon said. "I believe my grandfather collected for his own pleasure, not for financial investment."

"Well, there are so many things," she said, relaxing a little, as though she'd forgotten where she was. "I suspect some of the things may even have been stored away and forgotten."

"Go on," Damon urged, more intrigued with the pout of her lips than with what she had to say about the state of Rosewood's collection. That's what it was, he decided; a pout, not the truculent kind, but a thoughtful expression, full of concentration. She was too involved with her project at the moment to fight him.

"And what have you found?"

"Well, I've only just begun," she said.

She fought for her freedom again, and when he refused to give it she eyed him suspiciously. "If you'll release me, I'll show you what I've done so far."

"I suppose that's reasonable," Damon acknowledged, but she felt so good on his lap that he didn't want to let her go.

"Let me help you up, Miss Neilly." Anxiously, Uncle Cato crept forward and offered the lady his hand.

Damon released her, but kept the accounts ledger in place

on his lap to cover her arousing effect on him. He was surprised once again by how much he wanted her, how the tremble of the lace on her dress collar made him hard for what lay beneath it. He'd always thought of himself as a man attracted to full-bodied, sensual women, never the pert, cool, efficient sort, like Miss Neilly.

On her feet again, she demurely smoothed her skirts and took her pencil and the small book that Cato had retrieved for her. Opening her own little ledger, she held it out toward Damon and pointed to the list of items. "Should there be a fire or a hurricane or a flood, not only would there be great financial loss, but there'd be great historic and cultural devastation as well. No one, not your aunts nor any historical society, has a single record to account for it."

"I see." Damon noted the precise yet sweeping handwriting.

Each entry described in detail the condition of the piece; the artist; the history; and the source, if she had learned it. He doubted Aunt Isetta or Aunt Varina knew this much about what they owned. Miss Neilly had documented things in a very professional manner, as far as Damon could tell. He wondered if she'd done this kind of work before.

"Uncle Cato and I have already inventoried the drawing room, including the portrait of your grandfather."

She pointed to the heading written at the top of a page. "We were just starting with the library."

"What about the books? I know there are some valuable manuscripts here. Are you going to inventory them?"

"Oh, yes. I've noticed some fine editions," Miss Neilly said, glancing around at the book-lined walls. "I plan to work on the book collection after we've completed a listing of the art and historical objects."

"And you feel your background qualifies you to do this?" Damon asked, knowing full well that it was the kind of question about the past that unnerved her.

She paled and diligently studied the pages of her ledger.

"Miss Barrow gave all her young ladies a thorough education in the fine arts and history. I think I should be able to do an adequate effort for a first listing. Perhaps in the future you'll wish to bring in an experienced dealer to assign an accurate value."

"Perhaps," Damon agreed, but he saw no reason for that.

She closed the ledger with a snap. "Well, if you're satisfied, we shall leave you to your work."

Without waiting for a reply, Miss Neilly turned to go. "If we should interrupt you in the future, Mr. Durande," she said, pausing at the door, "please be so kind as to let us know at the outset. It certainly would save all of us and yourself from future awkwardness."

Uncle Cato opened the door for her. She headed for it, as if it was the gate to freedom, her little ledger clutched purposefully in one hand and her pencil in the other.

Damon knew he should be relieved that she was leaving, but something made him call to her. "Wait."

She stopped in the doorway.

"I think I could answer some of your questions about the library," he offered. He couldn't believe he was inviting her to return, but now that he'd suggested it, he liked the idea. "No reason for you to put off inventorying this room just because I'm here. I do know about some of the things, like the desk. I've heard it said that it was made for Governor Carondelet in 1792."

She stared at him over her shoulder as if she didn't quite believe what she was hearing. "You want to help me with the inventory?"

"Yes. I think it's a good idea. I'm glad you thought of it." Damon laid aside the plantation account ledger.

"It's not necessary," she stammered and blushed. "You really needn't trouble yourself."

"I don't mind," Damon said, wondering if her refusal came from a concern for his convenience or for her own desire to work unobserved. "I probably know the library better than anyone at Rosewood. Isn't that so, Uncle Cato?"

"Yeas, sah," Cato agreed. "Master Damon has spent many, many hours here."

"Well, then, of course we could use the help of an expert," Miss Neilly said with a tight, uneasy smile. "Actually, it shouldn't take long to do just the art and furniture today."

"Shall we start over here on the top shelf?" Damon asked. "I'd almost forgotten about these. My grandfather started a small collection of chess sets. When I was a boy I used to play with them as if they were armies."

"Very fine workmanship." Miss Neilly admired an intricately carved ebony knight on a rearing horse. "They were the cavalry, of course. I played that version of the game, too."

"Yes," Damon said, unable to keep the surprise and pleasure from his voice that she should share a boy's imagination. "Then I discovered the true game."

"You taught yourself?" she asked, her eyes wide with surprise. "My father taught me."

"All you need to know is in the books," Damon said.

For the next hour he took Miss Neilly around the room, describing the treasures of the library to her. At first he told himself his intention was to hurry her through the list-making, but deep down he knew he was lying.

Preparing the inventory was the perfect excuse to stand at her side, brushing elbows and leaning close to add the fascinating details he suddenly recalled. It was like discovering the few precious pleasures of his boyhood anew. He found himself elaborating on pleasant recollections he had buried beneath more hurtful things. He had forgotten there were gratifying memories at Rosewood, too.

Miss Neilly took down all the information with amazing efficiency, her writing crisp and clear, a slight sweep betraying her femininity.

When they reached the chess sets again Damon caught

himself searching for something else to add that might detain her for a few more moments.

"Well, that seems to complete this room," she said, snapping the ledger closed with a finality that disappointed Damon.

"Would you like some lemonade before you continue with your work?" she offered, her efficient-nurse manner suddenly replacing her curiosity about the objects in the library.

"No. I don't need anything," Damon said, his coveted solitude seeming far less precious now than it had an hour ago.

"Well then, I'll get on with my work, and let you get on with yours," she said, and started for the door. "Thank you for your help." Then she was gone, and Cato with her.

Damon stood alone in the library. The silence descended, muffled as it should be, but annoying. The figures in the accounts books no longer held interest for him, but Miss Neilly's did. Such a tiny little waist and such dainty black-slippered feet. And her company—undemanding and interested in what he had to say.

Library quiet swelled around Damon like an unwelcome companion, whispering emptiness. Something warm and vital was gone from the room, leaving him feeling desolate and restless.

Clearly he could recall the warmth of her body moving under his hands. He remembered the keen, sharp interest in her blue eyes, and the warmth of appreciation in her voice for each beautiful item they had inventoried.

Doubts poisoned his thoughts. Did Miss Neilly make the inventory for the reasons she gave or for another purpose? Damon wondered. What made her shift her clear, blue-eyed gaze away from his when he asked about her position in New Orleans? Was she truly a doctor's daughter and descended from a long line of South Carolinian bluebloods on her mother's side as she claimed? Aunt Isetta and Aunt

Varina were too easily impressed with old names and good manners.

The Turnbulls' party at the end of the week would provide Miss Neilly with the opportunity to prove herself an aristocrat. The Turnbulls spared nothing to feed and entertain their guests. If Miss Neilly was the blueblood she claimed to be, she would confirm her heritage at The Laurels.

But she was hiding something. He knew it. Something important. Conflict writhing in his belly like a snake, he sank into the library chair again. Why did he have the growing sense that he didn't really want to know the truth about Miss Cornelia Lind?

Five

"Isn't The Laurels a lovely plantation?" Varina declared as the Stirlings' open carriage clattered up the shell drive. They all craned their necks to gaze at the imposing Greek-style mansion, Augustine Turnbull's recently completed plantation home. To Neilly, the Greek-style house seemed to rise unexpectedly out of the Louisiana wilderness.

Varina and Isetta sat in the shade of Varina's lace parasol across from her and Damon.

"Yes, lovely." Neilly grasped the brim of her straw hat before the breeze could lift it from her head. She tried to smile in agreement. The house was magnificent, hardly the backwater sort of plantation she'd imagined when she'd agreed to accompany Miss Isetta to the barbecue. She hoped her smile hid her dismay.

Other arriving equipages fell into line with them. Matched teams of horses high-stepped. Shiny harnesses jingled. The drivers' colorful livery clashed against the driveway greenery.

"I knew you'd like it, Neilly." Varina waved at the carriage behind them. "Oh, look, there are the Carringtons. I don't see the Esterbrooks."

"They'll probably come by boat," Damon said.

Neilly stared at the house, paying little heed to the Stirlings' exchange.

The splendid neoclassic house stood on a slight rise cleared of trees, as if the Spanish moss might sully its pristine whiteness. Carefully manicured shrubs hugged the stone foundation. Marble columns and a rounded portico towered above the velvety green lawn and cast a bright, wavering image into a blue man-made lake.

Every detail of the facade was flawlessly balanced. Every leaf of the trees hung to perfection. Even the air was perfectly scented with bougainvillea.

Each detail bespoke money, influence, and connections beyond New Orleans or Louisiana. All Neilly could think of was how large the crowd was going to be.

A pang of misgiving about coming settled into an uneasy ache in her stomach. She took a deep breath to regain her calm. The barbecue was for local planters, she reminded herself. Among these Louisiana families it was very unlikely she'd meet anyone she knew—or anyone who knew her.

"This is going to be a delightful party," Isetta said, waving to more arriving guests in the carriage ahead of them.

Neilly's smile tightened. She wished she'd never concurred with Dr. McGregor. At first the barbecue had seemed to be just the thing for Aunt Isetta: the fresh air, a change of scenery, the pleasure of seeing old friends. Neilly would go, of course, to attend her patient.

Now that she could see how many people were attending, she wished she'd refused. She could only hope and pray that no one from Charleston would be a guest at The Laurels today.

"Olivia boasts that The Laurels has twenty-eight acres of gardens," Varina chattered. "It's laid out almost exactly like the gardens at Versailles. There's even a petting zoo, with tame deer, peacocks, pet squirrels, and such. Oh, look, there are the Esterbrooks. And the Turpins are right behind them."

Isetta leaned forward to confide in Neilly. "Olivia does give wonderful parties. Enjoy yourself today, my dear."

"I'm sure I will." Neilly's face ached from her forced

smile. She appreciated Isetta's generous admonition, but she intended to remain as unnoticeable as possible.

Isetta tapped her cane in Damon's direction. "And you, sir, remember everyone here will be eager to welcome you home. I know you don't believe it, but Olivia often asks after you fondly."

"Only because she still has one unwed daughter," Damon commented, his voice dry, a wry grin on his lips.

He lounged in the seat beside Neilly, his legs out-stretched, his thigh threatening to brush against the skirts of her new orchid gown. She was uncomfortably aware of his arm resting along the back of the carriage seat.

When she gazed at him her heart fluttered just a little. Absolutely nothing about him looked like the rugged bear of a man who had invaded Miss Isetta's bedroom two weeks ago.

She hated to admit it, but Damon looked positively dashing in his stylish dove gray coat and charcoal trousers—and his unfashionable Indian boots. The fringed tops clung to his calves and the supple leather slouched into folds around his ankles. He moved soundlessly wherever he went. Neither Aunt Isetta's raised eyebrows nor Aunt Varina's dismayed gasp could sway him from wearing his frontier footwear.

She also realized that the exotic boots marked him as the frontiersman and Indian fighter he'd become. Wearing them served as a silent reminder to all that he wasn't one of Louisiana's elite and had no desire to be.

But what really set off Damon's dark good looks was his yellow waistcoat. The fit emphasized the width of his shoulders and the narrowing of his torso at his hips. The pale color deepened his bronze complexion and contrasted startlingly with his black hair. No lady at The Laurels today would be able to keep her eyes from lingering on Damon Durande, Neilly thought with an unexpected pinch of disquiet.

"Well, I think they've finally got their youngest, Alice, betrothed now," Isetta snapped, bringing Neilly back to the conversation. She looked well today.

Neilly hoped the day's events wouldn't be too much for her patient. Day by day, Isetta seemed to grow stronger, her face always brightening when Damon walked into the room, her strength growing so that she took walks with him in the garden. Today her pale blue eyes were clear, bright, absolutely flashing with excitement and purpose.

"And I hear tell finding a bridegroom was no easy task," Isetta continued. "Nevertheless, Olivia and Auggie will be pleased to see you, Damon. I trust you will be on your best behavior."

Damon inclined his head. "As you say, the Turnbulls always entertain lavishly, and the least we can do is be good guests and enjoy their hospitality."

Isetta thumped her cane in Neilly's direction, nearly causing her to jump. "Smile, my dear. I don't want you worrying about me."

Peering around at the gathering crowd, Isetta muttered, "Today my health is Theo's affair. Where is he anyway? He should be here already. But you, my dear—you must mingle with the guests. Meet the sculptor."

"Don't worry about Miss Neilly, Aunt Isetta," Damon put in. "I've decided I'll give up gaming today to see to her diversion."

With an unpleasant start, Neilly realized that he was eyeing her again in the same speculative way he had during the drive.

"Wonderful!" Varina clapped her hands, almost dropping her parasol.

Isetta sat back in her seat and beamed. "Perfect."

"That's kind of you, sir," Neilly sputtered, a new clamor of panic churning up her stomach. Why was he so eager to bestow his attention on her? Except her visit to the library, he'd shown little interest in her. "You really needn't make such a sacrifice on my behalf."

"Nonsense, no sacrifice at all," Damon said, briefly touching Neilly's gloved hand. "It seems the least I can do after the devoted attention you've given my aunts. And it will be my pleasure to escort such a lovely lady."

Warmth spread from his touch, confusing her. She glanced away purposely to prove to herself that he had no effect on her. He was handsome, yes, but to think she found him attractive was silly, even ridiculous. He'd made it plain that he of all people at Rosewood would not hesitate to bring disaster upon her. Yet his hand against hers stirred a force in her that she couldn't explain.

She stammered, "I'm sure there are other ladies you'd rather attend—"

"Not a one." He grinned at her like the devil about to reap a soul.

Neilly stared at the house ahead of them and took a deep breath to regain control over the jumble of emotions that she didn't understand. She should never have agreed to come to this barbecue.

Olivia and Auggie Turnbull received their guests on the front steps of their palatial mansion, as was their custom, Damon remembered.

He waited in line with the his aunts and Neilly, thinking that this was the first social gathering he'd attended in over a year that required more of him than putting on a clean shirt and brushing the Texas dust from his boots.

He'd always liked the rollicking freedom of a frontier hoedown. But there were usually too few women—though he never had a problem acquiring his share—too little good music, and too much brawling.

As he dressed in his room at Rosewood he decided he didn't mind putting aside his buckskins for the Turnbull affair. The fine linen of his shirt and the silk of his cravat whispered soft and familiar against his skin. Even when he shrugged into his cutaway coat, he found an odd comfort in the fit, in the slight confinement across his shoulders and the exact length of the sleeve—sensations that reminded him of the Creole tradition of looking good and the Southern heritage of courtliness. But when he pulled on the hard-soled leather boots, he'd found them inflexible and uncomfortable, so he tossed them aside in favor of his fringed footwear.

The thing was, he realized as he glanced at Neilly, who stood beside Aunt Isetta and Aunt Varina in the receiving line, though he was dressed properly, he was lamentably ill prepared to test her. How on earth was he going to get Neilly to reveal that she was a fraud among the elite of Louisiana? What faux pas would give her away?

It was their turn to be received, and Isetta made the introductions.

"So pleased to meet you, Miss Lind." Olivia Turnbull lifted her gold lorgnette to her long, thin nose and with narrow eyes peered at Neilly: up, then down. Her gaze lingered on Neilly's face. Damon could see the old gal was impressed, as well she should be.

Neilly looked lovely, decked out as a proper Southern belle. Her fashionable orchid gown fit perfectly, nipping her waist and exposing her shoulders and the swell of her breasts well enough to tempt any living male. He clasped his hands behind him to keep from touching her. What the fit of the gown didn't show off, the color enhanced. It heightened the blue of her eyes, contrasted with her dark curls, and glowed rich against her translucent skin.

Aunt Isetta had insisted on having the garment made to replace the blue one ruined in the fire. To her credit, Neilly had refused the new gown.

The girl had pride, Damon admitted grudgingly to himself. He'd seen color stain her cheeks, her chin tilt stubbornlike, and her eyes gleamed as if she'd been mightily offended when Aunt Izzie had presented her with the fabric.

Curious, he'd lingered in the morning room long enough to hear her objection, her soft voice laced with genuine indignation. Blithely Aunt Izzie and Aunt Varina draped the fabric over Neilly's shoulders. Pleased with their choice and ignoring the girl's every protest, they'd rung for Mammy Ruby and her sewing basket.

Damon was glad his aunts had won. The sight of Neilly in her orchid gown was a pleasure to behold. From what he could see there was no lady present who could outshine her. Sure as blossoms drew bees, she'd be attracting the men. All the more reason to make himself her escort.

"The Carolinian Ashleys, you say? We were all so sorry to hear about the loss of Bay Haven," Olivia added, as if the loss of the seaside plantation to a hurricane had happened just last week instead of thirty years ago.

"Thank you," Neilly replied with a curtsy, a dip low enough to be respectful but not so low as to be humble.

Damon realized the task before him was going to be even more difficult than he'd suspected. She obviously knew something of the nuances of society. "I'm so pleased to be a guest at The Laurels," Neilly added.

"Cornelia is something of an artist, aren't you, my dear," Isetta said. "She does amazing sketches."

"Wonderful." Olivia peered even more closely at Neilly. "Then you and Mr. Hiram will have much in common. You will have a special interest in his work, which we are going to unveil this evening at the dance." She turned to the frail, earnest young man who stood next to her. "Peter, dear, we have a fellow art lover. Miss Cornelia Lind sketches, don't you, dear?"

At the sight of Neilly boredom fell from the artist's soft, pale face. Eagerness livened his features as he seized Neilly's hand. "I'm delighted, Miss Lind. We must get together for a tête-à-tête later."

The hell you will, Damon thought. He longed for a bucket of cold water to douse the lust glowing in Peter Hiram's eyes as the artist bent to kiss Neilly's hand. Damon was sorely tempted to step between them. Instead he rested his hand on the small of Neilly's back to move her away from the drooling artist. But his urging was unnecessary. Like a veteran belle, she slipped her hand away from the ogling man.

"Of course, Mr. Hiram," Neilly said, her polite smile never wavering. "I'm looking forward to the unveiling of your work."

Olivia turned to Damon.

"And you, Damon Durande, have been gone far too long. Your aunts have been in need of you and it takes a serious illness to bring you back from Texas. But here you are, handsome as ever. Alas, I regret I have no daughters left for you. Alice is promised, you know."

"To my great disappointment," Damon said, with suitable gravity, he hoped. "My best wishes to the happy couple."

"But you must convey your wishes to her," Olivia said. "She is here today and will be delighted to see you."

After spending a few more minutes with Olivia, Damon hastened to catch up with Neilly inside the door, lest she slip away from him.

Varina had already disappeared into the garden with a group of lady friends, and Theo was escorting Isetta to a chair under a tree.

"I couldn't help but overhear our hostess's gentle scolding," Neilly said as they strolled through the house and out onto the gallery. "I hope you feel properly set in your place."

"Olivia has always excelled at putting people in their place."

"Admirably," Neilly agreed, a smile of mischief twitching on her lips. "I suppose she was disappointed you didn't stay around to marry one of her daughters."

"I had no need for a piece of a Louisiana plantation," Damon said.

"Nor a wife?" Neilly asked, casting him a curious sidelong glance. "They are lovely girls. Well brought up, I should imagine. Trained to be dutiful wives. No doubt their husbands are very happy."

"I have no ambitions in that direction." Damon didn't like her line of questioning. It moved too close to home and too far away from his own goal. "And what about you, Miss Neilly?"

Neilly stopped at the edge of the gallery. "What about me?"

"Haven't you a need for a husband?" he asked, scrutinizing her reactions. "You've proven yourself an efficient household manager. And your looks are—not unpleasant to behold."

Neilly's gaze faltered. Silence loomed between them and stretched out into awkwardness. The smile slipped from her lips.

Damon waited.

"I'm not really a good candidate," she said, turning on him suddenly with a bare-faced honesty that stumped Damon. "My mother was something of a bluestocking. Though she instructed me in the manners of polite society, she was given to being critical of its values. My father was a doctor, and his view of womanhood encompassed much more than the manners of a drawing room. So you see, such an unconventional upbringing makes me less than qualified."

"Less than qualified?" Damon repeated. What a strange response. Her reply was so totally different from the sad-eyed hedging that Damon had anticipated. He'd anticipated some pathetic story of a lost, unrequited love, thus her dedication to caring for the sick.

"No suitors, then?"

She hesitated again, as if reluctant to reveal more. "Truthfully? I was betrothed once."

"Truthfully, I'd be surprised if you'd gone overlooked."

The off-hand compliment seemed to fluster her. Her cheeks pinkened and she turned away so that the brim of her hat hid her face. "It was an unsuitable match. I—we called it off."

Silence between them again. Questions crowded into Damon's head. Who had she been engaged to? Where? When? Why? Why had the fool let her go?

Suddenly she cast him a bright, almost brittle smile. The breeze toyed with her curls and her blush faded to roses in her cheeks. "It was a sad time. Must we talk of these things on such a fine day and at such a lovely party?"

He wanted to press the subject, but he thought better of it. Behind her sunny smile he sensed pain. He'd struck on something sensitive, and he couldn't bring himself to force her to reveal more.

At that moment a black-and-white-garbed servant hurried by toward the kitchen bearing a few glasses of sun-warmed champagne. Inspired, Damon reached for two of the glasses.

"Let's begin the afternoon by having some champagne," he said, handing a glass to Neilly. "Aunt Izzie ordered us to have a good time, Remember?"

"Yes, I remember. To your aunt's good health."

"Yes, to Aunt Izzie's good health," Damon repeated. "You know, the Turnbulls import only the best French wines."

Neilly sipped from her glass. Her long dark lashes fluttered against her cheeks. She looked up at him with an apologetic smile and handed back her glass. "I'm sure they do, but this has gone flat, don't you think? Perhaps it was allowed to sit out in the sun too long before serving."

"Yes, I can taste that myself," Damon stammered, surprised to find himself awkwardly holding two glasses again.

She smiled at him sweetly. "But I do so love good champagne."

"Well, then," he said, "I'll find some for us."

Silently berating himself, he headed off to find another tray of champagne. That hadn't been a very good test, he told himself as he deposited the glasses on another passing tray and reached for two flutes alight with golden bubbles.

Any young woman might have had an opportunity to taste fine wine, even develop a taste for it. It wasn't all that unusual to find imported wines in New Orleans or any number of other cities along the coast. But he was convinced he was following the right course. Somewhere, somehow, Cornelia Lind would tip her hand today. He was certain of it.

When he returned, determined to pursue his testing, he found Neilly in the center of a male throng, including John and Bradley Kenner and Nilges Esterbrook. The young planters hovered over her, grinning and slavering like foxes in a henhouse.

Theo eyed Isetta professionally as he handed her a cool glass of lemonade. He usually had no problem being objective about his patients, but in Isetta's case perhaps they'd been friends too long. Today he thought she looked well, even a little beguiling in a pale blue gown with her gray curls piled like a crown atop her head and blue cameo earrings dangling from her ears. It wasn't the fashion, Theo thought, but the style suited her.

"Thank you, Theo. That was very kind." She accepted a glass from him. "I'm glad you stopped to introduce the Kenner boys to Cornelia. Now sit. Talk to me for a while."

She sat as regal as a queen enthroned in a chair beneath a moss-draped live oak, her cane at her side. She'd taken to wielding the bloody thing more like a scepter than a walking stick, Theo observed. Izzie had always been a lady

who knew her mind, and she wasn't about to stop dictating
to everyone just because she was feeling a little under the
weather.

Theo sat down beside her. "The Kenner boys were about
to make fools of themselves and take the Esterbrook boy
along with them if someone didna make introductions."

He followed her gaze to the Kenner brothers, who were
jostling each other aside in an effort to impress Neilly with
their wit and flattery. "Damon may not thank me for making
the introductions, but I figure the boy needed to find his
territory threatened."

"He will thank you in time," Isetta said, a mysterious
look of knowing in her sharp blue eyes. "We always appreciate most the things that don't come to us too easily."

"True." Theo said nothing more as he watched her sip
from her lemonade. Her color was good and her expression
animated. He sat back in his chair. He couldn't help thinking she looked almost too well to be sitting in the shade
like an invalid. The cloud of apprehension that had hung
over him the past two months evaporated.

Izzie's illness had frightened him, had shaken him to the
core. His world had gone gray when he'd been called to
her side and found her pale and weak.

Long ago he'd learned to do his best for each patient,
and then to accept fate. But his powerlessness to help Izzie
had left him disheartened and frustrated and painfully aware
of how really useless he was in the face of the grim reaper.
He wouldn't even allow himself to think of losing her. What
good were his skills if he could not save his friends, the
people he loved?

"How are things going at Acorn Hill?" Isetta asked.

"Oh, fine. Fine," Theo said, aware that Isetta was purposely drawing him away from his gloomy thoughts. They'd
been friends too long, spent too many hours together beside
a slave's sickbed not to understand the turn of each other's

thoughts. "The cane crop looks good this year. The plaster is repaired and the house is almost ready to furnish again."

"You've done a lot with that deserted old place," Isetta said. She nudged him with her elbow. "Who would have thought all those years ago when you first came to Louisiana—your burr was so thick, we could hardly understand you—who would have thought that you'd become a planter one day."

"I always thought I would," Theo said, a little annoyed that Izzie, of all people, should have doubted his ability to become one of them.

"Theo? Tell me, who are those two pretty dark-eyed girls with the Turpin boy?"

"Oh, aye, the new bride. Isna she a pretty little thing? The taller girl is Annick LaBelle, Randolph Turpin's new wife. The smaller one is her cousin."

"A Creole girl married into the Turpins?" Wonder, more than surprise, filled Isetta's voice. "A quiet wedding, I suppose. That's why I hadn't heard about it."

Theo watched Isetta study the girl. "Isna like it used to be when we were young, Izzie. When the Creoles and the Anglos didna mix, ever."

Izzie turned toward him. "In the days when a doctor was considered little more than a tradesman and was just barely respectable enough to be admitted through the front door."

Theo couldn't resist smiling at the memory of his own humble beginnings. "Aye, 'tis past. The young people have the courage to cross those barriers now. Their parents have the wisdom to let it happen."

"But courage doesn't ensure success, does it?" Isetta asked. "Look at what happened to my sister, Rosalie. She had courage, but was it courage to be admired? After all these years, while she and her husband are dead and gone, Damon still suffers for his mother's defiance of Papa."

"A tragic end, without a doubt, but who's to say it

wouldna have ended just as sadly if Rosalie had taken the Anglo husband your father chose for her?"

"You might be right." Isetta sipped her lemonade in silence a moment more. "Theo? Do you think I was a coward?"

The question took Theo by surprise. He thought of protesting that he had no idea what she meant, but he did know. He knew exactly the hour and the day when Izzie's courage had failed her and had disappointed him, when she had bowed her head to her father's will and had altered the path of her life and his forever. But there was nothing to be gained by admitting to that now. "You? A coward? Izzie, you've never known a cowardly moment in your life."

"Bah! You and I both know that's not true."

"It doesna matter, now." Theo shook his head. "Donna trouble yourself over the past, lass."

"I never believed in doing that, Theo," Izzie said. "But when you're faced with death you realize all you have is the past. And it matters."

Six

John and Bradley Kenner stood on either side of Neilly, rocking on their heels, their frock coats pushed back, and their hands shoved in the pockets of their trousers. Nilges Esterbrook held center stage, gesturing wildly as he told some preposterous story about bear hunting.

Neilly smiled at the young planters as she listened, amused by their harmless flirtations. What a pleasure it was to be flirted with after so long. She'd been too young to appreciate the fun of it when she'd first been introduced into society. Now it was a diversion.

Their youthful camaraderie put her at ease. As her apprehension about the barbecue slipped away, she laughed with the young men at the silly outcome of Nilges's story.

"Durande, ol' man, there you are." John was the first to spot Damon returning with a glass of champagne in each fist. "We hoped you had deserted the lady and left the privilege of entertaining her to us."

Neilly met Damon's scowl with a steady smile. "These gentleman are most diverting. They've been kind enough to tell me about the exciting hunts in the parish."

"Durande, you lucky dog." Bradley Kenner made to slap Damon on the back, then seemed to think better of it. "You ride back from Texas to find a pretty little thing like Miss Cornelia under your roof. Miss Isetta should take ill more often, huh?"

Damon said nothing, but held Bradley's gaze for a long

moment. Despite the sunshine, the air chilled notably. Nilges Esterbrook excused himself and beat a hasty retreat.

"Of course Mr. Kenner is jesting, Damon," Neilly said, trying to ease the tension the young planter's unfortunate comment had created. "I was just telling these gentlemen how much Miss Isetta is improving."

"Is that what you meant, Kenner?" Damon baited.

Bradley blushed and stepped back. "Of course, I meant no insult, ol' man. I spoke in jest. Thoughtless of me, of course, just as Miss Cornelia said."

"So how many Apaches have you killed since your last homecoming?" John asked with an uneasy laugh, plainly attempting to turn the conversation away from his brother. "Miss Cornelia, has Durande told you about all his adventures? He makes it difficult for us mere planters to compete with him."

"I never count how many Indians I shoot," Damon said, allowing Neilly no opportunity to reply. He held up the two glasses of champagne he carried. They trembled in the strength of his grip. "But I do recall throttling two—a warrior in this hand and a chief in this one. I'd demonstrate, but I don't want to do damage to Miss Olivia's fine glassware."

Neilly frowned.

The Kenner brothers' eyes widened. They glanced at each other, apparently unsure whether Damon was joking or not. The joke won out. They brayed laughter.

Neilly snatched a glass from Damon. "Thank you, sir. I think that's quite enough about Indians."

"You will save a dance for us, won't you? Miss Cornelia." Bradley glanced uneasily at Damon again.

"How nice of you to ask," Neilly said. She loved to dance, and she wanted to accept Bradley's invitation. But she was also aware that she had not come to The Laurels to play the belle. "But I really must tend to Miss Isetta."

"I'm sure she'd give you leave to dance a cotillion with

each of us," John said bravely, ignoring Damon, whose scowl deepened with each passing moment.

"Well—"

"Miss Cornelia is in my company today, gentlemen," Damon said. With a tight, possessive grip on Neilly's arm, he led her away. "I hope this champagne is more to your liking, Miss Cornelia?"

"Yes, thank you." Neilly said between tight lips. She'd hardly had a chance to take a sip. "But did you really have to behave like that?"

"Like what?" Damon said. "I'm your escort today. I could hardly leave you at the mercy of those two scamps. They're spoiled sons of a rich planter, well known for their card-cheating and their fornicating, and I don't believe they've ever hunted anything meaner than an old 'possum."

"At their mercy," Neilly snapped. "I was hardly at their mercy, sir. Every lady here knows what those two are and how to handle them. Honestly! Throttling an Indian in each hand . . . Next I suppose you'll be telling people you prefer to eat cactus and sleep with rattlesnakes. Or vice versa. Shame on you."

Naked honesty passed over Damon's face, and Neilly knew instantly that he had done all those things. She forgot to take a sip from her champagne glass. "Did you really kill those two Indians, one in each hand?"

A look of pure innocence spread across Damon's face and he grinned. "No, but a friend of mine did."

Neilly stared at him, uncertain what to believe.

"Damon, dear," a feminine voice called from across the lawn. They looked around to see a pretty blond belle tacking through the sea of guests, her green hooped skirts billowing out under full sail. "Mama said you were here, you rogue."

She threw herself into Damon's arms. Neilly quickly recovered his glass of champagne before the contents splashed across their clothing.

"Hello, Alice," Damon said, accepting the lady's kiss on his cheek, then setting her away from him.

"What a sight for sore eyes you are, Damon Durande."

"You're looking well yourself, Alice," Damon said, his smile unreadable. "I understand best wishes upon your engagement are in order."

"Why thank you," Alice said, beaming. A healthy but unladylike ruddiness stained the round face she tipped toward Damon. Neilly realized with an unexpected pang of jealousy that the lady still had a crush on him. "I'm rather pleased to be promised at last, if I don't say so myself."

"I'm sure your gentleman is even more pleased," Damon said, all politeness and generosity. Neilly wondered if he'd ever returned any of Alice's feelings.

"And you are Miss Isetta's new companion?" Alice turned to Neilly, appraising her with narrowed eyes.

Damon made introductions.

With a quick greeting, Miss Alice dismissed Neilly, leveling her charm in Damon's direction and slipping her arm around his waist in a rather daring show of intimacy. "It's a delightful party, is it not? You're saving a dance for me tonight, aren't you? Now don't look at me like that, Damon Durande. I can see Miss Cornelia isn't a jealous sort of female. She won't mind if we take a turn 'round the floor."

Damon gazed at Neilly over Alice's head. Neilly could have sworn she saw appeal in his eyes, as if the frontiersman and Indian fighter was pleading for rescue.

Neilly smiled wickedly and shoved Damon's champagne glass back into his hand. "No, of course, I wouldn't mind at all. You two must have a dance."

"Wonderful." With a wave of her hand, Alice set sail for another guest.

"Thanks," Damon said, rather ungratefully. He took a long swig of his champagne as they gazed after Alice.

"You're welcome," Neilly said, smiling into her glass.

"I tried to save you," he muttered. "I bargained you'd return the favor."

"I didn't need to be saved," Neilly said, knowing the champagne had already gone to her head. She was getting reckless.

"Perhaps not," he said, taking her arm rather possessively and leading her toward another group of people. "But let's be safe. Let me introduce you to some respectable members of Louisiana society."

After the exchange with the Kenners—who could never keep their greedy hands off a pretty woman—Damon decided the safest course was to introduce Neilly to every elderly gentleman, dowager, and matron he recognized.

With a patience he never knew he had, he listened to the recitals of children and grandchildren's names, ages, and talents. He even took some interest in Olivia Turnbull's lengthy discussion about training a new hunter she planned to ride in the fall hunting season.

He watched as Neilly listened, too, sometimes asking questions and always sharing laughter over the little ones' precociousness. She never betrayed a flicker of impatience or a gleam of anything less than pure graciousness. In short, she behaved with all the tranquillity and composure of a genuine lady—and she seemed to be enjoying herself.

All the while he racked his brain for another test of Neilly's social skills. Stymied for what to do next, Damon led Neilly toward the food table. "Would you like something to eat? I'm hungry."

"Yes, breakfast does seem like a long time ago," Neilly agreed, setting aside her empty champagne glass.

Servants served up the dishes they requested—everything from roasted pork to barbecued shrimp—as they worked their way along the table. Damon turned the conversation back to the Turnbull daughter and her horses, which, to his surprise, seemed to interest Neilly. Craftily he slipped the wrong fork onto her fish plate and handed it to her without allowing the discussion to flag. This test was far more subtle than the champagne one.

He thought he did a rather fine job of it; then he stared at his own plate without interest and waited for her to begin.

With the first bite she didn't seem to notice that she was eating with a pewter fork that corrupted the delicate white fish flavor. Elation and disappointment assailed Damon, battering against his insides, extinguishing any appetite he'd had. She was going to reveal her common origins at last.

On the second bite she stopped in midsentence. She pursed her mouth in distaste, then examined her fork with sudden interest. "I do believe I've gotten the wrong fork," she said. "How odd."

She immediately turned to the table and politely asked for a replacement. She accepted a silver utensil and resumed eating. "That's better."

In a confusion of emotions, Damon set his plate aside and longed for some of Auggie Turnbull's fine Scotch. "You were saying about your first pony."

As they moved down the table, she spoke lovingly of her dapple gray pony while finishing her fish with the silver fork. A bowl of red caviar lay ahead of them. Damon would have staked money on the fork business, but caviar posed a good test.

When Neilly passed up the red salmon roe Damon thought he might have something on her at last. Every Southern belle worth her black velvet slippers knew she should like caviar.

A few steps farther down the table, she stopped at the next dish, heaped with shiny black fish eggs.

"Now, here's my favorite," she said, helping herself to a generous portion of black caviar. She leaned close to him to confide, "Russian beluga is my favorite. Would you like some?"

Damon nearly choked on his champagne. "No, thanks."

"Is something wrong?" Neilly set down her plate and gave him a solid thump on the back.

"No, no." Damon gently pushed her away. "I think I'm choking on crow."

"What?"

Damon shook his head in wordless frustration. He'd had enough fine champagne and fancy food. He decided that if Cornelia Lind was anything less than the lady she claimed to be, he wasn't likely to prove it today.

"I've introduced you to anyone who matters in this parish." Damon turned to Neilly with a suddenness that took her aback.

"Yes, and I might add you scowled mightily at every gentleman who looked like he would dare ask me to dance," Neilly shot back.

"Perhaps," Damon agreed. "But now I think you should entertain me, Miss Cornelia, with your choice pastime. What would you like to do?"

"To be honest, I've had enough of this crowd," Neilly said without hesitation. She hadn't seen a soul who even looked remotely familiar, but getting away from the new and curious faces was what she truly longed to do. "I'd love to see the petting zoo your Aunt Varina mentioned."

"The petting zoo?" Damon blinked at her. She could tell he'd never troubled to visit the zoo.

"Yes, but I'll understand if you'd rather join one of the card games in the house," Neilly said.

"No, the zoo it is," Damon said. "I'm a man of my word."

Neilly smiled at him. Somehow she already knew that.

The zoo, a tall fenced enclosure some distance from the house, was nearly deserted when she and Damon strolled up to the gates. The children had been lured inside for a

nap with promises of stories and treats, and most of the
ladies had joined them. Only a betrothed couple or two
lingered almost hidden in the shade of the trees and bushes.
The scene was cool and quiet, a respite from the crowded
house and lawn. The zoo animals satisfied with the treats
had also disappeared. Only a shy deer and a bold white
peacock remained.

One of the servants gave them birdseed. Neilly took some
and offered it to the peacock. The bird seemed to take a
fancy to her. With a flourish of tail feathers, he strutted
across the lawn for her, his tail in full show and his snowy
white head gleaming in the sun.

"No doubt he's related to the Kenner clan," Damon
drawled.

Neilly laughed. "Oh, I wish I had my sketch pad. He's
so elegantly perfect."

Damon turned to one of the ever-present servants and
ordered that drawing materials be brought. They were. Without hesitation, Neilly untied the ribbons of her hat, peeled
off her gloves, sat down on a bench, and began to translate
the bird's beauty onto paper.

She could feel Damon watching over her shoulder, but
she didn't care. The bird was too wonderful and the feel of
charcoal in her hands was too familiar and right. She drew
simple but faithful lines that brought the peacock's elegance
to life on the paper.

She knew her style was bold and strong, completely unlike the polite, thin drawings of the belles who named
"sketching" as one of their accomplishments. But she put
down what her heart and her eye dictated.

She felt Damon put his foot on the bench and lean over
her shoulder to get a better view of her work.

"Draw the deer," he urged. "See the white-tailed doe at
the lake edge?"

She flicked to the next page and pressed the charcoal
across the paper again, capturing the graceful lines of the

deer drinking from the lake. She was a little out of practice, she thought, but her hand and eye warmed to the task as she worked. The doe took shape on the paper.

"In the tree above the camellia bush, see the pair of doves?" Damon said, pointing to the tree beyond the peacock.

Again she flipped the page and drew, sometimes with her eyes on the subject while her hand moved independently on the page.

"Lady," Damon said quietly. Neilly could hear a touch of awe in his voice. "You can draw."

She flipped the page and began to draw again, holding the pad so he couldn't see what she was doing. "You know, I've had the strangest feeling all afternoon that there's something you want from me. Some questions you want to ask."

Damon straightened and backed away a step. "Why would I want anything more than the pleasure of your company?"

"That's what I'm asking you." She sketched as she spoke, studying every line of his austere face. "And there's something else I'd like to know. Now that your aunt is feeling better, are you going to leave?"

"Odd that you should ask that," Damon said. "I was about to ask you the same thing."

She paused in her work, frowned, then continued without looking up at him. "I shall leave when I'm dismissed by your aunt, since it's she who brought me to Rosewood. And you?"

"I'm pleased that Aunt Izzie is better," Damon said. "But there are things at Rosewood that need to be taken care of before I leave again. We might be sharing Rosewood's roof for some weeks yet."

"Yes, it sounds that way." She glanced up at him, hoping she was hiding her disappointment well.

But as she gazed at him she decided there was something about the strength of his mouth and the intensity of his eyes that she had not got quite right. She scowled down at her work and began to smudge some of the lines with her thumb.

"What are you doing?" he demanded finally. "Let me see what you've drawn."

"I'm filling in contours." She took one more stroke at the drawing, then turned the pad toward him. "There you are. What do you think?"

Damon stared at a portrait of himself. She'd drawn a harsh face shaded with a growth of beard and framed by hair grown too long. She had pictured him as he had appeared to her the day he'd burst into Rosewood. She'd drawn him as the rough frontiersman, a big, dark, bearish man quick to protect his own and slow to trust.

He scowled at the sketch.

She frowned and peered down at the drawing, too. "I know. Something about it isn't quite right. It's not really you."

Damon shook his head. "No, you've got it right. It's me."

"Neilly! Damon! What are you two up to?" Varina glided across the lawn, her hooped skirts swaying, her sun bonnet ribbons fluttering. A gaggle of dowager friends bobbed along in her wake. "Aren't the gardens lovely? And the zoo, too. Neilly, you've done a drawing of Damon. It's wonderful. May I have it?"

Damon seemed about to object, but Neilly ripped it from the book and handed it to Varina before he could voice his objections. "Yes, please take it."

"Thank you, Neilly." Varina held up the drawing for her entourage to admire. "I must show this to Izzie. We're off to change for the ball, and for the unveiling of Mr. Hiram's statue. Neilly, Izzie says you must come change for the ball, too."

"Yes, I'll be along." Neilly rose from the stone bench and gathered up her gloves and hat.

Damon took the sketchbook and asked the servants to

deliver the other drawings to the Stirling carriage; then he offered his hand to Neilly, as if to do so was the most natural action in the world. "We mustn't miss Hiram's unveiling."

"Or the dancing," Neilly said, placing her hand in his and taking pleasure in the way he closed his fingers over hers. "I love to dance, you know."

"Is that so?" He spoke with caution in his voice.

"Yes, and since you've spent the afternoon discouraging any prospective partners, the obligation of dancing with me falls to you." She grinned at him, aware that her eyes betrayed her vengeance. "I'll not give up a single round to Miss Alice. We might just dance holes into those Indian boots of yours."

Damon smiled back at her. "A price I must pay, I fear. But Aunt Izzie wouldn't want you to exhaust yourself."

"Oh, I don't think that's going to happen." She patted his arm reassuringly, a gesture that seemed to surprise him. "What is it called in horse racing when a horse gets stronger in the last half of the race? I think I'm getting my second wind."

She had indeed gotten a second wind, Damon thought ruefully as she glided across the ballroom floor in his arms. All the ladies had changed gowns. In place of the orchid garden dress Neilly wore a plum-colored ball gown. Fresh bougainvillea blossoms garnished her dark curls. After a quick survey of guests Damon decided no lady in glittering jewels was as lovely as his partner.

She fit perfectly in his arms, her waist easily grasped by his hand and her fingers warm and strong on his shoulder. She danced with him again and again, defying convention with a toss of her head, indifferent to old rules as only a princess could be.

They danced together all night. Her enthusiasm never

flagged and her feet never faltered, not even when he talked the orchestra—imported from New Orleans for the occasion—into playing some lively Texas jigs and reels. She tackled the steps and patterns he demonstrated like a natural-born hoedown dancer.

He liked the feel of her there, in his arms. The spirited foot-stomping didn't seem to embarrass her in the least, even when other ladies and gentleman deserted the floor for them.

It ended too soon, when Auggie Turnbull brought the dancing to a halt to announce that Peter Hiram's work of art was to be unveiled in The Laurels's entry hall. Amid murmurs of anticipation, the guests filed out of the ballroom.

Damon followed reluctantly with Neilly on his arm. He didn't care one whit what Hiram had carved in stone, but he could see the interest in Neilly's eyes. So they joined in the crowd gathered in the hall. He spotted Aunt Varina and her friends leaning over the upstairs banister to get the best view of the unveiling of the statue, draped with a white cloth. He saw Aunt Izzie and McGregor standing companionably arm-in-arm near the front door.

Auggie Turnbull raised his hands. An expectant hush settled over the guests. Lace fans fluttered in the silence as Auggie puffed out his thin chest. "Olivia, my dear, do the honors."

Mrs. Turnbull came forward. "As most of you know, three years ago we had the wonderful opportunity of meeting a talented young sculptor, Peter Hiram."

She swept a gloved hand in Hiram's direction, and the young man bowed in acknowledgment. The guests applauded him.

"Peter was just at the beginning of his career and about to embark on a tour of Italy to further his studies, and it was our great honor to become his sponsor. Now, after his hours of study and work, we have the privilege of premier-

ing his work here at The Laurels. Without further delay . . ."

Olivia Turnbull tugged the cloth cover from the eight-foot
white marble statue.

A chorus of cheers and scattered applause spread
throughout the crowd.

Then Damon stared at the piece, unimpressed. To him it
looked like one more curly-haired, bare-legged, athletic man
modestly draped in a Roman toga. The marble appeared to
be of good quality.

"What do you think?" Damon asked Neilly softly. He
took the opportunity to draw her a little closer and to catch
the scent of flowers and woman about her. "Just between
us. You're the artist."

"I think it's well done." Her tone lacked a certain admiration.

"Is that all?"

"It appears to be a competent copy of Apollo Belvedere
wearing a toga. The original Greek sculpture is a nude in
the Vatican's collection, I think," she added.

"A nude? Something your family allowed you to look
upon?"

"It was an artistic study," Neilly said, irritation in her
voice. "I'd like to have a closer look at Hiram's sculpture,
if you don't mind."

They lingered, allowing the crowd to view the sculpture
before wandering off to the midnight supper that was being
served on the gallery. Only Peter Hiram, a few admirers,
Aunt Isetta, and McGregor remained.

"May I congratulate you on a fine piece of work," Neilly
said.

"Why, thank you, Miss Lind," Hiram said, a smile of
pleasure and admiration lighting his face again, as it had
earlier in the receiving line. Damon reminded himself that
a certain amount of that was to be expected from the men

around Neilly. "Such praise from an art lover such as yourself is appreciated.

"I owe much to my sponsors, the Turnbulls, and to Mr. Minor, who will be displaying my work in New Orleans. Have you met Mr. John Minor? Miss Cornelia Lind, may I present Mr. John Minor. I told you about the lady who sketches earlier."

A small, squat, foreign-looking man stepped forward and held out his hand. "Miss Lind. I believe we've met. A few years ago I was agent for some art transactions with your father."

Minor had the sharp nose of a ferret and the dark, furtive eyes of a street thief. Despite his well-tailored clothes and his careful diction, his manner was too bold and too smooth for Damon's liking.

Neilly made no move to take the man's hand. Color drained from her face, and she stepped back on Damon's toe in her effort to escape. When Damon put his hand on the small of her back to steady her he could feel fear and loathing coursing through her.

"I'm Damon Durande." He took Minor's hand and shook it, rescuing Neilly from the need to touch the rude man if she didn't want to.

But he purposely blocked her retreat. He had no intention of allowing anything to happen to Neilly, but he wasn't about to miss this opportunity to learn more about her.

She pressed back against him and took a shallow, shaky breath. "Yes, I remember you, Mr. Minor."

"What a pleasant surprise to find you here, *Miss Lind,* so far from Charleston," Minor continued, as if her enthusiasm for the meeting matched his. "I understand you're staying at the Rosewood plantation. Thomas Stirling's art collection is legendary. What a delight for someone with such appreciation for art to be living in a house with so many antiquities and artistic treasures."

"Yes, it's a pleasure," Neilly murmured, casting a guilty glance over her shoulder at Damon.

"What sort of art do you deal in, Mr. Minor?" Damon asked. The thought that Neilly was somehow associated with this nefarious-looking fellow didn't please him at all. What did she have to be guilty about? "Do you represent sculptors? Painters?"

"I have no specialty, Mr. Durande. I handle sculpture like this fine work of Mr. Hiram's. Paintings, yes. Antiquities. Even excellent sketches like those of Miss . . . ah . . . Miss Lind's. I remember your work well, miss. I work with collectors of all sorts of fine art.

"And, Miss Lind, may I offer my belated condolences on the death of your father. A great loss, my dear," Minor continued to the growing discomfort of all who stood around him and Hiram. "So well thought of in Charleston. I'm surprised you left town."

"Well, I, uh . . ."

Damon studied her profile, awaiting her answer and trying unsuccessfully to read her expression.

"Oh, oh my! Oh my, Damon! Neilly!" At Damon's side, Isetta clutched at her chest, then grabbed his arm. "I have a pain in my chest. I think my palpitations are threatening. I feel faint."

Damon stared down at his aunt, his suspicions of Neilly immediately dismissed. "McGregor? Where are you?"

Neilly turned immediately to Isetta.

"Get her off her feet." McGregor appeared at her side. "Neilly, do you have a vial of her amyl nitrite?"

Damon swung his aunt up in his arms before she could swoon.

"Yes, right here." Neilly pulled open the plum satin drawstring bag hanging from her wrist. "Lay her out on the bench over there."

Damon headed for the marble seat against the wall, scattering Hiram, Minor, and the others from his path. He settled Isetta on the bench, and knelt down to support her head against his arm. McGregor sat down on the edge of the bench and took her wrist in his practiced fingers.

"This will clear your head." Neilly's satin gown rustled as she knelt beside Damon and broke a vial of yellow liquid into a handkerchief. She passed the fruity-smelling medicine beneath Isetta's nose. "Just take a little sniff."

"Ugh." Aunt Isetta turned her head to the wall and pushed the salts back at Neilly. "Is there a crowd still?"

"No," Damon assured her, conscious of how much store his aunt put into appearances. "They've gone out onto the gallery."

She rested in his arms: feather light, still, pale, her eyes closed. "How serious is this?" he asked McGregor.

"Her pulse is strong," McGregor said, his voice crisp and professional. "But it's been a long, exhausting day. I tried to get her to rest this afternoon, but she wouldn't."

"And I've ruined everyone's good time, now haven't I?" Isetta said without opening her eyes.

"Nonsense," McGregor said. "Three children have already been sick from eating too many eclairs, and one of the ladies with child fainted at the sight of rare beef on the buffet table. Your palpitations are hardly worth taking note of, my dear."

Aunt Izzie's eyes popped open. "That's a fine thing to say, Theo. Out of the mouth of my own doctor!"

"Well, I do think it's time you go home and get a good rest. I'll come along just to be certain this spell is past."

Isetta peered around the entry hall. "Are they gone? Hiram and that other little man?"

"Yes," Damon and Neilly said in unison. Their eyes met briefly. Neilly looked away first. Damon recalled all the questions he'd wanted to ask just before his aunt's spell. What did John Minor know about Neilly that frightened her so badly?

"Good, I'm glad they're gone." Isetta sat up and

smoothed her skirts. "I feel better now. Well enough for the trip home."

Relief eased through Damon. Aunt Isetta sounded more like herself now, and her color had returned. When he glanced at Neilly he saw the puckers between her brows smooth and her smile returned. But she avoided meeting his gaze again, and he knew it was because of the meeting with John Minor.

Cool, deadly fingers of suspicion spread through Damon as he rose to help his aunt to her feet. He had Aunt Isetta, Aunt Varina, and Rosewood to protect. No matter how prettily Cornelia Lind smiled or how well she danced, he could not let her charm beguile him from learning the truth.

Seven

"What have I heard about Peter Hiram and his art dealer?" Theo repeated thoughtfully, swirling the brandy in his snifter, playing for time. His mind was still on Isetta and her attack. He had to sort through his thoughts and fears to find an answer for Damon's question.

They sat in the library drinking, a small table between them. Candlelight glittered off the golden book titles as soft shadows wavered around them. Outside, the crickets and tree frogs sang a noisy chorus.

In the house silence reigned. Isetta was safely settled in bed and the servants were all asleep. Theo was satisfied that the danger had passed—this time.

"Theo, you travel every road and bayou of this parish in the course of a month. People come to your door," Damon said, his eyes dark and troubled. "You know both the fine families and the humble ones. You must hear things. What have you heard about John Minor?"

"Not much, really." Theo paused, reluctant to go on, uneasy about repeating what little he had heard. Damon had become rather obsessed with his questions about Cornelia Lind, and Theo did not want to feed the boy's suspicions. "As far as I know, John Minor is an art dealer from New Orleans, just as he claims."

"I knew you'd heard something." Damon leaned closer, staring into his brandy glass, his voice low and edgy. "Go on."

"Auggie Turnbull told me that Minor wasna the dealer they had originally wanted to work through. It seems the man has something of a tarnished reputation. But Hiram insisted."

"I suspected as much." A look of displeasure contorted Damon's face. He tapped the foot of his glass on the table. "What else?"

"Nothing." Theo sipped his brandy and shrugged. "I just know that none of the other families in the parish have dealt with the man. No one seems to have taken much of a liking to him."

"I didn't care for him either." Damon drained his glass, then stared into it thoughtfully. "I have another favor to ask."

"Ask."

"You said you were going to Charleston for a medical conference next week?"

"Aye, I'm leaving Monday," Theo said. "Provided Isetta doesna have another attack. I've asked young Johnson to come down from upriver to check on my patients. But I donna think your aunt's attack was very serious. Overall, I'd say her condition is improving."

"Does Neilly know where you're going?"

"I donna think I've told her more than the fact that I was going to a medical conference."

"Good. While you're in Charleston, find out what you can about Cornelia Lind," Damon said. "She claims her father was a doctor there and that her mother was an Ashley."

"Aye?" Theo frowned, unhappy with the thought of playing spy. "And is there anything else you expect me to learn that will help you?"

"I know that she was betrothed, and that her gentleman called it off." Damon shook his head. "That might have been some time ago, but the gossipmongers would remember such a scandal."

"Aye," Theo agreed. Especially when the lady was as

pretty and desirable as Neilly, he thought. They'd tell that bit of a tale over and over again.

Damon stared off into the darkness, his face taut. "Theo, did you see her face when she met Minor? This meeting was the last thing she expected or wanted. Surprise was written all over her, and something else. Embarrassment? Guilt?"

Theo looked down at his glass. "Damon, having an acquaintance with an art dealer of questionable reputation doesna mean she's here at Rosewood to do anything terrible."

"No, it doesn't," Damon agreed, facing Theo again. "But it's an odd coincidence, don't you agree? A girl of no apparent means and with Neilly's obvious knowledge of art has the good fortune to win a position at Rosewood.

"She comes here and worms her way into the affections of the mistress of the plantation. And what if she does an inventory of all the fine pieces? What if this inventory isn't an inventory, but a shopping list for a shifty dealer of art?"

"What you're saying is pure speculation!" Theo said, trying to allay Damon's suspicions. "Nothing more. The art world is probably just like our society here in Louisiana. It's very small and everyone knows everyone, good and bad. Association means nothing.

"I believe Neilly is everything she says she is." Theo set his empty snifter aside and softly pounded his fist on the table. He was a little offended that Damon didn't at least trust his judgment of the girl. "Just to prove you wrong, I will confirm Neilly's background while I'm at the conference in Charleston. I'll find out as much as I can and prove to you what a fine young lady she is."

"That's all I want," Damon said. "Thanks, Doc."

Neilly stood at the top of the attic stairs and caught herself yawning for the third time that morning. She hadn't been sleeping well, but she wanted to get an early start.

In fact, she'd hardly slept a wink since her encounter with John Minor at The Laurels two days ago. She'd enjoyed the elegant social affair, and she hadn't seen a single familiar face all day. She had come to the conclusion that she had nothing to fear at The Laurels. Then there he was—John Minor.

Her first reaction had been to turn and run, but Damon had blocked her path of retreat. What did he suspect, if anything? The sight of Minor had shaken her completely. It had almost left her babbling. The only person's face that would have shocked her more would have been that of Charles.

Neilly closed her eyes against the vivid memories of the unfortunate meeting with Minor. Damon couldn't know anything, except that she had been badly frightened. She had to believe that.

But there were other memories that kept her from sleeping, as well. The memory of Damon's touch lingered with her. It was as if he'd left some indelible mark on her with the brush of his hands. Dancing with him had been an unexpected, unparalleled pleasure.

No partner had ever swept her across the floor with such ease, with such perfect rhythm. Like a seductive invitation to something more. She was vaguely aware of what she desired and was annoyed that her body yearned for more of his touch.

Her head said "nonsense." Attentive as Damon had been, she sensed that he'd still reserved his judgment about her. He'd watched her so closely, testing her reactions to him, questioning what and who she was.

Then she'd walked into John Minor. Heaven knew what Damon had concluded from that awkward confrontation. With the guilt that must have been written all over her face and the information about her past engagement that he'd wheedled out of her, heaven knew what he suspected.

The next question was: If Minor knew where she was,

would Charles find out? No, Neilly told herself. Not likely. They didn't even know each other.

Her lack of sleep was clouding her perceptions.

Isetta's condition had also been keeping her up at night. She checked on the lady every hour during the first night, but each time she found her patient breathing deeply and sleeping soundly. It seemed Dr. McGregor had been right: The attack hadn't been a serious one.

Stifling another yawn, she convinced herself that Damon really didn't know anything. She had no serious reason to fear discovery. In fact, since Miss Isetta's most recent attack, Neilly's help was needed more than ever.

In the past none of the families she had worked for had scrutinized her story as closely as had Damon. Certainly her integrity had never been questioned: not once, not ever. She'd always left of her own free will, usually with good references, and only when her patient was on the road to recovery. Or when she knew Charles Ruffin was getting too close.

"Well, good morning, Miss Lind."

Neilly started and turned toward the source of the voice.

Claude Pugh greeted Neilly as he closed the door to his attic room. He was dressed for his day's work in wrinkled frock coat and limp cravat. His pale, intent gaze slid over Neilly in an ungentlemanly way that always irritated and unsettled her. "I certainly didn't expect to meet you up here so early in the morning."

"I'm taking inventory of the attic," she said, clutching her ledger against her breasts as if it were a shield.

"How very enterprising of you," Pugh said, continuing to stare at her far too intently. Then he gestured toward the crates. "I suspect it's been some time since an inventory has been done in this house."

"Actually, it's never been done," Neilly said. "Or so I'm told."

"So you have no old inventory to work against," Pugh said, seeming to take note of the point. "Such a lot of work on top of your other duties. Will you need to see my room then?"

"Oh, no, I don't think that will be necessary today, Mr. Pugh," Neilly said. She had no interest in his room. "I'm primarily concerned with the art and the antiquities."

"I see." Pugh stepped toward the attic stairway. "Then I won't keep you. The attic is hardly my favorite place. Good day to you, Miss Cornelia."

"And to you, sir."

Pugh brushed past her. He smelled sweet and musty, of stale liquor and unwashed clothing, and she was relieved when he disappeared down the stairs.

Morning light filtered through the trees and into the attic dormer windows. Golden shafts struck the floor, raising the dust into swirls of glittering particles.

When Neilly had come up the stairs she'd noted with a housekeeper's eye that the stair rail had been dusted. The stairs and the hallway to the dormer rooms where Mr. Pugh lived had been swept. No other cleaning appeared to have been done in the storage area.

"Miss Neilly, you up here?" Cato called up the stairs. "Cleo said you wanted to talk to me."

"Yes, Cato," Neilly said. "I have some questions about some of the crates up here."

Soon Cato joined her. "There's things in storage up here that Master Stirling never even took out of their boxes after he come home."

"Is that so?" Neilly said. "Why not?"

Cato shook his head. "Trip after trip. He always brought loads of things back to Rosewood, 'til he stopped traveling. Then we just covered it and left it alone like he told us."

"When did he stop traveling?" Neilly asked, surveying the cartons and crates with a new eye.

"After Miss Rosalie and Master Louis died, and when Master Damon come to live with us. Them was unhappy days. We—I don't talk about that time."

"I see," Neilly said, a little disappointed that Cato wouldn't tell her more about Damon's parents. "Heavens, I hardly know where to start."

"Well, them things there are the things Master Thomas brought back from his travels to New York and Europe," Uncle Cato said, pointing to a stack of sturdy crates. "Those pictures against the wall, them are paintings that he decided he didn't like no more."

"I see some furniture back in the corner there." Neilly gestured.

The old servant paused, "Them are Miss Rosalie's things. Master Thomas ordered us to burn them things when she run away to marry Master Louis. Said he didn't want to see no more of her frippery around the house, but Miss Isetta told us to hide them in the attic. I don't know if those is things that you want in your list."

"Thank you, Uncle Cato," Neilly said, knowing without a doubt and with no good reason—except curiosity about Damon's mother, the infamous disinherited heiress to Rosewood—that she was going to start on Miss Rosalie's things. "I don't think I'll need any more help this morning. Just let me know when Miss Isetta wakes up."

"Yeas, Miss Neilly." Uncle Cato descended the stairs, his old joints popping and creaking so loudly, even Neilly could hear them.

Already the air hung hot and heavy in the attic, and by midday she knew the storage room would be unbearable. That was why she had decided to begin work early. Time enough for breakfast later.

She took a scarf out of her apron pocket and tied it around her head, tucking the ends in at the base of her neck, tignon-style. Then she weaved her way between pine crates, draped furniture, and dusty hatboxes to the dark corner of the attic that Uncle Cato had pointed out. She pulled off the cover to find a girl's furniture and treasures.

Neilly wondered whether Damon knew his mother's

things were up here or if he cared. Propped in the corner
stood a rolled-up Oriental rug. Next to that the tallest piece
in the corner was a cheval glass. A burled wood chest of
drawers stood in front of the mirror with a brass birdcage
sitting on top of it. Boxes of books and baskets filled with
girlhood odds and ends sat at its feet.

Old Master Thomas had removed his daughter from
Rosewood as completely as he could, Neilly thought, and
hastily, too, from the look of the way things had been
thrown together. She drew up a stool and began to sift
through baskets of delicate china figurines, ornate perfume
bottles, and richly dressed dolls. In the cedar chest she
found a lace bedspread, a bed canopy, and a demure white
damask gown. Neilly held it up, wondering if it had been
a confirmation dress or a first ball gown.

A couple of the boxes appeared to have been disturbed
recently. The dusty top layer of books—mostly novels of
adventure and romance—had been shoved aside in an effort
to look at others. Neilly leafed through a number of well-
fingered catalogues from exclusive shops in Boston,
Charleston, and even London. She hoped vaguely to find a
diary or perhaps some letters, some kind of insight into the
girl. At the bottom of one of the boxes all she discovered
was an ebony gargoyle.

Puzzled, she held the gothic creature up to the sunlight.
The grotesque, big-eared monster stared back at her, pulling
a comical face much like a schoolchild's insulting grimace
made behind a teacher's back. What troubled her about the
wooden piece was that gargoyles were usually carved out
of stone and cluttered the facades of gothic churches.

"Rosalie had a pair of those."

The words startled Neilly so that she almost dropped the
ebony figure. Turning, she saw Varina at the top of the attic
stairs. "Oh. I didn't hear you come up the stairs."

"I'm sorry, Neilly. I didn't mean to startle you. I just
came up to tell you that Isetta is awake. But there's no

hurry. She can't be very sick, from the way she's tapping out orders with her cane."

Varina crossed the storage room. She was already dressed for the day, with her work gloves tucked into the pocket of her gardening apron. "I always thought those things were horrible little things, but funny all the same."

"I know what you mean," Neilly agreed, holding up the gargoyle to the sunlight again. "Ugly, but fascinating. Doesn't it make you wonder what the medieval workmen dreamed about?"

"Elijah said the same thing," Varina said, coming to a stop by the box Neilly had been going through.

"Elijah?"

"Our carpenter. He's the free man who helped you and Damon out of the burning guest house."

"Oh, yes. Elijah." Neilly clearly recalled the big man with strong hands who had pulled them from the fire.

"Rosalie found a picture of a gargoyle in one of Papa's books and asked Elijah to make a pair for her to use to hold up her books. He made them from some remnants of wood that he had." Varina laughed, as if pleasant, long-forgotten memories of her sister were fresh again.

"Rosalie was like that. She liked pretty little novelties. She was always off shopping for something odd or new, studying all those catalogues. But I'd forgotten about the gargoyles until just now. Where's the other one?"

"I only found one," Neilly said, peering into the bottom of the box again to make certain that she hadn't missed the other gargoyle. "I wondered why it showed no signs of wear."

"It's not an antique. It's just the result of a girl's fancy," Varina said wistfully. "She was only fifteen when Elijah made them for her. Three years later she ran away, and five years after that she was dead. Maybe Elijah knows where the other one is." With a shrug of her shoulders, Varina added, in a hushed voice, "Don't tell Isetta about them. She ordered everyone to stay out of Rosalie's things."

"I won't say a word to Miss Isetta," Neilly said, her interest in the lone gargoyle renewed. So Damon's mother had liked homely, medieval creatures and read novels and played with fine dolls.

Reluctantly, Neilly rose from her stool, she wanted to know more about the piece, but now wasn't the time to investigate. "It's probably not worth anything. But I'll see what Elijah knows about it. Speaking of your sister, I'd better see how she's doing this morning."

It was midafternoon before Neilly was able to leave the house to seek out Elijah. She left Miss Isetta and Miss Varina occupied with a caller: their nearest neighbor, Violet Esterbrook, who had come to see how Miss Isetta was faring after the swooning spell at the barbecue.

Neilly wrapped the gargoyle in a towel, tucked it into a basket, and set out to find the carpenter. Following Cleo's directions, Neilly found Elijah's log cabin on the edge of the row of slave quarters that lay 'round the bend in a narrow track just beyond the kitchen and the laundry house. She'd walked nearly a quarter of a mile from the plantation house on a well-worn path. As she'd walked, Neilly had heard the slaves singing as they worked in the fields.

This time of day the cabins were nearly deserted. The able-bodied workers were in the fields—where Damon was. Old, grizzled women sat in their rockers and swapped stories while their hands worked at the sewing and spinning in their laps. Only toddlers played with rag dolls and puppies in the dust beneath the trees. From one of the cabins came the slap and thunk of a busy loom.

Neilly nodded to the women and they nodded back.

Elijah's cabin was easy to find, just as Cleo had said. Wooden planks and whole logs cluttered the yard around the small, square log cabin. Carpenter's tools, a saw, and an ax lay on the workbench under a lean-to, out of the weather. A round whetstone stood nearby.

Neilly stopped to look at the other things in the strange yard. As she stared at the sawdust and litter, the sound of two voices reached her from the cabin, voices speaking in low, hushed tones. One was a deep, gravelly man's voice and the other that of a young woman.

"Just one more kiss, woman," the man said. Elijah's voice, Neilly thought.

"There's no time," the woman protested.

"It don't take no time, baby," Elijah said, his voice thick with desire.

The woman murmured something so low, Neilly couldn't understand the words.

"Not much. Let me show you."

Then Neilly heard a cry. She couldn't decide if it was a sound of protest or one of surrender. Should she leave, or should she go to the lady's rescue? Silence followed. She started toward the doorway to save the woman.

"Miss Violet will miss me soon," the woman said. She sounded breathless now, but unharmed. Neilly stopped in her tracks.

The woman continued. "She's been good to us, honey, and Miss Stirling, too. I don't want to do nothing to change that."

"I know, baby." Elijah's voice sounded tight, as if he was in pain. "It won't be much longer. We're close now. I promise, we is so close."

Another soft cry, which Neilly decided wasn't a protest. She had a vague idea of what was probably happening in there now, and she knew it was private. She backed away from the door.

"It's hard for me to believe it's really going to happen."

"It will, baby. It will. We's both going to be free soon."

Neilly stopped, her curiosity overcoming her sense of propriety. She turned an ear back toward the cabin.

Eight

"How much more do we need?" the woman questioned. "Tell me again."

Neilly stood perfectly still, lest her footfall on the grass alert the couple inside the cabin.

"Only forty dollars," Elijah said.

"Forty dollars. It sounds like so much money. Let's just run away. You and me."

"Too dangerous. It ain't worth it. We is so close now. Have faith in me, baby. Be patient."

"If you love me, you won't take much longer to get the money," the woman cajoled.

A soft moan filled the silence. Neilly started away again, sorry that she had eavesdropped. Whatever was being plotted was none of her affair, and she didn't want to hear more. In her haste she walked right past the only window of the cabin.

"Miss Neilly, is that you?" Elijah called. "You looking for somebody?"

Neilly halted, inwardly chiding herself for not having had enough sense to leave when she'd first heard the voices. There was nothing for her to do but turn and face Elijah. He was standing in the cabin doorway. "Well, yes, I was looking for you, Elijah, but I'll come back."

"No, miss, please, I was just leaving." The woman stepped out from behind Elijah, a tall, elegant woman with smooth skin and an oval face. Bold brown eyes met Neilly's gaze. The woman smiled without warmth and bobbed a curtsy. "I'm Alma, Miss Violet's maid."

"Hello, Alma."

"But not a maid for long," Elijah said, his voice impassioned. He slipped his arm around Alma's waist. "You is going to be free like me soon. You going to hold your head up high."

"I already hold my head up high," Alma told him, her nose in the air. "But the lady here don't need to know about our doings."

"Miss Neilly is a lady who will understand," Elijah said, determination and pride lighting his face. "I'm buying Alma's freedom. Miss Isetta and Master Esterbrook agreed to it. We'll be free and married soon."

"That's wonderful," Neilly said, caught up in the pleasure she could see in their faces. "I'm glad for you."

"It just seems to be taking so long to get the money," Alma complained, leaning against Elijah, a longing invitation softening her eyes as she looked up at him and fingered the homespun cloth of his shirt.

Elijah frowned. "I know. But it won't be much longer. I promise."

"I got to go." Alma pulled away from Elijah and put her hands to her head to straighten the neat white tignon tied over her hair. "Miss Violet will be looking for me, and it won't help us none to make her cross."

With a look almost painful to behold, Elijah watched Alma stride away toward the plantation house. Neilly waited. Once Alma turned and waved to him; then she disappeared around a bend in the path. At that moment Neilly's heart ached with envy. How fortunate they were to have each other. They could face the world together, knowing someone stood at their side. Neilly's parents had loved each other like that.

As if he'd suddenly recalled that Neilly was there, Elijah turned to her. "Sorry, Miss Neilly. What can I do for you?"

Neilly took the gargoyle from the basket and unwrapped it. "I was looking through some things in the attic and found this. Do you remember it? Miss Varina told me that you made a pair of them, and I was wondering where the other one was."

Elijah took the wooden figure from Neilly and examined it carefully. "Yeas, I remember this. Lawdy, I carved it a long time ago, before I'd earned my freedom. Miss Rosalie came to me with a picture in a book from her daddy's library. I made a pair, all right. From some wood left from a fireplace mantel I made for one of the neighbors. I never saw them again after I gave them to her."

"Oh, what a shame," Neilly said, accepting the gargoyle from Elijah. "They wouldn't be of value for anything except a novelty, but I think they're rather distinctive."

"That's what Miss Rosalie liked, unusual things," Elijah said with a shake of his head. "She was something special. Had ideas of her own. Got fancies, like that gargoyle. A lot like her father that way. I suppose that's why they didn't get along."

"Is that so?" Neilly prompted, hoping that Elijah would be more talkative about Rosalie than Cato or Cleo had been. "I understand he refused to allow her to marry Louis Durande."

"Yeas, but it wasn't until after she drowned in the boat accident that he shut himself up in his room and wouldn't come out no more," Elijah said.

"What boating accident?" Neilly asked. No one had ever mentioned a boating accident.

"The one that killed Miss Rosalie and her husband, Master Louie," Elijah said, as if she should have known.

"That's how Master Damon's parents died?"

"Miss Rosalie was gone a lot," Elijah said with a shake of his head. "She'd get Isetta or Varina to take care of Master Damon and then she'd go off with her husband on shopping trips to Paris. But Damon's father liked his boats. The

day they died they was sailing Master Louie's new boat—
what do they call it?—A maiden voyage, and a storm come
up. Their bodies was washed up three days later."

"Oh, how tragic," Neilly said, shocked. She stared down
at the gargoyle in her hand, the fancy of a young girl like
so many other young girls, with a carefree heart and an
imagination full of sweet and ugly visions.

"Oh, yeas, and Master Damon, him only a boy then. He
found their bodies washed up on the riverbank." Elijah nodded. "Yeas, miss. It was a mighty terrible thing."

"Damon found the bodies of his own parents?" Neilly
asked. The pain and grief Damon must have suffered from
such a discovery would have been overwhelming for a child.

Elijah nodded again. "That was the beginning of the end
for the ol' master. He was never quite himself again. Started
staying in his room all day and sending out his steward to
do all the work around the plantation. My mammy—she's
gone now—she worked in the big house then and she'd
come down here and tell us all the strange happenings."

"So Thomas Stirling withdrew from the world to mourn
the daughter he'd disinherited?" Neilly mused aloud,
pleased to glimpse a soft side of the dictator of Rosewood.
But her imagination refused to comprehend how Damon
must have suffered.

"Well, that's not what *he* said," Elijah said. "He said she
got what she deserved for disobeying her father."

She should have guessed, Neilly told herself.

"He wouldn't even have her buried in the family cemetery on the hill out there," Elijah said, gesturing in the direction of the cemetery plot Neilly had seen from a distance.
"Had her buried in the church plot, 'mongst strangers. Master Louie's family buried him with their people. Seems the
ol' folks had their way in the end. Neither family wanted
that marriage, love match or not."

"How much of this did Damon know about?"

"Nobody worried about keeping nothing from the young

master," Elijah said with another shake of his head. "His ears were nary spared a word of it. But he never spoke of it. Leastways, not to me. He would come down here and work with me sometimes. Good worker. Good pupil. Sometimes we went fishing. We always got on jis fine. But he kept all his thoughts about his mother to himself."

"Then his grandfather ordered him out of the house?" Neilly asked, eager to fit all the pieces into the puzzling story.

Elijah grinned. "But Miss Isetta had her way of not always hearing what her daddy said—even when he shouted in her ear. She and Miss Varina took care of Master Damon. They did their best for him, and he always comes back when they need him."

"So I understand," Neilly said. No wonder Damon had such strong feelings about sleeping under Rosewood's roof.

She turned the gargoyle over in her hand. What did he think of his mother? Had her indifference toward her son left him wary and suspicious of others?

"Miss Neilly? You want me to make you another one of these?" Elijah looked around the yard. "I don't know if I can find the same wood, but there might be something around here."

"No, I was just curious about the piece." Neilly weighed the ebony gargoyle in her hand. "I'm afraid what's been lost is irreplaceable."

The sad strains of a piano sonata faded, echoing melodically through Rosewood's music room, where they had retired after dinner. From the window Damon watched Isetta hover over the ivory keyboard and sigh, her thoughts obviously somewhere else. Varina dozed in the chair across the room.

Neilly sat on the sofa, a faraway look in her eye, apparently lost to the music. She was dressed in a pretty pale yellow gown that gave her an air of sincerity. He liked it.

When Isetta played the last notes of the piece he applauded her performance. Neilly joined him. Varina started awake and added her approval.

"Very fine, Aunt Isetta. A few weeks away from the instrument doesn't seem to have affected your skill," Damon said.

"I quite agree," Neilly said.

"Oh, yes, but that piece was a little sad, don't you think, Sister?" Varina said. "Play something happy for us. Please."

"No, I'm not in the mood to play something happy," Isetta snapped. "When did Theo say he'd be back?"

"Not for three weeks." Slightly alarmed, Damon stepped away from the window. "Why? Do you feel unwell?"

"No, no." Isetta shook her head and waved him away. "Nothing like that."

Damon shot Neilly a questioning glance. She shook her head to assure him that his aunt was telling the truth. Relieved, he returned to his position, leaning against the windowframe, where he could view the garden.

Daylight had faded, leaving a pool of golden light around the piano while darkness gathered in the corners of the room. Varina's flowers layered the breeze from the garden with wonderful scents. Outside the crickets had taken up their evening song. Uncle Cato tottered in and began to light the candles.

"No, Uncle Cato," Isetta ordered with an imperious wave of her hand. "We're not staying here. I'm exhausted."

Without breaking his dogged stride, Cato doubled back in retreat.

"Would you like to retire, Miss Isetta?" Neilly suggested, rising from her chair.

Damon turned to study his aunt again. He couldn't imagine what was troubling her.

"Not just yet." Isetta's eyes narrowed when she appraised

her nephew. "Damon, you seem to find the garden fascinating this evening. Why don't you take Miss Neilly for a walk?"

"Yes. Yes," Varina agreed, eagerly sitting forward in her chair, her eyes lighting with anticipation. "You and Neilly must smell the fragrance of the roses. They're wonderful right now. A walk in the garden is just the thing."

Across the room, Neilly met Damon's gaze, a wariness in her fine blue eyes. She'd been uneasy around him ever since the scene with the art dealer at The Laurels. She'd hardly allowed herself to be alone in the same room with him. He'd missed the challenge of her company.

It seemed that Varina and Isetta were playing right into his hands. A few moments alone with Neilly wasn't a bad idea, Damon thought. He wanted to talk to her about John Minor. The least he could do was offer her the opportunity to explain that awkward meeting. "What an excellent idea, Aunt Isetta."

"I hardly think it necessary for Damon to entertain me this evening," Neilly protested, appealing to the two ladies in the room. "He's already devoted more time than necessary to my amusement."

Damon stepped away from the window, annoyed with her lack of enthusiasm and curious about the expression of alarm that crossed her face. "Is the prospect of a walk in the garden with me so terrible?"

"Well, of course not. It's just that—"

Isetta stood up from the piano stool. "Good. It's settled then. Varina will see me to bed, won't you, Sister? Good night."

"Good night, Aunt Isetta," Damon said.

"I'm coming, Sister." Varina grinned at Neilly and Damon before she followed Isetta from the room. "You have a good time now, you two."

Neilly stared after the sisters with the expression of

someone who had just found herself deserted in the face
of the enemy.

"It appears they've left you no choice." Damon swept
his hand toward the door. "After you."

She hesitated. Then she smiled at him bravely, with a lift
of her chin, and marched past him out the door.

Cool darkness closed around them.

"Is that a new gown you're wearing?" he asked as he
led the way into the garden shadows.

"Yes. Well, now that Mammy Ruby has my measure-
ments she can't seem to stop sewing for me," Neilly explained. "But I intend to repay your aunts. I've made it
clear the gowns are not gifts, and they certainly aren't part
of the arrangement we had."

"It's all right, Neilly." Damon squeezed her hand. "It's
not the cost of the gowns that concerns me. I just want to
tell you how lovely you look in that shade of yellow."

"Why—why, thank you," she stammered.

"Is it so difficult to accept a compliment from me?" He
couldn't see her face in the darkness, but her obvious surprise exasperated him. "You didn't have any problem accepting compliments from the Kenners."

Neilly stopped and withdrew her hand from his. "Was
there some particular reason why you wanted to talk to me?
May I answer some questions about your aunt's condition?"

"I have another topic in mind, but let's find a place to
sit."

"Why can't we talk here?" she asked.

"Sitting would be more comfortable, don't you think?
There's a nice place over here that offers a view of the
continents."

"Yes, I know where you mean," she said. "You can see
the statues of Europa, Asia, and the Americas that can't be
seen from the drive."

She followed him to the white wrought-iron bench under
a weeping willow. They ducked under the feathery boughs.

Damon brushed fallen leaves from the seat. When he finished Neilly sat down, carefully arranging her skirts, and Damon joined her. The bench was so narrow that it was impossible not to sit thigh-to-thigh, but she was doing her best to avoid the contact.

Just to thwart her attempts, Damon slipped his arm along the back of the bench, closing the distance between them. He leaned close enough to feel her warmth and to smell her lilac scent.

"Uncle Cato told me that you started inventorying the attic this morning. Will it take long?"

"Uh, well, as a matter of fact there are some interesting pieces up there," Neilly said, holding herself erect and avoiding eye contact. "I found a pair of Chinese vases and an ebony chest inlaid with ivory and mother-of-pearl. There are crates that your grandfather never unpacked."

"That sounds like him.

"It will take some time to sort through everything. Unfortunately, I found little background material on the items for the provenance, unless some histories are packed with the things." Neilly chattered on, so involved in describing her work that she seemed to forget to be wary of him.

She leaned back against the bench as she talked. Damon watched her closely, amused by her enthusiasm and animation. She liked working on the inventory. Her pleasure and excitement showed in her gestures and in her voice.

He listened with half an ear, taking pleasure in having her close to him, her body in his grasp as she had been on the dance floor at The Laurels. The skin of her arm was warm and smooth under his hand, and he could smell the womanliness beneath her lilac scent.

As he gazed down at her, he considered what liberties she might have allowed her betrothed. Had the man kissed those deliciously delicate collarbones or nuzzled her throat? Damon wondered with a growing ache in his groin. Had she allowed her promised one to tongue her ear or to slip his hand up her skirt?

"Tell me about how you and your father happened to know John Minor," Damon said, coldly interrupting his lusty longings.

She blinked and leaned away from him.

"Ah, it was just as Mr. Minor said. He and my father had some dealings over a few imported pieces, I believe. It was a very long time ago. I don't remember much about it."

Her sudden memory loss was troubling. She refused to look at him, and Damon knew there was more to this relationship between Minor and her father than she wanted to tell. "Did John Minor know your betrothed?"

She sat erect and caution edged her voice. "Why? What does Mr. Minor have to do with the inventory?"

"You tell me."

"I hardly know the man. He was an acquaintance of my father's who called at the house once or twice."

"He's a man of bad reputation."

"Oh? Am I responsible for his reputation?" Neilly snapped. Even in the dark Damon could see the gleam of anger in her eyes. "Because I know a man of bad reputation you feel I must bear the same?"

"That's not what I said."

"I'm sorry if people have taken advantage of your aunts' generous nature," Neilly said, her anger in full flame now and her reserve about being alone with him plainly forgotten. "But I am here to help them. I hardly think it's fair of you to suspect me of some offense because of what has happened in the past. Or because I happened to have met a man of questionable reputation."

Just enough light fell through the lacy cover of the willow to show him the defiance in her features, to reveal the sweet, somber line of her lips and the outraged honesty of her eyes. The way she put it, his suspicions were unfair.

What's more, they didn't have an iota of effect on how desirable he found her.

Lord, he wanted her to be the paragon his aunts believed her to be. He hooked a finger under her chin and bent to kiss her.

She pulled away at first, a soft murmur of surprise escaping her lips. Then she softened, kissing him back, moving her lips against his, to Damon's pleasure. She leaned into him, spreading her hands on his thigh. His body responded with a raw rush of desire.

Encouraged and aroused, Damon deepened the kiss, thrusting his tongue into her mouth.

The liberty seemed too much for Neilly. She pushed against his leg, arching her back against his hold. But her first willing response had kindled his passion. He threaded his fingers through her dark curls, preventing her escape. He devoted himself to exploring the pretty little corners of her mouth, then venturing into her depths.

He'd given her little warning of what he wanted. He knew he'd startled her, but he wasn't going to let go now. He'd wanted to kiss her like this since their first night alone on the gallery.

The fact that she might not be what she seemed mattered little when he held her in his arms. Nothing mattered but the sweetness of her mouth.

She struggled against him again, her efforts more forceful this time.

He released her.

She was off the bench in an instant. But he caught her wrist just in time to keep her from escaping into the darkness.

"How dare you," she railed in curiously hushed tones, as if she were incensed but afraid of being overheard. She fought against his grip. "Let go of me."

"No." Damon remained where he was but tightened his

hold on her, silently cursing the darkness. He longed to see her face and confront her squarely.

"I demand to know your intentions," Neilly said, her pull against his grip unrelenting.

"I was merely seeking the good-night kiss I never received after the barbecue," Damon lied, annoyed with her virtuous wrath. "After all, you spent a good deal of the evening at The Laurels in my arms. You didn't seem to mind a bit."

"We were only dancing!" she whispered. "Let me remind you that I agreed to go to that affair only for the benefit of your aunt. I am not here at Rosewood for your amusement. I'm here because—I need this position."

In the dim light from the upstairs rooms of the house he caught the glimmer of angry tears on her cheeks and of desolate confusion in her face. His male indignation deserted him.

"Why do you need the position, Neilly?" Damon asked, desiring an answer to her question almost as much as he wanted to possess her. "Why did you choose to come to Rosewood? At first I thought you were here to take advantage of my aunts. But there's more to it, isn't there? Neilly, are you running away from something?"

She looked so defenseless and vulnerable that for a moment he believed she was going to tell him.

"No. What would I have to run from?" She shook her head. Sweet fierceness transformed her features. "Now let me go. I must go see to your aunt."

"I'll let you go in a minute," Damon assured her, dissatisfied with her answer. His question had hit on something. Her agitated denial was proof, but he felt like a cad for upsetting her. He had not behaved like a gentleman. Still, he couldn't resist pressing the small advantage he had left. "At least tell me if you enjoyed the kiss. I think you did."

"I did not." She gasped. "I can't believe you're asking me that."

"You definitely kissed me back." Damon shook his head. "I won't let go until you admit it."

She sniffed. Damon watched her wipe away angry tears with the back of her free hand.

"Well, maybe a little." She tugged against his grip again, then relented. "You are an attractive man, you know, in a rough sort of way."

"Ah, that accounts for it," Damon said, unable to keep the wryness from his voice. A smug smile touched his lips. He liked thinking she found him attractive. "Maybe your response means we like each other."

"Not at this moment." She still whispered, as if she thought all the world was listening.

"But you did admit to liking the kiss," Damon reminded her.

"Sir, I believe you are toying with me."

"Never," Damon vowed, uncertain whether he truly meant it but determined to make her forget her tears. "I'm just asking for assurance that you're not going to hold my ungentlemanly conduct against me."

"I don't believe this." She stared at him openmouth for a moment. "Just what are you asking?"

"For some token of your forgiveness," Damon said.

She was silent for a moment. "Do your aunts know you behave like this with ladies?"

Damon chuckled, but her question made it plain that she thought this was some flirtatious game of his. "Are you going to tell on me? I swear I've never asked any lady's forgiveness, never, before you. Besides that, I can't afford to have you take offense and leave Rosewood with Dr. McGregor away."

"That's reassuring," she said ruefully. But her resistance to his grip eased a little. The understanding that he couldn't and wouldn't send her away seemed to console her a bit. "What sort of token?"

"A kiss of forgiveness," he said. If she thought it was a

game, he'd play a game. He rose from the bench and offered his cheek. "Only a small one."

"I see." After a thoughtful moment she leaned toward him, allowing him to draw her close again. She touched his cheek with her lips, warm and soft. When he expected her to pull away she didn't. She leaned nearer, her eyes closed, her nose brushing along the line of his jaw.

With painstaking control he turned his head slightly, brushing her nose with his. His whole body reacted to her nearness, demanding that he crush her close again. But he checked the urge.

When she still didn't withdraw he kissed her brow and pulled her even closer, until her skirts clung to his buckskin boots and her breasts were pressed against his ribs. He savored her sweet offering—never allowing himself to give in to the need to take more.

It was an oddly gratifying exchange, though far softer and sweeter than the satisfaction his aching groin demanded.

She'd done more than just submit to his kiss; she'd lingered near and offered him tenderness and closeness. And he realized that was what he wanted from her—almost as much as he desired her body.

She pulled away at last. The cool night settled on him. They stood apart.

"So you have your token," she said, sounding a little breathless. "I think I should go back to the house now."

"Yes, of course," Damon said, reluctantly releasing her. She walked away rubbing her wrist, her steps hurried on the garden path.

As he watched her go, he wondered if she understood just how sweetly seductive had been the token she'd bestowed on him.

He also realized that he hadn't learned a bit more about her and John Minor.

Nine

Mercy, when was she going to learn to stay clear of Damon Durande? Neilly shut the door of the house and leaned against it, trying to catch her breath and to put her thoughts back in order. She had never behaved so shamefully in her entire life, kissing a man like that.

She put her hand to her swollen lips. Charles had kissed her the way Damon had once, using his tongue, and she had thought it the most disgusting experience of her life. She had practically sputtered in Charles's face. But Damon had been right about their kiss: She had enjoyed it. She had enjoyed it a great deal.

She would have taken more pleasure in it, though, if she hadn't been certain that he was trying to make a fool of her. Trying to embarrass and humiliate her. She knew meeting John Minor had done nothing to reassure Damon about her background. She wanted him to trust her, had even hoped they might become friends of sorts, for Isetta's sake. Then he'd betrayed her like this.

Closing her eyes, she said a silent prayer that no one in the house had seen them kissing. What would the ladies think? What would the servants think? Such impropriety justified immediate dismissal in most respectable households.

"That's all I need," Neilly groaned to herself. What was worse, she had the humiliating feeling that everyone had been aware of her weakness for Damon long before she realized it herself: Miss Isetta, Miss Varina. Now that she thought about it, she'd even seen Uncle Cato and Cleo exchanging knowing glances.

It was almost as if some plot was afoot to—to what? To pair Damon with his aunt's paid companion? Such a match would be highly unsuitable for a man of Damon's station, Neilly thought. For a moment the hard-and-fast rules of Southern society reassured her.

Then she remembered how Miss Isetta had beamed when she'd mentioned ever so casually that her mother had been an Ashley of the famous Bay Haven Ashleys. Neilly groaned again. Would they think that connection qualified her to marry into the Stirling family?

Neilly shook her head. No, she was being silly. Even if the aunties had concocted such a plan, Damon would never consent to it.

If he knew of the plan.

The whole idea was just too crazy. Preposterous. Mad. Who would ever think that an independent, dashing bachelor like Damon would look twice at a drab bluestocking like her? She started up the stairs, but the thought that a plan might be afoot wouldn't die. It was just the kind of thing those two idealistic, scheming, sweet little old ladies would think of.

What better way to keep Damon at Rosewood than saddle him with a bride? They were trying to throw Neilly and Damon together. And what part was Damon playing? Did he know what his aunts were up to?

She stopped halfway up the curving stairway. Of course he didn't know, Neilly concluded. He plainly enjoyed his bachelorhood. Though he adored his Aunt Isetta, and recognized some of her faults, he was most likely blind to others. He'd never suspect Isetta and Varina of trying to wed him to a member of the household.

So what was she going to do?

She was going to see to Miss Isetta's welfare.

At the end of the hall light streamed from beneath Isetta's door. Neilly rapped on the door and peeked in to discover Isetta perched at her writing desk by the window, playing a game of solitaire. Varina sat nearby, sipping a glass of sherry.

"I didn't expect to find you out of bed," Neilly said as she entered the room. "Are you feeling all right?"

"Izzie is fine," Varina said, coming to her feet. "We were just cele—taking a little sherry for medicinal purposes."

"Did you and Damon have a good—walk in the garden?" Isetta asked, placing a black card on a red one.

"Yes. Since you're up, I wanted to talk to you about Damon and me."

Isetta hesitated before she laid down the next card.

"Would you like a glass of sherry, Neilly?" Varina asked, reaching for the decanter on the bedside table.

"No, thank you."

"Well, what about you and Damon?" Isetta said, turning to Neilly.

Neilly took a deep breath. It would serve no purpose to be oblique about this. "It occurred to me, after the way it seems that Damon and I are always being thrown together, that perhaps you are—well, are you trying to make a match between us?"

Varina gasped.

Isetta laughed, a dry, light dismissive sound. "And what on earth gave you that idea, my dear?"

"The way you insist that I dine with the family, that I accompany you to the Turnbulls' barbecue. Then you sent Damon and me to walk in the garden. You nearly pushed us out the door together."

"Oh, dear," Varina sat down heavily in her chair. "I was afraid of this."

"Well, you might as well know the truth." Isetta sighed and put aside her cards. "Varina said you were too bright for this to go on much longer."

"I said that?" Varina asked.

Neilly let out a long slow breath. "You're admitting to matchmaking, then?"

"Oh, no, not matchmaking, dear," Isetta said, turning to her cards again. "We'd never put a lady of your refinement in that awkward position."

"Not matchmaking?" Varina sat up, her eyes wide, the sherry in her glass slopping onto her silk dressing gown.

Isetta gestured to the footstool at her side before she picked up the stack of cards and resumed her play. "Sit down, Neilly, and I'll explain."

Neilly sat, watching Isetta deal out her cards while she listened.

"You know, of course, that Damon is the true heir to Rosewood. You heard much of the story at the dining table the night the guest house burned."

Neilly nodded.

"You know that he professes to dislike Rosewood."

Neilly nodded again. "I think I've heard him use the word 'hate.' "

Isetta glanced at Neilly briefly. "Indeed. Now that I'm ill I've had to face a few things. One is the disposition of Rosewood. Father told me on his deathbed he did not want the plantation to go to Rosalie's son."

"So you promised it wouldn't." Neilly knew deathbed requests were powerful things.

"No, I didn't promise him anything," Isetta said, the harshness in her voice surprising Neilly. The lady slapped a card down on the desk. "That sour old man, rest his soul, had ruined too many people's lives by then, and I wasn't going to promise anything I wasn't sure I'd be willing to carry out.

"But I was young enough at the time to think I should carry out his wishes. So when I drew up my first will I made Arthur, Mirabelle's son, the heir to Rosewood, just as Papa wished.

"But not long ago I had a change of heart." Isetta looked at Neilly. "When you get older the desire to honor tradition grows stronger.

"I believe Damon is Rosewood's true heir. The plantation should be his. He is his grandfather's grandson in more ways than any of us would have ever guessed. Did you know Papa defied his own father and came from Virginia to carve this place out of the Louisiana wilderness? Thomas Stirling was a frontiersman, a builder, just as Damon has become in his own way. But what do you think Damon would do if I told him Rosewood is his?"

"He cares about Rosewood," Neilly said, memories of Damon's concern for the ledgers and records still fresh in her mind. "But if you offered it to him, he'd probably refuse it."

"Exactly." Isetta returned to her game. "And that's where you come in."

"Me? How?"

"We want him to love Rosewood as much as we do," Isetta said, her eyes intent on the cards again. "So Varina and I decided we needed someone to help him learn to love Rosewood. That's you."

"Yes, you, Neilly," Varina said. "Izzie knew you were the one the minute she saw your self-portrait."

"Wait." Neilly scooted the stool closer to Isetta. "Let me make sure I understand what you're telling me. You brought me here to help you make Damon love Rosewood?"

"That's it, precisely," Isetta said.

"Yes, that's good." Varina's head bobbed in assent. "I like that."

"You're not trying to inspire a suit between us?"

"With Damon a confirmed bachelor?" Isetta exclaimed. "Hardly. And his head and heart full of painful memories of his mother's unhappy demise? No, that would be foolish, wouldn't it? He'd be angry if he thought we were trying to match him up with a wife. He'd be gone in a flash."

"In a flash," Varina agreed with a frown.

"I can't tell you how it would set my heart at ease to know that Damon had come to love Rosewood and would be here to carry on after me," Isetta said with a sad wag of her head. "We think you care about Rosewood enough to be just the person to bring him around, to win him over to an acceptance of what is rightfully his."

"Well, I admit it seems to be a good cause, but I hardly think I'm qualified to be the one to win him over," Neilly said, flattered that they had such faith in her but eager to distance herself from their plot as quickly as possible. "Damon knows his own mind, for the most part. Maybe someone to tutor Damon in the value of Rosewood's art would help. Someone like Peter Hiram."

"Oh, no," Varina said, shaking her head vigorously.

"No," Isetta said. "Turnbull's sculptor would never do."

"Never," Varina echoed.

"Why don't *you* begin by giving him some art history lessons tomorrow?" Isetta said. "I think you'll find him cooperative."

"I don't think so," Neilly said, rising from her stool. She'd often tutored fellow students at Miss Barrows's academy, and she'd been good at it. But giving Damon lessons was quite another matter. "I'd be glad to help you select a tutor if you like, but I don't think I have much to teach Mr. Durande."

"I'm disappointed," Isetta said, laying down another black card. "Perhaps you'd like to think about it?"

"No, I'm certain of my answer," Neilly said, going to the door and putting her hand on the knob. "I came to Rosewood to be your companion. I just don't think it's really proper for us—for Damon and me—to be involved in any other—projects. And please, no more suggestion of things like walks in the garden."

"Not unless you wish it, dear," Isetta said, flipping over

another card and snapping it down on the table. She didn't appear especially disappointed, Neilly thought.

"Thank you for your understanding," she said, then added her good night and left, closing the door behind her. She mentally reviewed what she'd told the two sisters as she walked to her room. She'd made herself perfectly clear, she thought, and she was satisfied that she was no longer any part of a plot to keep Damon at Rosewood.

When Neilly was gone Varina turned to her sister. "That was absolutely inspired, Izzie. I think she believed every word you said."

"I know," Isetta said. She turned the deck face up and began to shuffle through the cards. "It was bound to happen. They are bright people. One of them was certain to suspect something sooner or later. Where is that ace?"

"I hope she doesn't mean what she says," Varina said, hugging herself. "The air positively hums when they are together in the same room."

"It's called sexual attraction," Isetta said.

"Don't be vulgar, Sister," Varina scolded. She wanted to think of it as romance. "From the way they were kissing in the garden this evening, they'll lose their hearts to each other soon. Don't you think so?"

"Not if either of them thinks we're matchmaking." Isetta frowned and sorted through her deck again. "Not if other things interfere. We don't have forever to make this match happen."

"Do you think she will change her mind about tutoring Damon?" Varina asked.

"I hope she won't be able to help herself," Isetta said, still searching for the ace.

"Do you think Damon will let her?"

"Under the right conditions, yes, I think so," Isetta said. "Where is that ace?"

Varina stepped to the desk and idly peered at the cards. She detested cards. She could never remember which suit was what or which face card was where. But Izzie could, and she knew more games of solitaire than anyone else. However, this game looked to be a draw. "I'm afraid you're not going to win, Sister."

"Of course I'm going to win," Isetta said. "I always win. Even if I have to cheat."

The next morning, in answer to a summons, Damon stepped into his aunt's darkened bedchamber. The air hung close around him like that of a sickroom, and the sharp, bitter odor of medicine assaulted his nostrils.

Apprehensively, Damon closed the door and waited for his eyes to adjust to the dim light. It wasn't like Aunt Isetta to allow him to see her abed. He'd only found her there once, on the day he arrived. Since then she'd always been convalescing in the morning room by this time of day.

Through the shadows he saw her lying against eyelet lace-covered pillows, her gray hair tucked under a frilly cap, her eyes closed, and her blue-veined hands folded across the counterpane. Even on such a warm morning Aunt Isetta was well-covered with quilts. Her face was pale, almost ashen. Damon looked around the room, but Neilly was nowhere to be seen.

"Good morning, Damon." Varina was bending over the bed. She stifled a sneeze and hastily tucked a small box of something behind her skirts. A falsely bright smile quivered on her face. "Thank you for coming so promptly."

"I came as soon as Uncle Cato said Aunt Isetta wanted to see me."

"This isn't one of Izzie's better days, but it's nothing to worry about. Dr. McGregor said she'd have one now and then."

"Damon?" Isetta's eyes fluttered open. "There you are, dear."

"Does Neilly know you're not feeling well?" Damon asked. "Should we send for Dr. Johnson?"

"Heavens, Neilly just left," Varina said. "She'd been in here fussing over Izzie all morning."

"I just need my rest, dear," Isetta said, her voice so weak and thin, Damon had to move closer to hear her. "But first I need you to do something for me. Come sit beside me."

Damon settled on the edge of the goose-down mattress.

"I know your concern is with the accounts and the progress of the crops, harvest, and shipping, but would you please show Neilly the paintings under the stairs?" Isetta toyed with the lace edging of the counterpane. "She is doing a fine job with the inventory for us, but I don't think she knows about the paintings under the stairs. The ones Father reserved for private showing."

Damon said nothing for a moment as he tried to recall which paintings his aunt meant. "Oh, the nudes and Poussin's work on *Aurora's Seduction of Cephalus.*"

"Precisely." Isetta bit off the word with surprising energy. "I'd like to know what she has to say about them."

"Perhaps Varina could show Neilly the paintings," Damon hedged. He was hesitant to present the works to Neilly, partly because of their subject matter, partly because he believed those paintings were among the most valuable at Rosewood, partly because he wasn't certain how she'd react to him this morning.

"Oh, not me," Varina protested with a flutter of her hands. "I can't keep those paintings sorted out in my head."

"If it's propriety you're concerned about," Isetta said, "the paintings are as proper as Hiram's statue. I didn't see Neilly swoon away at the sight of that."

Damon thought Peter Hiram's sculpture considerably less risque than the Poussin painting, but Aunt Isetta was right about Neilly's cool appraisal of a bare-legged male. She hadn't so much as blushed, nor was she the swooning type.

"Neilly told me she wanted to finish the inventory of the first floor today," Isetta said, reaching under her pillow and bringing forth a skeleton key. "This is the only key to the room under the stairs. I think you must show the Poussin to her today. You'll find her in the drawing room."

With that, Aunt Isetta settled into her pillow, closed her eyes, and seemed to fall asleep.

Damon sat back and looked askance at Varina, who shook her head, apparently as puzzled as he. "She must have her rest," Varina reminded him.

His aunt's request seemed an odd one. Yet, if anyone was going to show the valuable paintings to Neilly, perhaps it should be him.

Damon paused on the threshold of the drawing room, where Thomas Stirling's portrait hung. He'd been at Rosewood for nearly a month and had managed to avoid stepping into the room until now. The drawing room was his grandfather's territory.

His grandfather's favorite chair sat near the fireplace, and his favorite things—the Andrew Jackson sword and his silver cup—shone on the mantel. Above them hung Grandfather's portrait. Damon's grandsire gazed down on him with disapproval. Damon glared back, resentful of the self-doubt the dead man could still stir in him.

". . . and then Master Jackson, he handed his sword to Master Thomas across the dining-room table," Cato said, his words cutting into Damon's thoughts.

Uncle Cato, Pugh, and Neilly stood in front of the fireplace, staring up at Andrew Jackson's sword. The old butler was telling his favorite story, one Damon had heard many times.

"In this house, in Rosewood's dining room here?" Pugh asked, without taking his gaze from the sword.

"Yeas, sah. In the dining room in this house it was, and Master Thomas was always mighty proud of this sword and of the fact that Gen—I mean President Jackson called him friend in front of all the important parish families."

"Did he say any more about the sword?" Neilly asked as she scribbled in her small ledger. "Where it was made or anything of that nature?"

"Said he defended New Orleans with this sword, Miss Neilly. Said that he killed an English officer with it, he did. And it's here at Rosewood."

"I think of all the treasures Grandfather imported and collected, he was proudest of that sword," Damon said. All three heads turned toward him. "I think it was a little tarnished when ol' Hickory handed it to my grandfather, wasn't it, Uncle Cato?"

"Well, yeas sah, it wasn't so bright as it is now. Your Aunt Varina put the shine on it, she did. Shines it every week now, just like she does your grandfather's cup right here."

"I don't know how to put a value on something like that," Neilly said, shaking her head in bewilderment.

"What was he like?" Pugh asked. "I mean President Jackson?"

"Well, sah, he and Master Thomas looked a lot alike," Uncle Cato said. "Tall men, thin. With that look around their mouth. Tight. Strong hawk kind of nose. A sharp jaw. You know the look of a man who's going to have things his own way or else."

"I know," Pugh said, reverently. "Many people here and abroad would pay a good deal of money for a military relic like that."

Damon eyed Neilly closely, but she seemed too absorbed in her note-taking to notice him. As she wrote he peered closer, searching for signs of their disagreement the night before. He hadn't slept a wink, annoyed with himself for pressing her for a kiss and not learning what he wanted to know. But she looked fresh as a morning flower. Had the kiss of the night before been so easily forgotten? he wondered with irritation.

"And to what do we owe this visit to the house, Mr. Pugh?" Damon asked, eager to get rid of the man. He wanted to be left alone with Neilly.

"Sir," Pugh said, with a glance in Neilly's direction, "I must speak to you about something in confidence."

Damon walked Pugh to the door where they were unlikely to be overheard. "What is it?"

"Mr. Durande, I don't know how you're going to take this."

"Spit it out, man."

"Your grandfather's ghost was seen in the cemetery last night."

"The ghost of my grandfather?" Damon almost laughed at the image of his dignified ancestor reduced to loitering in a lonely cemetery. Then his superstitious Creole blood prompted him to reconsider the sighting. "Who saw him?"

"Mammy Lula," Pugh said. "She came to me this morning. Said she saw the ghost in the cemetery last night, way after the moon had set. She was walking home from helping one of the girls with a colicky baby."

"Exactly what did she see? How did she know it was Grandfather?"

"She was distraught, Mr. Durande," Pugh said. "Practically babbling nonsense. That's not like her. She saw something, all right. She said his shroud hung in tatters and he was standing at the cemetery fence. She couldn't see his face and he didn't make a sound, but she knew it was him."

"My grandfather has been dead for almost fifteen years," Damon said. "I haven't heard any stories about his ghost in that time."

"There've been none till now, sir," Pugh said. "The story has spread like wildfire. I'm afraid I can't get anyone to mow the cemetery now. I didn't want you to think I was allowing the family graves to be neglected."

"I understand. Thank you," Damon said, dismissing Pugh. "I'll see to it myself."

Damon turned back into the drawing room. Mammy Lula had been with the Stirlings as long as he could remember, and she wasn't a teller of tales. Nor was she inclined to be superstitious—beyond the horseshoe she'd hung over the kitchen door for good luck.

Damon smiled to himself. Maybe Grandfather really *had* climbed out of his grave when he'd moved into the house. If so, he was certain they were destined to meet sometime.

In the drawing room Neilly was still scribbling in her notebook. Her dark curls had fallen into a frame for her face, and her brow was furrowed in concentration. Damon forgot about the ghost story.

"Well, that information about the sword was most enlightening," Neilly said as Damon approached her. Memories of the stolen kiss in the garden stirred him. She snapped the ledger closed. "I'm continually amazed at the variety of treasures in this house."

"Well, I have more to show you," Damon said, holding up the key. "Aunt Isetta reminded me that there are some paintings you may have missed."

"Oh, I missed something?"

Damon ushered Neilly out into the hall. She came willingly, lured with the mention of more artwork. "Yes, the private viewing gallery."

"Why a private gallery?" Neilly asked.

"See for yourself." Damon unlocked the door and stepped back to allow Neilly to enter. She hesitated on the threshold, plainly wary. Damon thought she was going to refuse to enter alone with him after their exchange in the garden, but after a moment she stepped into the dim room.

* * *

Neilly surveyed the narrow chamber quickly. It wasn't much larger than a dressing closet and was lit only by a small, round window. On the walls hung several paintings, each covered by velvet draperies.

"This isn't the best setting for the display of paintings," she said. As she looked around the isolated room, she had second thoughts about viewing the works with Damon. "You said Miss Isetta wanted me to see this artwork? Today?"

"Yes. These pictures aren't exactly what Grandfather thought should be on exhibit for general viewing." Damon lit an overhead lamp that cast a better light on the artwork. Then he turned to Neilly. "Between you and me, I promise to do my best to be a gentleman today."

Neilly bowed her head in acceptance of his pledge but said nothing. His avowal was probably as close to an apology for his behavior in the garden as she was ever going to get.

He pointed to the painting nearest the door. "Why don't we start?"

He drew open the first set of curtains.

A lush, rounded body in shades of pink and golden peach filled the canvas. Downy white wings sprouted from the figure's shoulders and golden curls capped the head. A dimpled smile captured the viewer's attention.

"But it's only a cherub," Neilly said, laughing with delight. "What a charming piece of work, too. A smiling little angel. From the looks of it I'd guess this is a study for a larger work. It does have a sensual quality, but this is hardly erotica."

"You must admit, Neilly, not every lady has your educated perspective," he pointed out, smiling at her.

"But I can't imagine that any lady would find that smiling creature offensive," she said, jotting down the painter's name and asking Damon about the source and the date of purchase. He told her what he knew.

148 *Linda Madl*

"What else is here?"

Damon opened the next set of curtains on a picture of a couple having a picnic. The lady's luscious decolletage was bared right under the gentleman's nose. Their faces glowed with desire.

"What do you think?" Damon baited.

"Of course some ladies might think the subject matter a bit inappropriate," Neilly said. The picture stirred strange, warm feelings in her breasts and lower down. Suddenly she was wondering what it would be like to lie on a blanket with Damon and let him put grapes in her mouth like that. "But it's just a picnic, not even based on a classical tale, is it?"

"Nor is this one." Damon pulled the curtains on the next picture to reveal a canvas full of naked women bathing in a river.

Neilly studied the grouping of nude females in silence.

"Well? Tell me about it."

She blushed. "Actually, it's a very good study by a painter who isn't much appreciated right now. But he will be in the future."

"What about it makes it so?"

"The composition, for one thing," Neilly said as she took notes in her ledger. "The colors. The use of shades of one color is not popular now, but the technique has its appeal. And the simplicity of line."

"But that must be credited to a woman's figure, not any great discovery on the part of the artist," Damon countered. She could feel him studying the blush in her cheeks.

"Well, yes, if you think about it in a dispassionate way, you will realize that the human body is a very beautiful thing," Neilly said, trying to concentrate on her note-taking. "That's why artists like to use the human form in their work."

"Indeed, it's the dispassionate part that most of us have trouble with," Damon said. He touched her elbow to move her to the end of the narrow room, and his touch lingered, burning through the fabric of her dress and into her skin. "Which brings us to the last painting."

He opened the curtains on the last picture under the stairs.

Grasping hands, longing looks, and ripe bodies—male and female—filled the canvas. No matter how innocent the viewer, neither the gender nor the intent of the figures could be mistaken.

Neilly gasped. "It's a Poussin. *Aurora's Seduction of Cephalus*. But it can't be the original. That's in France."

Forgetting Damon, she stepped forward, peering at it more closely.

"I don't think it's signed and it appears unfinished," Damon said.

"It's a preparatory study," she muttered to herself as much as to him and stepped back again. "But this may be the most valuable artwork you have in the house. I don't believe it. A real Poussin here."

"So what's going on in this frolicking little scene?"

Neilly blinked at him and felt the heat of her blush return. Damon moved to stand behind her, as if he wanted to get a better view of the artwork. But his nearness warmed her body, and her neck seemed suddenly naked, bare to his eyes.

"It's a classical story, of course," Neilly said, gazing at the painting again.

"Of course, and who is this young man?" Damon asked, one hand settling casually on Neilly's shoulder. She tensed under his hand, but he didn't remove it. Nor did she brush him away.

"Well," Neilly stammered, "this beautiful youth is Cephalus, who was married to the lovely Procris, a favorite of Diana, the goddess of the hunt. See the javelin he carries? That was a gift to Procris from Diana and, with pride, Procris gave it to her beloved. It never missed its mark."

"The best kind to have," Damon said. "Is this Procris?"

"No, this lady is Aurora—you can tell from her bright hair—she is trying to seduce Cephalus away from Procris."

"And a fine job of it she seems to be doing," Damon said, obviously admiring the invitation in the angle of her hips. "Does she succeed?"

"No, Cephalus loves Procris and he ignores Aurora."

"Clearly a man to be admired in the face of such temptation," Damon said. "Did Cephalus ever regret his decision?"

"Yes, he did," Neilly said sternly. "While Cephalus was away, and before he could tell Procris of what had happened, a friend of Procris came to her. This friend told her that she'd overheard Cephalus in the woods begging a maiden to take away the heat that burned him."

Damon quirked a brow and gave her a sidelong, skeptical look. Neilly's blush warmed her face again.

"Honestly, this is a classical story," she scolded.

"I'm trying to think classical, honestly I am," Damon vowed, attempting to pull his grin back into a look of innocent interest.

"Procris's friend thought badly of Cephalus, just as you did," Neilly said, unable to keep the reproach from her voice. "But that was just Cephalus's way of speaking to the wind in the heat of the day when he liked to nap."

"Oh, of course. I say the same thing to the wind myself."

Neilly drew away a little and frowned over her shoulder. "Do you want to hear the rest of the story or not?"

"Yes, please continue."

"Poor Procris loved her husband desperately and after Aurora's early attempt to seduce him she was vulnerable to every threat. She believed her friend's version of the tale."

"What did she do?" he asked.

"She slipped into the woods and hid near the place where her friend said the tryst had taken place. When she heard Cephalus speak to the breeze as he always did she sobbed.

"Hearing the sob and thinking it was some wild animal, Cephalus threw his javelin—the one that never missed its mark—into the bush. Procris cried out and Cephalus found her, dying. Before she died he explained the truth about the breeze, so she died happily."

Damon frowned. "A died-happily-ever-after story."

"Well, you know mythology," Neilly said with a shrug.

"No, I don't," he said. "And I don't think I've missed much."

Neilly stepped away and turned toward him. Damon dropped his hands to his side.

"The lesson in the story is that one should trust the people he or she loves," she explained, choosing her words carefully.

"Or don't lend your magic javelin to your husband, as Procris did," Damon said.

"I don't think you should dismiss it that easily," Neilly persisted. "When you love someone, you have to trust him. If you don't trust, love dies. In Procris's case, her suspicions caused her own death."

"It's just a painting," Damon said, the slight smile he'd been wearing earlier gone. "So what do you think of these paintings?"

Neilly sighed. "I think you or your aunts should build a long hall onto the house to display them in the proper lighting. A room with lots of windows and perhaps a view of the gardens."

"Well, that's something to think about," Damon said. "I shall speak of it to Aunt Isetta."

Outside the room in the entry hall, Neilly heard the front door open. Uncle Cato exclaimed a surprised greeting.

Footsteps rang on the brick floor and a childish voice cried out, "Oh, I hate those lions, Daddy. When this is our house I want to paint over those ugly things."

Neilly and Damon turned to the door as Cleo's long elegant face appeared.

"Master Damon, Miss Neilly, Uncle Cato sent me to tell you Master Arthur Sitwell and his son, Vincent, are here."

Ten

The news of Arthur Sitwell's arrival made Damon curse and turn away from Neilly. When he rounded on her again he hardly seemed the congenial man who had just sparred with her over Rosewood's paintings. His face had become harsh, cold, and remote. His dark eyes glistened hard and black.

"Not a word to Arthur about this inventory," he commanded. "Do you understand? All he needs to know is that you're here seeing to Aunt Isetta's welfare."

Neilly nodded, curious about the implications of that particular instruction.

Damon stopped when he reached the door of the tiny art gallery and turned to Neilly again. His handsome mouth was pressed into a thin line of distaste. "And be sure he knows your connection with the Carolinian Ashleys. That will keep him properly respectful."

Neilly nodded again as she slipped her ledger and pencil into the drawer of a side table. That done, she followed Damon out to meet his cousin.

Varina had already swept into the entry hall and begun to hug everyone. "How good to see you, Arthur, dear."

"Yes, Aunt Varina, we just couldn't stay away a moment longer, knowing that Aunt Isetta is ill," the man, dressed in a white linen suit, was saying as he stiffly submitted to Varina's show of affection. "My wife couldn't leave her sister, who has a new baby. But here we are, Vincent and I, to do what we can."

Neilly lingered on the edge of the group, out of the way but able to see everyone. She wasn't about to miss an opportunity to meet this cousin she'd heard about: Arthur Sitwell, Mirabelle's son, Thomas Stirling's youngest grandson. The heir to Rosewood.

What a pallid heir he was, too, Neilly thought. She couldn't help comparing him to Damon's tall, dark good looks. Sitwell was shorter, and fair to the point of being pale: hair, complexion, and light gray eyes set in an unremarkable face.

Neilly wondered if he ever ventured into the sunlight for more than a visit to his tailor. The exquisite cut of his coat and the intricate knot in his neckcloth marked him as a man who loved his clothes. His weak chin and narrow shoulders gave him a feeble appearance countered only by his air of pompous self-importance.

Neilly knew she wasn't going to be fond of this man, nor the boy at his side. Ten-year-old Vincent, as he was introduced by Varina, was a miniature image of his father, with the addition of a petulant pucker to his mouth.

"So you are Aunt Isetta's companion," Arthur said after Varina had completed the introductions. "How does Auntie fare? I was surprised to learn from Uncle Cato that she is still abed. Our auntie is absolutely dauntless, isn't she, Damon? Nothing keeps her down."

"If you were really concerned, Cousin, you'd have been here weeks ago."

Damon cast all of them a withering look. "If you'll excuse me I have work to do elsewhere."

"Well," Arthur said with an injured air. "Cousin Damon never was one for the niceties of being a gentleman."

Neilly recognized the truth in Arthur's words; yet she admired Damon for not being so two-faced. He was not pleased to see his cousin; no one could doubt that. At the same time she watched Damon leave the house with a sense of loss. She was acquainted with him well enough now to know he would never linger in the company of someone he disliked.

"I'm so glad you're here for a visit, Arthur," Varina said, regaining her cheerful smile and ruffling Vincent's hair.

The boy swatted his aunt's hand away. "Stop that."

Varina's smile failed her again. "Sorry, I see you're too grown up to be treated like a child these days. How long will you be staying, my dears?"

Neilly didn't need to hear Arthur's answer to know their visit was going to be too long.

"I'll be right there, Cleo," Varina said, sweeping into Isetta's room. "I need to find the Venetian glass vase. You know, the green one with a dolphin worked into the stem. I want to cut the flowers for the dinner table. I'll be right back."

Varina closed the door. "Where is Neilly?"

"In the kitchen, seeing to the dinner menu," Isetta said. She wore a dressing gown and her nightcap and sat at her writing table with maddening calm, her cards laid aside, untouched.

"Izzie, what are we going to do? Arthur and Vincent have been here three days, and we haven't seen Damon except for brief appearances at the dinner table," Varina complained, concerned that Isetta didn't really understand how awful things were turning out. "He's hardly spoken a word to Neilly."

"Damon and Arthur have always mixed like oil and water," Isetta said thoughtfully, tapping her silver-headed cane on the carpet. "You know that's why I delayed writing Arthur about my illness in the first place. And when I did I sent the letter the slow way. I suspected he'd be here as soon as he thought I might have a foot in the grave."

Varina noted the healthy glow of annoyance in her sister's cheeks. "You'd better apply more rice powder before you receive anybody else. You're looking entirely too well."

"Thank you, Sister, I'll remember to do that," Isetta said, staring out the window.

"Maybe you could get well all of a sudden," Varina suggested. "Then Arthur and Vincent would leave."

"Then *everyone* would leave," Isetta reminded her. "Anyway, I don't think a miraculous recovery is credible, especially with Theo away. We need his word to make it official. And Theo's becoming more difficult to fool."

"Oh, Izzie, what are we going to do?" Varina crossed the room, plopped down on the chair by the window, and wrung her hands in despair. She'd been watching Neilly go about her duties the last three days. The lilt had gone from the girl's step and a slight preoccupation furrowed her brow. "I think Neilly misses Damon as much as we do."

"I've noticed," Isetta said. "I've also noticed that Damon has made no attempt to move out of the house. He may not like Arthur, but he won't give ground to him either."

"That's true." Varina considered Izzie's observation for a moment. The thought of Damon standing by them against Arthur felt good. Then she remembered the other reason she had come to Izzie's room. She got to her feet and began to search for the green glass vase. "It's not here."

"The dolphin vase? No, I haven't seen it," Isetta said. "Did you ever find the Empress Josephine snuff box with the Tudor earrings? I noticed you didn't wear them to the Turnbulls's barbecue or ball."

"No, I didn't find them," Varina said with exasperation. Izzie *would* have the bad taste to remind her of the missing jewelry and box. "But I know they're here in the house somewhere. Some morning they'll turn up where I left them. You'll see. Now, what are we going to do about Damon and Neilly?"

"I'm not certain." Isetta resumed tapping her cane on the

floor. As if inspired, she nodded. "Cato told me that we need wine for dinner tonight. Would you ask Damon to go to the wine cellar and select a few bottles? Nothing like a good vintage to mellow everyone at dinner."

"Well, of course I'll ask him, but I don't see how that's going to solve our problem," Varina said, impatient with her sister's apparent lack of concern. "Damon's in the library. Where's Arthur?"

"He's with our great-nephew, what's his name? Virgil?"

"Vincent," Varina corrected.

"You know who I mean. They are out touring the warehouses with Overseer Turner," Isetta said. "That family is taking stock of Rosewood like bankers processing assets for a loan.

"Now that you mention it, Arthur does act a bit like an assessor, and I don't like it either." Varina picked up the Wedgwood vase from the mantel. It would have to do until the green Venetian glass turned up. Vase in hand, she headed for the door. "I'm off to find Damon."

She discovered him in the library just as Izzie had said, and he agreed to select a wine. When he left the house she returned to the garden and began to cut roses.

A late afternoon peace settled over the garden, and Varina was soon lost in clipping fresh blossoms for her arrangement. She shut out thoughts of missing vases, of Damon and Neilly's romantic future, or of Arthur and Vincent's greedy assessments. She just reveled in the beauty of her flowers. When insistent fingertips struck Varina's shoulder she nearly jumped out of her skin.

"Lawdy, Uncle Cato! You just scared me out of ten years of my life."

"Yes, Miss Varina. I'm sorry, but Master Damon, he hasn't come back from the wine cellar. And, well, it's been a long time since he left saying he'd be right back."

Varina checked the watch she'd pinned to her garden

apron. Cato was right; it had been some time. "Why don't you go see if he needs help? Or send the punkah boy."

"Won't nobody go, Miss Varina," Uncle Cato said, shaking his head. "Not after Mammy Lula saw the ghost in the cemetery."

Varina almost dropped the small clippers she'd been using. "Ghost? What ghost?"

"Mammy Lula saw him, your papa's ghost in the cemetery a few nights ago," Cato said.

"Papa's ghost." Varina tucked her trembling hands in her apron pockets to hide her reaction from Uncle Cato. But her heart beat so violently, she was certain he could see the flutter beneath the bib of her apron.

"Master Damon sure knowed what he was talking about when he said Master Thomas would turn over in his grave if he slept in the house. Master Thomas done crawled out of his grave."

"So it appears," Varina mumbled. Damon's words returned to her immediately. A man like Thomas Stirling would never die easy, especially if something was not to his liking at Rosewood. She'd told Isetta their plot would make Papa angry. "Who else knows about the ghost?"

"Master Damon and Mister Pugh and everyone down in the quarters," Uncle Cato said, referring to the slave cabins around the bend in the road.

"Does Miss Isetta know?"

"Oh, no, miss, I don't think she knows," Uncle Cato assured her. "Wouldn't be good for her condition, now would it? We kept it from Miss Neilly, too."

"Of course," Varina said. "No need to trouble the girl."

They jumped when they heard someone calling Varina's name from far away. Varina grabbed Cato's arm. He grabbed hers, and they waited in paralyzed fear.

The camellia bush behind them rustled. Neilly emerged from the thicket of leaves. "There you are, Miss Varina and

Uncle Cato. I was just wondering where the wine is for dinner."

Varina and Cato glanced at each other, relief on their faces. They released each other.

"Is something wrong? Miss Varina, you look pale."

"Oh, no, my dear," Varina hastened to assure Neilly. "I'm fine. Damon went to the wine cellar to select a wine and he hasn't returned."

"Let's send someone for him."

"No one will go," Uncle Cato said, glancing uneasily at Varina.

"Why not?"

Varina took a deep breath and told Neilly of the sighting of Thomas Stirling's ghost in the cemetery.

"What a charming story for All Hallow's Eve." Neilly smiled at Varina, an expression of gentle amusement. "Don't worry. I'll go after Damon. I know where the cemetery is. If the ghost of Thomas Stirling is lurking about, he'll have to answer to me."

Neilly strode away purposefully. Varina admired the girl's youthful courage. Once she'd longed to possess such spirit and dauntlessness, to be able to face the world with such confidence and energy. But she was too old to aspire to those virtues now. With age came resignation. Varina sighed. With age came wisdom, too; the wisdom to know that Papa's ghost wasn't going to be easily satisfied.

The Stirling family cemetery rested atop a grassy swell shaded by a wreath of pine trees. In the side of the rise, away from the river, stood a weather-stained door set in a stone portal. It served as the only clue to the existence of Rosewood's wine cellar.

In the earliest days of the plantation the cellar had provided a food cache. Later, because the plantation lacked suitable cool storage, Thomas Stirling had ordered the underground chamber modified to accommodate his taste for fine wine.

Neilly knew little of the cellar and had only seen the iron-fenced Stirling family plot from a distance. White marble slabs, sad-faced cherubs, and grieving winged angels studded the graveyard. The square pink marble mausoleum of Thomas Stirling dominated the graveyard.

As she approached the hill, she wondered where Mammy Lula had spotted the ghost of the old master of Rosewood. In the daytime the cemetery appeared a peaceful place, a serene setting for eternal slumber. But at night, with the wind whistling through the pine needles and the shadows dancing in the moonlight, Neilly could see how someone might think she saw a ghost.

She wondered how long Damon had known about the supernatural sighting without saying anything to the ladies. Of course, she expected him to protect Aunt Isetta and even Varina, but she was surprised that he had not shared the information with her. In fact, he had spoken only a few perfunctory words to her since the Sitwells had arrived.

He stayed away from the house during the day and appeared at dinner only out of obligation and respect for his aunts' wishes. She also suspected that if Isetta showed any improvement, he would be on the road to Texas so fast, he'd leave the Spanish moss flying in the rush of his departure.

What a shame if he left. Neilly was becoming as convinced as Miss Isetta and Miss Varina that Damon belonged at Rosewood. He saw to each of the plantation's operations with great concentration and care, sometimes even working besides the slaves to finish a task—the kind of dedicated attention given by one who loves what he is doing. He'd even risked his life to save Rosewood's account ledgers. She couldn't imagine Arthur Sitwell risking his new cutaway coat for anything at Rosewood.

She wished Arthur and his spoiled son would leave. Their

presence did nothing to comfort Miss Isetta. But it had created a tense and unpleasant atmosphere in the house. Neilly had seldom suffered through meals as strained as the past three dinners with the Sitwells and Damon. Arthur bemoaned the lack of social life on the river and expounded at length upon fashion: the most current suit-coat styles, the most-sought-after new furniture, the most desirable architects. Did he have plans to make over Rosewood or dismantle it? Neilly wondered. At the head of the table she caught Damon glowering a murderous gaze at his loquacious cousin.

Ten-year-old Vincent had endeared himself to the servants by tormenting Cleo. The first time he dropped his napkin, Neilly thought it was a simple accident. Cleo good-naturedly picked it up and handed it back to the boy. Then, as Cleo moved around the table to fill the water glasses, Vincent's napkin once more slipped to the floor.

When Cleo poured water into Varina's glass before retrieving it for him immediately he called her attention to it. "I've dropped my napkin. Can't you see that? Fetch it."

With a bland expression unnatural for Cleo, who always smiled as she worked, she picked up the napkin and placed it in the young master's lap.

Vincent giggled the moment Cleo left the room. Arthur noticed nothing and turned the conversation to cravat knots. Varina settled back in her chair and yawned, and Neilly feared she might doze off. Damon toyed with his food and said little.

The meal progressed. Uncle Cato brought in the meat course as Arthur expounded on the merits of the cutaway jacket as opposed to the frock coat.

The next time Cleo came into the room to remove the plates, Vincent's napkin flopped on the floor for a third time. Cleo, with both hands full of dirty dishes, glanced at it and hesitated.

"Don't trouble yourself, Cleo," Damon said, laying aside his own napkin. "I'll take care of it."

Vincent's giggle ceased. His eyes grew wide as Damon rose from his chair looming majestically at the head of the table. Uncertainty flickered across Vincent's face as he looked at his father, who chattered on as though he hadn't seen what happened. Then Vincent cast a sidelong look at the napkin on the floor. Neilly thought he was considering retrieving it himself, rather than leave the job to his dark cousin.

But Damon snatched up the linen square before the boy could move. Damon smiled at Vincent, a chilling, thin-lipped expression that rendered everyone at the table silent—even Arthur. Damon shook out the napkin and stood over the boy.

"What are you going to do?" Vincent piped, his childish voice brave but quavering slightly.

"I'm returning your napkin, which you seem unable to keep in your lap."

"It's just a little game he plays with the servants," Arthur explained. "Keeps them on their toes."

"Charming," Damon said, holding the square up by two corners. Stepping behind Vincent, he pulled the napkin under the boy's chin and tied it.

"Not too tight," Arthur exclaimed, almost rising from his chair.

"Is that too tight?" Damon asked Vincent with cold solicitousness.

"No," Vincent choked out, running his forefinger between his neck and the napkin to test the fit, his eyes nearly bugging out of his pale face. "It's fine."

"Good," Damon said. "We don't want this nasty thing to get away from us again, do we?"

"No, sir," Vincent said, his voice meek but his glare resentful.

Damon sat back down and the meal resumed in silence. Neilly was not looking forward to another dinner like that.

A shift in the wind billowed her skirts, dismissing memories of the unpleasant scene. A cool shadow fell over her. She looked up to see a giant thunderhead thrust its golden crown across the sun. Its dark underside skimmed the treetops. Moist air caressed her face and the scent of rain tickled her nose.

She'd better stop woolgathering, she decided. Hitching up the hem of her skirt, she quickened her steps toward the cellar.

She found the entrance under the moss-draped live oak at the foot of the cemetery hill. The door stood ajar. So Damon was still here, Neilly thought, noting that the grass around the entrance lay flattened, probably by soft leather boots.

The black latch rattled and iron door hinges squeaked as she opened the door wider. Dankness assaulted Neilly's nose.

"Who's there?" Damon called.

Neilly saw him sitting in a circle of candlelight on a bench pulled up to the rough table littered with wine bottles.

"It's me," Neilly said, hesitating in the doorway, waiting for him to invite her in. The weak light gleamed off the dusty bottles resting in the wine racks behind him and made feathery shadows of the grass roots dangling from the cellar ceiling.

He smiled at the sight of her, his lopsided smile of pleasure that surprised and warmed Neilly, reminding her how much she'd missed their private conversations during the last week. He rose from the bench where he was sitting. "Come in. What brings you here?"

"Miss Varina wondered what happened to you up at the house." At the far reaches of the ring of light, Neilly saw a spiderweb waver in the draft from the open door. On the dirt floor below, a shiny black beetle scuttled for darkness.

With a little shudder, she wondered what else lived in the darkness.

"Have I been that long?" Damon looked at the bottles on the table as if he'd just been called back from a long distance. "I was surprised by what I found here. Did you bring your inventory by any chance? There are vintages here I never imagined Grandfather owned. French, would you believe that? It seems he held no prejudice when it came to wine or art."

"I didn't bring my ledger," she answered. "And I don't know anything about wine." Neilly moved to the table, wondering if Damon had been sampling from the bottles, but as she neared him she saw that his eyes were clear.

Damon regarded her in surprise. "You certainly have a taste for good champagne."

"Well, I know what I like," Neilly explained in exasperation. "I never had to make the selection. Where did you learn about fine wine? Surely not in the wilds of Texas."

"Actually, I learned from a distant but generous cousin in England," Damon said. "He also shared with me his knowledge of horses. An expertise I plan to make use of someday—in Texas."

"Have you made a selection?" Neilly asked. Despite the cool respite the cellar offered from the heat outside, she wanted to get Damon out of there as soon as possible. "I think a storm is about to break."

"Would you take this decanter and the goblet? I'll take these bottles. I'd ask Uncle Cato to bring these things, but he wouldn't come to the cellar after he heard about Mammy Lula's seeing the ghost in the cemetery."

"Why didn't you tell me about the ghost?" Neilly asked. "I don't believe in them, but I need to know about anything that might affect Miss Isetta."

Damon paused in gathering up the things from the table. "I didn't think about that. I don't think Isetta would be particularly frightened. I doubt she believes in ghosts. Even Grandfather's ghost."

"You believe in ghosts?" Neilly could hardly keep the astonishment out of her voice. Damon seemed like such a worldly man: practical, pragmatic, and without superstition.

"Let's say I don't disbelieve," he said, then added with a charming smile and a shrug. "Must be my Gallic blood. But I think it's possible that a person's spirit might be so strong, so closely attached to things in this life, that it cannot or will not leave."

"Like your grandfather?" Neilly asked, thoughtfully considering Damon's opinion. "And his attachment to Rosewood?"

"This is grim conversation for a summer afternoon." Damon gathered up the remaining bottles. "Let's get these wines back to the house before the storm breaks."

Without argument Neilly took up the decanter in one hand and the goblet in the other and waited for Damon to blow out the candle. Just as he bent to extinguish the flame, an unexpected gust of wind surged into the room, pulling at Neilly's skirts and snuffing the candle. Before she could reach out to catch the door, iron hinges screeched, rending the air like the unearthly wail of a banshee. The door swung shut with a resounding thud.

Neilly stood in complete darkness, her breath caught tight in her throat. "Damon?"

"It's just the wind," he said. She heard bottles clink as he set them on the table again and felt him move to her side. He found the old metal latch ring and rattled it. Nothing happened.

"Jammed," was his only comment.

Neilly heard him throw more effort into each pull on the latch, but the door never budged. As her eyes grew accustomed to the darkness, she could make out the thin strip of daylight leaking beneath the door.

"The latch seems to be caught on the outside," Damon explained at last, his voice even and unexcited.

Neilly could make out his profile in the darkness.

"You mean we're locked in?" Despite his reassuring calm, she fought back rising panic. "What shall we do?"

"Stay where you are until I get the candle lit again. With some light I'll have it worked loose in no time."

She did as he instructed, listening to the clatter of a tinderbox. A spark flashed in the darkness, and the candle flared to life again, revealing Damon's familiar face. Neilly finally released her breath, somehow reassured by the light of the candle and Damon's confidence.

"Move away from the door," he said, carrying the candle closer. "Sit on the old sofa, why don't you? We'll be out of here in a moment."

Neilly did as he said, too unnerved to argue or to offer any helpful suggestions. The best she could do was stay out of his way. She settled onto the musty velvet of the discarded sofa to wait and watch.

He lugged at the pull ring, pitting his strength against the thick cypress boards and whatever held it on the outside. He braced himself against the stone doorframe with one Indian-booted foot and hauled at the latch. He knelt down and tried coaxing the latch with gentle touches and cajoling words. Despite Damon's best efforts, the door refused to give way.

"I'm surprised that rusty latch fell into place so easily," Damon said, peering at the latch ring again. What are our chances that it would fall accidentally so that it can't be moved?"

Cold fear curled restlessly in Neilly's belly and she rose from the sofa to join Damon at the door. "Are you saying some one locked us in here?"

"No, I'm not saying that at all." Damon stood up and shook his head. "It had to be the wind, just as I said."

A low rumble of thunder shook the ground under their feet, as if to punctuate his words.

She did not want to be in a subterranean chamber when the rain began to seep under the door and drip from the roots dangling overhead.

Neilly's meager courage dissolved and she jumped up from the sofa. "Maybe if we shout and pound on the door someone will hear us."

She began to hammer on the solid cypress with her fists and to holler in a very unladylike fashion. Odd circumstances demanded extraordinary action. "Hello? Hello? We're locked in the cellar."

Damon put a hand on her shoulder. "Neilly, I don't think that's going to help, and you're going to exhaust yourself."

Neilly stopped, her hands throbbing already. "But what's going to happen to us?"

He turned an apologetic smile on her. "I'm afraid you're trapped here with me for a while. Until someone at the house thinks to come looking for us. Meanwhile, this is the safest place we can be in a serious storm."

"So it would seem," Neilly agreed, recalling the fear on Uncle Cato's face. It would take a team of horses to drag him anywhere near cemetery hill or the cellar—storm or no storm. Isetta was napping. Varina would be lost in her gardening until Cleo reminded her that it was raining, and she should come into the house.

"The only thing to do is make the time pass pleasantly until someone misses us," Damon said, looking around the room. "How about a lesson in wine appreciation? You taught me about art; I'll teach you about wine."

"Well, I'm not certain that's appropriate right now," Neilly said, in no mood for social chitchat over a glass of wine.

"What *is* an appropriate pastime for a lady and a gentleman who are locked in a wine cellar?" Damon asked, beguiling Neilly with his lopsided grin. "Aunt Isetta probably knows a card game just for such an occasion, but we're without cards. Or her instruction."

Neilly smiled in return, her fear fading a little. "I wouldn't be surprised if she doesn't know of just such a game. All right, teach me to appreciate wine. It's bound to make the time pass more quickly. Someone will have to come after us sooner or later if they want wine with dinner."

Damon pulled the table over to the sofa and Neilly sat down. "I'm going to enjoy sharing this wine with you here much more than sharing it with Arthur in the dining room."

He grinned at her as he pulled the cork from the first of the bottles he'd selected.

Neilly didn't have to ask what Damon meant about Arthur. "Have you and your cousin always been at odds?"

Damon glanced up from the bottle of wine he was opening with a surprised lift of his brows. He pressed his lips together before he spoke. "Yes, I think so. Since before we were born, probably. Since the day my mother was disinherited and the day a year later when Mirabelle married the man Grandfather had chosen for my mother."

"Mirabelle married Rosalie's chosen suitor?"

"Well, he was acceptable to Grandfather until he committed the dreadful sin of taking Mirabelle to New Orleans to live," Damon said, his tone even and surprisingly without bitterness. "To my grandfather even that was a lesser transgression than marrying a lazy Creole. I don't think Grandfather ever saw Arthur, his chosen heir.

"I first laid eyes on my cousin at Grandfather's funeral fifteen years ago," Damon said. "I was fifteen. He was only twelve, but even then he was taking stock of the plantation like a steamer captain checking off a manifest."

A slow smile spread across Damon's face as some forgotten memory surfaced.

"What happened?" Neilly prompted.

"We ended up in a fight." Damon's grin broadened. "It wasn't even a fair one and I knew it. I was bigger and more experienced. Arthur didn't have a chance, but he wouldn't back down. So we slugged it out in Mammy Lula's kitchen garden compost pile."

"Oh, Damon." Neilly laughed at the image of a meticulously dressed Arthur rolled in cold tea leaves and rotting vegetable peels. "You ruined his fine coat, no doubt."

"And my own," Damon said. "But it was worth every stinking minute of it."

"What did Isetta say?"

Damon shrugged. "Boys will be boys. Aunt Mirabelle swore she'd never come back to Rosewood, even if it *was* Arthur's legacy. Too uncivilized here, she said."

"Has she?"

"No. As a matter of fact, she and her husband died two years later of yellow fever," Damon said. "But Arthur has continued to visit Rosewood at long intervals. I went away, too; first to college, then on to Europe. But enough about my cousin. I am going to teach you about wine."

"What do I need to know?" Neilly asked, determined to forget that they were locked in a dank, dark cellar.

"This red is from France." Damon carefully poured the wine into a decanter. "Like most reds it needs to be decanted. Which is what I'm doing now."

"I see stuff in the bottom," Neilly said, peering at the bottle, a little repulsed by what she saw. Through the green glass the candlelight plainly revealed a dark sludge.

"Just a little sediment. That's why we pour the wine off into a decanter." As Damon poured, the heavy sediment lagged at the bottom.

"This will be a dry red wine, not a sweet drink like the sherry my aunts prefer." He splashed a small amount of the ruby red liquor into the goblet for Neilly. She reached for it.

"Oh, no, not so fast. Wine-drinking involves more than just swilling the stuff down."

Neilly frowned at him in mock offense. "I assure you, sir, I never *swill* anything."

"No, of course not." He chuckled. "Forgive me. I did not mean to imply such. Appreciating a fine wine takes time and care. A sort of ritual, if you will. Not unlike enjoying a fine piece of art."

"I see. Then, what more is there to this ritual after decanting?"

"Hold the glass up to the light to see that the wine is clear."

The candle flame leapt through the rich red liquor, magnified by the curve of the goblet in Damon's hand. The wine glowed ruby red, rich and mellow. Neilly stared at it, quite hypnotized by the lush color and light. "What do you think?"

"About what?" Neilly shook her head to throw off the spell. "Oh, the wine is too lovely to drink."

"But we're not ready for that yet," he said, eyeing her in that appraising fashion that always gave her gooseflesh. She shivered.

"Are you cold?"

"No," Neilly said, too quickly. "I mean yes, a little. I hadn't intended to spend any time in the cellar when I walked out here."

"Me either. Here, take my waistcoat," Damon said, shrugging out of the gray damask vest that he often wore when he was working around the plantation. "This should give you some warmth."

Neilly gratefully allowed him to drape the garment around her shoulders, his large hand resting briefly, almost intimately, on her back.

"Better?"

"Yes, thank you." Under his scrutiny, under the power of his hands, her gooseflesh multiplied. To keep him from recognizing the effect he was having on her, she pressed the conversation on. "So, you were saying that we've seen that

the wine is clear and has a good color, but we're still not
ready to drink it?"

"No." Damon took up the wineglass again. "Now we
test the bouquet. Umm, this is very nice."

He passed the glass just below his own nose. "Here, you
try it."

Neilly reached for the glass, but Damon took her hand
in his, away from the glass.

"Sniff," he said, and passed the goblet just beneath her
nose.

She obeyed. A light fragrance almost as delightful as a
scent of flowers filled her head. "This is wonderful. Like
a garden almost. Champagne doesn't smell this good."

"No, it doesn't," he said with an understanding grin on
his face.

"Are we ready to drink it now?" Neilly asked. "My nose
tells me this is going to taste good."

He leaned closer to Neilly, slipped his arm around her,
and held the glass up for her to sip from.

"Thank you, sir," Neilly said, grinning at him with more
courage and sipped slowly, delighting in the light, dry flavor
that suffused her mouth and the sweet fragrance that filled
her head. His nearness banished her fear of the cold darkness of the cellar. The wine warmed her insides, all the way
down. Wine drinking could be a wonderful experience, she
thought, a more engaging event than it had ever been in
the past.

"You're right," Neilly said as soon as Damon took the
glass from her. She licked the last of the liquor from her
lips, then smacked them, rather unbecomingly, she suspected. But Damon smiled at her with a pleasant, self-
contained expression that she liked. She didn't care if she
had smacked her lips. "There is more to appreciating wine
than just sipping at it. Or swilling it."

"Indeed." Damon reached for another bottle. "Now, here
we have a German wine, something from the Rhine River

valley, I believe." He began to open the bottle and tell her about the vineyards on the banks of the Rhine River.

Time slipped away as they sampled that bottle. Neilly was only vaguely aware of the storm raging outside. Thunder rumbled through the ground beneath their feet another time or two. Barely noticeable. Once they heard the wind soughing through the branches of the live oak outside the door. Otherwise Neilly almost forgot they were trapped.

She found herself smiling a lot and laughing a good deal and warming up so much that she let Damon's waistcoat slip from her shoulders. Still she made no effort to move away from him. She didn't mind his thigh resting against hers as they sat on the sofa. She didn't give a thought to sharing the glass with him. It seemed the only logical, friendly way to taste wines.

"There's something else about wine tasting that I haven't told you yet," Damon said after they had tasted the third bottle. "The best wines hold their flavor on your lover's lips."

Neilly became quiet. After all the witty words that had just been falling from her lips, she couldn't think of a thing to say to Damon's remark.

"It certainly can add a new dimension to a fine wine." He leaned closer, his mouth nearing hers. Inviting. Strong. Tempting. Firm and masterful. "Shall we try this tasting tradition, too?"

Intrigued, Neilly almost puckered her lips in response, then caught herself. With a jerk, she drew away, pressing her back against the tattered arm of the sofa, her hands firmly spread across his chest, holding him at bay.

"I think that's one tradition we should forgo," Neilly said, unwilling to allow things to get away from her as they had in the garden.

A smile of regret softened Damon's face. He looked just disappointed enough to make Neilly consider changing her mind, yet something dangerous glinted in his eyes.

"If you say so." He returned to studying the wines on the table.

She stole a quick sidelong glance at his handsome face. The dangerous gleam was gone, and he was intent on the wine labels.

After all, what harm could a little kiss do? she thought. *Harm? Remember the garden?* her conscience shouted back. *It starts with a little kiss. Next thing, you lose all your self-discipline. Then his hands are on your—*

Damon's head came up. "What? Did you say something?"

"Me?" Neilly shook her head and tried to shut off her wayward thoughts. She must have been thinking too loudly.

He picked up a fourth bottle. "This is a French white . . ." he continued.

The kissing tradition was forgotten. Soon they were both laughing over some silly thing Neilly had said, untroubled by the locked cellar door.

The candle flared, illuminating the room so brightly for an instant that the flash hurt Neilly's eyes.

Then the flame died and total darkness engulfed them.

Eleven

Startled by the sudden blackness, Neilly cried out and clutched Damon's arm. The dark was so complete, she couldn't even see the table or the bottles that sat right in front of them. No light seeped under the door now. But Damon was next to her, solid and steady.

"The candle has burned out." He placed a steady hand over hers. "That's all. You're not afraid of the dark, are you?"

"Oh, nothing like that, but I don't suppose you brought a spare candle?" Neilly asked, trying to keep her apprehension from her voice. The pleasant warmth of the wine ebbed away into the darkness. She wasn't especially afraid of the dark, under normal circumstances. But cellar dark seemed particularly unpleasant.

"No spare," Damon said. "I hadn't intended to stay this long. But nothing is going to happen to us here."

"I'm not so sure." The memory of the spiderweb in the corner and the crawly beetle returned to Neilly. "Other things consider this hole in the ground home."

"Nothing will bother you as long I'm with you," Damon said, male bravado and amusement rich in his voice. But she believed him. He wasn't the kind of man who promised—or threatened—anything he couldn't do. He pulled her closer.

She let him.

"How long have we been here?" she asked, her voice

quivering. "Surely someone in the house has missed us by now. It's so dark outside, there's no light under the door."

"Darkness came early, with the storm."

"Oh," Neilly groaned. "What if the river is rising?"

"I doubt that it is." Damon's lips brushed her temple, warm and reassuring. "I've never known the river to get this high."

Neilly leaned against him in the darkness and she turned her face up to his, longing in vain to see his features. He touched her cheek, his callused fingers stroking lightly, tenderly across to her jaw.

"You're afraid, but you're not crying," he said. "Like in the garden."

Neilly shook her head, embarrassed that he would bring up their confrontation in the garden. "I only cry when I'm angry."

"Or hurt," he added. "I'll remember that."

She felt his lips brush against her cheek this time, and she knew he was searching for her mouth.

In the garden the moonlight had given the world a glow nearly as plain as day. All the windows of the house had looked down on them, watchful reminders of her responsibilities to Varina and Isetta.

Here in the darkness no one was watching. Damon was near, warm, tangible, and caring. His arms provided a protective circle around her when she needed it most. When the dark was closing in and panic threatened. Her senses sharpened. He smelled of pipe smoke and red wine. The heat of his body seeped into hers, inviting her to snuggle closer.

Hesitantly, she slipped her arms around his waist, pressing her breasts against the hard wall of his chest, and offered him her lips.

He accepted her invitation, his mouth moving across hers, his warmth and tenderness touching her like a gentle dew urging her to give up her sweetness. Better than anything they had shared in the garden.

"Can you taste the wine?" she asked, realizing only after she'd said it how provocative it sounded.

"The wine is good," he murmured, with a smile in his voice, his lips against hers. "But your own sweetness is better."

Neilly's defenses melted, trickling away with her fear. There was danger in this. He knew more about what he was doing than she, but his kiss stirred sensations too glorious to deny. His hand stroked down over her shoulder, brushing ever so lightly against her breast, sending an unexpected thrill through her stomach. She gladly sank against him, unashamed and tingling with newfound pleasure in a man's touch. She opened her mouth to his.

Damon's low groan revealed his delicious appreciation. Without releasing her, he pushed her gently down on the sofa, pressing the length of his body along hers. She welcomed the weight of him as much as the renewed force of his mouth on hers. It made her feel wanted, needed, and cherished. He captured her head between his hands, his fingers tangled in her curls, and his tongue probed her mouth. She'd never been kissed with such passion before. Eagerly, she returned his forays, wanting to taste him as much as he seemed to want more of her.

When he released her they both panted for breath.

"Darlin', you taste better than any wine," he whispered, with that faint Texas drawl creeping into his voice. He trailed his fingers along her mouth. "I wish I could see your lips. All red from the wine and a little swollen from that kiss."

Neilly licked her lips. Tender. Sensitive lips that tingled and burned. She slipped her arms around his neck and threaded her fingers through his thick hair. "Will you kiss me like that again?"

But he had already nibbled his way to her ear, tracing

the shell with his tongue, then trailing light kisses down her neck. Neilly's belly did a sweet somersault. She closed her eyes and soaked up the delight of the feathery kisses he bestowed on her shoulder. The buttons at her throat seemed to fall aside beneath his skillful fingers. Her bodice had slipped from her shoulder. Each opened loop exposed more and more of her to Damon's lips. Each kiss lured her deeper and deeper into the bliss of his embrace. She yearned for his hands and for his mouth on her, everywhere.

But when his hand gently cupped her bare breast her good sense rose above the passion. Her well-educated brain struggled against the sweet pleasure of his touch. "Damon, what are we doing? I'm not sure that this is prop—?"

"Shh, darlin', we're making love," Damon whispered reassuringly. "Sweet, gentle love."

"But I'm not sure we should make—oooh!"

His moist breath drew a tight, tingling desire into the crest of Neilly's breast. Her senses reeled, though she tried to cover herself with her camisole, but he gently pulled her hand away. His tongue drew such pleasure through her, she ached for him to cover her other puckered nipple with such perfection—and he did. The sweet thrill brought a sigh to her lips.

Reason battled the emotions begging her to surrender to his intimate touch. Damon would leave Rosewood—and her—as soon as Isetta admitted to good health. But logic had no strength against the ache his tongue nurtured deep inside her. No man's touch had ever reduced her to such mindless weakness. No man's caress had ever made her long to open herself to the mysterious need to satisfy that deep aching.

Damon moved lower, abandoning her nipple, kissing her ribs as he kneaded her sensitive breasts. Good sense fled the battle scene, deserting her heart and inebriated body to every seductive strategy Damon chose to practice on her.

A soft cry of disappointment escaped Neilly. Damon returned to her throbbing breast. She threaded her fingers through his hair and sighed surrender.

Reason's defection became a release, like being set free to bestow generously what she longed to give. Why fight Damon's desire for her when she longed to be wanted by him? He held her, touched her, praised her with endearments and with his hands and mouth. He caressed her with kisses that made her skin sing with pleasure. She needed no good sense to know the rightness of that.

When his hand slipped up her leg the heat of his palm on her thigh flooded through her, sweeping away the last of her resistance. She was lost in a world of caresses and kisses, warm and tingling, sweet and bright.

He kissed her deeply again, his hand slipping up farther, loosening tapes at her waist, stroking her skin as he tucked her skirt around her waist and parted her undergarments. The air of the cellar felt cool on her bare thigh, but the heat of Damon's hand brushed the chill away.

Neilly ached for his touch in all of the forbidden places. She was disappointed when he took his hands away and grasped hers. He placed her fingers on the buttons of his shirt. For a moment she didn't understand that he was urging her to explore him, too. The idea that her touch might please him as much as his thrilled her delighted Neilly. She almost giggled as she grappled with his buttons.

"Slow down, darlin'," Damon said with a chuckle. But she was already peeling the shirt from his chest. At last she could trace the muscles she had only touched and massaged through a layer of clothing. She longed to see the contours that her hands were already familiar with.

His skin was warm and firm and his chest hair tickled, crisp between her fingers. She remembered how dark and curly it was when exposed at his throat, thick and masculine. When her hands slipped lower, discovering the powerful muscles of his narrowing hips, she realized he had already unbuttoned his trousers. Brushing his hard, hot arousal startled her. Unprepared to go farther, she halted her exploration. She sensed that in daylight he would not look like the cold marble nude males she'd seen.

His fingers sought her secret place and found it. The first touch, though gentle, sent shock through Neilly. She tensed in Damon's arms, but he whispered reassuring words to her. He tenderly stroked her moistness through the soft, sensitive folds of her femininity. He urged her to open up to him. Under his hands the shock mellowed into a new, powerful longing. Neilly wanted him inside her.

There was no going back now. She reached for his shoulders and pulled him to her.

She was prepared for the pain when Damon first thrust into her and she bit back any sound of her discomfort. But she had not expected to feel him stiffen and curse. She went still under him. What had she done wrong?

"My God, Neilly, why didn't you tell me?" He rested his forehead against hers, his breath ragged and the cords of his back hard and taut beneath her hands. "Oh, darlin', this shouldn't have happened like this."

"Why not?" Neilly asked, confused. "You said you wanted to make love. It's what I wanted, too."

He said nothing.

"It really wasn't so bad."

He remained silent, his breathing still uneven. Neilly began to fear she had done something wrong. She shifted under his weight. "Is there more? Should I do something more?"

"Oh, there's more," he whispered into her ear, his voice still ragged. He stroked her temple with his thumb. "So much more. Move with me, Neilly. If it doesn't hurt you, darlin'. With your hips. Slow and easy."

Neilly followed his example. He groaned again, but it was a sound of pleasure. Emboldened, she lifted against him, allowing herself to take pleasure in the fullness she felt as he moved deeper inside. The pain was gone. They fit together with gratifying precision, a mutually pleasurable coupling. So close their hearts almost touched, and she wanted it to go on and on.

Damon traced kisses along her cheek until he reached her lips. Then he claimed her mouth with his, gliding his tongue between her lips. Probing. Penetrating.

"There is more, Neilly. You deserve to have it all the first time. I want to give it all to you."

What more did he want to give? Neilly wondered, her senses too full to imagine anything more.

His hip movements changed; he thrust in a circle, stirring deeper into her. Neilly felt him touching her womb, and she arched against him and instinctively wrapped her legs around his, drawing him deeper. The urge to move with Damon took her, requiring no thought, only response. Pleasure glowed inside. She could feel a deeper heat awakening inside her somewhere where Damon sought his satisfaction—and hers.

Damon feathered kisses across her lips and whispered something hot and breathless and encouraging. She strived to please him and reached to find what awaited them. She lost herself in a spiraling journey, following her need until the crest broke over her, sweet and bright in her belly, tingling through her limbs, clutching at her pounding heart.

She cried out and offered herself up to him.

Damon shuddered, pouring himself into her. Neilly knew her pleasure was his, too. Damon murmured something reassuring into her ear and she sighed. They both relaxed, settling into the sofa, Damon's weight still pleasant and comforting.

Neilly had almost fallen asleep when Damon left her. Nearly bolting off the sofa, he was up and pacing around the dark cellar. Neilly struggled to sit up, cold and alone. She smoothed her skirts back in place. She could hear his soft boots pad across the earthen floor and stop, followed by the rustle of clothing. In her mind's eye she could see him with his back to her, tucking his shirt into its proper place and rebuttoning his trousers.

Neilly tried to do the same with her bodice. She wondered if she'd bled. She prayed that if there was blood, it would be confined to her petticoats and not stain her skirt.

Still, Damon was silent. She waited, longing for him to come sit beside her, kiss her, and tell her how special the joy was that they had just shared. He didn't return.

When he did speak his scolding tone caught her unawares.

"Darlin' Neilly, the first time should not happen like this. It should be in the privacy of a room in the comfort of a bed."

"Are you going to give me a lecture about waiting for my wedding night?"

"After what just happened I don't feel in the position to lecture anyone."

She was still so wrapped in the fuzzy cocoon of the pleasure they had just shared that she could hardly think of what to say to him. Why was he angry at what had just happened?

"Why didn't you stop me?" Damon went on, puzzlement and indignation in his voice. "Why didn't you tell me there's never been anyone else?"

"Why did you assume there had been?" Neilly countered, indignation coming to her rescue at last.

"Because—" Damon began. She could hear him pacing in the darkness and knew he didn't want to admit what he was about to confess. "Because if I'd put a betrothal ring on your finger, as your fiancé must have done, I'd have proceeded to seduce you at the earliest opportunity."

"And what if I'd refused?" Neilly interrupted, not particularly flattered by his confession. "Did you ever think of that possibility?"

"After the way you kissed me in the garden, no, never." This time Damon sounded almost as bewildered as she felt.

"Obviously you did refuse him. So why didn't you stop me?"

Neilly shook her head, thankful for the cover of darkness.

"I didn't stop you because I didn't want to stop you," she managed to say evenly, though the ache of humiliating tears was rising in the back of her throat. "I made a choice. I wanted to be held in your arms and I wanted to hold you."

Damon made a sound that resembled agreement, but he said nothing more.

Neilly started to work on her buttons, slipping each one into its proper place, she hoped, with trembling fingers. In the darkness she tried to ignore her growing fear. She'd always suspected she'd take a lover someday, because she'd come to understand a little of her own passionate nature. But she'd always assumed her lover would return her affection.

A sudden pounding on the cellar door interrupted her efforts.

Neilly jumped guiltily, losing hold of the last button.

"Are you dressed?" Damon whispered, across the cellar.

"Yes, I think so," Neilly answered, fumbling for the wayward button again. She fastened it and ran her fingers down the row on her gray broadcloth bodice. All seemed to be in order, but it was impossible to be certain in the dark.

"Damon? Neilly?" The voice was Varina's. "Are you in there, dears?"

"Yes, we're here, Aunt Varina," Damon said. "The latch is jammed. Can you work it free?"

The scraping of the latch being worked reached them.

"Damon?" Varina called again. "The latch is hopelessly jammed. Elijah is going to have to get a tool to pry it loose. You'll be out in a moment."

Damon called back that he understood.

Neilly heard his footsteps come back in her direction, and she felt the springs sag as he sat down beside her. She moved away, but he managed to find her hand in the darkness and squeezed it.

"Are you all right?"

"Yes, of course," Neilly said. Her tears were gone now, her bodice buttons fastened and her pride in place. "I wish I could be more certain about my hair."

To her surprise Damon touched her head and let his hand slip down the back of her neck. "Most of your combs seem to be in place. I don't think anyone will be too suspicious of a few stray tendrils under the circumstances. But I was really asking if you are in any discomfort."

"I told you, I'm all right," Neilly said. He didn't need to know that she was already sore. She tried to pull her hand from his grasp, but he wouldn't release her.

"Neilly, I—" he began, but Neilly stopped him. Somehow her fingers found his mouth even in the darkness.

"Don't say you're sorry, Damon. Please don't say that. Because then I'll have to be sorry, and I'm not."

Damon gripped the ancient iron latch in his left hand and lifted the rusted iron bar with some effort. Metal scratched against rusted metal, then clanked into place, solid and immovable by anyone on the wrong side of the door.

"Wouldn't have taken much effort," Elijah said, peering over Damon's shoulder. "Most anybody could've slammed that door and locked you and Miss Neilly in the cellar. Big person or li'l. But it weren't no accident."

"But why?" Arthur demanded. The three men stood on the edge of the gallery, contemplating the hardware Elijah had pried off the cellar door.

The storm had moved on, leaving the last of the day's light to filter through the thinning clouds.

Varina and Cleo were gathered near Rosewood's back door, fussing over Neilly. A soft blush stained her cheeks and a dark, unruly tendril had fallen across her brow. She looked remarkably collected as she assured Varina that no harm had been done.

He wanted to say something to her. To thank her for not telling his aunt that he'd plied her with wine, then bedded her like a thoughtless brute—with all the caring of a stag in rutting season.

No, he wanted to say more to Neilly than that, but he wasn't sure what the words were yet.

"The women don't need to know that this was anything more than. the wind blowing the door shut," Damon said. He didn't want Neilly or his aunts thinking anything was wrong.

"So, who's your enemy around here, Damon?" Arthur asked, hooking his hands in his green brocade waistcoat in a know-it-all gesture. As if this incident proved something despicable about Damon to which he'd been privy all along. "Who do you owe money to? Or did one of your Indian friends track you to Rosewood to settle a score?"

"I don't have the slightest idea who would have locked Neilly and me in that cellar," Damon said, glad the women were out of earshot. He glared at Arthur. "But when I find out who it was, he'd better be miles from here."

Arthur stepped back, obviously offended. "Are you implying something, sir?"

"Only that the man who did this will have some tall explaining to do."

Vincent skipped along the gallery to join the men. "Did the ghost lock you in Cousin Damon? I bet the lightning struck Great Grandpapa's mausoleum and called him out of his grave. I'll bet he locked you up for stealing bottles out of his wine cellar."

"What nonsense," Arthur scolded, glancing guiltily at Damon.

"All the servants are talking about it. They say that Great

Grandpapa has come back because Aunt Isetta is going to give Rosewood to Cousin Damon instead of you, Papa."

Arthur's face fell, disappearing into his weak chin; then anger flashed in his eyes. "Is what Vincent says true, Durande? Have you talked Aunt Isetta into changing her will? Is she leaving Rosewood to you instead of me?"

"This is the first I've heard of it," Damon said, mildly amused with his cousin's outrage. Losing his legacy must be a maddening thought to Arthur. At the same time Damon was annoyed by mention of a will. Aunt Isetta's demise wasn't a subject that he cared for. "What makes you think I'd want the damned plantation?"

"Why ever not?" Arthur asked, his pale blue eyes widening in disbelief. "There's enough artwork in the house to buy a complete wardrobe for every season, right down to silk underwear. For my wife, too. Money enough to assure a man of a warm welcome in all the best gambling salons and race tracks. To send Vincent off to the best schools."

"But I don't want to go anywhere," Vincent said.

Arthur ignored his son. "I can't believe Aunt Isetta has changed her will. I'm going to see about that right now." He strode off down the gallery and into the house, his boot heels ringing on the floor. Vincent tagged along.

Damon knew he had to stop them before they upset Isetta.

He shoved the latch back into Elijah's hands. "Thanks for your help. Put a padlock on the cellar door for now."

All Damon could think of as he took the backstairs two at a time was the waste if Arthur inherited Rosewood—a waste of Thomas Stirling's lifetime and work. Of a beautiful house, of a profitable plantation that supported many families, and of the fine pieces of art that would disappear— simply to appease this one small man's vanity.

Twelve

By the time Damon reached the top of the stairs Arthur was already attempting to argue his way into Aunt Isetta's room—to no avail. Neilly was at the door, stalwart and as unflappable as ever.

"Please understand, Mr. Sitwell, your aunt is in delicate health," Neilly was saying as she gripped the doorknob to prevent Arthur or Vincent from brushing past her. She'd tucked the loose tendril behind her ear and spoke calmly, as if this confrontation was just another daily exchange.

"But I must see her now." Arthur's voice rang out in a high, petulant pitch. He backed Neilly against the door, looming over her as much as his slight stature allowed him to.

Neilly met his demanding gaze but remained unmoved. "I think not."

"That's enough, Arthur," Damon said, amazed at her courage and loyalty. After the way he'd treated her in the cellar he could hardly believe she was still on his side, still defending Isetta and Varina. "If Neilly says this isn't the time to talk to Aunt Isetta about Rosewood, then this isn't the time."

"I will not be put off about Aunt Isetta's will," Arthur said, whirling on Damon. "Not by this girl or by you."

"I saw Auntie playing cards in there when Cleo left the room this morning," Vincent volunteered at his father's side.

"See there," Arthur said with a huff. "If Aunt Isetta is

well enough to get up and play cards, she is well enough to talk to me about Rosewood."

Damon turned to Neilly. "Is she awake?"

"Yes, and she wants to see you—and me," Neilly said, a blush blooming in her cheeks. "She's heard about us being locked in the cellar."

"Then we will see her and set her mind at ease," Damon said.

"If she can see you," Arthur shot back, "she can see me."

"For God's sake, Arthur, she's an old lady in bad health," Damon snapped. "Humor her. Don't you have that much charity in your heart?"

"Don't start making me out the villain here, Damon."

Neilly interrupted. "Miss Isetta's weak heart is the villain, Mr. Sitwell. She can only take so much excitement, and I'm sure you wouldn't want to risk another attack before you and she have settled affairs to your satisfaction."

Arthur paled. "No, of course not."

"I didn't think so." Neilly offered Arthur a beguiling smile, not unlike the sweet, patient one she'd bestowed on the Kenner brothers at The Laurels, Damon thought. "Damon and I will see her briefly, as she requested; then we'll ask her if she's up to seeing you and Vincent."

"All right," Arthur replied with reluctance. "But you won't take up all her time? Drain her of all her energy?"

"I think she just wants to be assured that we're all right," Neilly said, glancing uneasily at Damon. "Why don't you and Vincent wait out on the gallery, Mr. Sitwell? It's cooler out there."

Arthur agreed, taking his son by the hand and leading him out onto the gallery.

As soon as they were out of hearing, Damon moved closer to Neilly and turned his back on the Sitwells so they couldn't see his face or hers.

"Thanks for heading Arthur off," Damon said, thinking

Neilly appeared more nervous with him than she had been while confronting Arthur and Vincent.

She put trembling hands to her hair. "What is your aunt going to think? I must be a sight."

Mud still caked the hem of her skirt, and that unruly tendril was about to escape from behind her ear. Damon resisted the urge to tuck it back for her. He thought she looked absolutely ravishing, especially for a woman who had just been—well—ravished.

He let his gaze slide over her, remembering the satiny smoothness of her skin, the ripe fullness of her breasts, the sweet virgin tightness of her body.

"You look fine considering the circumstances." Damon made himself look away. If he didn't practice a little more self-discipline, he was going to be the one who wasn't presentable enough to go into his aunt's room. "I'm sure Aunt Isetta will think so, too."

But he couldn't help glancing at Neilly one more time before they went in. It was then he noticed that the last three buttons of her bodice were incorrectly matched with their button loops.

"Whoa, darlin', your buttons are all out of order," he whispered, touching the jumble of buttons and loops at her waist.

"My, oh my!" Neilly hurried to set them straight. Her cheeks glowed pink. "I'm glad you saw that before your aunt did. She may be ill, but she doesn't miss much. Are they right now?"

"Perfect. You look as beautiful as a freshly loved lady can," Damon added.

Her blush deepened to crimson. "I feel like a hussy," Neilly protested, refusing to look at him now. "What on earth are we going to say to your aunt?"

He longed for a moment alone with her instead of these stolen seconds in the hallway with Arthur and Vincent loitering on the gallery.

"I don't mean for you to feel like a hussy," Damon said, and meant it. Neilly was a lady, no matter what else she might be. He'd known that ever since that day at The Laurels.

He didn't care what they told Aunt Isetta. He longed to tell Neilly that what they had shared in the cellar was something as new and unique to him as it was to her. Something he didn't understand yet. But words seemed too meager, too hollow to hold the fullness of his feelings.

"We're going to assure Aunt Isetta that everything is all right," Damon said. "There's nothing for her to be worried about. How does that sound? Does that make you feel better?"

Neilly nodded.

"Ready?"

When Neilly nodded again Damon opened the door.

Isetta was propped up in bed with her imperial silver-headed cane in her hand. Instead of the frail woman Damon had expected to find she looked like Elizabeth Regina in a bed cap receiving her court. Varina stood at her side like an obedient retainer.

"Well, what is this I hear about the two of you being trapped in the cellar for over three hours?" Isetta inquired, her eyes narrowing as she scrutinized them.

Damon forced a smile to his lips. "Neilly came to find me and the wind blew the door closed. The lock jammed; then the storm broke."

"Then the candle burned out," Neilly added, going straight to the bed to straighten the covers and fluff the pillows. She moved as gracefully as ever. Damon couldn't keep from recalling the sweet taste of her neck and the warm silkiness of her thighs.

"We were left in total darkness," Neilly continued as she smoothed the quilt and tied back the mosquito netting.

"I take it no harm came to you, then?" Isetta said, looking at Neilly with particular interest, her gaze penetrating.

"No harm." Neilly touched the buttons at her waist before she added, "A cellar is the safest place you can be in a storm, you know."

Damon tried to catch her eye, to reassure her. But she busied herself with gathering up Isetta's playing cards.

"Well, I'm glad to know that no damage has been done," Isetta said, wrinkling the counterpane Neilly had just smoothed.

"There is another matter, Aunt Isetta," Damon said, all too aware of his cousin in the hallway. "Arthur insists on talking to you about Rosewood—and your will."

Isetta said nothing at first, only tapping her cane on the floor. "So he's heard the rumor about the change."

Damon frowned. "I wish you'd informed me."

"I meant to talk to you about that before the word got out," Isetta said, still tapping her cane. "I can see that you are not pleased with the change."

"Grandfather made his wishes known long ago, and I have no quarrel with them."

"Do you want to see Arthur take over Rosewood?"

Damon paused. He couldn't lie about this. "No, but I don't belong at Rosewood either. Grandfather made that clear to me."

Isetta sank back on her pillows. "Oh, Damon, don't you think you might come to feel differently some day?"

"I'm sorry to disappoint you," Damon said. He'd made his place in the world already, and it wasn't on this plantation. "I'll do whatever I can to help you, but Rosewood is yours."

"I understand, dear," Isetta said, closing her eyes.

Neilly touched his sleeve. "Let her rest."

The door opened behind them and Arthur stuck his head in. "Will she see me now?"

"I don't think this is the time," Neilly answered firmly. "She's very tired."

Arthur burst into the room before Damon could shut the door in his face. Vincent slipped in at his father's side.

"Aunt Isetta, I want to know about this rumor that you have changed your will," Arthur demanded.

"Neilly told you this wasn't the time," Damon said, his voice low and threatening.

"It's all right to let Arthur in," Isetta said, her pale blue eyes popping open, suddenly focused and icy sharp. "There's no time like the present to deal with business."

Arthur stalked to Isetta's bedside. "I know all about the promise you made when Grandpapa died. My mother was here and heard every word. If you give Rosewood to Damon, you defy your father's last wish."

"My decision is made, Nephew," Isetta snapped with gusto.

Arthur blushed at being addressed so.

"I'm sorry that neither you nor Damon like the change, but the new will is written and witnessed and safe and secure in my attorney's vault," Isetta said. "Arthur, I recommend you treat your Cousin Damon with more respect if you think you may have any need of his support in the future."

"I can't believe you're going to betray a deathbed promise," Arthur cried. "One made to your own father."

"My decision is made." With that, Isetta settled back on her pillows and waved a hand, dismissing them all.

Damon held the door open for his cousin. "You heard the lady. Out."

Arthur scurried out and turned on Damon in the hall after the door to Isetta's room was closed.

"Let's you and I settle this," Arthur said.

"What's to settle?"

"The point is, you don't want Rosewood and I do," Arthur said. "We can work something out. Aunt Isetta need never know."

"We have nothing to work out." Damon shook his head,

unamused by his cousin's desperate appeal. "I'm not making any deals with you, Sitwell, now or ever."

Damon told Uncle Cato that no wine was to be served at dinner. Whatever he and Neilly had to say to each other should come from a clear head, he told himself as he smoothed the corner of the tablecloth. Then he straightened the fork beside Neilly's plate, something he'd never done before in his life.

He wanted to believe he didn't know why this dinner alone with her was so important, but he knew. This afternoon, he'd taken advantage of her—an unmarried lady under his protection. He owed her something.

But he was beginning to realize that there was more to his feelings than obligation. He cared about Neilly. Damon frowned to himself. That was the hardest thing for him to face. She was the first woman who had ever stirred this overpowering sense of responsibility in him and something more. As uncomfortable as the feeling was, he couldn't turn his back on it.

He'd always thought of love as a dark tangle of emotions that held you hostage, made you vulnerable, and brought you pain. That's what had happened to his mother and father. That's what had happened to him. He'd vowed love would never afflict him. He didn't need the complication of a woman. In Texas female companionship without it was easy enough to find. He'd been satisfied with that.

But Neilly had given him so much more than mere companionship. She'd cared for Aunt Isetta, who could be difficult. She'd stood toe-to-toe with Arthur, which was definitely beyond the call of duty, and she'd given of herself to him—in more ways than their embrace in the cellar. He simply couldn't think about her in the same way he had before. He didn't feel about her as he had before. The feeling made him strangely happy, lighthearted and strong. The emotion made him feel as awkward as a boy.

When he heard Neilly's footsteps in the hall he turned to the door, eager for her company. His heart beat more rapidly than it had since he'd faced his first Comanche.

"Good evening," Damon said as soon as Neilly appeared in the dining room doorway.

The soft pink gown she wore gave her a rosy glow. Her dark curls were all in place on the kissable nape of her neck. She paused, shy, unsure, beautiful. Damon held his breath for a moment, afraid of frightening her away.

She glanced around the room, her gaze settling on him at last. "Where is everyone?"

"The Sitwells are dining in their rooms tonight," Damon said, realizing for the first time how much she'd come to mean to him, how desolate he would have been if she'd refused to come to dinner. "And as you know, Aunt Isetta and Aunt Varina decided to take a tray in Isetta's room. That just leaves the two us."

"Alone?" She looked so apprehensive that Damon began to fear she really was going to turn around and leave him. "Maybe I should take a tray in my room also."

"Nonsense. Uncle Cato will be disappointed if he doesn't get to serve us in here," Damon said, going to the place set for her and pulling out the chair. He wasn't about to give up without a fight. "Cleo will be serving, too. Let me seat you."

Still she hesitated.

"You know, if I were going to romance you, I should have wined and dined you first."

"You already did the wine part," Neilly said, a hint of humor quirking at the corner of her mouth.

All was not necessarily lost, Damon decided.

"So let's do the dine part." He gestured to her chair.

Neilly eyed him with skepticism.

Just as Damon was convinced that she was going to turn

and disappear, she stepped into the dining room. With resolution she strode toward him and her chair.

Damon seated her, sat down across the table, and smiled
to hide his relief.

She busied herself with her napkin. Damon saw her
hands trembling.

"I need to know something," she began without looking
up at him. "It's important to me."

"Know what?"

"If anything about my position here at Rosewood is going to change because of what happened this afternoon."
She lifted her head and studied him.

He saw that despite her calm gaze she was frightened.
He realized she feared he was either going to dismiss her
or to take unfair advantage of the situation. What had she
said about needing this position? Maybe this wasn't the time
to declare how he felt. She might misunderstand his intentions.

"What do you want, Neilly? How do you want us to go
on from here?"

"I want what happened to remain private between us. As
if it never happened."

A sudden rush of disappointment engulfed Damon. He'd
wanted her to know that their few moments together had
altered his outlook on love. But she was refusing to hear
that. "Then nothing happened in the cellar."

"Thank you," Neilly said. He heard the genuine relief in
her voice. When she took a sip from her water glass Damon
noticed that her hand was steadier.

"Then we'll say no more about it," Damon vowed, glad
to have reassured her. "Tonight we have the rare opportunity to enjoy our meal in peace, without Vincent's enter-
tainments."

"That won't be difficult, will it?" Neilly smiled at him
across the table, and Damon knew he was going to have
trouble keeping his promise.

Thirteen

Their conversation took a prosaic turn. They discussed the progress of the crops and the welfare of the livestock. Damon was glad to stay on neutral topics. As they talked, Neilly's eyes met his more frequently over the dining table, and she seemed to grow more comfortable in his company.

She did justice to the etouffee, the only French dish Isetta favored and had been allowed on the menu after Thomas Stirling died. By the time Uncle Cato served Mammy Lula's special bread pudding for dessert they were able to return to the subject of the storm.

"What did you discover when you looked at the latch?" Neilly asked as she toyed with her dessert. "Do you think someone locked us in the cellar deliberately?"

Damon started to deny the possibility, then reconsidered. He wanted to be honest with Neilly, at least about this. "I think it's probable that someone closed the cellar door and dropped the latch."

"But why?"

"I haven't any idea," Damon said with a shake of his head, "other than Vincent's ghost theory."

"I heard him say that." Neilly laughed good-naturedly.

"Who else could it be?" Damon asked, pleased to see her smile. "A pretty harmless ghost, I think. What danger was going to come to us in the cellar?"

Neilly looked down at her plate and blushed.

"I mean other than what—" Damon began, then realized

how cavalier his words sounded. "What I want to say is that we weren't ever in any danger of bodily harm."

Damon cursed inwardly. His Texas friends thought him smooth as glass with the ladies. They'd sure get a laugh out of seeing him now, blushing and stammering over every sentence like a gawky schoolboy.

"What I'm trying to say is that no one had anything to gain by locking us up in the cellar," Damon said, completely exasperated with himself. "What could happen? Either someone was going to miss us, as Aunt Varina did, or, at the very worst, I was going to have to dig us out."

"I see what you mean." Neilly put down her spoon. "Even a ghost had nothing to gain, really. In that light, the whole thing seems like a strange prank. So you don't think we had anything to fear?"

"Nothing that makes any sense," Damon said.

"No, I can't think of a reason for anyone to lock us in the cellar either." Neilly took up her spoon and picked at her pudding again. "It was probably just the wind, as you said."

Damon also attacked his pudding and said no more about the latch. If Neilly was satisfied with casting the wind as the culprit, he wasn't going to worry her with other candidates.

Neilly caught herself daydreaming again, staring off into the rafters of the attic like a moonstruck girl. Annoyed with herself, she glanced down at her ledger, on top of the shipping crate. She hadn't made an entry in it for the last hour. She was only fooling herself into thinking that she was working on the inventory.

All she seemed to be able to think of was Damon. Of his smile, his touch, of the deep resonance in his voice when he spoke her name. These days a word from him could send shivers down her back.

He'd been a perfect gentleman this past week: courteous, thoughtful, attentive, and proper. At moments she almost wished he wouldn't be so proper. She almost wished that she hadn't asked him to forget what they'd shared in the cellar. The truth was, she longed to feel his warm hand on her bare shoulder and his lips on her breasts again.

Neilly tried to shake off the memory. But her body ignored her head, again. A few intimate moments in the dark cellar had altered everything.

Now she understood why society made rules: why young ladies had chaperones, why ladies and gentlemen wore gloves when they danced, why they were never left alone in the dark. A myriad of rules kept men and women from touching, skin to skin, heart to heart, because society knew the secret.

The purpose of it all was plain now, Neilly realized. Society's married ladies and upstanding gentlemen in their tight corsets and starched collars knew passion simmered beneath the surface. They all knew, but never spoke of, how sensitive a woman's skin was to the touch of a man. How easily the stroke of a man's hand could stir forbidden desires, weaken well-bred defenses, and conquer good sense. Neilly knew now, too. She longed to experience all of it again at Damon's hand.

She frowned, impatient with herself. What she wanted and what she needed didn't seem to fit together at all. She should be thankful that Damon was keeping his promise. He hadn't breathed a word about what had passed between them in the cellar. She still had her position at Rosewood.

But in their agreed-upon silence the experience hung between them. She could feel Damon watching her, desire in his eyes, when he didn't think anyone else would notice. She caught herself eagerly listening for his entrance into the dining room each evening.

Nothing was the same where Damon was concerned, and she wasn't sure if she was sorry about that or not.

Purposely pulling herself back to her task, Neilly tucked her pencil into her apron pocket and ran her finger down along the last entries. She'd itemized all the Chinese vases in the crate. Thanks to her lack of concentration, she decided she wasn't going to get much else done this morning. She rose from the stool where she'd been sitting while she unpacked and inventoried the crate from Hong Kong and headed for the attic stairs.

The sunlight flooded through the dormer window, shining onto the pile of Rosalie's things in the corner. Something black gleamed bright and rich, catching Neilly's eye.

"What's this?" She threaded her way between the crates, the round hatboxes, and the dusty furniture to the corner. On top of a box of books sat a pair of ebony gargoyles. The one she had shown to Elijah was there, grinning up at her over its left shoulder. The other, the missing piece Neilly had never seen before, grinned at her over its right shoulder.

A chill slithered down Neilly's spine. "Where have you been?"

She picked up the creature and examined its dark leer. The pieces matched, both the carving style and the wood grain. She was holding the pair. "I'd swear you weren't here last week when I went through Rosalie's things. Then you appear, like magic. Where have you been?"

Neilly looked around for evidence that other things had been moved, but she saw nothing disturbed. Who could have been in the attic since she'd been up here? Mr. Pugh? His room was at the other end of the attic. Why would he bother with these things? He'd professed to hate the attic and spent as little time here as he could. Cleo? What would she want with the gargoyles?

The door at the bottom of the attic swung open and Uncle Cato appeared, huffing and puffing. "Miss Neilly, Dr. McGregor has returned. He's with Miss Isetta now."

"Thank you," Neilly said, replacing the gargoyle. Thank heavens the doctor was back. Isetta had been doing well, but Neilly was relieved to know the doctor would be at hand if the lady suffered another attack. "I'll be right there, Uncle Cato."

She touched the ebony creature's mate. What a strange thing, the reappearance of a missing gargoyle, she thought, a little like a ghost appearing from the dead.

"I hope you enjoyed yourself in Charleston," Isetta declared as soon as Theo entered her room. Varina followed him in and closed the door.

Theo ignored Isetta's ungracious welcome. He noted that her color had grown healthier than when he'd left for his meeting, and her eyes sparkled bright and alert. Her voice resonated, strong and clear. She sat up in her bed with her cane at her side and her playing cards strewn across the bedside table. Her mouth twisted into one of her splendid, frosty grimaces. Theo could see Isetta was in a fine state, a surprisingly healthy condition.

"I'm glad to see you too, Isetta." Theo sighed wearily. He was exhausted from the long trip. Bad weather at sea. Bad food, dubious company, and little sleep. He hadn't really expected Isetta to appreciate his effort to get back in a timely fashion, but a little warmth in her welcome would have been nice.

Theo sat down beside the bed.

Varina wisely remained near the door, out of range of Isetta's sharp tongue. Theo wondered how Isetta had been to live with during the past few weeks.

"You're looking better." Theo opened his doctor's bag. "I'd hoped to find you stronger when I returned."

"Well, I don't feel any better." Isetta shoved his heart listening device back at him. "You can keep that thing to yourself. It's not proper for a man—even a medical doctor—to put something like that against a lady's chest.

"Neilly's care has been superb, and I'm glad you're back,

but I'm still weak as a puppy by noon every day. I'm sick of it, Theo. What are you going to do about it?"

"I have not a thing to offer you but advice," Theo said. He tucked away the heart listening device and grasped Isetta's hand so he could take her pulse. She offered no resistance to that.

Instead of the weak, uncertain beat that Theo expected, Isetta's pulse beat rapid and strong beneath his fingers. This condition of hers made no sense. "I can only advise that you get plenty of rest."

"I've been resting. Just makes me stiff when I do get up."

Theo went on. "You must avoid anything that causes you to be anxious."

"Arthur has been here for two weeks," Isetta said. "That's about as much anxiety as I can take."

"I'm sure having a guest is unsettling."

Theo regarded Isetta in silence. It had occurred to him that she might be suffering from something other than a heart condition—something such as a need for more attention. But that seemed unlikely. In the past, when Isetta wanted notice she demanded it and got it. She was not a lady to beat around the bush. So what was going on here? Theo wondered. Why did she complain of weakness while her pulse beat vigorously?

"What is it, Theo?" Isetta asked, her voice lowered so that the others in the room couldn't hear. Though he'd finished taking her pulse, he had not given up her hand, nor had she withdrawn it.

"Your ailment puzzles me, lass," Theo admitted. "I canna explain the weakness you complain of. 'Tis a mystery to me."

"Don't trouble yourself over that, Theo," Isetta said, patting his hand between her own. "I know you're a good doctor and if there was anything you could do, you would do it.

"And Theo?" She beguiled him with that sudden, sweet girlish smile he'd fallen in love with the first day he'd stepped through Rosewood's door. "I'm *so* glad you're back. You aren't going away again for a while, are you?"

"No, lass," Theo said, realizing how much he'd missed Isetta's company, cranky or otherwise. "I donna find myself inclined to leave home again any time soon. I'll be staying where I belong for a while. It wasna a good trip."

Theo strode into the library, where he'd agreed to meet Damon after examining Isetta. When he heard the library doors close soundly behind him, he turned, expecting to find Damon, but found Arthur Sitwell instead.

"I want to know, Dr. McGregor, just how serious Aunt Isetta's condition is." Sitwell's face was tense and white. "I have a right to know my aunt's true condition."

Theo had only met this nephew of Isetta's once, years ago. From what he could see, manhood had not mellowed the boy's pomposity or churlishness. He was Mirabelle's son through and through. She'd always been greedy and vain and selfish, Theo thought, and her son was walking in her footsteps.

He found himself disinclined to tell Arthur Sitwell much of anything. Isetta would let her nephew know what she wanted him to know. "Your aunt appears to be stable. I recommended bed rest and avoiding any drain on her energies."

"Oh, good," Arthur said, relief in his voice. His pale brow puckered. "You don't think a fatal attack is imminent?"

"I don't think so," Theo said, without adding that he actually suspected Isetta might—if it struck her fancy—outlive them all just to be contrary.

The door burst open and Damon stood in the doorway, glaring at his cousin. "Arthur, what are you doing here?"

"I was just getting the truth from Dr. McGregor," Arthur

said, smoothing his hair. He walked around behind Theo, as if to keep out of Damon's reach. "I can hardly believe anything you tell me, Cousin. Dr. McGregor says her condition is stable."

"I'm glad to hear it," Damon said, no emotion in his voice.

"Then she must be well enough to discuss the issue of the will," Arthur said. "Would you agree, Doctor?"

"No, absolutely not," Theo said, a little alarmed by the thought of Isetta's final will and testament. He would not have Sitwell pressing Isetta about such a thing. "No discussion of a will. That's final."

"You heard Dr. McGregor," Damon said, gesturing toward the open library door. "Now will you excuse us, Arthur."

Arthur stepped toward the door but paused to shake a finger in Damon's face. "Listen to me, Cousin. I don't care what you or the doctor say. I'm not about to let Aunt Isetta die with her will as it stands."

"Get out," Damon ordered, his voice so cool and even, it gave Theo a chill.

Arthur's eyes narrowed. Without a word of farewell, he marched out the door.

Damon closed it soundly behind him. "Now, McGregor, what do you have to tell me?"

"How about a brandy?" Theo suggested. He wanted something strong, something that would wash away his anxiety and numb his nerves. He hoped it would do the same for Damon. He'd broken bad news to people many times in his life. It was part of being a doctor: part of dispensing medicine, giving advice and meting out diagnosis. Life and death. But he'd never become accustomed to it, and he certainly did not know how to do it with a passionate man like Damon.

"Sit down," Damon invited as he handed a snifter of amber liquid to Theo. "So, what do you have to report? I suppose Neilly had to leave Charleston over some scandal having to do with a broken betrothal."

Theo shook his head and gulped down a healthy portion of his drink.

"What then?" Uncertainty crept into Damon's voice.

"Nothing." Theo took another gulp. "And I mean nothing. As far as I could learn, there never has been a Cornelia Ashley Lind living in Charleston or studying at Miss Barrows' Academy for Ladies."

Damon stared at him in silence for a moment, then sat down in the chair across from him. "What about her father? What about Dr. Lind? Surely someone remembered him?"

"No doctor by such a name has practiced in Charleston," Theo said. "I asked, Damon. Believe me, I searched. I even asked about the Ashleys."

"And?"

"Supposedly the last survivors fell on hard times. No money, illness. They've all died off a few years ago."

Abruptly, Damon rose from his chair and paced the length of the library.

When he stopped in front of Theo again the disbelief on the boy's face was heartbreaking. He'd been so willing to believe the worst of Neilly before Theo left; now he looked stunned.

"I even asked some of the doctors' wives if there'd been any scandal about a broken betrothal among the doctors' families," Theo offered. "If there was one, 'twas kept quiet, and only the most powerful families can do that. I'm sorry, Damon. I'd give most anything to have'na found this out."

Damon shook his head. "There must be some explanation."

"I've tried to think of one." Theo drained his glass. "I believed everything she told me. We all did. You're the only one who thought her story should be confirmed. I hate to admit it, but you were right. We donna know who she is."

Damon drained his snifter. "Either Cornelia Lind is not her real name or she never came from Charleston."

"Or both," Theo added. "We're not the only ones she's lied to, remember. I saw her references, and Cornelia Ashley Lind was named in all of them. I'm sure the ladies and gentlemen who wrote those letters hadna inkling that she wasna who she said. And they took her into their homes, just as Isetta has."

"Damn," Damon said, closing his eyes. The shock on his face hardened into sharp, angry lines. "Damn! She deceived us all."

"You'll give her a chance to explain, won't you?" Theo asked, uneasy about the harshness he saw in Damon's face. "Donna be too hard on her. She's been a good nurse and companion to your aunt. She has demonstrated that her skills are real. There must be some explanation, but I canna imagine a respectable one."

"I can't either." Damon walked to the window and turned his back to Theo. "But I have to know the truth."

Damon never heard the library doors close as Theo left. His head was too full of Neilly, of her image, her scent, her sighs, her touch. The suspicions he'd first had when he'd arrived began to crowd out all those sensations. Now all his early questions clamored for re-examination in the light of day. There was no pleasure in being right, he thought.

Only last night he'd made love to her again in his dreams. She had filled his head and his heart every day since they'd been locked up together. It had been so easy to forget his early suspicions.

What did he know about her?

She was from a society family; her performance at The Laurels confirmed that. He knew that she'd never given herself to any man until him. That act of innocence and integrity had captured his heart.

She'd remade this room, the library, into a new and welcoming place, and she had delved into the collections to discover things about Rosewood that he'd either forgotten or had never known. She'd brought comfort to Isetta and Varina. She'd revived laughter at the dining-room table and put smiles on Cato and Cleo's faces. How could he credit her with evil intentions when she had given him and Rosewood so much?

Damon shook his head again. If she cared enough about them to do all that, how could she lie? Why was she at Rosewood? What did she mean when she said she needed this job?

John Minor had seemed to be the only person who knew her, recognized her from Charleston. Damon closed his eyes and tried to remember every detail about the meeting with John Minor. The surprise and shock had been plain on Neilly's face that day, and she'd refused to shake the man's hand. Yet Minor hadn't contradicted a word of hers and had called her by the false name she'd given them all. He had even talked about her father and offered condolences. But John Minor was a man of dubious reputation, and Neilly had never denied knowing him.

So why was Neilly at Rosewood? Living under a false name. Carefully making a list of all of Rosewood's treasures. Damon could think of no good reason. Was she running away from something? Or was she here to find something?

Then a thought hit Damon with such a wallop that his knees went weak. He sat down behind the desk. He'd almost declared his feelings for her that night in the dining room. Fortunately, he'd had the sense to bide his time. His confession might have played right into her plans, whatever those were.

Damon stared at the empty snifter on the desk and

thought about pouring himself a brandy, but he didn't want anything to dull his senses. Neilly had just ripped out his heart and twisted it into a knot, and he wanted to remember every painful second of the experience. She'd made a fool of him. If it hurt badly enough this time, maybe he'd not be so asinine again. He'd been right all along; the entanglements of love were not for him.

When the library door opened he didn't even look up. "Uncle Cato, tell Miss Neilly I want to see her."

"Here I am." It was Neilly's voice.

Damon's head came up. His eyes narrowed as he stared at her, waiting to see the stranger he knew her to be. But she stood in the middle of the room, smiling, sweet and prim and so familiar in her everyday gray gown and white lace collar.

"Dr. McGregor said he was pleased with your aunt's condition. I think that's good news, don't you?"

Damon rose from his chair, scrutinizing her for a clue, some sign in her eyes or hint on her face that she had come to Rosewood under false pretenses.

All he saw was a lovely woman with smooth skin and a wealth of innocent passion.

"What's the trouble?" she asked, her smile fading as she stepped closer. Concern filled her voice. "Did Dr. McGregor have something more to say? What is it? What's wrong?"

"Do you know where Theo has been?" Damon asked, maintaining a deadly calm tone.

"He went to a medical conference," Neilly said. "My father attended meetings like that from time to time."

"McGregor went to a conference in Charleston."

"Oh, how nice." Uncertainty flickered in Neilly's expression. She clasped her hands over her apron and looked down at the floor. "Charleston is a lovely city in the spring."

Damon leaned closer across the desk, studying her pale, drawn face. "Yes. When I found out McGregor was going to Charleston I asked him to learn something more about you and your father."

Her head came up slowly and her eyes widened in surprise.

"You understand these are my aunts, the dear ladies who raised me. I will spare no one to make sure they are safe."

"Yes, so you have said before," Neilly snapped, a glimmer of anger shining in her eyes. "But how dare you ask Dr. McGregor to spy on me?"

"Why does that trouble you?" Damon challenged. "Is it because no one in that fine city has ever heard of Dr. Lind or of his daughter, Cornelia Ashley Lind?"

When she said nothing Damon pressed on. "Would you like to explain why?"

Neilly looked away, studying the Constable painting over the fireplace. "It's rather complicated to explain."

"Perhaps you would like to try," Damon prompted, unable to keep the sarcasm from his voice. "Surely you have some tale ready to smooth over difficult moments when your first lie fails you."

"It's not like that," Neilly said, swinging around on him. Defiance gleamed in her blue eyes, but he could see she was chewing on her bottom lip.

"Then how is it?" Damon demanded. "I am waiting to hear the truth."

"All I can say is that as much pleasure as I have taken in the lovely things at Rosewood, I have no designs on them. And I've never done anything to harm your aunts. You know that."

"Then why the false name?" Frustrated with her lack of answers, he raked his fingers through his hair. He longed to hear some logical excuse for coming to Rosewood under false pretenses. "And what is your connection with John Minor? I want the truth."

"Oh, Damon." Neilly sighed and turned away. She passed a hand over her face and her shoulders slumped. She looked small and fragile, bewildered and confused. "The truth will damn me."

"And your lies haven't?" Damon's anger wavered. "For God's sake, Neilly, what in the hell did you think was going to happen? Did you honestly believe you'd go on living here and we'd never find out? That no one would ever ask these questions?"

"Yes, all of those things," Neilly said, without looking at him, her voice small and quiet. "I thought Rosewood would be a wonderful place to live forever and I'd hoped— well, then we got locked in the cellar and—I don't know what I expected."

For a moment she looked so lost and defenseless, he wanted to dismiss everything McGregor had told him and go to her. But he held himself still. He wasn't going to let his passions rule him this time. "Neilly, all I'm asking for is the truth."

"I wish there was a truth I could tell you," she said without turning to him again. "But I have nothing to offer that would make you feel better about why I'm here."

"Nothing?" The heat of Damon's anger returned. He stood behind the desk, uncertain if his exasperation stemmed from her lies or from her refusal to defend herself.

"Don't you have anything to say for yourself, Neilly?" Damon asked. "Neilly? Is that your name? Won't you even tell me what your real name is?"

She looked at him, injured pride and anger in the set of her chin. "My name is Cornelia, just as I told you. People who know me well call me Neilly."

"I'm glad to know that," Damon quipped. "I think we should talk about this later, when we've both had time to reconsider the situation."

"I have lied and been found out," Neilly said, her chin still set. "What is there to reconsider?"

Head held high, she walked out of the library and closed the door behind her.

* * *

Neilly felt a gaze on her back and turned to see Thomas Stirling's portrait glaring at her from the shadows of the drawing room.

On impulse she walked across the hall and closed the drawing-room doors behind her. She rested her head against the wood and listened to Damon come out of the library and go out the back door. Her eyes were dry, but the sobs rose in her throat, cutting her breath into short, staccato gasps. She covered her mouth to smother the sound.

An odd dank smell assaulted her nose. When she turned around, looking for the source, she found Thomas Stirling glaring down at her from above the fireplace. Anger rose in Neilly at the sight of him.

"You," she said aloud to the patriarch of Rosewood. "Damn you! I've had my fill of men with power and money, like you."

She noticed that the silver goblet was sitting to one side of the mantel. Marching to the fireplace, she set the cup in the center where it belonged. She glared up at the portrait.

"I've made my mistakes, sir, but this is your fault, too. You were vengeful and shortsighted and selfish. You threw away the love of your daughter and your grandson. Damon—he'll never trust anyone, not completely.

"Do you know what would happen if I told him the truth? He'd be more convinced than ever that I came to Rosewood for some nefarious purpose. You are to blame. You turned your back on him, proving that no one he cared about could be trusted."

Thomas Stirling said nothing, but his eyes followed Neilly as she roamed around the room.

Outside the birds sang in Varina's garden, and the Lafayette clock ticked away on the mantel.

Neilly heaved a defeated sigh. Railing at a portrait of a

man dead for fifteen years was hardly going to solve her problem.

She had to think what to do now. She should have known when she met Minor at The Laurels that it was time to leave Rosewood. But life on the plantation had been too comfortable. After three years of running from Charles she'd enjoyed Rosewood's tranquillity. She'd even fooled herself into thinking that her relationship with Damon didn't need to change anything. How easy it had been to be lulled into thinking that perhaps she could live down what had happened in Charleston. When the time was right and they knew her well enough to understand, she would have told Isetta, Varina, and Damon the whole truth.

But the promise of that cozy future was gone now.

The only thing to do was leave as quickly and as quietly as possible, without upsetting Miss Isetta and Miss Varina. She saw no other solution. She'd think of some excuse that wouldn't alarm them. Hopefully, Damon would honor that. He didn't want his aunts upset either. Cleo could handle things until a new nurse was found, and Dr. McGregor had returned in case an attack did occur.

Poor Dr. McGregor, Neilly thought. She had liked to think of him as her friend, and he probably had been until he'd discovered there'd never been any Dr. Lind.

She paced around the room once more, longing to say good-bye. She touched a few treasures that she had described in her ledger.

The Lafayette clock chimed the hour. The river packet to New Orleans would arrive soon, she calculated. She had no more time to mourn past pleasures or a future that would never be.

She'd best be on that steamboat when it pulled away from Rosewood's landing.

Fourteen

"This is the last of her luggage, Master Damon," Elijah said, easing Neilly's small trunk off his shoulder and onto the cart for the journey down to the landing.

Damon tossed one end of the rope across to the carpenter and they pulled it tight across the trunk, two bags, and a battered portfolio. When Uncle Cato had come to tell him that Neilly was leaving Damon had assumed she'd be leaving in two or three days. He'd never known a woman could travel so light or pack so quickly. His mother had always taken days to fill trunk after trunk for a trip.

He couldn't help but wonder if Neilly's swift, efficient departure came with practice or from owning so little. Either way, she certainly seemed bent on making a quick, clean break. Maybe that was for the best, Damon decided.

He was tightening the last knot in the rope when he heard the rustle of her skirts.

"Elijah, have you heard the packet's whistle yet?" she asked. She stood in Rosewood's entrance, wearing a green traveling suit, one of her gowns that looked as if it had been selected and worn often by a younger lady. She was so intent on pulling on a glove, Damon knew she had not seen him.

"No, miss," Elijah said. "I ain't heard nothing yet."

Damon thought he'd never seen her face so pale and somber—the line of her mouth so vulnerable. That thought only served to remind him of how much light and change she'd brought to Rosewood in the three short months she'd lived there. Where was that serenity going to go when she stepped out of the door?

Damon walked around the cart and up the steps.

"Oh, I didn't expect you to be here." She straightened her shoulders. "I told Miss Isetta that a distant relative is ill and has sent for me."

Damon nodded and looked away, down the shady drive toward the Mississippi River. He couldn't bring himself to look into her eyes. His anger was spent now. He was empty inside and had nothing left to say to her. "How did Aunt Isetta take it?"

"She made me promise that I'd return as soon as I could. She and Miss Varina were very kind. Neither is particularly upset. No palpitations. Miss Isetta's condition seems to be no worse for my leaving."

"Good," Damon said. He'd feared an unpleasant scene with Aunt Isetta. But he should have known Neilly would figure out how to take her leave without upsetting her patient. He should have trusted her to do so. She really did seem fond of his aunts, and he knew they adored her. He saw no reason to tell them anything to make them feel otherwise.

He took the envelope out of his pocket and held it out to her.

Neilly looked at it but made no move to take it. Somehow he'd known she would be reluctant to take money, and he'd thought of just tucking it into one of her bags. But that left too much to chance.

"It's your wages," he explained. "You earned them, and you're going to need them."

Her lips thinned into a tight line. She nodded, accepted the envelope, and stuffed it into the bag that hung from her wrist.

Damon watched her buttoning her gloves, a little cold fear stealing around his heart. He was afraid he was losing something very important, and he was powerless to do anything about it. He didn't even know her full name.

When she finished pulling on her other glove she raised her gaze to his. "Will you promise to do something for me?"

"Perhaps."

"You will take care of your aunts," Neilly said, meeting his gaze for the first time since their confrontation in the library. "Don't desert them to Arthur. No matter how much you miss Texas, they need you more."

Damon stared at her, a little surprised that she would think him capable of such a thing. At the same time he was also awed that this young woman, at the point of farewell, would plead for the cause of her patient. "I won't desert them, to Arthur or anyone else."

"Good." She nodded. "I'll feel better knowing that."

Damon wanted to say something more, about how he felt about her, about how she'd made him feel alive and a part of Rosewood, but no words offered themselves up. He closed his mouth and watched her start down the steps.

She stopped on the bottom riser and turned back to him. "And one more thing."

Damon nodded, conscious now of all sorts of things that seemed destined to remain unsaid between them. The kisses and the intimacies that would go unshared.

He started down the steps toward her. "What? What do you want, Neilly?"

She captured his gaze once more.

"I think it's only fair for you to know that your aunt's illness might not be as serious as she lets us believe." She spoke softly, so that no one heard but him.

Astonished, Damon closed the distance between them. "What do you mean?"

She shook her head, as if she was sorry she'd revealed anything. "I'm not certain, but I think your Aunt Isetta is only as ill as she needs to be for her purposes."

Neilly looked up into his eyes. No deception clouded her gaze. "What purposes?"

"I'm not sure," she said, shaking her head again. "Just know that the people of Rosewood love you, Damon. They care for you more than for their own selfish whims. Not everyone is like your grandfather. Not everyone throws away the love of the people around them. Think about it, for Isetta's sake."

The words hung in the air between them, though Damon tried to absorb what she was saying. He knew he needed more time to understand.

The plaintive steamboat whistle pierced the silence and echoed down the river from the north.

"Steamboat's acoming, Miss Neilly," Elijah called from beside the luggage cart.

In a few minutes the packet would nose into the Rosewood landing to unload mail and supplies and to pick up goods. Damon knew Neilly would board it and he would not stop her.

Her lashes fluttered. She seemed suddenly uncertain of herself. Before he realized what she was doing, she stood on tiptoe and kissed his cheek. A sweet, shy, girlish kiss, but a bold gesture from a woman he had accused of being a liar. A generous kiss from an impostor who had refused to disclose her identity.

Before she could start away, Damon grasped her arms and pulled her to him. "We can do better than that."

He pressed his lips against hers with no concern for who might see them kissing on the front steps of Rosewood: Elijah, Cato, Cleo, Arthur or Vincent.

He took her with his mouth, his hand on the back of her neck to prevent escape. He savored her lips, and teased her tongue, and delved into the corners of her mouth. Her warmth flooded through him. He pressed deeper and pulled her closer, cherishing the soft, round feel of her body against his.

He wanted her to remember forever that he was the man she'd allowed to touch her deepest secret places.

She gasped for breath when he released her. Her hand grabbed at her hat to keep it from falling off. He held her a moment longer to steady her, so she wouldn't stumble off the step.

He held her gaze. "I'll be here when you're ready to tell me the truth," Damon whispered. He released her and walked back into the house without looking back. He didn't think he could bear to see her walk down the drive, away from Rosewood and him.

The house stood silent and sleepy in the twilight, as if some vital part of it had stolen away.

Varina summoned her courage, looked straight ahead, past the vicious fangs of the wallpaper lions guarding the library, and tapped on the door. Everyone in the house knew Damon was in there, but no one had been brave enough to interrupt him since Neilly had said farewell. Since the packet had whistled its departure and headed down river over two hours ago.

Varina wouldn't be bothering Damon if Uncle Cato and Elijah hadn't pressed her—if Isetta hadn't insisted they must know what was going on.

"Come in," Damon said, a distracted note in his voice.

Hesitantly, Varina pushed the door open.

He sat at the desk, invoices and manifests scattered across its surface. The quill pen stood in the inkstand and the accounts ledger remained unopened. His hair was mussed, as if he'd been raking his hand through it, and his cravat was untied, as if he'd found the air in the room too close.

Varina walked in, aware of Father's portrait in the drawing room directly across the hall, glaring at her back. "She left all of them."

"Who left all of what?" Damon said, looking perplexed, as if he truly didn't know who she meant.

"Neilly," Varina said, suddenly annoyed with him. She and Isetta were certain there was more to Neilly's hasty departure than the excuse she'd given them. They both wondered about Damon's part in it, but they'd agreed not to press him about what had transpired. "She left all of her new gowns. The plum ball gown and the lavender lawn, all neatly folded in the clothes press. And here's the inventory. That's a good sign, isn't it? That means she'll be back, doesn't it?"

"Perhaps," Damon said, taking Neilly's small ledger from Varina and laying it aside. He stared out the window, a faraway look in his eye.

Guilt? Varina wondered. Isetta had blamed it on a lovers' quarrel. Nothing to worry about, Isetta had declared. They'd be back together soon. Varina wasn't so certain. Lovers didn't pack up and leave every time they quarreled, did they?

"Wasn't that odd?" she continued. "How Neilly received that letter from her sick cousin *before* the packet arrived with the mail?"

Damon busied himself with a stack of papers on the desk. "Yes, odd."

"Master Damon?" Now that the lions had been breached, Cato hobbled in with an envelope. "Elijah say Miss Neilly sent something to you."

Elijah appeared at the doorway. "She said you paid her too much, Master Damon. And she said to tell you that she didn't want no more than what she earned."

Varina watched as Damon stared at the envelope in Uncle Cato's hand for a long moment. He looked both surprised and disappointed to see it again. Slowly, he accepted it from Uncle Cato and stuffed it in a desk drawer.

"You gave her extra pay?" Varina prompted.

"I thought she might be able to use some extra cash,"

Damon said. "God knows, she worked hard enough. And she's a woman alone. You know . . ."

"Well, our Neilly has her pride," Varina reminded him.

Damon nodded. "But it's not going to pay the bills if things get difficult for her."

"Why would they get difficult?" Varina asked, sensing that Damon was getting at something she didn't quite understand. "Neilly seems very capable of taking care of herself. She's going to stay with a sick cousin."

Damon closed his eyes and shook his head. Varina didn't think she'd ever seen her nephew look so heartsick. When he spoke his voice was low and husky, like that of a man in pain.

"Just because Neilly's intelligent and a doctor's daughter doesn't mean she knows everything about how to take care of herself."

"Well, she promised to come back," Varina said, hoping to ease Damon's mind a little. "And she left the address in New Orleans where we can reach her."

She reached into the pocket of her gardening apron for the notepaper that Neilly had scribbled on and began to unfold it. Damon seized it like a starving man grabbing at a crust of bread.

He smoothed it out on the desk and read it in silence. Then he looked up at Varina. "I know this street. It's a nice neighborhood."

"I thought so," Varina said, smiling at him, glad to know he agreed that Neilly was going to a respectable place and would be staying with family.

"Wait." He looked at the address again—to make note of the house number, Varina thought. To her surprise, angry disbelief hardened the lines of his face.

Damon crumpled up the address in his fist. "But if this street is long enough to reach this house number, her cousin's parlor is in the middle of Jackson Avenue."

Uttering an oath, he hurled the ball of paper into the fireplace.

Puzzled, Varina stared down at the wadded note the reason for Damon's unhappiness finally dawning on her. "Oh, dear. We don't really know where Neilly's gone, do we?"

Damon never made a conscious decision; he just began to avoid the house except to eat and to sleep. He found numerous things to be done in the fields, at the mill, the stables, the landing, the warehouses—one was being re-roofed. Pugh could manage the account books just fine without him being at Rosewood every minute.

Aunt Isetta's health remained constant. McGregor visited her every day and reported to Damon that he was encouraged by the fact that her condition hadn't worsened. But she complained of missing Neilly. He also reported that he was having no luck finding a companion to take Neilly's place, which didn't surprise Damon. They might have to look for someone outside the parish. After Neilly, no one was going to seem quite right, especially to Aunt Isetta and Doc.

"No advertisements in the newspaper," Damon cautioned as they leaned against the track fence, watching the trainer put a chestnut colt through his paces. A layer of clouds grayed the sky above. A cool breeze ruffled through the trees. The sunless indifference of the day suited Damon's mood just fine.

"Agreed, no advertisements," McGregor said. After a moment of silence he asked, "What did she have to say for herself when you told her you knew she was using a false name?"

"Nothing," Damon said, unwilling to talk about the scene with Neilly. Review only brought pain and anger he couldn't explain or resolve.

McGregor shook his head. "I wish she'd told us her side

of it. I canna help but think the circumstances aren't as black as her lies made them seem."

"What difference would it have made?" Damon said, his wounds festering under the doctor's questions. "She wasn't even honest about where she was going when she left. I don't much appreciate her lies, or being made a fool of."

Damon could feel McGregor's eyes on him.

"I donna think making fools of anyone was ever Neilly's intention," the doctor said. "That's not like her."

When Damon said nothing McGregor went on. "Aye, her lies look bad, but from the things she did here at Rosewood, from the way she took care of your aunts, worked with the servants, cared for the house, she didn't mean anyone harm. No, sir, I wouldna call that being made a fool of, son. No, not a'tall. Whatever her faults, she deserves that you think better of her than that."

Damon smarted under McGregor's gentle reprimand. He wondered if it would satisfy the good doctor to know that since Neilly had left his nights had been sleepless. His dreams had been jumbled and chaotic—accusing him with vague images of Neilly alone, confused, walls closing in on her, and she not knowing which way to turn.

She might have lied to gain a position at Rosewood, but her plight was his fault. He deserved every bit of the guilt. He'd sent McGregor to find a hole in her story, and the doctor had. And then what had he done? Made accusations, demanded answers, expected explanations that she found impossible to share. Besides that, Damon simply could not dismiss the possibility that he might have gotten her with child that stormy afternoon in the cellar.

Lord knew he had no intentions of becoming a family man, but he wasn't a man to duck his responsibilities either. If they'd conceived a child, he'd do his part. That was why he'd wanted Neilly to have the money.

Damon almost winced when he remembered how quickly she'd returned it. If she'd known what was in the envelope when he'd handed it to her, no doubt she would have slapped him in the face with it. Instead she'd sent Elijah back with the overage.

What had he expected to buy with it, anyway? Some peace of mind? That was beyond price, he was learning.

Though she'd promised to return, Damon knew she never would—not even if she needed his help. As Aunt Varina had reminded him, Neilly had her pride.

"Dr. McGregor. I need to talk to you, sir." Arthur walked toward them from the direction of the house, picking his way carefully through the dust, ruts, and horse manure. His boots gleamed from a fresh polish. He was all decked out in a gray suit coat, a double-breasted purple waistcoat, a spotless cravat, and a gray top hat. He'd crimped his fair hair into curls over his ears. At his side trotted Vincent, dressed just like his papa, crimped curls and all.

Damon thought the Sitwells' funeral-going getup a good sign. "Where are you off to, Cousin. You're not leaving us so soon, are you?" It lightened his mood to think of his cousin leaving Rosewood.

Arthur frowned. "Of course not.

"We're off to call on the Esterbrooks, Cousin Damon," Vincent said.

"Never fear, Durande," Arthur added. "I wouldn't leave my poor, sweet aunts at your mercy. Which is the reason Vincent and I sought you out, Doctor. You seem to be spending a lot of time here. Is Aunt Isetta worse?"

"Well, sir, I'm spending a lot of time here because your Aunt Isetta is something of a special patient to me," Mc-Gregor began. It was a statement Damon was a little surprised to hear the dignified doctor make aloud. McGregor went on to report on Isetta's health.

Damon happened to glance down at Vincent, who promptly pulled an ugly face at him. He really didn't relish the thought that they were related by blood. Without comment, Damon excused himself and started to walk away.

"Don't go far, Cousin," Arthur called after him. "When I'm finished with Dr. McGregor I have something to discuss with you."

Damon halted. The tone of Arthur's order was enough to make Damon call for his horse and ride off for three days at least. But curiosity stopped him, curiosity and caution. He wasn't about to leave Arthur to his own, unobserved devices at Rosewood for too long. Damon did call for his horse, but he decided to wait for his cousin to finish with McGregor before riding very far.

Arthur wasted no time. As soon as he was satisfied with McGregor's report, he dismissed the doctor and approached Damon at the stable door.

"Where did you hide the dueling pistols?" Arthur demanded.

The questions took Damon by surprise. "Why? Has some lucky fellow called you out? They're locked up in the gun cabinet in the library."

"I know that's where Grandpapa was supposed to have kept them," Arthur said, his face puckered with impatience. "But they're not there now. What did you do with them?"

"I haven't done anything with them," Damon said, annoyed at being questioned.

"I thought you'd know what happened to them."

"What do you want with them, if you're not calling anyone out?" Damon asked, his annoyance turning to curiosity.

"Nothing," Arthur said, casting Damon a look of total innocence. "Dueling is barbaric and illegal. But those pistols are worth a great deal of money. Aren't they the pistols used by Aaron Burr and Alexander Hamilton?"

"I think the Hamilton family disputes that," Damon said mildly. Arthur was up to his usual toting up of the riches at Rosewood.

"Nevertheless, they'd be worth a lot of money to someone," Arthur said.

"Who were Aaron Burr and Alexander Hamilton?" Vincent asked. "Did they duel? Was it bloody?"

Vincent covered his chest as if he were mortally wounded, staggered, and fell on the grass. "Did one of them linger on for days and days with all his relatives gathered around his bed before he choked up a big glot of blood and died? Then his eyes rolled up into his head like this?"

The child demonstrated with his eyes.

"Something like that," Damon said, amused by the boy's dramatics. "That's how most duels end, unfortunately."

"I'll explain about Burr and Hamilton later," Arthur said, dragging his son up from the ground and dusting off his breeches. "Well, Cousin, I take it you don't know where the guns are."

Vincent's face brightened. "Did you sell the pistols to get extra money, like Papa thinks you did?"

"Hush, Vincent." Arthur caught his son by the collar and pulled the boy behind him.

Damon was not in the least surprised by Vincent's accusation. Arthur didn't think any better of him than he thought of Arthur, and he didn't think his cousin would stop at much to cast him in a bad light. "I'll see what I can find out about the pistols for you. But don't credit me with your own greedy intentions, Sitwell."

Fifteen

Damon waited until late that evening to look for the missing pistols. After everyone had retired for the night, including the Sitwells, he went to the library. Taking the key from the desk drawer, Damon opened the gun cabinet and found the pistols missing, just as Arthur had told him. The teak box had been wrapped in felt and stored in the bottom of the cabinet with both pistols lying inside.

Damon had last examined them the day he and Neilly had inventoried the library. He remembered clearly being at her side when he'd shown the pistols to her. She had entered the pistols in her ledger, describing their intricate brass fittings and smooth ebony hand grips in detail. With apparent interest, she'd listened to him tell about the tragic Burr versus Hamilton duel, though he knew she'd heard the tale before. All Southerners had.

Puzzled by the missing guns, Damon locked the cabinet again. No strangers had been in the house for weeks. Nothing else was missing, Damon reasoned. Or had the absence merely gone unnoticed?

Damon pulled the inventory ledger from the desk, where he'd put it the day Neilly had left. He flipped through the pages, finally finding the entry he sought. He touched the letters she'd inscribed on the page.

It was no love letter, but suddenly he was lost in memories of Neilly. How he'd wanted to set her down on his lap again and take ungentlemanly advantage of her.

How many nights after their intimacy in the cellar had he lain awake and envisioned her sweet body covered by a sheer cotton gown, pink where her breasts strained against the fabric, dark and mysterious where the cloth settled in the valley between her thighs?

He'd ached to steal her out of her room and carry her to his bed while she still lived under Rosewood's roof. He'd stripped that gown away and run his hands along her body without the confines of a corset or the hindrance of a camisole or the barrier of drawers.

Something primal told him she belonged to him now. Her place was at his side—naked in his bed, ready to make love—and when they were exhausted to rest beside him, sharing her dreams.

A noise in the hall disturbed him. Footsteps and whispers. Candlelight and shadows hovered outside his door.

"Who's there?" Damon called, curious but not alarmed. He rose from the desk and went to the door. He thought everyone in the house was abed at this hour, but when he pulled the door open he found Uncle Cato and Aunt Varina standing at the foot of the stairs. Varina was wearing her dressing gown and Uncle Cato was in his shirtsleeves, a sight Damon didn't think he'd ever seen.

"Oh, Damon," Varina said, her hands dropping away from the tray Uncle Cato had been about to hand her. "I'm sorry. We didn't mean to disturb you."

"No, sah, I was just bringing Miss Varina and Miss Isetta their warm milk to help them fall asleep," Uncle Cato said. "Can I get you something, sah?"

"No, I was just surprised to hear someone up and about," Damon said. "Aunt Varina, could I talk to you for a moment?"

"Of course, dear," Varina answered, as if her nephew requested midnight conversations with her all the time. "Uncle Cato, will you take the milk up to Miss Isetta?"

"Yes, miss," Uncle Cato said. "I'm on my way."

Damon opened the library door for Varina, and she stepped in ahead of him.

"Is something wrong, dear?" She tucked her hands into the wide sleeves of her flowered dressing gown. "This is about Neilly, isn't it?"

"In a way," Damon admitted. "I don't want to worry Aunt Isetta with what seems to be going on."

"No, of course not, dear," Varina said. "I won't say a word to her."

"It's been called to my attention that some things in the house, some valuable things, are unaccounted for. I wondered if you'd missed anything?"

Varina gazed at him in silence, dismay on her face. Damon sensed that she was debating about telling him something. "You have missed some things?"

"Well, now that you bring it up, there are a few items I haven't been able to find for some days, well, perhaps for several weeks.

"Weeks?" Damon prompted. His aunt was known to misplace things from time to time, but it wasn't likely that the items she referred to would be misplaced for weeks. "What things?"

"Well, my Tudor earrings in the Empress Josephine snuffbox," Varina enumerated. "I wanted to wear them to the barbecue at The Laurels. That's when I first missed them."

"Neilly had been here how long then?"

"Oh, I think about a month," Varina said. "I never mentioned them to her. I don't think she even knew they existed. I'm sure she never entered them in the inventory."

Damon shook his head. "What else?"

"Well, one day, after Arthur and Vincent arrived, I was looking for the Venetian glass vase, the green one with the darling little dolphin fashioned in the stem . . ."

"That's gone?"

"I haven't been able to find it yet," Varina said. "It used

to be on the hall table, but I've searched the house. Then there were the gargoyles."

"What gargoyles?"

Varina looked up at him, obviously reluctant to go on. "Your mother's ebony gargoyles used for bookends. Neilly found one in the attic, but she couldn't find the mate. She said they probably weren't valuable because they weren't antiques, but she thought they would mean something to the family. She was going to talk to Elijah about it, but I don't know if she did."

Damon stared at his aunt. Did Neilly know that things were missing? Or were things missing because of her? That seemed unlikely. Why tell his aunt one was missing if you intended to steal the other? None of what Varina said made much sense, except that the things—some of them quite precious—were suddenly missing from Rosewood.

He glanced down at Neilly's inventory on the desk. What other valuables were missing and had gone unnoticed?

His silence seemed to make Varina uneasy. "It's a big house, Damon," Varina said, giving a little nervous laugh. "Sometimes I think things scuttle off by themselves. I know it sounds silly, but . . ."

"Things don't scuttle off by themselves, Aunt Varina." Damon smiled and shook his head. "It's much more likely that someone took them."

Varina gasped. "Oh, no. You don't mean you think Neilly . . . ?"

He could hear the astonishment and injury in her voice, and he felt like a cad.

"Surely you don't believe that Neilly stole from us?"

"I don't know what to think," Damon said.

"Well, I know Neilly's no thief," Varina said. "Why would she make a list of things, then take them? That's not the kind of thing Neilly would do. She's more sensible than that."

Damon shook his head, this time trying to shake off his

warring emotions. He was angry with Neilly for her lies, but his anger fought against the longing to know where she was and if she was all right. He didn't want to believe any of the growing suspicions that kept planting themselves in his thoughts.

"Well, I know the address she gave us was wrong," Varina said. "She probably confused the numbers in her concern over her cousin. But I know you could find her, Damon, if you went to New Orleans. You found all those other people for us—the French maid and the inventor who absconded with the advance money Isetta had given him."

Damon smiled ruefully. Varina made it sound so easy to go to a city like New Orleans, a city of alleys, courtyards, and narrow dark streets, and find a needle in a haystack. A needle that had no intention of being found. Neilly had made that clear enough. With the false address she'd left them, he had no clue of where to begin his search—if he did decide to go.

"Didn't I hear you say you wanted to ask our New Orleans agent to find a new accountant to replace Mr. Pugh?" Varina asked.

"Yes," Damon said. "What's that got to do with this?"

"You have business in New Orleans, don't you?"

"Yes, but—"

"I think you should go to New Orleans, find Neilly, and ask her about the list and the missing things," Varina said. "Ask Neilly. Make her tell you the truth."

Damon closed the inventory ledger. Even if he couldn't pry the truth out of Neilly when he found her, he could at least assure himself that she was all right.

Varina put her hand on his arm, and Damon was surprised by the glint of determination in her faded blue eyes. "Go find that girl. I know you want to. And it isn't just to ask her about these missing things.

"And don't worry about Isetta. Theo comes by every day

now. I know she'd agree with me when I say she'd feel much happier if she knew you were going to find Neilly."

Damon said nothing. He didn't think there was much chance of bringing Neilly back, but Aunt Varina's suggestion had merit. A trip to New Orleans would answer a lot of questions.

He needed answers. He needed to know whether he'd fallen in love with a liar and a thief.

Neilly waited alone on the banquette across from the dusty parade ground known as Jackson Square. It was mid-morning. The mist had cleared and the levee bustled with people of all colors and walks of life. Merchants. Trades-men. Fishermen. Sailors. Farmers and their wares on the way to the market just down the street.

She'd been on the corner several minutes with her port-folio tucked under her arm, but Rene had not shown him-self. The only passersby had been regular mass-goers. She was beginning to think of going away and coming back later. A lady alone on a street corner was too conspicuous.

Another well-dressed gentlemen walked by and leered indecently—the third one to do so. He stopped and tipped his hat. "Perhaps I can be of service to you, my dear. Escort you somewhere? Buy you a meal?"

"No, thank you, sir," Neilly said, scowling him down. "I'm waiting for my husband. Perhaps you passed him. A tall gentleman. Large. Broad-shouldered."

She held out her hands to demonstrate the impressive breadth of her alleged husband's shoulders. Thank heavens she was wearing gloves, so the man couldn't see that she wore no wedding ring. "He always wears a kind smile, though he has a bit of a jealous nature," she confided.

The man frowned at her. Plopping his tall hat back on his head, he muttered some excuse and hurried down the street, dodging a farmer's wagon as he went.

Had these men no sense of propriety? Neilly railed to herself. It was morning, far too early for the ladies of the evening to be out! Where was Rene anyway? she wondered, looking up the street toward Rue Bourbon.

"I'm counting on you, Rene," Neilly whispered to herself.

Two weeks in New Orleans and she still hadn't found a paying position. Another payment was coming due soon. She almost had enough cash to make it. If she could just get another position *soon,* she'd be able to earn the balance.

If. Her life seemed to be haunted by the word these days. If she'd been able to stay at Rosewood, there'd have been no problem about the money. If she'd taken the extra money Damon had given her, she'd have enough for the payment. She shook her head. She wasn't going to think about that again. She'd done the right thing in returning the extra money to him. She wasn't going to think about Damon again, either, about his wonderful dark eyes, his warm touch, his teasing lips.

In spite of her best resolve, forbidden thoughts of him drifted through her head at the oddest moments, leaving her feeling unaccountably warm, alone, and forsaken.

Luck had been with her so far. Mrs. Robards had had an unexpected vacancy on the day Neilly returned to town. The landlady who had been kind to Neilly during her first stay in New Orleans was proving to be so again. Like this morning; she'd slipped Neilly the newspaper after she'd finished with it. Those little kindnesses mattered when your resources were low, Neilly thought. So far her savings were holding out.

She glanced down the street again in the direction of the Rue Bourbon, where she knew Rene LaBeau had an attic room over a bakery. Still no sign of him. The levee was busy with arriving steamboat passengers, people with money to spend; travelers who wanted to take drawings and paintings home with them as souvenirs.

"Neilly, what are you doing here so early?"

"Rene." Neilly turned in relief to find him standing behind her, his cravat crooked and a cowlick of red sticking out from the crown of his head. Under each arm he carried paintings and easels, like all the street artists did.

Neilly was so glad to see him, she almost planted a kiss on his cheek. "I was beginning to wonder if I'd misunderstood you last night."

Neilly had stopped to admire Rene's work one afternoon when she'd arrived in New Orleans for the first time, and they'd struck up a conversation. He was a young artist from a Creole family, though his red hair and beard hinted at some Scottish or Irish ancestry. He was a few inches shorter than Neilly.

Immediately they found they had art in common, and their instant friendship had grown, untended and unfettered by the presumptions and expectations of polite society.

"No, I'm sorry," Rene said with a disarming grin. "I overslept. But before you scold me, I have something for you."

He leaned his burden against the brick wall, took something from his coat pocket, and, with a bow, offered her a fresh fried square pastry wrapped in a napkin.

Neilly's reprimand about drinking too many spirits died on her lips. She was hardly innocent of that sin herself, she recalled. The scent of the fried pastry sprinkled with white sugar tickled Neilly's nose and set her stomach to growling. She pressed her hand to her abdomen to cover the sound, but Rene's smile told her he'd heard.

"The baker always gives me a few extra in the morning, *lagniappe,* and I figured you hadn't been eating," he said, a knowing gleam in his eye. "Old lady Robards is generous in her fashion, but not with food."

"Thank you," Neilly said, the words coming straight from her heart.

"Eat. Eat. We artists have to look out for each other." Rene blushed and shrugged. "Sorry I can't offer you coffee."

Neilly smiled, touched by his generosity and at being called an artist, as if she were his colleague. Then her stomach growled again, and she stepped back into the shade of the brick wall to enjoy her pastry.

She tried not to bolt down the square French doughnut, but her appetite was powerful. The best she could hope for, she decided, was to avoid getting telltale sprinkles of powdered sugar all over her lips and down the front of her gown.

"Yes, about last night, I had a few drinks," Rene admitted as he worked at setting up the makeshift easels he used to display his artwork. "But you don't need to scold me. It wasn't enough to interfere with my work."

Neilly gulped down a bite because she did want to scold Rene for not taking care of himself, for not having more respect for his talent and himself. He was a gifted painter who deserved a rich patron and European art tours like the one the Turnbulls had given Peter Hiram.

"So, what's in your portfolio, Neilly?" Rene asked as he finished setting up his booth. "What do you have for me to sell? Your drawings always attract so much attention, I become jealous."

Neilly laughed and licked the white sugar off her fingers. "You flatter me, Rene. I only have a few things, some animals I drew while I was away." She took the drawings she'd made at The Laurels out of her portfolio and set them on the wobbly easel Rene had erected.

He nodded. "Deer. A pair of doves. Ah, the peacock is wonderful. Elegant. Simple. But not to the ornate taste of our times; you know that, Neilly."

"I know, but maybe someone will like it."

"Do some more of the city," Rene suggested, "if it's money you want to make. People always liked your rendering of the St. Louis cathedral."

"Perhaps I will if these sell," Neilly said. She didn't want to admit that she was out of paper, and her charcoal supply was running low.

"Did you try to get into the galleries on Rue Royale?" Rene asked, thoughtfully studying the peacock again.

"It's always the same old story with the galleries," Neilly said. They'd discussed the difficulty of getting into the exclusive art and antiquities establishments on Rue Royale before. "They don't take a woman seriously, even a woman supposedly representing her invalid brother's work."

"Invalid brother?" Rene threw back his head and laughed.

Neilly grinned, not proud of how accomplished a liar she'd become over the last few years. "I tried telling them the truth. When that wasn't successful I tried every heart-wrenching story I could think of. Nothing worked."

Rene nodded. "They look at the work, then ask whose letter of recommendation you have to present."

"Precisely," Neilly said.

"Your drawings will sell here on the street," Rene said, scrutinizing the right-hand corner of each sketch. "You have signed these, haven't you? Yes, I see it here: C. L. Carpenter. They're worth more signed. And you don't want me to tell the buyer anything about you? Are you still concerned about a gentleman looking for you?"

"Yes," Neilly said, sorry that she had to ask a friend to lie for her. She hoped that Charles Ruffin had given up his search for her by now. It had been almost three years since she'd refused his proposal, but he was not a man to give up anything easily. Three years of trying to escape him had taught her that. "If anyone asks questions, just tell them you . . ."

"I'll tell them I don't know anything about you," Rene said. "Not where you're from, or where you live. All I know is that you're an artist whose drawings I bought to sell along with my own paintings. Wild horses won't get any more than that out of me, Neilly."

"Thank you," Neilly said, bestowing a quick kiss on his stubbled cheek. "And thank you for including me as one of you. I can't tell you how happy it makes me to be considered a real artist."

Rene grinned, his white teeth gleaming and the beginnings of his beard shining golden in the morning sun. A blush began at his cravat and spread across his ruddy face. He took Neilly's hand and kissed it. "You are one of us, Neilly, we free spirits of the street. Never doubt it."

Neilly left, a smile on her lips and optimism in her heart. She also had Mrs. Robards's newspaper tucked under her arm. On a bench in the shade of a tree she settled down to study the classified advertisements. Some income from her drawings would be helpful, but she needed a larger sum of money to make up the balance of the coming payment.

She chewed on her lip, disappointed by the small number of advertisements listed. She needed a job desperately, but the newspaper offered nothing promising. Summer was a slow time in the Crescent City. Many affluent families traveled north to escape the heat and the possibility of yellow fever outbreaks.

Idly she leafed through the rest of the paper, scanning the society column and a few business items. A name caught her eye, a name that made her heart beat crazily. She peered at the article more closely, praying she'd misread the type.

"Mr. Charles Ruffin of Charleston, Virginia, will meet with New Orleans bankers and investors this month to discuss building a railroad, a new mode of transportation, in Louisiana. He is a well-known investor in steam-powered engines. Mr. Ruffin is an engineer and a member of a socially prominent Charleston family. While visiting our fair city, he will be feted by . . ."

Anxiously, Neilly skimmed through the article, looking

for the name of the hotel where Charles would be staying, but none was mentioned. Resisting the panic blossoming in her belly, she quickly folded the paper and threw it in the trash basket next to her. She wanted to be rid of anything that had to do with Charles Ruffin. She sat stone still on the bench, waiting for the illogical fear and loathing to pass.

Charles had no idea she was in New Orleans. At least it was unlikely that he knew she was here. All she had to do was make the payment to the Ruffins as stipulated, and everything would be all right. Charles would be busy with high society.

He'd stay in only the best hotel in town. He'd never stroll the streets of the French Quarter, or shop in the market, or promenade on the levee with the common crowd. He'd be occupied with earning the goodwill of the wealthy families. Occupied? He'd be obsessed. He went after everything with a fixation that was frightening.

Neilly took a deep breath. She was safe. Nothing to fear. Poverty offered anonymity, if nothing else. They moved in entirely different circles now. It was unlikely her path and Charles's would ever cross.

"Mr. Durande, what a pleasure to see you, sir," the hotel desk clerk said, his smile of welcome genuine. Damon wasn't surprised to be recognized. He and his aunts always stayed at the Lafayette House when they were in New Orleans.

All at once the little gray-haired clerk's smile faltered and his narrow mustache twitched. He lowered his voice, as if he feared something was wrong. "Were we expecting you, sir? I'm afraid we don't have your usual suite available."

"This trip is rather impromptu," Damon explained, a little disappointed not to be able to have his usual accommodations. The rooms on the fourth floor were comfortable and familiar, but he didn't intend to spend much time in them. "My aunts aren't traveling with me on this trip so I don't need anything as large as a suite."

"Oh, I see." The clerk's face cleared and his smile returned. "Please sign our book. I'm sure we have something for you."

"Fine. I just need the necessities." Damon penned his name in the guest book. Though he was bone-deep weary from the trip downriver, he was eager to get his lodgings settled, and then to begin his search for Neilly.

Once he'd decided to come to New Orleans, he'd packed a single bag and boarded the next packet. The idea was to find Neilly and return to Rosewood without delay. Isetta's condition seemed stable, but Arthur and Vincent were still visiting—still counting their anticipated legacy. Damon didn't like the idea of Isetta and Varina having to deal with Arthur alone.

Abruptly, a tall, well-dressed man thumped his fist on the counter beside Damon.

"Key to suite 417," the man demanded, drumming his fingers on the polished mahogany desk. "Quickly, I say! I'm running late and I have an important dinner engagement."

"Oh, yes, sir." The clerk immediately forgot Damon and scurried to find the key.

Damon recognized the number and was just a little curious about who was staying in the Stirlings' usual suite. Guarding his scrutiny, he glanced sideways at the brusque hotel guest.

He was nearly as tall as Damon, but thin in a graceful, fashionable way. His sandy brown side whiskers and mustache were trimmed to the latest fashion. In the crook of his arm he carried a brown top hat that perfectly matched the brown of his frock coat. The cut of the garment bespoke the excellence of his tailor. He appeared in every way to be a gentleman. But it was his manner to which Damon took exception. The man spoke with unpleasant curtness, exuding power and influence.

The man glanced back, his mouth pursing in distaste at the sight of Damon's Creole countenance and his Indian boots. Dismissing Damon, he handed his hat to his servant and turned back to the desk clerk.

The slight didn't bother Damon. He'd met this man's like in boarding school. They were always tyrants in their own society, revered and bowed to for their wealth and family connections. But they never survived long on the frontier. Either they mended their ways or something got them. Indians and rattlesnakes were democratic in that way. Neither cared who your tailor was.

"Yes, Mr. Ruffin. Here's your key, sir. May I get you anything else, sir?"

"Send a barber up right away," Ruffin said. "And I want the good one. I think his name is Joseph."

"Yes, sir," the clerk said. "Right away."

Without so much as a nod of acknowledgment, Ruffin strode away, his personal servant scurrying behind him.

In the middle of the lobby, Ruffin stopped, as if a new thought had just occurred to him. "Clerk, send up your house detective, too."

Alarm crumpled the clerk's face. "Is there a problem, Mr. Ruffin?"

"Here? No," Ruffin said. "I'm looking for someone, and I want them investigated."

"He will be right with you, sir," the clerk said. Then he turned to Damon. "I'm sorry for the interruption, Mr. Durande. I'll be right back."

He disappeared into the back room for a moment. Then messenger boys ran out of the room in all directions.

The desk clerk reappeared and began searching the room key board again. "Now, here we are, Mr. Durande. We have a delightful room for you on the third floor."

"I take it," Damon said, "that Mr. Ruffin is someone of importance?"

"Oh, yes, sir," the clerk said. "Mr. Ruffin is a very influential businessman from Charleston. He's organizing a railroad to run right here in Louisiana. Knows a lot of important people here in New Orleans, and in Baton Rouge, too. Quite a gentleman, he is."

"So I noticed." Damon accepted the room key, thinking a detective was something he might need. But the idea of involving a stranger rankled. Finding Neilly was far too important to be left to a hireling. Damon longed to talk to her himself, to study the expression on her face, to read the color of her dark blue eyes.

In his room he left his bag where the boy dropped it and sat down at the writing desk to begin his search for Neilly.

His inquiries went out by messenger the evening of the first day. Then he hit the street. By the end of the second day Damon found himself pacing the levee in frustration and wondering if this search was folly.

The discreet inquiries he'd sent out to Stirling friends and acquaintances about needing a companion for Aunt Isetta had yielded nothing. Several families were out of town. The ones who weren't had no names to offer him, but had warmly invited him to dinner. He'd hastily declined on the excuse that his aunt was ill and his trip a hasty one.

Next, in the vague hope that perhaps Neilly had confused the number, as Varina had suggested, Damon had walked the street Neilly had given in the false address. But the street ended two blocks too soon at Jackson Avenue, just as Damon had told Varina. The houses in the district were all homes of well-to-do, prominent New Orleans merchants and property owners. If Neilly had joined one of these households, chances were good that one of the Stirling contacts would have heard of it and said something—unless they were out of town.

Undaunted, Damon had walked through the market several times on the theory that Neilly might have to shop for food, at least for herself. All he'd found was a crowd with people of every color and every shape of eye. He also saw a profusion of the exotic and prosaic: game, vegetables, fish, fruit, and flowers.

His nose was assaulted by the smells of rancid meat, rotting fish entrails, and sour milk. A gentle tug on his coattail warned him of the pickpocket. When he'd turned on the scruffy-looking fellow who was pressing closer than necessary even in the market crowd, the thief had sprinted off—empty-handed.

New Orleans was a city Damon enjoyed visiting about once every three years. He preferred dusty, open country and Indians on the warpath to the Crescent City's noise and avarice.

He'd continued his search with a stroll along the levee every evening, hoping Neilly would be one of the many promenaders who came out after sunset. She was never there.

He'd walked Rue Royale and toured all the galleries, thinking she might have tried to sell her work. It wouldn't have surprised him to run into John Minor, perhaps with Neilly on his arm. But Damon found nothing of Neilly's or of Rosewood's in the galleries. Nor did he see John Minor.

After more than three days of searching he found himself walking the levee for the twelfth time and making a serious assessment of his efforts. He even wondered if Neilly had stayed in New Orleans. Damon scanned the ships that lay tied three abreast on the levee, flags of all countries flying from their masts. She had enough money from her wages to buy a one-way ticket to almost anywhere.

In his gut he was almost certain that she'd stayed in New Orleans. He rejected the possibility that she'd just sail away, not after the love and care she'd given Isetta and Varina. Neilly wouldn't do that.

With little more than instinct to go on, he turned his back

to the river and looked at the cathedral and the grassless parade ground, flanked by the newly completed upper and lower Pontalba buildings, the ornate wrought-iron work fading into the gathering shadows.

A black-clad nun glided across the parade ground at the head of a bevy of uniformed schoolgirls. It was late for such a group to be abroad, and no doubt they were hurrying to reach home before dark descended.

When the little swarm reached the far corner a pair lagged behind, peering at the works of a street artist. Alerted by some invisible instinct, the nun turned. White hands made a sharp gestures in the air—which Damon suspected corresponded to some sharp words—and immediately the laggards deserted the artist.

Damon had seen enough. He hadn't thought to look for Neilly or her works among street artists. What made him think she'd be in the galleries? Her acquaintance with John Minor? Her innate lady-likeness? Or simply that he didn't want to think that she'd been reduced to consorting with street vendors?

Damon marched down off the levee toward the street artists. He crossed the street oblivious to the loaded wagons and carts moving briskly along and began his search anew. He didn't rush his examination of the works at each booth, but he did not linger either. Twice he refused to sit for an artist. They seemed determined that he needed a portrait. One tried to sell him a ghastly painting of a steamboat exploding on the river. But he saw nothing that bore any resemblance to Neilly's distinctive drawings. Nothing.

By the time Damon reached the end of the street where the last artist's booth in the block stood, night shadows were gathering. The young man had started to dismantle his display, but the lamplighter appeared and lit the street lamp overhead. Yellow light suddenly bathed the stall.

"Wait, please." Damon stepped onto the banquette, determined to see as much as he could before the artists dis-

appeared to wherever they went at night. "I'd like to see
your work."

The red-haired young man straightened from his task of
packing up and smiled a friendly smile. "Of course, sir.
That's what I'm here for. Is there something in particular I
can show you? I have other works not on display."

"I'm looking for charcoal drawings," Damon said, his
attention already caught by the black-and-white sketches
displayed next to the oil paintings. "Like these here."

"Yes, these sketches are the work of a colleague," the
young artist explained.

Damon had been disappointed so many times in the last
two and a half days, even in the last hour, that he could
hardly believe what he was looking at. This discovery was
too good to be true. The drawing of the deer and the pair
of doves he was looking at were the very sketches Neilly
had done the day of the barbecue at The Laurels. "What's
your name?"

"I'm Rene," the redhead said. "If you would like something a little different, I have another work by that artist.
Here, take a look at this."

Damon snatched the drawing of the peacock out of
Rene's hand. He held it up to the light of the street lamp
to get a better look. It was Neilly's work, no doubt about
it, and in the corner she'd left blank at The Laurels was
inscribed C. L. Carpenter.

Sixteen

Carpenter was Neilly's real surname, Damon realized as
he stared at the peacock sketch. Had McGregor found nothing about Cornelia Lind because he was looking for information about Dr. Lind instead of Dr. Carpenter?

"What do you know about the artist?" Damon asked,
careful to keep the excitement out of his voice.

"Carpenter? Not much." Rene picked up a portfolio.

"Is she living around here?"

"She? What makes you think the artist is a woman?"
Rene asked, busying himself with packing up his work in
a way that convinced Damon the artist knew something.

"Where is she?" Damon demanded, just barely holding
himself back from grabbing Rene's threadbare lapels and
shaking the truth out of him. "She's here in New Orleans;
this sketch proves it."

"If you're asking about the artist, I couldn't tell you."

"Where is Cornelia?"

"I don't know who you're talking about." Rene swiped
the peacock drawing out of Damon's hands. "I simply
bought these drawings to sell because I thought people
would like them."

Damon searched the redhead's face. He had no doubt that
the artist was lying. Rene knew exactly where Neilly was,
but he wasn't talking. Damon curbed the growing urge to
throttle the truth out of the little man. Threats would probably get him nowhere.

"Look, I don't mean Neilly any harm, if that's what you think." Damon tried to sound reassuring. "Would you give her a message for me?"

"Why do you insist the artist is a woman?" the street artist asked, obviously determined not to give anything away. Without waiting for an answer, he began to stash his remaining pictures into a portfolio. He added, "Anyway, I'm nobody's messenger boy."

"Then for God's sake tell me where to find her," Damon ranted, his patience worn thin. He was so close, he could almost feel her presence. Another thought occurred. "Information can be valuable."

"I sell artwork, not information." The artist held out Neilly's drawing. "You want the peacock or not?"

Damon wrestled with his anger, pinning it down inside where it would do the least harm. Violence would only ensure that he found out nothing from Rene. "What are you asking for the drawing? Does she get any of the money?"

Rene's gaze flickered over Damon in an assessing way. "Ten dollars. I assure you I always pay a colleague a fair price for work."

Damon's temper cooled a bit. Apparently Rene was going to persist with his lie. He was only protecting Neilly the way any friend would, any besotted friend. Damon couldn't fault him for that. But he had to ignore a new, unpleasant sensation—jealousy. He dug into his pocket and handed over twenty dollars. The artist's eyes widened.

"Make sure she gets her proper share," Damon warned.

Apparently unable to speak, the artist nodded. With practiced hands, he rolled up the peacock drawing, tied a short length of string around it, and handed it over to Damon.

Without another word Damon left, only going far enough away to become lost in the shadows beneath the Pontalba's balconies.

The redhead gathered up his things in haste, as if he thought Damon might change his mind and return for the money. Then, with a quick look over his shoulder, Rene trotted off down the street.

Damon followed through the dark lanes, his Indian boots soundless on the stone banquette. Near the corner of Barracks and Royale, the artist entered a lodging house built around a courtyard and over a bakery. The smell of frying pastries still lingered on the summer air.

Damon loitered in the dark long enough to satisfy himself that Neilly wasn't there. The lodgers he spied through the windows, open to catch the night breeze, appeared to be young men, artisans of one kind or another. The only woman on the premises was a turbaned Creole lady, obviously the landlady and wife of the baker, who had probably long ago retired for the night.

Disappointed, yet relieved, Damon stood in the darkness—summer lightning quivering in the night sky above—staring up at the lighted lodging-house windows. Neilly was not in that lodging house, but she must be near. At last he had a connection with someone who had talked to her recently—recently enough to have acquired these pictures from her. Damon was close to finding her now. All he needed was patience and a little more luck.

"He was here," Rene hissed at Neilly the moment she appeared on the street corner. He grabbed her hand and pulled her into the shade of the wall.

"What? Who are you talking about?" Neilly stammered, Rene's excitement catching her by surprise. She looked up the street and down as frantically as Rene did. She saw nothing, no sign of Charles. It was late in the day but not yet sunset, and the streets were quiet.

"The man you said is searching for you."

Neilly's heart tripped over a beat. Charles Ruffin was on her trail again. How had he learned she was here in New

Orleans? She touched Rene's shoulder. "When was he here?"

"Last night." Rene urged Neilly to stand behind his stall and out of sight. He shielded her from the street.

Neilly obeyed. "Is he here now?"

"No. I've been watching for him all day, but I haven't seen him again. He might have believed my story about not knowing where you are, but I can't be sure. He paid me this for your peacock drawing."

Rene held out the money in his paint-stained hand.

Neilly stared at it, speechless for a moment. "Mercy. There must be twenty dollars here."

Charles had never taken any interest in her work, let alone placed a monetary value on it. But Rene put the twenty dollars in her hand. She held two months' rent for Mrs. Robards in her hands, if not enough to make the balance of the payment she owed the Ruffins.

"Neilly, tell me what kind of trouble you're in," Rene pleaded. He took her hands in an earnest appeal. "Maybe I can do something to help you."

"You've done more than anyone should ask of a friend." Neilly shook her head. She didn't want to involve Rene in her unsavory affairs. She remembered only too well that her former fiancé could be vengeful. "Was Charles unkind to you? He can be—ugly."

"I wouldn't call it ugly, exactly," Rene said, obviously holding back the details of what had passed between him and Charles. "But he wanted like hell to find you, Neilly. He made that clear. I don't think there's much he'd stop at to do it. But he didn't scare me."

"Good," Neilly said, not entirely convinced that Rene was telling the truth, but she appreciated the brave face he put on for her benefit. She squeezed his hands.

"What shall I do if he comes back?"

"Tell him you heard I've left town," Neilly said, anxious to distance Rene from Charles. "I know. Tell him I went to

San Antonio. He hates the West. I'd better take my pictures with me."

"Why? He's discovered them already, and I might be able to sell the others. You said you need the money."

"Oh, yes, I do need the money," Neilly said, her anxiety growing. "You haven't seen him around since last night?"

"No. He doesn't seem like the type who'd stroll the streets."

"No, not Charles," Neilly agreed. He wasn't the sort who strolled the streets at morning or night. That's why she'd felt safe enough with her pictures displayed at Rene's booth. If Charles went out at night, it was usually in a carriage with friends—acquaintances—to seek the pleasures of the evening. The encounter Rene described sounded odd.

Neilly caught herself searching the parade ground and the walk under the Pontalba balcony. She couldn't overcome the feeling of being watched, but she saw no one looking in their direction.

She counted out Rene's consignment fee and handed it to him.

"No, no." He held up his hands, refusing to take the money from her. "We artists take care of each other, remember."

"Rene, this was our agreement."

He shook his head adamantly. "Go buy yourself a good meal and stay away from here for a while. Be assured your gentleman won't learn anything from me."

Neilly bent to kiss Rene on the cheek. "Thank you."

She turned back down Rue Chartres, not particularly frightened but unwilling to walk out into the open parade ground. The shadows of the narrow streets seemed friendlier.

After she'd gone only a few steps from Rene's booth she heard him call her name. She turned.

"He's here," Rene called softly. "I see him coming across

the parade ground. He must have been watching. Go. Go.
I'll delay him if I can."

Neilly looked in the direction Rene pointed only long
enough to see a figure loping across the dusty ground in
front of the cathedral. That was all she needed to see. She
picked up the hem of her skirts and raced down the street
and around a corner. She wasn't foolish enough to think
she could outrun a man, but she could make it difficult for
him to catch her.

Damon had been up at dawn, despite the long vigil he
had kept the night before. He gulped down some hotel coffee and headed for the square in front of the cathedral.
Neilly would have to return to the street artist's stall sooner
or later, and he'd be watching when she did. He stationed
himself out of sight in a doorway across the parade ground
and prepared to stay as long as it took—days or weeks—to
spot her.

The day dragged by, long, hot, and sultry. He was forced
to take up a different position several times before a suspicious resident or shopkeeper called the police.

He watched the red-haired artist set up his stall on his
usual street corner at about noon, and he did a slow business. Many people stopped to admire the artwork and to
talk to him, yet few bought anything.

By late afternoon Damon was beginning to think Neilly
wasn't going to appear. His feet hurt and his stomach complained. He could feel his temper turning sour. Surely she
would have to come tomorrow, he reasoned. She must need
the money he'd paid for her drawing. He was debating
whether he should remain and follow Rene home again on
the chance that the artist might stop by Neilly's lodgings.

As Damon speculated on this point, Neilly stepped out
of a side street. Her appearance was so sudden and unexpected, Damon almost didn't recognize her at first. She was

wearing one of her prim gray gowns and a plain bonnet.
The graceful way her skirts swayed when she walked caught
his eye.

The sight of her made Damon step out of the doorway,
eager to get a better look. But he checked his impatience,
remembering to keep himself concealed in the shadows.

She appeared thinner than he remembered, and paler. No
roses bloomed in her cheeks.

He watched Rene pull Neilly behind the display easels.
The artist must suspect that Damon might be watching. But
he could see enough of what was going on between them
to see that Neilly got her money.

Their discussion seemed long and serious. Both kept looking over their shoulders, up and down the street and out into
the parade ground—in Damon's direction. He cursed. If he
started out into the open toward them now, Neilly would flee.
But if he waited too long, she would get too far ahead of him.
She knew where she was going better than he did. He waited.
With some luck she'd walk in his direction.

She didn't. Instead, she kissed Rene on the cheek. Damon
refused to let himself think about that. Then the artist sent
her off down Rue Chartres. Damon cursed again and
charged across the parade ground after her. There was no
time to lose.

Rene saw him coming and ran to call a warning to Neilly.
When Damon reached the artist's corner Rene stepped into
his path. Damon shoved the little man aside and charged
down Chartres, but all he saw was the hem of a gray skirt
disappear down another narrow street. The market was only
a couple of blocks away.

Damon cursed again. He knew without a doubt that
Neilly would try to lose him in the crowd.

Neilly rounded the corner of Rue Chartres and St. Philip
and headed for the market. Charles hated nothing more than

a noisy, smelly crowd of common people speaking languages foreign to his ear: Swedish, Dutch, Norwegian. This late in the day it wouldn't be as busy as in the morning, but the throng of people would slow him down—if not put him off altogether.

Without hesitation, she reached the market and waded into the crowd, having little care for the condition of her skirt. She dodged around a juggler juggling oranges and edged her way ahead of a fisherman lugging a basket of shrimp. She weaved her way through the audience gathered around some out-of-tune musicians and hurried around a fortune-teller's stall and nearly knocked over a booth of green leather goods.

Halfway down the length of the market, Neilly turned to see if she could spot Charles behind her. Standing on tiptoe to see over the crowd, she could spot no top hat, no elegantly dressed, well-barbered gentleman barging through the crowd—cursing one and all for delaying him. But she did see a tall dark-haired man forging through the horde of people. When he saw her looking his way, he called her name.

Astonished and confused, Neilly whirled and pressed on, heading for the levee. But the contradiction between what Rene had told her and who she'd just seen muddled her thoughts. It wasn't Charles who was following her: It was Damon.

She reached the edge of the crowd, ducked around the corner of a building, and stopped. She leaned against the stone wall and attempted to sort out her thoughts. Her breath rasped through her in harsh gasps. Her mind reeled with the realization that it was Damon pursuing her through the crowd. He was the last man on earth she needed to see right now. Why was he following her? A man who had no faith in her. A man who never would. But why was he here?

She pressed her hand to her stomach, trying to control

her breathing, dreading every horrible possibility that raced through her mind. She had to know.

Damon charged around the corner and ran several strides past her. Neilly stepped out from her hiding place.

"Damon?"

He stopped in his tracks and whirled around. When he saw her a rainbow of emotions crossed his face. Neilly recognized surprise, relief—and anger. He started toward her.

"Stay there," Neilly said, putting her hand out to emphasize her words. She was suddenly afraid to be near him. They had not parted under the best of circumstances. Still, he looked so good, so solid, so broad-shouldered and strong—and so very furious.

"What do you want?" she asked, ignoring gawking market-goers. No doubt she and Damon made a strange pair: the lady in a worn gray gown and the hatless gent in a black frock coat and fringed Indian boots. "Has something happened to Isetta?"

Damon raked his hand through his hair and glared at her as if she should know. Under his eyes dark circles told of his lack of sleep. Strain etched lines at the corners of his mouth. Neilly's heart went out to him in spite of herself. Whatever had brought Damon to New Orleans, it was not good news. Suddenly the breeze off the river seemed chilling. "Oh Damon, tell me, what is it?"

Damon glowered at an unfortunate passerby who showed more than a polite interest in their confrontation. Under the heat of Damon's glare, the man slunk away.

"Aunt Isetta is about the same," Damon said, restraint in his voice. "She sends her affection."

"Oh, thank God." Neilly's knees went weak with relief and she reached for the stone wall to steady herself. "Mercy, I was so afraid something had happened to her."

For a moment that had been the only reason she could imagine for him seeking her out—that Isetta had suffered another serious attack or worse. "And Varina is well? Are Arthur and Vincent as charming as ever?"

"Oh, never fear on that account," Damon said. His face softened and he stepped closer. "Not much has changed at Rosewood, except that you're not there. But I need to talk to you. Let's go where we have more privacy."

A new thought occurred to Neilly as Damon continued to move closer. "It was you who bought the peacock drawing?"

He took her arm. "Of course. Who did you think it was?"

His grip was warm and unyielding as he steered her away from the market.

"Never mind," Neilly said, her mind still spinning between what she knew about Charles Ruffin being in New Orleans and Damon trailing her through the market.

"Let's go to my hotel," Damon suggested, already maneuvering them along the crowded banquette.

Neilly planted her feet. A hotel was entirely too improper and entirely too likely a place to find Charles Ruffin. "No, not your hotel."

"Why not?"

"Because a lady doesn't visit a gentleman in his hotel," Neilly stammered. Under Damon's amused scrutiny she blushed.

"I can think of less proper places we've been than in a hotel lobby sipping lemonade, Miss Cornelia," Damon said, lifting a skeptical brow. "Miss Cornelia Lind Carpenter. That is your name?"

"Well, yes," Neilly had to admit, another blush warming her face.

"I think you owe my aunts and me an explanation about a few things," Damon said, starting off down the banquette again, towing Neilly along.

"Yes, but that isn't why you're here," Neilly persisted, certain from the gravity of his expression that he hadn't come to New Orleans to satisfy his curiosity about her name.

"No, it isn't," Damon said, negotiating their way around a wagon-load of baled cotton. "We need to discuss questions about the inventory."

"Oh, that dratted thing," Neilly said, following Damon through the crowd, disappointment slowly eroding her pleasure in seeing him again. "I might have known that's what would bring you to New Orleans. You know I only started it to help your aunts."

"I believe you," Damon said, but Neilly doubted that he did. At least not from the way he dragged her along. She didn't like the direction they were taking: toward Rue Royal, where the nice hotels did business—where Charles would stay.

Neilly stopped. "All right, I'll answer your questions. But let's go to my lodging house, shall we? I think Mrs. Robards will provide us with something. It will be a quieter place to talk."

Damon stopped and looked down at her. She couldn't help thinking again how pleased she was to see him, in spite of everything. Despite the dark circles under his fathomless eyes, he looked absolutely wonderful to her. Tanned and vital. Neilly looked away, praying her thoughts weren't too plain on her face.

"All right, let's go to your lodging house, if you'll be more comfortable there," Damon said. "Which way?"

Neilly pointed out the direction and they started off. They made polite conversation as they walked. Neilly couldn't keep herself from stealing sidelong looks at Damon. After all the bleak days in New Orleans, his deep voice was music to her ears and his forceful presence lightened her soul. She realized with a wrench of her heart how much she had missed Rosewood—and Damon.

When they rounded the corner of Neilly's street Damon's

grip tightened on her arm. He assessed the shabby neighborhood. "Neilly, couldn't you do any better than this?"

"It's not that bad, Damon," Neilly said, determined not to let him pity her. "Honestly, it's a nice street. Mrs. Robards is very clean, strict, and proper."

Her steps lagged as she realized that the street was in an uproar. In the gathering darkness dogs barked. Children ran to and fro, calling to one another in French. Housewives stood on their front steps to gape, while servants took overlong to shake tablecloths out of the windows.

The object of their interest was the carriage sitting before Mrs. Robards's lodging house: a hired carriage, a grand one with a matched team in shiny black leather and brass harnesses. No such equipage ever entered this neighborhood, not even a hired one. Neilly hoped it belonged to some acquaintance or family member of one of the other girls boarding at Mrs. Robards. But in her heart she knew better.

She stopped to face Damon before they reached the lodging-house gate. She was afraid of who she might find awaiting her in Mrs. Robards's salon. She was even more afraid of having Damon meet her visitor. "I think you were right. I should meet you at your hotel—tomorrow."

Damon stared at the coach, his expression dark. "Why not now?"

Unnerved, Neilly searched for an excuse, something logical, something that would make sense to a suspicious man. Her mind went blank.

Behind her, the iron courtyard gate screeched open and Regis, Mrs. Robards' gate boy, stepped out onto the banquette. "Miss Carpenter. Miss Carpenter, Mrs. Robards wants to see you right away. You have a gentleman caller."

"I think we'd better see who it is, don't you?" Damon said firmly, taking Neilly's arm and leading her toward the lodging house. "Tell Mrs. Robards that Miss Carpenter is coming."

Seventeen

Neilly took a deep breath for courage and hoped that Damon hadn't noticed how frightened she was. With dragging steps and Damon's hand on her arm, she walked through the rusting iron gate, along the covered passage, and into the lodging-house courtyard.

A drooping palmetto filled the dry fountain in the center of the uneven flagstones. White paint peeled from the window shutters and the gallery banister above. She turned to Damon, stopping him before they entered the house, afraid for him to see more.

"You know, I really think we *should* meet at your hotel. Go on. I'll see you there later."

"Oh, no," Damon said, his eyes on the salon doors. He pressed Neilly toward them. "We're here now. Let's see who your caller is."

Before they reached the doors Mrs. Robards bustled out.

"Here she is." Sally Robards was a dark-haired, well-endowed widow who prided herself in the honesty of her establishment and of her lodgers—and in the same breath requested a month's rent in advance. But she was a warm woman and, in an offhanded way, she took a motherly interest in the females staying under her roof.

She frowned when she saw that Neilly had an escort, and surveyed Damon from the top of his head to the fringe of his Indian boots.

"This is most awkward," Mrs. Robards said, a frown pulling at her mouth. "You already have a gentleman caller who has been waiting to see you for over an hour. I asked him if he would care to leave a message, but he insisted on waiting."

"This is Mr. Durande," Neilly began, making introductions, but her mind was on the man who had hired the coach. It could only be Charles. How like him to insist on waiting. How like him to take over the salon and enlist the help of the landlady.

Before she was finished introducing Damon to her landlady, Charles Ruffin stepped out of the salon into the courtyard. He smiled when he saw Neilly, the smile that had made her heart flutter once long ago. He smiled as if he was truly glad to see her after nearly three years. Neilly's heart sank.

"Hello, Cornelia." Charles stepped forward, nudging the chattering landlady aside.

He was dapper as ever: the sandy-hued mustache perfectly trimmed and waxed, the cut of his coat snug, his spit-polished boots gleaming in the light of the courtyard lantern. Charles always made an impressive appearance.

"It's been a long time since we last saw each other, my dear." He reached for Neilly, as if to greet her with a kiss.

At her side she felt Damon stiffen.

A rush of defiance and anger coursed through Neilly. She sidestepped Charles. This man, her former fiancé, had ruled her life once, then ruined it. He had ruined her father's life, too. How dare he greet her as if she were his long-lost love. "What is it you want, Charles?"

He frowned, plainly offended by Neilly's cool greeting. "Is that all you have to say to me, my dear?" Then his steely gaze fell on Damon. "I don't believe we've met, sir. Introduce us, Cornelia."

"We've met," Damon said, with an icy aloofness of his own that surprised Neilly. He failed to offer his hand to shake. "You just don't know my name. I'm Damon

Durande, and I'm as curious as the lady about what brings you here to see her."

"I don't mean to be rude, sir," Charles said, in a tone that implied it was Damon who was being rude. It was the haughty kind of insult Neilly remembered Charles delivering so well. "My business is with Miss Cornelia."

"We'll talk later, Damon," Neilly said, anxious to send him away to safety. Charles was only getting into his best form, a form Damon would never tolerate from anyone. Neilly would rather take Charles's sly insinuations than see these two have a set-to—or worse—in Mrs. Robards's courtyard. "Go on. I'll send a message to your hotel."

"No, I'll wait here," Damon said, his voice even and smooth, as if he had suddenly acquired the patience of a saint. "Take your time."

"Sir, I haven't seen Miss Cornelia for three years and we have private business to discuss," Charles said, his forbearance obviously strained. "Surely you understand."

"Perfectly," Damon said. "I've been looking for the lady for some time myself, and I don't intend to let her out of my sight either."

"Damon? Please," Neilly pleaded.

"Mrs. Robards will entertain me while I wait, won't you, dear lady?"

Neilly was about to dispute the idea when she saw Sally Robards blush under Damon's disarming smile. "Why, of course, sir. This way to my salon. May I offer you a glass of claret? You must tell me what brings you to New Orleans."

"You won't be long, will you, Miss Cornelia?" Damon said. To Neilly's astonishment he bent down and kissed her on the cheek in a familiar, possessive way that she knew would provoke Charles.

Damon's devilish parting glance told her he knew it, too.

"So where did you meet your—quaint escort?" Charles

asked, his mouth twisted in derision, his eyes on Damon's fringed boots. "Pick him up on the levee, did you?"

Neilly ignored the remark. "How did you find me?"

"I finally learned the alias you've been using from one of your lawyer's secretaries. I'm afraid the new young fellow Mr. Smith has hired is easily inebriated."

Neilly wasn't particularly surprised that the information had finally slipped out, but she was disappointed. Mr. Smith had been as eager as she to keep her father's name clear of scandal and to help her avoid Charles. With his help she'd succeeded in keeping ahead of her former betrothed for three years.

"If it's the money you're concerned about, Charles, I have the payment, almost," Neilly said, knowing she was going to have to face this dilemma sooner or later. "I'm just a few dollars short, but I thought perhaps you would accept what I have for now."

"Oh, Cornelia, even someone as naive as you knows business isn't done that way." He offered a small smile of disappointment. "That's a charming little bonnet, Cornelia. I want to see your face. Take it off."

"I like wearing my bonnet," Neilly said, her head held high. "Don't change the subject. I do know that compassion exists in the business world, Charles."

"Perhaps, but compassion is not entered in the ledger under assets," Charles said. "It does not accrue value. Let me be honest with you, my dear: I don't like this payment arrangement."

"You made that clear at the time the judge arranged it," Neilly said. At the time she had suspected the Ruffins would be satisfied with nothing less than her hide.

"It's so materialistic," Charles continued, as if he hadn't heard her. "I imagine that after these years of making your way alone, moving from household to household, scrimping the money together, always counting on the generosity of strangers—I imagine you've had time to wish things were different. Time to regret refusing my alternative proposal."

"In truth, sir, I've never given your outrageous suggestion a second thought," Neilly said, familiar anger and outrage growing inside her. But her old fear was gone.

"Surely there have been moments when you wished the slate wiped clean and you were free of the debt," Charles said. "I'm offering you that opportunity again."

"I have no interest in your offer," Neilly said. "It is rude and ungentlemanly and insulting."

"Precisely, and I think you misjudge the value of my proposal," Charles said. "Besides dispensing with the debt, I'm offering you a life of ease."

Charles leaned closer, practically crooning his temptations into her ear. "Think of it, Cornelia. A townhouse of your own, clothes, servants, horse and carriage. You would live quite comfortably under my protection."

"I would live as your mistress, Charles," Neilly corrected. "That proposal was not acceptable to me when you first made it, nor is it acceptable now."

"Darlin'?" Damon suddenly appeared, a glass of claret in his hand.

"Are you finished talking with Ruffin yet? You must come taste Mrs. Robards's fine claret. It's really quite wonderful."

Neilly knew that was untrue. Mrs. Robards's claret was cheap and sour as vinegar.

Charles glared at Damon. Damon smiled back, as amiable as an angel.

"Charles and I have not concluded our discussion," Neilly said, praying that Damon had not overheard anything.

"Oh, sorry to interrupt," he said, without a single note of remorse in his voice. "It is a little stuffy inside. I'll just sit over here on the bench with Mrs. Robards and enjoy the evening air."

Charles continued to glare at Damon as he sat down with Neilly's landlady. "Who is that fellow?"

"A friend," Neilly said, secretly glad of Damon's interruption. It had given her a moment to think. "Charles, I'm sorry that our betrothal became such an embarrassment to you. When I accepted your offer of marriage I had no idea how things would turn out. But a lot of things have changed since our betrothal. You can't possibly think I would consider this second offer seriously."

Charles's face darkened. "You owe me, Cornelia. I risked my entire family's disapproval—especially my father's—to make you my promised, and what did you do? You and your father stole from us."

"I don't consider becoming your mistress an acceptable solution to the problem," Neilly said, recognizing the unholy light of obsession that glinted in Charles's eyes. A little frightened now, she stepped back from him. "I will make the payments as the court ruled and as was arranged through Mr. Smith."

"What payment is this?" Damon appeared at Neilly's shoulder again. She silently cursed those boots that allowed him to move so soundlessly across the courtyard flags.

Charles took a deep, weary breath and lifted his chin to peer along his narrow, aristocratic nose at Damon. "You, sir, are a nuisance."

"I've been told that before." Damon's smile widened and turned frosty as a November morn. "Particularly by my grandfather."

He paused for a moment.

Neilly feared he was going to add some insult just to annoy Charles. He didn't.

"Explain these payments to me," Damon said.

Neilly started to explain, as briefly as possible. He would never understand what had happened in Charleston, and he didn't need to know the details of her predicament.

But Charles interrupted, pulling an expression of long-suffering. "Miss Carpenter owes my family a considerable amount of money. A very large sum decided upon by the courts of South Carolina. Despite her hard work in the many households in which she's been a companion or whatever, she can't seem to come up with the money. I think she's not asking a high enough price for her services."

Embarrassment heated Neilly's face. Charles made it sound as if she'd been employed as little more than a prostitute.

Damon said nothing, but his expression closed.

"Don't listen to him," Neilly said, touching Damon's arm. She didn't care about the insult to herself. "I have the money and I will fulfill my obligation just as I've been doing for the last three years."

The two men glared at each other, completely ignoring her.

"You insult the lady, sir," Damon said. Neilly heard the deceptively cold, dispassionate edge in his voice.

Neilly didn't like the sound of that phrase. "Damon, there's no need for you to take my part in this. I have an attorney."

"Are you going to call me out, Durande?" Charles's unruffled challenge frightened her even more. She'd heard rumors that he'd killed at least one man in a duel—not a fair duel. He smiled coldly at her, letting Neilly know nothing would please him more than to shoot someone she cared for. "Let's meet at the traditional place, the Dueling Oak, at sunrise. We'll take care of the matter then."

"Hell, why waste time finding some damned tree?" Damon said, as if he'd never heard of New Orleans' infamous dueling site. "Let's call for the guns and have it out here."

"Damon! Charles!" Neilly stepped between them. "Stop it. Both of you. This is ridiculous."

Damon yanked her away from between them.

"Not here, Durande," Charles sputtered, disquiet showing

in the pinch of his lips. "If we're going to do this, we'll do it the civilized way."

"Since when has shooting each other at point-blank range been civilized?" Damon demanded. "I call for it here and now. I'm the injured party. I set the time and place."

"That's enough, gentlemen," Mrs. Robards cried, rising from the bench where she'd been watching them. A few girls had gathered along the railing of the gallery above. The men were providing Mrs. Robards and her lodgers with better entertainment than they'd had in months, Neilly suspected.

"I'll have no fighting or dueling in my courtyard," Mrs. Robards declared. "This is a proper lodging house, gentlemen. I have the delicate sensibilities of my young ladies to consider."

"Mrs. Robards is right," Neilly said, icy fear heavy in her stomach. She stepped between the two men again. This time Charles dragged her out from between them, nearly wrenching her arm from its socket.

"Has she told you the truth about what she and her father did?" Charles asked.

Neilly groaned. This was what she'd been afraid of from the beginning. She knew without a doubt that if Damon knew the whole truth, he'd turn his back on her forever, and she couldn't blame him. "Damon, it was an unpleasant court battle. The issue was complicated and some bad feelings developed."

Damon remained intent on Neilly's former betrothed. "Make your point, Ruffin."

A wicked smile spread across Charles's face, as if he knew he'd hooked his prey at last. "Your name is Durande? Yes, Durande, a fine old Creole family. I remember now. One of the younger sons married a Stirling girl. The Stirlings of Rosewood."

"Damon, there's no need for you to listen to any of this." Neilly was not particularly surprised by Charles's knowledge of Damon's family tree. Most Southern aristocrats retained a mental catalogue of who married whom.

"Your thieving father would be proud of you," Charles said, his evil grin spreading under his pointed mustache.

Neilly saw doubt flicker across Damon's face.

"I haven't told Damon the truth, Charles," Neilly said. Strain thinned her voice, making it sound weak and strange even to her ears. "There's nothing for you two to fight about."

"Wait, Neilly." Damon leveled his gaze at Charles. The conviction on his face made Neilly forget the threat of a duel.

"Neilly has been a good companion to my aunts and she has run the house with as much care as if it were her home. She is loyal and strong and caring. I know all I need to know. What kind of payment do you want, Ruffin?"

Neilly could hardly believe her ears. She stared up at Damon, almost ready to ask him to repeat the words. *I know all I need to know.*

Ruffin smiled a wide, cold, knowing expression. "So, Durande, she's seduced you into believing her sad story."

"I'm sorry, Mrs. Robards, but that's one insult too many," Damon said.

Neilly never saw his fist. She only felt him push her aside as he gathered strength for the blow. Then fists flew in a blur.

Damon's knuckles cracked against Charles's jaw. Charles threw a punch and missed. Damon's second blow sent Charles sailing through the air. He landed on the seat of his finely made pantaloons. A trickle of blood trailed from the corner of his mouth. He gaped at Damon in astonishment.

"No more of that," Mrs. Robards cried, placing herself between the two men. "Get out, or I'll send for the police."

Charles raised himself up on his elbows. "I might have expected something that uncouth from you, Durande."

"Oh, come on, Ruffin. A bully like you has been in a few dirty fights. Your style is different, that's all. You're spoiling for a duel, so let's fight."

Slowly, Charles crawled to his feet, his glare unwavering. He gestured to his personal servant, who ran forward to brush the dust off his master's pants. "I only duel with gentlemen."

Damon laughed this time. He wasn't fooled by Charles's cowardly insult, anymore than Neilly was. But she clutched Damon's arm with all her strength. She feared he'd go after Charles again. The desire to fight hummed in the tension of his hard muscles. Any excuse would be good enough for him to take on Charles again.

Charles moved with stiff dignity, despite the lopsided droop of his mustache and the scuffs on his shiny boots. Coolly he took his top hat from his servant and held it in the crook of his arm, as if in defiance of his ruined appearance. He squared his shoulders, but the belligerence seemed to have been knocked out of him. Still Neilly knew better than to jump to conclusions about Charles.

"You'll get your money, Ruffin," Damon said, his voice clear and decisive. "The entire amount. Put what's due in writing and send it to my agent here in New Orleans—Harvey, Allen and Watkins in Canal Street. I'll notify him to write you a bank draft and the business will be done."

Charles plopped his hat on top of his mussed hair. "It's not going to be that simple, Durande."

Then he strode out of the courtyard. With every step the dust of humiliation flapped from his coattails.

Still clinging to Damon's arm, Neilly stared at him in awe. She'd heard little of the two men's exchange after what Damon had said about her. The words echoed through her mind. *He knew all he needed to know.* He believed in her!

She'd known since that afternoon in the cellar that she

cared about Damon a great deal. She knew that she'd fallen in love with him.

At the moment loving him was the only thing that mattered.

The throbbing pounded something fierce in Damon's hand as he allowed Mrs. Robards to usher him and Neilly into the salon, where a lamp was burning. The room was cramped with furnishings: a sofa, a pair of mismatched Spanish chairs, and a scarred spindle-leg table.

But all Damon was aware of was the pain in his knuckles. He flexed his fingers. No bones seemed to be broken, and he smiled to himself despite the ache. The sight of Ruffin sprawled on his ass made the discomfort worthwhile.

"Shall I call a doctor?" Mrs. Robards asked, staring down at Damon's hand, her eyes wide with alarm.

He glanced at his knuckles and realized for the first time that they were split and bleeding. He reached for his handkerchief. "No, I'm all right."

"But we'll need some ice, Mrs. Robards," Neilly said, taking charge in her gentle, confident way. "Please."

"Of course. I'll send it right in." Mrs. Robards disappeared in the direction of the kitchen.

"She likes you," Neilly said, taking something from her reticule. "She didn't ask Charles if he needed a doctor."

Damon located his handkerchief in his pocket, but Neilly had already taken his hand and started to wrap it in her small, inadequate square of lace-trimmed linen.

Her touch was tender, but her hands were cool and her lips pursed tight in concentration.

"I feel like a medieval lady bestowing her colors on her favorite knight," she said, a faint smile on her lips.

"I feel like a knight receiving a great honor," he said, partly to make her truly smile at him. His handkerchief would have made a better dressing, but he decided wearing hers was a good deal more satisfying.

She smiled at him finally—a lovely, sweet smile of gratitude that made Damon forget about the throbbing in his hand. "Thank you for standing up to Charles."

The overwhelming urge to kiss Neilly assailed Damon right there, with the salon door open. He squelched the desire. There were things he had to know. He'd better find out the truth before he touched her again. He loosened his cravat with his uninjured hand. "You've got some tall explaining to do."

Neilly nodded, her face still and tense but her eyes shining with some emotion he didn't understand. "Yes, you deserve to know the truth."

"Sit down and don't move until you've told me everything."

Obediently, she untied the ribbons of her bonnet and laid it aside. Then she sat down on one of the rickety Spanish chairs, her face still pale and tense.

Damon sat down on the worn velvet sofa across from her. "I want to know about everything that Ruffin hinted at. Just what sort of payments are you making to him, and for what? What did he mean by those remarks about your father?"

"It's rather complicated," Neilly began, her shoulders slumped, as if the story weighed heavily on them. She evaded his gaze.

"I'll do my best to understand," Damon assured her, knowing she couldn't possibly comprehend how much he wanted to understand. Ruffin could insinuate about Neilly's sins to hell and gone, but she'd chosen to give herself to him. Damon found that he could believe in that above all else.

She looked up at him at last. "From the beginning?"

Damon nodded.

Neilly took a long, shaky breath. "My father was the

physician to Charles's grandmother some years ago. She was ill for a long time. Papa was often in their home. Almost every day. In fact, there wasn't much that Papa could do for the lady, but the family wanted him to see her frequently. So he did. Sometimes I went along."

"Go on."

"The Ruffins are very wealthy, as you probably know. They own many plantations and several Charleston warehouses."

"I've heard," Damon said, remembering the awe and respect in the hotel clerk's face when he spoke of the Ruffins.

"Well." Neilly looked very uneasy and stared at her hands trembling in her lap. "My mother was also very ill. She had a weak heart, much like Miss Isetta. I did my best to nurse her. But she grew weaker. Then we heard wonderful things about the healing powers of a spa in Austria."

"Your father wanted to take her there?"

"Yes, but it was a very expensive trip. At the same time as my mother's health worsened, Charles had made it known he was interested in courting me. I don't know why."

Damon knew why, but he merely gestured for her to go on.

"People told me I was the luckiest girl in Charleston. Society feted us. The older Ruffins considered me barely a suitable match. My father was only a doctor, but Mama was an Ashley." Neilly looked up at Damon imploringly. "I never lied about that."

Damon nodded. "Go on."

"Mother's condition worsened, and we became concerned about her having the strength to make the trip to Austria."

Neilly was silent and thoughtful for a moment, as if she was uncertain of how to continue. She glanced apprehensively at Damon. "I don't know how to tell all of this."

"Just tell it, Neilly," Damon said, relieved at last to be hearing the truth from her lips. "I don't want any more lies between us."

Damon hadn't thought it possible for her to turn paler, but she turned white as a sheet as she stared at him uneasily.

"Let me guess." He wanted to make it as easy for her as possible. "Your father did something dishonest?"

He was beginning to understand what lengths a man might go to if he were desperate enough, if he loved enough.

Neilly nodded and stared at her hands in her lap.

"He stole the money for the trip from the Ruffins?"

Neilly's head came up slowly and she considered him for a moment. Relief washed over her features and she nodded eagerly. "Yes, he stole the money, and from the Ruffins. They had so much, I guess he didn't think they'd miss it."

"Didn't you wonder where it came from?"

Neilly shook her head. "He told me he'd managed to get a loan. I never thought to question him. I was only a girl. I didn't know how these things worked. And there were loans from people who wanted to help."

"So you made the journey to the spa with your mother."

"Yes. Charles didn't want me to go, but Mama needed a nurse and I wasn't going to miss being with her at a time like that. Then he wanted to go with us, and it took both Papa and me to convince him that wouldn't be appropriate."

"Did the spa help your mother?"

Neilly's face brightened. "She did improve at first. We stayed several months in Europe. Papa and I were really heartened by her improvement.

"We enjoyed the sights. We saw some works by the great artists. I did sketches. It was a wonderful few months." A wistful smile played across Neilly's face.

"What happened, darlin'?"

"She died." Damon waited for the tears, but none came. "She died in Germany in her sleep. It was very peaceful, and Papa and I were so glad we'd had that time with her."

Neilly paused, and Damon decided not to rush her.

She chewed on her lip before she went on. "Those were

dark days for Papa and me. I truly feared that Papa might do something rash, he was so beside himself with grief."

Then anger flared in her eyes. "If it wasn't bad enough that we had to bring Mama home in a casket, the Ruffins were waiting for us in our own drawing room the day we returned. There was Charles, his father, and their lawyer— Charles knew our housekeeper and had talked his way into the house. They'd discovered the theft, you see."

"The cad didn't waste any time, did he?" Damon asked, wishing he'd had an opportunity to hit Ruffin again.

"They couldn't even wait until Mama had been laid to rest." Neilly sniffed and a tear rolled down her cheek. She hastily brushed it away.

Damon reached across the distance between them and took her hand. So small, cold, and shaking. "Did they jail your father?"

"No, thank heavens," Neilly said. "Papa had helped so many families in town over the years, including the judge's wife and the sheriff's son. Those people used their influence on Papa's behalf. Still, the Ruffins wielded a lot of power."

"How did Charles behave after your father stole the money?"

"That was the thing," Neilly said, her tears disappearing. She sat a little straighter in her chair, her eyes bright with indignation. "Charles and his family were outraged because of our betrothal. They seemed to feel Papa's offense was some kind of betrayal on my part. They wanted the whole affair kept quiet. Charles broke off our engagement. He was terribly humiliated.

"The judge suspended jail time for Papa, but he did fine him and require that the money be paid back to the Ruffins."

"That is the sum you are making payments on?"

"It was a rather large sum, and Papa died about six months after the trial. He just pined away for Mama. Of course I inherited everything, and I'm responsible for the debt. We Ashleys honor our debts."

"Nonsense," Damon said. "You didn't commit the offense."

He squeezed her hand, annoyed with Neilly's father for leaving his daughter in such straits. "What about you and Charles?"

Neilly glanced at him with a look that said Charles was a subject she'd rather not discuss. "Charles seemed unable to put the whole thing behind him. There were rude letters and inappropriate gifts."

"Suggestive gifts," Damon filled in for her. When she nodded he suppressed his anger. "Go on."

"So I talked with Papa's lawyer, Mr. Smith, and made arrangements to take care of Papa's debt. I was frightened, but I knew it had to be done. I gambled on the Ruffins' desire to keep the affair quiet. I packed my bags, got two letters of reference from families in town, and set out on my own."

"Did Charles follow you?"

"Yes, he searched for me. Charles can be rather persevering. But I managed to stay ahead of him—until now."

"So you've been working as a companion since then?"

"Yes," she said simply. "For the last three years."

"Your letters of reference are genuine?"

"Of course," Neilly said, staring at him in complete innocence. "How else would I have gotten them?"

Ashamed of his earlier suspicions, Damon said nothing.

"Mr. Smith, my lawyer, warned me not long after I left Charleston that Charles was looking for me," Neilly continued, a look of distraction on her face. "He had no good reason for contacting me. I'd managed to elude him until now."

"And what did he want?"

Neilly blinked at Damon, and the little color that had

returned to her cheeks drained away. "He is demanding the money be paid."

"He shall have it," Damon said, not entirely satisfied with her answer. "Was there anything else he wanted?"

Neilly opened her mouth to say something more, but just then Mrs. Robards bustled into the room. "Here is the ice you requested, dear. I'm sorry it took so long; I had to send out for it."

Neilly wrapped the ice in a towel and sat down next to Damon to press the cold pack against his bloody knuckles. The scent of lilacs assailed him. The warmth of her nearness stirred his longing to possesses her again.

He couldn't help thinking, as Neilly held his hand between her own, that if Ruffin had pursued her for the last three years, he wasn't likely to drop his interest merely because someone handed over a bank draft.

Eighteen

They lingered over supper in Mrs. Robards's salon as long as Neilly could manage. She purposely ignored how low the lamp had burned. She leaned across the table, eager for news of Rosewood and to soothe her fears with the strength of Damon's presence. She longed for his touch, but Mrs. Robards's vigilance and the table stood between them. So she asked about Isetta's health and Varina's rose garden, about Cleo, Cato, and Elijah. She desperately needed to hear about home—or the place that seemed like home.

Damon indulged her. She listened to his every answer and was pleased to know that all was as well as could be expected. He rested his injured hand on the table and leaned toward her. He answered her questions with interest, throwing in details to make her laugh. The conversation flowed between them without any hesitations.

When all seemed to have been said about Rosewood and the lamp burned lower, Neilly finally admitted, "I was glad to see you today."

"Were you?" Damon said, leaning back in his chair, his gaze turning cool and skeptical. "You ran from me as if I was the last person on earth you wanted to see."

"Yes, but you see, I thought you were Charles," Neilly said, disconcerted by the withdrawal of Damon's warmth. "When Rene told me the man I had warned him about had purchased the peacock drawing I could only think that it was Charles."

Damon nodded. "Rene, the street artist?"

"Rene is a friend." Neilly couldn't keep the smile of pride from her lips. "A fellow artist."

"Do artists kiss fellow artists?" Damon toyed with a spoon on the table and frowned.

"Rene has been a real friend to me." With a jolt, Neilly realized that Damon was jealous. For a moment she was annoyed with him. Then she reminded herself of the boy whose mother had practically deserted him, whose grandfather had cut him off from any affection. Her heart softened.

"I met Rene when I first came to New Orleans. We became fast friends. Never lovers, Damon. You're the only lover I've ever had. You know that." Neilly looked away, but she could feel the heat flooding into her face.

"I know that," he agreed without looking at her, but the hushed tones of his voice enthralled Neilly. "I intend for it to stay that way," he added.

The lodging house had grown dark and quiet, except for Mrs. Robards's occasional commotion just beyond the salon door, to remind them they weren't alone.

"I'd better leave," Damon said. He reached across the table to touch her hand, then rose from the sofa. "I'll be back tomorrow. We'll take the afternoon packet back to Rosewood."

"Damon, I don't know," Neilly began. She shook her head. "I'm glad you know the truth, but I'd be so embarrassed if your aunts knew."

He frowned at her. "I'm not going to tell them anything. If you won't come for my sake, then come for Aunt Isetta's. She and Varina miss you. I think you're an important part of her recovery."

Neilly thought how good it would be to defy the lions in Rosewood's front hall again, to listen to the falling rain from the gallery and to stroll through Aunt Varina's lovely gardens.

And then there was the money she owed Damon for paying off the debt due to Charles. He'd said nothing of that. "I've grown very fond of your aunts, Damon. I would like to do what I can to help."

"Good," Damon said, his face suddenly unreadable. "I'll be back tomorrow after I've arranged things with Harvey, and we'll be on our way back to Rosewood."

He bent down to kiss her, a sweet, longing kiss. Warmth and desire flooded through Neilly, tingling from her belly downward. She slipped her arms around his neck, wantonly pressing her body against his. When their lips parted she sighed and clung to him, reluctant to let go after so long without him.

For once she wished Mrs. Robards wasn't so proper and strict with her rules about gentlemen callers. She realized with a thrill that now that she loved him, spending the night in Damon's arms was what she wanted more than anything.

"Tomorrow night we'll be back at Rosewood with only a few feet of gallery between us," Damon whispered against her ear. Neilly wondered with a start whether he'd read her scandalous thoughts.

"Yes," Neilly said, blushing, her head full of memories of their first encounter on the gallery, the feel of Damon's hard muscles under her hands. She wanted him to kiss her again, but he released her hands and started for the door.

"Damon," Neilly called after him.

He turned at the door. "Yes?"

"Take one of Mrs. Robards's servants with you," she said, suddenly recalling how dark the streets of New Orleans were at night.

He laughed. "I'll be all right, darlin'. I've been in more dangerous places than New Orleans after dark. See you in the morning."

And he was gone.

Neilly stared after him, peering into the dark uneasily. Those more dangerous places Damon spoke of didn't have Charles Ruffin lurking in the shadows. She couldn't dismiss the uneasy feeling that her former betrothed might not have said his last word yet.

In her room she opened the window shutters that had been closed against the sun. The breeze of Lake Pontchartrain breathed into the room, blowing it clear of the stuffy heat. Rays from the street lamp below lit the chamber well enough for Neilly to undress and pull on her thin nightdress. She crawled into bed, arranging the mosquito netting for protection, and lay down without pulling the sheet over her.

She was drained, physically and emotionally. The meeting with Charles had shocked her. She'd known he'd be ugly if they ever met face to face. She'd expected him to be insinuating and belittling. Disgracing her was exactly what he'd intended to do from the beginning.

Then she remembered Damon coming to her defense, standing beside her with his head held high and confidence ringing in his voice as he vowed he knew all he needed to know. When he hardly knew anything of the whole sordid tale—or of what Charles had just demanded of her.

"Mercy," Neilly whispered aloud to herself. She hoped Damon meant what he said, because she had a lot to tell him yet, before he knew the whole truth. Maybe she'd been a fool to let him put the words into her mouth. She would tell him the truth, in time. But somehow it still seemed safest not to let him know everything.

Tomorrow she'd get on the packet with him, not because it was wise or because she owed Damon and his aunts money now, but because she wanted to see Miss Isetta and Miss Varina again. Because she wanted to be with Damon, for a little while longer at least.

Content with that thought, Neilly drifted off to sleep with the breeze stirring the mosquito netting over her head and pleasant fantasies playing through her dreams.

* * *

A screech woke Neilly. She hauled herself out of her peaceful dream about the ducks swimming on Varina's garden pond. Why on earth were the fowl making that strange sound? When she opened her eyes her room was quiet, and she realized the unpleasant sound might not have been part of her dream. She sat up and listened. She waited, not knowing what to do. Mrs. Robards's house was normally quiet at this time of night.

The sound came again, rending the silence. Iron against rusty iron. The sound of the courtyard gate just below her room being swung open. This time the grumble of demanding voices followed the screech.

She heard Regis, who slept in a little alcove near the gate cry out her name, his voice full of fear and warning. She heard a smack, followed by a foreboding quiet.

Neilly tore aside the mosquito netting and jumped out of bed. Hard-soled boots thundered up the stairs to her room. She reached for her clothes but realized they wouldn't help her defend herself. She reached for a shoe. The door of her room banged open. The light of the lantern blinded her.

Shrinking back against the bed, Neilly shielded her eyes against the light and squinted at the invader. A stranger stood at the door: a big man, not tall, but broad, massive, wrapped in a sinister black cape.

"Is this her?" The stranger held the lantern up higher and toward Neilly, as if to show her to someone following him.

The man in the hall shoved the lantern carrier aside and advanced into the middle of Neilly's room. She stared up at the intruder and her heart pounded in fear and dismay.

"Charles!"

"You're going with me, Cornelia." He grabbed Neilly by the wrist and ripped the shoe from her hand. "You've made a fool out of me and the Ruffin family for the last time.

We're going back to Charleston, and you'll learn your place."

Charles's viselike grip clamped onto her wrist, and Neilly stumbled after him out of her room and down the stairs. In the courtyard she saw some of the girls peeking out of their doors. Mrs. Robards followed Charles, her face white and drawn.

"Where are you taking her?" the landlady demanded. "You can't drag her out in the street dressed like that, in only a nightdress. And no shoes. If the police see her, they'll have questions to ask for sure. Here, let her take this cape. Someone fetch her slippers."

"She will be in my private carriage," Charles said, as if that should be enough for any woman. "But all right. Give her the cape. I'll not have strangers gawking at my mistress."

The landlady stepped forward with an old cape, one left in the gate room. One of the girls appeared with Neilly's slippers. Charles's henchman dropped them at Neilly's feet.

"I'm sending word to Mr. Durande," Mrs. Robards whispered as she tied the cape ribbons at Neilly's throat. "He told me to send for him if there was any trouble."

So Damon had suspected Charles might turn up again, Neilly thought. She opened her mouth to tell Mrs. Robards to warn him about Charles's henchman, but Charles pulled her away from the landlady's embrace.

"Let's go," Charles said, roughly seizing Neilly's elbow.

"Where are you taking her?" Mrs. Robards demanded, with more courage than Neilly would have given her credit for.

Charles eyed the lady suspiciously. "You've been paid for your silence, madame. Why do you want to know more?"

"So she can send my things along, Charles," Neilly explained.

"Yes, to send her things along," Mrs. Robards agreed.

"You're not going to need your things," Charles said, shoving Neilly toward the courtyard gate. "I'll take care of providing what you need when we get to Charleston."

Charles pushed Neilly into the carriage, climbed in, and sat down beside her. His grip on her wrist never eased. He knocked on the roof and the carriage rolled away from Mrs. Robards's lodging house.

They had hardly lurched around the corner when Charles ripped open Neilly's cape and grabbed her by the waist. He shoved her into the corner and, without preamble, pressed his mouth against hers. His tongue sought entrance. He smelled of garlic and tasted of bitter absinthe. Neilly clamped her lips together and tried to turn away. She mewed as noisy a protest as she could and pushed at his shoulders. He threw his leg over her to prevent her from kicking him and grasped both of her wrists. Then he forced her hands behind her back and bound her before she realized what he was doing.

"How dare you!" Neilly ranted, squirming against his hold, repulsed by the feel of his greedy hands groping for her breasts, covered only by her thin cotton gown. His touch repulsed her. She tried to scream, but he clamped a hand over her mouth and panted against her cheek. With his other hand he squeezed her nipple painfully.

"Oh, feel that. You're already hard for me."

Incensed, Neilly fought him. He pinched tighter.

"Be still, my love, and it won't be so bad for you," he said. His breath nearly made Neilly sick, but she obeyed. Slowly, he took his hand from her mouth, and his head slipped down against her body until his cheek rested on her sore breasts. He stroked her thighs. The loathsome heat of his hands burned through the thin cotton. A cold frisson of fear sliced through Neilly. Every part of her turned tense and wary.

"Don't get any silly ideas in your head about screaming again, Cornelia," Charles warned. "I'll put a gag in your mouth if I have to. No one will see it with a cape hood drawn over your head."

With great effort, Neilly tried to calm herself and searched for something to say to Charles that would help her.

"Your running is over, you know," he continued. "You're returning to Charleston with me. You'll become my mistress and everyone will know it."

"I never agreed to this proposition of yours," Neilly replied, praying that talk would gain her time.

"It doesn't matter whether you agreed or not," Charles said. "By the time we get to Charleston your reputation will be ruined. The entire town will know that you shared a cabin with me on the return passage from New Orleans. That will leave little doubt in anyone's mind about what you've sunk to."

Neilly stared at him in disbelief. "I'll go to the police."

"You think they will believe you? A spurned mistress seeking revenge?"

Neilly remained still and silent. What he said was true. The authorities would never believe anything she said against a Ruffin.

Charles continued to stroke her thighs. "Did you sleep with him?"

"Who?" Neilly asked, nearly paralyzed by the helplessness of her situation.

"Durande. You slept with him, didn't you?" Before she could answer he sat up, reared back, and slapped her so hard, her head thumped against the side of the carriage.

She was so stunned that anyone would strike her that she felt no pain.

"After keeping me at arm's length for years you slept with some damned Creole planter."

He seized her by the waist again, and Neilly scrambled deeper into the carriage corner. From the maniacal light in

Charles's eyes she had no doubt about what he intended next.

"Not here, Charles," she pleaded. "Please, not here. Let's wait until we reach—reach our destination. You know, a bed, where we can be more comfortable and it will be like a honeymoon."

He stopped, then lazily stroked her thigh again. "Would you like that? A little romance? The pretense of a honeymoon?"

"Yes, and I think you would like it, too," Neilly said, knowing that she was teasing him in ways she didn't quite understand, but that it seemed to be working. A light of interest sparked in his pale blue eyes.

"Did he teach you things in bed?"

Neilly coyly fluttered her eyelashes.

"Good. You can show me what he taught you," Charles said, his voice deep with satisfaction. "Then I'll teach you more things. I'll give you the taste of something really good."

With an unholy grin, Charles knocked on the roof of the carriage. "Faster. Faster. We haven't got all night."

Neilly stared at the stony face of the man beside her and wondered if she'd won herself some precious time in which to escape, or if she'd sealed her own fate in Charles's bed.

"You're sure the man in the top hat didn't say where he was taking Miss Carpenter?" Damon asked young Regis as they stood in the cloakroom off the hotel lobby.

The breathless boy's chest heaved so from his sprint through the New Orleans streets, he could only shake his head.

"Damn," Damon muttered. He'd been dozing in his room—fully dressed—because he'd half expected something like this from Ruffin. He'd been on his feet immediately when the night clerk had pounded on his door and

summoned him downstairs. But he'd expected Ruffin to
come after him, not Neilly. He should have known the man
would take the coward's way out.

"No, sah, didn't say where," Regis panted, shaking his
curly head. Even in the low light of the cloakroom Damon
could see the boy's right eye was nearly swollen shut.
"Nothing, 'cept he said Miss Carpenter wouldn't need her
things in Charleston."

"That's it. That's what I needed to know." Damon dug
into his pocket and pressed a generous tip into the boy's
small, callused hand. "Go home and take care of that black
eye."

"Yes, sah. Thank ya, sah."

Damon didn't go back to his room. He headed straight
out the hotel door and down the street for the levee. There
was no time to spare. Somewhere along the rows of boats
tied at the river's edge was a paddle wheeler with boilers
building steam for the voyage to Charleston. He intended
to find it.

New Orleans thronged almost as noisily by night as by
day. Though the evening levee promenaders were gone,
they'd been replaced by sailors—some on watch, some on
leave—fishermen, gamblers, stevedores unloading newly
arrived boats, and others who did their business by night.

Damon weaved his way in and out of the night crowd
and around the stacks of shipping crates, barrels of molasses, bales of cotton, and clumps of fish baskets. He asked
the destinations of boats that seemed about ready to leave.
At the same time he watched the street below the levee,
looking for Ruffin's hired carriage. He was fairly certain
he wouldn't miss it. Carriages were relatively rare in the
streets of New Orleans because almost everyone walked
where they were going.

A forest of ship smokestacks and flagpoles reached into
the sky. Fires burned in braziers on decks and along the
levee. Fish stew cooked in black iron pots, the spicy aroma

flavoring air already heavy with the stink of rotten wood and engine grease. Torchlight glittered off the narrow alleys of water between boat decks.

From one boat came the voices of sailors singing a foreign, homesick-sounding song. Farther down the levee, he heard banjo plucking and the clatter of dancing feet.

By the time Damon had reached the boats tied near the market he was beginning to wonder if Regis had been mistaken about what he'd heard. Damon had found no steamers headed for Charleston, and he hadn't seen a single carriage.

He stopped to look up and down the levee again. Had he missed them? Had Ruffin some other plan for getting Neilly out of the city? Then he saw a coach pull up to the levee near the parade square. Ruffin's manservant and a big man climbed down off the driver's seat. The big man opened the carriage door and dragged a woman from inside. The size was right for Neilly, but the hood over her head made it impossible for him to be certain. Ruffin climbed out of the carriage after the woman, his hand gripping her cape-draped elbow.

Damon charged down the levee toward them, shoving sailors and fishermen out of his way.

Ruffin saw him coming and dragged the woman up the levee and down toward a paddle wheeler Damon hadn't passed yet. She resisted, struggling against Ruffin's hold. Damon heard Neilly's voice. "No, I'm not going with you, Charles."

A couple of deckhands on a neighboring boat straightened from their work to stare at her with mild curiosity.

Damon sprinted for the gangplank to the paddle wheeler just ahead of Ruffin.

"Oh, Damon!" Neilly cried, renewing her struggle against Ruffin. The hood slipped back from her face. "Am I ever glad to see you!"

"You're not going anywhere with this lady," Damon said, blocking Neilly and Ruffin's path.

Ruffin frowned. "Believe me, Durande, you don't know what you're doing. You're better off without her."

"That's between Neilly and me," Damon said. "But you're not taking her anywhere she doesn't want to go."

"Be careful, Damon," Neilly said, tipping her head in the direction of the big man following her. "He has help."

Damon had already noticed the thug. He suspected Ruffin would never have attempted something like this without help.

"Before you put yourself at risk for the lady," Ruffin began, "let me tell you what I'm sure she hasn't told you herself."

"I know the truth," Damon said, glad that he and Neilly had talked earlier.

"I don't think so," Ruffin said, his eyes narrowing. "I don't think you—keeper of the legendary Rosewood—would be here if she'd told you everything."

"Oh, Charles, don't," Neilly pleaded, straining against Ruffin's hold again. She shook her head and the cape hood fell completely away. Damon saw the bruise on her cheek and realized for the first time that he hadn't seen her hands free of the cape. "Damon, don't listen to Charles."

"She got into Rosewood by playing nurse and companion, didn't she?" Charles asked.

Damon said nothing.

"You see," Charles continued, smiling slyly, "that's how their confidence scheme worked. Neilly and her father got into our house through their good works and then substituted a copy of a painting for the real thing in my grandmother's room. My poor sick grandmother's room!"

Damon's insides clenched. He glanced at Neilly, longing to hear her deny Ruffin's story. She looked away.

"They sold the original to an unscrupulous dealer," Charles said. "Then they skipped off to Europe to spend the money. My family was stunned. Embarrassed. Neilly and I were promised, you see. Then she betrayed our trust."

"Is that how it was, Neilly?" Damon asked.

This time she met his gaze, and he knew from the pain in her eyes that Ruffin was telling the truth.

"Damon, I didn't understand what was happening," Neilly pleaded.

"Have you discovered what's missing from Rosewood yet?" Charles baited.

Damon took a deep breath, seeking the cool control that was always his salvation in moments of trial. Had his first instinct about why Neilly was at Rosewood been right? Worse yet—had she lied to him even while they'd been nestled up in Mrs. Robards's cozy salon?

"You find my story enlightening, don't you, Durande? Ruffin said. "Admit it."

Damon mastered his expression. "Yes, it would seem I have my own account to settle with the lady."

"Damon?"

Ruffin jerked Neilly's arm to silence her. Damon concentrated on Ruffin's face, taking in every ugly, well-groomed facet of it. He felt the cool composure he needed settle over him.

"She was my betrothed, Durande," Ruffin continued. "Don't you see? That makes her betrayal doubly treacherous. Doubly humiliating. Now it's my turn to humiliate her. Not many people know what happened, but those who do will understand. She'll be safe in my protection. Her debt will be paid. She's a thief. I don't have to make an honest woman of her. But she'll be known as my mistress."

Damon stared at Neilly, comprehending at last the full extent of her dishonesty with him. She met his gaze for a moment, and he sensed that there were things she wanted to say but wouldn't. Not here in this place, at this time. She shook her head and turned away.

"Maybe you're right, Ruffin," Damon said, his self-discipline perfectly in place. "Now that I know the truth. I won't stand in your way. Take her back to Charleston, with my blessing."

Bowing slightly, Damon stood aside, no longer blocking the gangplank.

Neilly's head came up and she stared at Damon, her mouth open, her heart sinking. He'd been her only hope. She knew he must feel betrayed, but she'd prayed that he'd meant what he said about believing in her. She'd believed that he had enough of a sense of justice to help her escape Charles.

But now he stood aside—gave his blessing to this kidnapping.

Charles laughed and gripped her arm, squeezing it painfully through the cape, and urged her up the gangplank. Without looking up at Damon Neilly brushed past him, walking along the narrow way, her mind numbed by growing terror and confusion. She'd have to think of some way to escape on her own. She held her head high, seeing the name of the paddle wheeler painted just below the bridge, but the letters meant nothing.

Just as she was about to step onto the deck, with the assistance of the deckhand, she heard Charles choke. He tugged at her arm briefly. Then his hand was gone.

When she turned she saw Damon grasping the back of Charles's cravat. The fabric cut into Charles's chin. His eyes bugged out and his arms flailed in the air. Damon grabbed the seat of Charles's pants and bodily threw him down the gangplank into his thug's face.

Neilly stumbled backward into the arms of a deckhand. Damon reached for her. "Let's go."

Bruno threw Charles over the gangplank rope and charged up the incline.

"Behind you," Neilly warned, unable to free herself from the surprised deckhand.

Damon turned to meet the thug head on. They both tumbled off the gangplank and into the water on top of Charles.

"Untie me," Neilly demanded of the deckhand, who staggered as he tried to steady her. She shouldered him in the gut. "Untie me."

The deckhand stared at her uncomprehendingly until he realized her wrists were indeed bound behind her. He reached for his knife and cut her loose.

Neilly dashed down the gangplank, thinking to come to Damon's aid somehow.

"Call the police," she cried as she ran. She had no idea how well Charles might defend himself, but Bruno looked solid as a stone wall. He probably packed a punch as powerful as a mule's kick.

Neilly looked to the deckhand, but he shook his head. "I ain't calling no police."

She turned to a pair of passing fishermen for help. They stopped to watch the fight and took the moment to light their pipes.

"Fight!" Neilly cried at them. They puffed on their pipes and nodded, admitting to their mild interest.

Frustrated, Neilly turned back to see the three men who had brought their fray onto the levee. She winced as Bruno landed a blow on the side of Damon's head. But Damon swung back, landing several blows in Bruno's gut. To Neilly's surprise the big man went down on his knees. But Charles was on Damon in an instant. Clutching his belly, Bruno scrambled to his feet and fell on Damon, too. She had to do something.

"Help!" Neilly cried, desperate now. Damon would do fine against one opponent, but he didn't stand a chance against two.

"Have you no shame?" Neilly goaded the pipe-smoking fishermen.

The two had lost interest in their pipes now and were watching with more enthusiasm.

"Two against one," Neilly railed at them, so angry she was jumping up and down. "That's not a fair fight. Have you no honor?"

"Two against one, huh?" one of them said. He consulted with his partner, who seemed to agree. "No, that ain't fair."

The two stuck their pipes in their belts and waded into the fray. On the way, one called to their fellows on the fishing boat down the way.

"Yes," Neilly cried, relieved to see help of any kind on the way. She saw a scrawny sailor ram his shoulder into Bruno's ribs. Bruno "rumphed" and fell over backward.

From behind she heard other voices. She turned to see hands from the steamboat run down the gangplank and dive into the brawl. The growing din—shouts, curses, and cries of pain—brought more onlookers.

A crowd of men gathered on the edge of the fight and began to exchange wagers. Then another few joined the fracas. Neilly found herself ducking wild punches in the midst of a noisy brawl. She'd lost sight of Damon. Around her stranger slugged stranger. For all she could tell, they just fought for the sake of fighting.

She scurried to the edge of the brawl, looking for Damon or Charles among the writhing mass of arms and legs. Where she found one, she knew she'd find the other. She scampered one way along the edge of the fray, then the other, until she spotted them—locked in combat and rolling on packed sand.

She stepped back from the chaos, considering the best way to stop them. Her foot stubbed against a bucket full of some dark liquid. In the torchlight it was difficult to tell if it was oil or water or molasses.

From the marketplace beyond the levee Neilly heard the shrill of a police whistle. On second thought she realized she had no desire to face the authorities, let alone Charles again.

Neilly decided any liquid would do. She grabbed the

bucket and scurried toward the brawling crowd. She took careful aim at Damon and Charles. With the practiced swing of a veteran housekeeper, she showered them with the contents of the bucket—fish heads.

Stink filled the air. A potent invisible cloud engulfed the fighters, a cloud so strong, the men near Charles and Damon lurched away and began to gag.

Others clamped hands over their noses. Many fighters surged away down the levee toward fresh air. Damon and Charles rolled apart, each of them choking and wiping fish heads and slime from their eyes and faces.

"What the—?" Damon crawled to his feet, brushing muck from his clothes. Water and scales dripped from his hands and his hair. "Who in the hell—?"

Neilly threw down the bucket and grabbed his slime-covered hand. "Let's go."

Damon blinked at her. "Where?"

"Let's just go, Damon," Neilly urged, watching Charles's manservant hurry to his master's rescue. Bruno was nowhere in sight. "Do you want to try to explain all of this to the police?"

Damon followed her gaze to Charles and his servant. The shrill whistle of the police echoed again, closer this time.

"Let's go," he said, and prodded her up the levee and toward the safety of the street below.

Nineteen

"You lied to me *again*, Neilly," Damon ranted, his head nearly touching the low beams of Mrs. Robards's laundry house. He paused just long enough to dredge a fish head from his coat pocket; then he leaned over the smooth clothes-folding table and glared at Neilly. She noted with concern the bloody cut over his brow and the swollen bruise on his lower lip. "I told you no more lies between us, and you just kept telling them anyway."

"I did not." Neilly lifted her chin, too proud to allow him to call her a liar when she wasn't. "Not exactly. You asked if Papa had stolen *money* for the trip, and I said yes. He did take the painting to get the money."

"That's shaving the point, Neilly, and you know it," Damon said. "And you didn't explain what Ruffin wanted from you either."

"Off with your pants, Mr. Durande," Mrs. Robards interrupted. The landlady stood beside a copper tub full of steaming water. She had welcomed them into her boarding-house with a look of relief and open arms—and no apparent guilt about taking Ruffin's money. "I don't care who lied to whom. I just know that you stink to high heaven, sir, and I want that fishy smell out of my laundry. The sooner the better!"

With a grin and a chuckle, Regis lifted another bucket of hot water off the stove and poured it into the tub.

Damon glowered reproachfully at Neilly and reached for his belt.

She decided this was not the time to argue with him. "You'd better take your bath."

She turned away from the stove, where she'd been helping Regis heat water, ducked under a clothesline, and headed for the door.

"Don't go anywhere, Neilly. This isn't settled yet."

She halted, her back still to him. "I can't very well argue with a naked man, now can I?"

"I'll fix that." Mrs. Robards swiped a sheet from the shelf and hung it over one of the clotheslines crisscrossing the room, separating Neilly from Damon and the tub. "There. I think you two had better air your differences."

"I agree," Damon said. Neilly heard the clank of his belt buckle.

"Keep talking and give me those clothes," Mrs. Robards said. "My back is turned."

Neilly could hear Damon shrugging out of his rank clothes. She didn't need to see him to know how the muscled contours of his chest glistened in the lamplight, his arms flexed hard and round as he shed his shirt. But she couldn't quite bring herself to picture the rest of him, lower down, though she wanted to. She only had the memories of her explorations in the dark cellar to know how the rest of him looked.

He didn't seem the least embarrassed about stripping down in front of Mrs. Robards, who'd become matronly and domestic. The landlady handed each piece of clothing—coat, waistcoat, shirt, pants—over the sheet to Neilly.

"Burn them," she ordered.

"Can't you just wash them?" Damon asked.

"There's no saving these garments, Mr. Durande," Mrs. Robards declared. "I'll send Regis to your hotel for fresh things."

With delicacy, to keep the smell from rubbing off on her

clean nightgown, Neilly fed each stinking garment, even Damon's drawers, into the fire.

Behind her, she heard water slap against the sides of the tub as Damon eased himself down into the soapy bath.

"Lord, this hot water feels good," Damon said. She could hear the slosh as he leaned back in the tub. "You know, Neilly, it really wasn't necessary to throw the bucket of fish guts on us. I would have had the best of Ruffin in just another couple of minutes."

That wasn't how it had appeared to Neilly at the time, but she refrained from saying so. "I apologize for any inconvenience," Neilly quipped, annoyed with his assertion. She turned from the stove to find Mrs. Robards holding Damon's fringed boots over the sheet.

"Burn these too, dear," the landlady whispered.

Neilly stared at the boots, the ones Damon had worn with such pride and stubborn independence to The Laurels barbecue. At the soft soles that enabled him to move silently. She fingered the smelly Indian-style fringe that defied the expensive good taste of all the planters. At the moment, the offer to burn them seemed too good to be true. Too tempting for even a saint to resist. Neilly grabbed them.

"No, not my Texas boots!" Water sloshed again. Over the sheet, Neilly glimpsed Damon rising from the tub—an angry Neptune emerging from the stormy sea.

She threw open the stove grate and lobbed the slimy boots into the roaring flames.

"Especially your boots, Mr. Durande," Mrs. Robards said, not the least perturbed by Damon's naked protest. "New Orleans is full of fine bootmakers. I'm sure tomorrow any number of them would be glad to see you well shod."

Damon cursed under his breath. Water splashed against the tub again as he sank into it once more.

"Now, can I get you a glass of claret to enjoy with your soak?" the landlady offered, as if she entertained men in the bath frequently. "My late husband always enjoyed a good glass of spirits with his bath."

Damon was silent for a moment. Neilly knew he was seething over the loss of his boots, but she didn't care. Maybe he would forget about Charles's accusations and her half truths if he had something else to vex him.

"No claret," Damon said finally, the words more growled than spoken. "I don't suppose you have any cigars?"

"Heavens no! I buried them with my dear husband. They're the only thing that stinks worse than fish heads."

Neilly peeked over the sheet to see Damon shaking his head, all the while muttering something to the water about crazy women, burned boots, and the sin of burying good cigars.

When he caught her looking at him he glared back. "I won't forget your part in the demise of my boots."

"Honestly, they were beyond help."

"Umph," was his only response. He seemed already preoccupied with another matter. "Can you at least provide me with a room for tonight, Mrs. Robards?"

Mrs. Robards clasped her hands before her in an attitude of piety. "This is a respectable boardinghouse, Mr. Durande."

"I know that," Damon said. Neilly could hear him lathering up the soap on his skin. "But suppose Mr. Ruffin should return tonight? Not to mention the fact, how am I to get back to the hotel when you just burned my clothes and boots? It's a little late to send Regis out, don't you think?"

Mrs. Robards's mouth formed an o. "I see what you mean."

"Of course, I'm prepared to compensate you generously for the inconvenience of having a man under your roof."

"Well, I suppose, in light of the unusual circumstances, you can stay in the room upstairs, over the laundry," Mrs.

Robards said, with a speculative glance in Neilly's direction. "I believe it's prepared."

"Thank you, Mrs. Robards," Damon said, flashing the landlady that charming lopsided grin of his. He had charm to offer every woman he met except her, it seemed to Neilly.

Mrs. Robards simpered. "Well, you and Cornelia have a lot to talk about."

She and Regis left the laundry, closing the door on them. Neilly reached for the cape she'd draped over a chair while she'd helped with the water. "Well, I'd better be going, too."

"You're not going anywhere until we talk about this," Damon said, his tone forbidding her to object. "I found the story Ruffin told very interesting. His version made a lot of things fall into place."

"I was afraid it might." The laundry suddenly seemed too warm and close to Neilly. She opened the window shutters, but the breeze did not soothe her much.

"Tell me again why you came to Rosewood," Damon said.

"Because Rosewood's collection is legendary," Neilly said, resigning herself to telling the story she knew he wouldn't believe. "All I wanted to do was see the works your grandfather had collected. Besides that, I needed the job to pay off the court settlement. Your aunts are known to be somewhat reclusive, so I knew I'd be safe from Charles."

"Rosewood was a place to hide?" Damon said, his voice quiet, matter of fact, almost sympathetic. Then he added, "But things are missing from Rosewood, Neilly. Dueling pistols and vases."

"But, I didn't take them," Neilly vowed. "You saw my luggage. I took just what I brought with me. I didn't take any of the dresses I couldn't pay for."

He was silent.

She went on, "See why I was afraid for you to know the truth? It's too easy to make me the culprit."

"Did you paint the forgery left in Ruffin's house?"

"That's exactly what Charles wanted you to think," Neilly said. "And you're playing right into his hands."

"Well, did you paint it?"

"No, I did not paint the forgery they found in Ruffin's house," Neilly asserted, a little too loudly. "Oils have never been my medium. I don't know where Papa got the copy. He never told me anything about it. We weren't working a confidence scheme on all the wealthy families, either. Why would you rather believe him than me?"

Neilly could hear Damon climbing out of the tub.

"The towels are on the table," she said, gathering up her cloak again. "I'm going to bed."

She reached for the door latch.

"You're not going anywhere." Damon's hand locked around Neilly's. Dripping wet and wrapped in only a towel, he loomed over her. Every fiber of her tingled to life with his powerful nearness. He stood so close, she could feel the heat of the dripping hot water against her skin.

"I meant what I said about Ruffin returning. I'm not letting you out of my sight again tonight."

"But Mrs. Robards—?"

"I think Mrs. Robards understands perfectly well," Damon said, leading Neilly back into the room with him, away from the door. "We're staying in the room upstairs. No one will know we're there except her and Regis."

"Is it Charles you're really concerned about?" Neilly asked. "Or are you just making certain I don't leave?"

"Some of both," Damon said. Neilly's anger with his lack of trust flared again. "You're going back to Rosewood with me tomorrow to make Aunt Isetta happy, if nothing else. And you'll stay until we discover where the missing items have gone. And you're going to repay me for my boots."

"I'll repay you for your boots and the dresses and the

debt to Charles," Neilly conceded, still too hurt and angry to let him steer her away from the issue. "But you said you believed in me. You said that you knew all you needed to know to believe in me."

"That's before I had Ruffin's version of the story to compare with yours."

"No, it was before you knew anything of my story," Neilly corrected him, her anger winning out. She turned the full blast of it on him. "It was when you knew me only from your own experience. You knew I loved your aunts and Rosewood and would never do anything to harm them. You believed in that. Damon, you believed in me."

"I still want to believe in you," Damon said, his voice soft and husky. "But you are not making it very easy. Every time I ask you to tell me the truth you lie."

"But the truth leads you to all the wrong conclusions." Neilly purposely turned away. She wanted to erect a cold wall between them, a wall that would shut out all her feelings for him, protect her heart, and abolish her yearnings. But there was no wall. Damon stood so near, the heat of his bare skin burned into hers. She longed for him to touch her, to feel the strength of his hands on her shoulders.

But she knew his touch could not brush away the lies that stood between them. "If I had told you the truth about Father, about how he had stolen artwork from the Ruffins, you would have decided that I had come to Rosewood to do the same thing."

Damon remained silent. Still wrapped in only a towel, he made no effort to move away. Neilly dared not look at him, for fear she'd betray her longing for his understanding—for the acceptance and the excitement of his naked embrace.

"You see, that's why I kept the truth from you." Neilly tucked her trembling hands beneath the cape she carried.

"I see what you're getting at," he said, leaning over her to whisper the dismissive words into her ear. His breath tingled along her neck. "I don't want to talk down here in the laundry room anymore."

He took her hand in a firm, warm grip, too strong to be resisted. While she'd truly feared Charles, she didn't believe for a moment that Damon would harm her. But his mood had become frighteningly unreadable. He picked up the candle on the table and started for the stairs.

His naked feet padded soundlessly on the steps. Neilly followed, confused. "I don't see how talking upstairs is going to change anything."

"It'll be safer there, and no one will overhear us."

With a jolt she realized he was going to force her to stay with him. While she'd longed—even dreamed—of experiencing intimacy with him again, she wasn't certain this was the time or place to renew their physical relationship. "Just what is it you want from me?"

"The truth, Neilly," he said, without turning to look at her or loosening his grip on her hand. "That's all I've ever asked."

He ushered her into the room, closed the door, and turned the key in the lock.

"Are you locking out Charles or locking me in?" Neilly asked, unable to keep the bitterness from her voice.

"What I want is to lock out the whole world," Damon said and turned to her.

Unable to wait any longer, Damon tossed the key aside and pulled Neilly into his arms, as he'd wanted to do since they'd faced each other on the banquette.

To his satisfaction, she only held back for an instant; out of surprise, he supposed. Then she came to him with her face upturned, her lips moist and inviting. He kissed her deeply, savoring her warmth. Then she was kissing him in return, every bit as willing and responsive as she had been in the cellar.

She slipped her arms around his neck and pressed herself against him. Her tongue teased his with tempting eagerness and considerably more confidence than during their first encounter.

Damon groaned with pleasure and slid his hands down her sides and up the sweet curve of her tapering back.

When he released her they both gasped for air. Damon put a finger under her chin and peered into her face.

"One last time, darlin'," he said. "Is there anything more I should know? Have you told me everything?"

"Everything." She looked up into his eyes and nodded. "You know the whole story. I swear."

Damon couldn't resist smiling as relief washed through him. His arms tightened around her. Then he saw the dark spot on her jaw. When he drew his finger across it lightly she winced. "Damn Ruffin. He hit you, while you were tied, of course."

Dark thoughts stirred, bringing things to mind that he didn't even want to acknowledge. "What else, Neilly? What else did that bastard do?"

"He was rough enough to frighten me, Damon; that's all," Neilly said. She laid her head against his chest, hiding her face. "Honestly, I just want to forget about Charles."

Damon wanted to strangle the man. Instead he lifted her face to his to kiss her again, tenderly. "Then we'll do our best to forget about him."

Slipping his hands down the soft length of her body, he decided it wasn't that difficult to forget about Ruffin. Only a thin linen towel separated them. Cupping her bottom to press her closer, he savored her mouth. He relished the roundness of her in his hands and the pressure of her belly against his arousal.

He had no intention of letting his lust get the better of him this time. Neilly deserved better than he'd given her in the cellar. Tonight he intended to make real love to her.

Suddenly, she pulled her arms from around his neck and

brushed them down along his ribs. The feathery sensation, coupled with the soreness in his muscles, made Damon draw a sharp breath.

Neilly frowned. "You're sore from the fight. Maybe this isn't the time for us to . . ."

"This is the time," Damon said quickly, lest she get the wrong idea. "Believe me, darlin', this is the time. And I don't want anything between us, nothing. No lies."

"No lies," she agreed.

"No petticoats or drawers. No nightgowns."

"No nightgown?" she repeated, wide-eyed. "Nothing?"

"Not a shred of anything between us," Damon said, "but the truth."

"Not even a towel?" she asked, a look of seduction stealing into her smile.

Damon laughed softly. He liked her style: sweet, frank, and alluring. He dropped the towel to the floor. Without giving her time to appraise him, he untied the ribbons of her gown and began to pull it up over her hips. Neilly lifted her arms to help. At first the gown came off easily. Damon gathered an amazing amount of fabric in his hands. When he was about to pull the last of it over her head, baring her skin to his touch, the fabric snagged on something and ripped.

The sound stopped Damon.

"It's caught on a comb in my hair," Neilly explained.

Through the gauzy cotton, he watched her search for the comb. Suddenly, the gown fell free. He threw it to the floor.

"Good riddance." Damon slipped his hands under her bottom and lifted her up until her breasts, already swollen and taut, nearly reached his mouth.

"Open up, darlin', and wrap you legs around me." She did as he urged, her thatch tickling his belly and her heat rubbing moist against his skin.

Wrapping her arms around his neck, she offered her breast to him and crooned encouragement that he didn't need. His mouth closed over the bud, teasing it into a taut hardness that made Neilly moan and pull at his hair. She arched against him. His own excitement grew dangerously close to the edge of control. The need to bury himself inside her was overpowering.

He carried her to the narrow bed. Beneath a canopy of mosquito netting nubby with frequent darning, he sat down with her straddling his lap.

He kissed the earlobe that seemed so near and so tantalizing. She offered her throat and he indulged himself in tasting her fragile collarbone, first one side, then the other—warm and delicate and scented with Neilly. She shivered under his lips.

"This time we have all night, darlin'." He stroked Neilly's thick, dark curls away from her face, enjoying the silky tickle of her tresses between his fingers and against his shoulder.

But the heat of her burned against his thighs, driving him mad. He slipped his hands beneath her and lifted her to suckle her breasts once more. He ached for the sweet relief her body offered. Still, he hesitated to lower her onto him.

"Yes," she whispered, trust in her eyes, tenderness in her touch when she caressed his shoulder. He eased her down.

Just as he had thought, she was ready for him. Her body, satiny and moist, accepted him, slipping down over him inch by delicious inch.

A groan of pleasure escaped Damon. He looked into her face. In the soft candlelight her skin glowed white. Her dark lashes lay against her cheek and her lips were parted. She was as lost in the satisfaction of coming together as he.

Damon lay back on the bed and stroked Neilly's thighs. "Move, darlin'."

Her breasts swayed as she responded to his direction. Damon grasped her around the waist, helping her find the rhythm that grew between them and in them. He lost himself in stroking her deeply, savoring the pressure of her satiny warmth clutching at his aching shaft.

The vision of her above him, her face betraying a passion as intense and burning as his, strained his control. But he clung to it, taking pleasure in the consuming torment that grew and spread through him with each intimate stroke. A man tortured this way could die happy, he thought. When her spasms began he tightened his grasp on her waist and deepened his thrust. With her gasp of pleasure and the clutch of her body came his release. The excruciating joy wrung a cry from him.

Neilly sank down onto his chest, her sighs tickling his chest hair. He wrapped his arms around her and watched a bashful smile play on her lips. Sharing herself with a man was still new to her, he reminded himself.

"Now you know *everything*," she whispered against his chest.

Damon tensed. "What's that?"

"When I'm with you I turn into a wanton."

Damon laughed and kissed the top of her head. "I'm glad you saved that revelation for me."

Her shuddering sigh of satisfaction was incredibly sweet.

They crawled the rest of the way into bed and slept briefly. Damon awoke with Neilly spreading her hand across his chest and combing her fingers up through his crisp curls, teasing him with a new sensation.

"You're right; it's better without clothes." With her fingertips she traced the cut over his brow, and when she touched the split in his lip he winced. "Did it hurt when we kissed?"

"Not a bit," Damon lied. "Promise me something, Neilly."

"Anything."

"You'll never lie to me again. Not about anything important."

"I promise." Neilly silenced him with a light kiss on his bruised lip.

Summer heat lightning brightened the room for an instant, and a new moist breeze brought the scent of rain with it. The candle flame died. The tattered mosquito netting canopy fluttered above them. Damon realized that the moon was gone and a storm was building. The silent lightning flashed again, lighting Neilly's naked body lying against him. He lifted her face to his and rained kisses across her face as he slid his hand down her body and between her legs.

He caressed her thighs until they parted for him. Then he sought the warmth hidden in the petals of her womanhood. She caught her breath when his fingers invaded her, but she clung to him. When she gasped he knew he'd found the secret, sensitive bud that he sought. He caressed it. She melted in his arms, opening for him, not in invitation but in surrender. "It is good, isn't it? he asked. "Tell me."

Neilly's only response was a whimper.

Damon rose over her and entered her, holding back the urge to take her in one magnificent thrust. Even though she was willing, he didn't feel she was ready for raw passion yet. He eased into her little by heavenly little, losing a bit of himself each time he penetrated deeper and deeper. At last he was buried in her hot passage.

A momentary fear of vulnerability lanced through him— a fear that had never troubled him with any other woman. Neilly moved urgently beneath him. Damon responded, forcing himself to loosen his grip on his need for her, allowing her to possess him in a way he'd allowed no other woman.

He urged her to lose herself with him in the carnal dance. She did, her movements drawing him deeper into her embrace. At last Neilly shuddered and cried out in her release. Damon shed his shadowy fear and gave into his own surrender. Amid the sweet, soaring climax he shared with Neilly, he knew he was bound to her forever.

Damon drifted with Neilly in his arms. He wondered at how much more comfortable a narrow cot shared with her was than his big, solitary feather bed at Rosewood. He slid his hand across her belly and spread his fingers across the place where a child would grow.

"Neilly?"

"Ummm." She was half asleep already, cuddled close, smelling of lilacs and musk.

"We've been together before," Damon began, wondering how she was going to react to his words. "You could be with child."

"But I'm not." She stirred, snuggling closer into the shelter of his body. Her eyes never opened.

"Are you certain?"

"Yes, certain," she murmured, nearly asleep again.

Until tonight, Damon almost said aloud, but didn't. Why trouble her with the thought? But the prospect of Neilly carrying his child had intrigued him from the first moment it had come into his head at Rosewood when she'd left them.

The vision of Neilly's curly dark-haired, blue-eyed sons and daughters dancing around the Christmas tree in Rosewood's hallway threw a new, tempting light on fatherhood—on marriage.

He'd never intended to be a papa. He hardly remembered his own father, and his grandfather had refused to have him under the same roof. He didn't know the first thing about how to be a good father. But if he ever became one, he'd never turn his back on his children. Never.

He drifted again, drowsy but unable to fall asleep. His body was sated but his heart still troubled. Although he couldn't condemn Neilly for hiding incriminating facts, he wished he could be certain that he knew everything—knew the entire truth. He wished he knew who was stealing from Rosewood.

He touched the dark bruise on her cheek. She sighed and slipped an arm around his waist. Whatever questionable scheme she'd been mixed up in, he felt certain he could learn how to live with it—as long as she told the truth. As long as she returned to Rosewood with him.

Neilly awoke slowly from a dreamless sleep, too sluggish to move at first, but aware that Damon was missing from the bed beside her.

Hushed voices caught her ear; then she heard the door close softly. The sounds of paper being folded and the ring of hard-soled boots on the floor reached her ears. A little alarmed by that unexpected sound, she rolled over to find Damon peering down at her through the mosquito netting. He was fully dressed in a snowy white shirt with a cravat, blue coat, and gray trousers.

"Wake up, slugabed." He grinned uncertainly, looking every bit as good this morning as he had the day before, when he'd chased her down through the market. Memories of the fight with Charles and their night together stirred a thrill in her belly. She smiled back at Damon, wondering vaguely how lovers treated each other in the morning.

Damon planted one foot on the bedframe for her to admire. "What do you think?"

Neilly blinked and sat up, staring at the shiny black Hessian boot that clung to his strong, elegant calf. "They're very nice. But do you like them?"

"I liked my old ones better," Damon said, regarding his new boots with reservation.

"Well, they look very—refined." Neilly couldn't help smiling at him even more broadly. As good as Damon looked in the boots, she couldn't quite imagine him wearing fashionable Hessians for long. The rigid, hard leather soles didn't seem to fit his temperament.

"But that's not all, darlin'," Damon said, reaching for the

parcel on the table. "I have something for you." He ripped
open the tissue wrapping. "To replace the gown we ripped
last night."

"But where? How? You didn't send out Mrs. Robards for
a gown? Damon, this is hardly proper."

"No, of course I didn't send Mrs. Robards." Damon
shook his head. "The dear lady loaned me some of her
husband's clothes, so I've been out shopping already. I
bought this in a shop near the hotel. The silk made me
think of your skin. Of your thighs, to be exact."

Heat flooded into Neilly's cheeks. If she remembered correctly, Damon had awakened her during the night and they'd
made love one more time. He'd kissed the insides of her
thighs until he nearly drove her insane with the desire to
feel him inside her again. And when he had come inside
of her she'd thought she was going to die of the pleasure.

Tossing aside the tissue, Damon parted the mosquito netting and sat down on the edge of the bed, holding up the
ivory, lace-trimmed gown for her approval. "Those sweet,
sensitive thighs of yours should be covered by only the best
silk."

"You're embarrassing me," she scolded halfheartedly as
she admired the sheer gown.

"It's too late to be embarrassed." Damon placed a brief
kiss on her mouth, a cool distracted kiss; then he rose from
the bed, leaving the garment in her hands. "You needed a
new gown anyway."

In silence he paced the barren chamber restlessly, as if
the night and the nightgown were already forgotten. Neilly
watched him uneasily.

"Get dressed and pack your things," he instructed, staring
out the window. "I need to meet with my agent to give him
instructions about the bank draft for Ruffin, and about selecting a new accountant for Rosewood, before we leave
this afternoon."

"You won't have to see Charles, will you?" Neilly asked,

dismayed by Damon's sudden coolness. She gathered the bedsheets closer, feeling a distinct coolness settle over her—along with a sense of shame.

Last night she'd thought he shared her feelings and she'd given her heart to him without even thinking about what would come next. In the light of morning she sensed she might not like what lay ahead of her.

"My agent should be able to handle Charles, as well as notifying the authorities that need notifying," Damon said. "When we leave New Orleans today you will no longer owe the Ruffins anything." Damon turned from the window.

"And I will owe you instead," she said, feeling the need to complete the thought he'd left hanging unsaid in the morning air.

She pulled the sheet closer, wishing she'd had an opportunity to dress and a moment to prepare herself for this discussion of business matters. With great effort, she marshaled her thoughts and her pride into order. "Make no mistake, Damon. I'm grateful for your help. I view this as a loan, and I will certainly pay it off at the earliest opportunity."

"I expect no less," Damon said, regarding her from the window, his gaze as dark and inscrutable as that of a stranger. "You said Ashleys always honor their debts. So there is no question about you returning with me. You will be working off the loan. Your duties will be the same as they were before. We are in agreement?"

"Yes, of course," Neilly snapped, despite the rebellion and the hurt churning inside her.

When they'd talked of returning to Rosewood yesterday she'd truly wanted to go. She longed to see Isetta and Varina, to sit in the rose garden and to walk through the entry hall jungle once more. But in the light of morning her enthusiasm dwindled.

Her joy in finding happiness with Damon evaporated.

"So, we're going to treat last night just like our tryst in the cellar? We'll forget that any of it happened?"

"Oh, no, I'm not forgetting anything, Neilly," Damon said, speaking cautiously and folding his arms across his chest. Neilly studied him carefully. He had retreated behind that unreadable expression of his again. "But I don't intend to speak of what is between us until other things are settled."

"Such as Isetta's health and my debt," she prompted.

"Among other things," Damon replied, obviously unwilling to share with her exactly what was on his mind.

"And the thief?" she asked. The slight hardening around his mouth told her all she needed to know. "You don't believe me when I say I've had nothing to do with the missing things."

"I believe you've never meant my aunts any harm." He reached for her cloak. "Let's go. I'll escort you to your room. After you're dressed and packed we'll be on our way."

With a sinking heart, Neilly wondered if he had believed in what they'd shared during the night. For a moment she thought of asking him, then she decided not to. She couldn't bear to hear him attempt to placate her with some silly answer.

She'd given of herself because she loved him, and that would have to be good enough. "I can manage on my own, thank you. If you don't mind leaving the room—"

"I prefer no further delays." Damon held up the cape.

Annoyed, but certain that arguing would only be a waste of energy, Neilly tucked the silk gown under her arm and tightened the sheet around her. She stepped out of the bed into the protection of the old cloak that Damon wrapped around her.

Twenty

Sunlight streamed through the window of the quarters cabin at Rosewood, providing good light for Theo McGregor to stitch by.

"This is a pretty nasty injury," he said, tying the last suture in the long, ragged gash in Elijah's left arm. The carpenter hadn't so much as winced while Theo had sewn eleven tight stitches in the deep cut.

Without being asked, Isetta handed him the scissors to cut the thread. She had insisted on leaving her room to accompany Theo to treat Elijah. Theo had permitted the outing only because Isetta had always taken satisfaction in seeing to the welfare of her people. Besides that, he thought the fresh air and exercise would do her good.

"Will it keep him from working, Doctor?" Alma sat at Elijah's side, her pretty high brow puckered in concern.

"Nothing's going to keep me from working, baby," Elijah said, reassuring her with a smile. "Don't you worry none neither, Miss Isetta. I'll finish that arbor for Miss Varina. Ol' Elijah has worked with cuts on his arms before. On his fingers and toes."

"I'm not worried about that," Isetta said.

"I think you'd better take it a wee bit easy with this injury, Elijah," Theo warned, eyeing Alma. He'd heard that Elijah was trying to buy Alma's freedom, but Theo had his reservations about the girl. For all her airs and refinements, there was something willful and grasping about her. He wondered if Alma was good enough for the hardworking carpenter. "Keep the wound clean and let Miss Isetta know at the first sign of infection."

"This should have a fresh dressing every day, shouldn't it, Theo?" Isetta asked.

Theo nodded, pleased to see her taking charge as she used to do.

"You come to the house tomorrow, Elijah, and Varina or I will see to dressing that properly, you hear," Isetta instructed, shaking a bony finger at Elijah. "We can't let that injury get infected and hold back the best carpenter in Louisiana."

"Yeas um," Elijah said. "I don't want this to hold me back neither."

He grinned at Alma, and she gave him a dazzling smile in return. Theo suspected the exchange meant that completion of the commission Elijah had taken for the doors of a New Orleans church would bring the money needed to buy Alma's freedom. He hoped Elijah knew what he was doing. She was a comely thing, but Theo suspected that with her maneuvering ways she was going to break the heart of every man who sought her favor.

"Well, I believe that takes care of everyone we needed to see today." Theo gathered up his needles, scissors, and suture thread and closed up his doctor bag.

"I believe it does," Isetta said, taking up her cane.

She remained silent until they were outside Elijah's cabin and out of earshot. Then she started in on Theo.

"I can see it in your face," she began as they walked toward the house. The deep shade of the path offered a cool respite after sitting in the sunlight to work. They strolled along, taking their time. "What have you heard, Theo?"

He shook his head. Isetta had always been able to read him like a book. "I donna think it means anything, lass."

"I'll decide that. Out with it."

"I was called to set a leg over at Esterbrooks' yesterday,"

Theo began. "A mule kicked the poor fellow. Snapped the leg just—"

"Theo, get to the point."

"The word over there is that Alma has another man."

"What? Who?" Isetta stopped and faced Theo. "No, let me guess. The blacksmith? He's the envy of every plantation owner in the parish."

"He's working himself into an early grave to buy his own freedom and Alma's," Theo said.

Isetta muttered an unladylike oath. "I can't say as I'm surprised. Violet Esterbrook sets great store by Alma, but I always had some doubts about the girl's character."

As always, Theo overlooked Isetta's cursing. "Elijah is a grown man, and free. He can do with his life as he pleases."

"But we can't just stand by and let him waste his efforts on some little—strumpet," Isetta said, outrage glinting in her eyes. "She'll break his heart. You saw him. He loves her."

Theo said nothing, leaving his silence to suggest agreement.

"Are men always such fools for love?" Isetta asked.

He studied her for a long moment. Her color was high and her voice strong. Her stride betrayed too much energy for her to truly need the cane she insisted on carrying. Her heart ailment was certainly one of the strangest conditions he'd ever seen.

Isetta met his searching gaze. Then she let her own slide away, as if she was afraid of betraying more than she cared to reveal. "Well, are they?"

"Aye, I'm afraid love makes blind fools of men," Theo admitted. "And more often than they care to admit, I suspect."

"Do you think Elijah has any idea about the other man?"

"I think he only knows that he loves her, and he thinks she loves him."

"What's her game?" Isetta asked. "Do you think she's going to take whichever man buys her freedom first?"

"I suppose that's the plan," Theo said with a shrug.

Isetta stepped out with more spirit this time. "We could tell Cleo, and she could whisper it to Mammy Lula, who would make certain that the word got to Elijah."

"They probably all know about Alma already," Theo said. "You know how they gossip back and forth between plantations. They may have tried to talk to Elijah, and he's closed his ears to anyone who tells him bad things about the woman he loves. On the other hand, knowing about another man might only make him do something foolish, like pushing his work too hard and risking another injury."

"I suppose you're right," Isetta said, plainly disgusted to be powerless in the situation.

During the silence that followed, Theo decided to change the subject. "What do you hear from Damon?"

"Nothing." Exasperation filled her one word. "He's been gone nearly a week."

"A week isna so long, lass," Theo said.

"It's an eternity if you have Arthur Sitwell and his son underfoot. And yesterday Arthur came home with that art agent, John Minor."

Theo nodded in sympathy. Isetta had never liked Mirabelle's son, nor his friends. Damon was the apple of her eye. Theo had to admit, between the two men, he'd much rather spend an evening with Damon than Arthur. "You know, if I didna know better, I'd almost think your strength has returned just to spite Arthur."

"It has," Isetta said, no deception in her voice. "Every time I see him and—now that art dealer is helping—they reckon up the value of piece after piece of Papa's collection. I just get stronger."

"If I'd known that's what you needed, I woulda written Arthur myself after your first attack," Theo said with a chuckle. "Has he said more about your will?"

"Nothing since the incident in the garden."

They had reached the edge of Rosewood's garden and

now they saw Varina come out of the drawing-room door. She waved to them.

"Varina seems better today," Theo commented. "I was a wee bit troubled by her hysteria the other evening."

"And Uncle Cato's, too," Isetta added. "You know, neither of them will leave the house after dark now."

"What has Arthur had to say about the sighting?"

"Very little. That is strange for Arthur, isn't it?"

Theo said nothing more as they neared the house. If Arthur had any intelligence, he'd mind his tongue for the sake of Isetta's health. If anything happened to Izzie, Rosewood would go to Damon. Though she looked more vital than she had in weeks, Theo still worried. Doctors knew the heart was a fragile organ, delicate and unpredictable. Relapse was always a possibility.

Damon reached for Neilly's arm, steadying her on the wobbly gangplank. "Have a care, darlin'. Don't fall into the river so I have to explain why I brought you home soaking wet."

"I was just trying to get a good look at Rosewood." A wistful smile touched Neilly's lips. "It has always seemed like hom—"

She paused, blinking away her smile, as if she was afraid she'd betrayed herself. "I mean, Rosewood has always seemed a special place."

Her admission eased Damon's conscience. He wasn't proud of using her indebtedness to him to ensure her return. He'd been secretly relieved that she'd consented to come back to Rosewood with so little argument. If her pride had turned her stubborn, he might have been forced to use Ruffin's tactics—kidnapping.

"I always like to get that first glimpse, too," Damon admitted. "I happen to know you can't see the house from here. We'll be able to get a good look from the top of the riverbank."

"I thought you always hated Rosewood," she said, attempting to withdraw her hand from his. He resisted letting her go.

"Oh, no. When I was a boy I couldn't think of leaving Rosewood even for the bright fun of New Orleans."

"Then when did you start to hate it?" Neilly asked, genuine curiosity in her eyes.

"Later."

"After your grandfather ordered you out of the house?"

"Yes, after that," Damon said, trying to recall just when the sight of the house had begun to offend him. It hadn't happened overnight, but had grown over time. As he'd matured, he'd come to understand the depth and harshness of his grandfather's decision, despite Isetta and Varina's love and kindness. He'd been turned out by his grandfather. He didn't belong at Rosewood and never would.

Behind them, the packet's deckhands unloaded Neilly's luggage and the crates destined for Rosewood. Three of Mammy Lula's kitchen girls appeared on the wagon track at the top of the bank. They had come to pick up the food supplies ordered from downriver. Surprised, they waved to Damon and Neilly, who waved back. Then one of them turned and disappeared.

"They'll be expecting us at the house," Damon said. "I hope everything is all right."

"Yes, me, too," Neilly said, starting up the track. "Assuming all is well, what are we going to tell your aunts and Dr. McGregor?"

"I don't see any reason to tell them anything, except that your cousin has recovered from her illness and you've agreed to return to continue with your attendance on Aunt Isetta."

"We're not going to tell them the truth?" Neilly asked, reproach in the arch of her brow.

"Don't give me trouble over this, Neilly," Damon warned. "They are only vaguely aware that something is amiss, and I don't want either Isetta or Varina alarmed."

"I understand," Neilly said. "Really, I do. But how are you going to determine who the thief actually is?"

"I'm not sure," Damon said. He released her hand, suddenly unhappy with the intrusion of the unpleasant subject. "Speaking of the thief, what was that about the gargoyles of my mother's that Aunt Varina was talking about."

"The gargoyles?" Neilly stopped in the middle of the path. "I almost forgot about them. That was the strangest thing."

"What? Tell me," Damon urged.

"Well, I found one of a pair," Neilly said. "A lovely, strange little thing carved out of ebony. Miss Varina told me it was one of a pair made by Elijah for your mother."

"Go on."

"I asked Elijah about it, and he confirmed what Miss Varina had said, that there was a pair."

"So?"

"I couldn't find the mate," Neilly said. "Then, one day, there it sat on top of a box of your mother's things I had already inventoried. Damon, I know it wasn't there before."

"What do you think that means?"

"I'm not sure," Neilly said. "At the time I didn't know that there were other things missing."

Damon looked up toward the top of the path. "Here's Pugh, come to pick up the mail."

The accountant stopped in his tracks at the edge of the greenery, apparently surprised to see them.

Behind them, the packet whistle shrilled, echoing across the river. The unloading done, the deckhands shouted and began to crank the gangplank up. Engines thundered. Fire, smoke, and cinders spewed from the twin smokestacks as the stern wheeler pulled away, its paddle wheel churning against the river current.

Amid the noise, everyone on the bank waved to the passengers aboard the packet, heading up the river for other plantations. Passengers at the railing waved back.

"Welcome back to Rosewood," Pugh shouted over the noise, his strange pale eyes hooded. "I'll send someone for your luggage."

"Thank you, Mr. Pugh," Neilly said. Damon noticed that she seemed uncomfortable under the accountant's gaze.

"How are things at the house?"

"As well as can be expected, Mr. Durande," Pugh said, his manner as evasive as always. "It's been rather eventful since you've left, sir. Mr. Sitwell has invited an art dealer to stay at Rosewood to evaluate the works."

"Oh, and who might that be?" Damon frowned, impatient with Pugh's indirectness and eager to know more.

"A Mr. Minor," Pugh said. "He was visiting at The Laurels, and Mr. Sitwell invited him to Rosewood. A very knowledgeable gentleman, from what I hear."

Damon felt Neilly stiffen at his side.

"I'd also like to say that I have the account books all in order, Mr. Durande," Pugh added.

"I'm glad to hear it." Damon took Neilly's arm and escorted her past the accountant. "We'll discuss business later."

"Yes, sir," Pugh said, and made his way down toward the river, where a stack of crates and a mailbag awaited him.

"Does Pugh know you're replacing him?" Neilly asked.

"He knows his position is temporary," Damon said. "I made that clear as soon as I saw the condition of the books. I wonder what's been going on in the house."

"Miss Isetta must be all right," Neilly said, "or Mr. Pugh would have said something."

"That's true," Damon said, but he quickened his step. "But I don't like the idea of John Minor being here."

"Nor do I." Neilly matched his step. Neither of them

could take their eyes off the front door of the house at the end of the drive.

The familiar sight of Rosewood ignited an unexpected spark of joy in Damon. He slowed his stride, amazed by the pleasure the sight of the gracious white house gave him. Neilly slowed, too. He could feel her stealing a quick look up at him. He wondered how plain his feelings were on his face.

"You know, while I was in New Orleans I missed the funniest little things about Rosewood," she said, as they started to walk toward the house once more. "Like the way the sunlight falls through the fan window over the door and brightens the hallway in the mornings."

Damon said nothing. Neilly's admission reminded him of how he'd missed the spacious dining room that always smelled of Mammy Lula's fresh bread. He quickened his step. She hitched up the hem of her skirt and walked faster, too.

"And in the afternoon I missed the coolness of the east gallery where Miss Isetta likes to take her lemonade," Neilly said.

Damon immediately thought of the upstairs gallery that overlooked Aunt Varina's rose garden, where he used to wait in the shadows for Neilly to come out of her room. He lengthened his strides.

"I even missed the library," Neilly said, nearly trotting to keep up with him.

"Yes, the library," Damon agreed, suddenly realizing how glad he was to be coming home. And realizing something more: how pleased he was that Neilly had missed Rosewood, too. Bringing her back was like closing a circle that had been incomplete, only he'd never known that until now.

Neilly smiled up at him—the first smile he'd seen on her face since they'd left New Orleans. She pulled away from his grasp and ran up the steps ahead of him. "Welcome home, sah."

Damon stopped at the foot of the steps and grinned back at her. "Welcome back, Neilly."

Suddenly the front door flew open and Varina rushed out. "Neilly, oh Neilly," she cried, her arms open wide to crush Neilly in her embrace. Cato followed her out onto the porch.

"Damon, I'm so glad to see you," Varina sobbed over Neilly's shoulder. "After the horror of the last few days the sight of you two together is more than I ever hoped for."

"Miss Varina, what is it?" Neilly hugged the lady close. Damon studied his aunt's face, concerned about the dark circles under her eyes. "What's wrong? You look as if you haven't slept in a week."

"Damon, you were right," Varina cried from the security of Neilly's arms. "Papa rolled over in his grave and he's returned to haunt us. I've seen his ghost."

Neilly had no time to admire the wallpaper jungle in the hallway or to savor the sunlight falling through the fan window. She had all she could manage in calming Miss Varina, who sobbed out her terror in her arms.

"Papa came for me in the garden," Varina babbled.

"Exactly what did you see in the garden?" Damon asked.

"No questions now," Neilly pleaded, more concerned about where the smelling salts had gotten to than what had been seen. Varina was nearly hysterical.

"I told Isetta that Papa wouldn't like what she's doing," Varina sobbed.

"I think we'd better talk with Isetta," Damon said, leading the way upstairs.

Neilly agreed. She'd calmed Miss Varina and settled her in the sofa in Isetta's room. Only then did she greet Isetta with a kiss on the lady's cool, dry cheek. She thought Rosewood's mistress, reigning from her sickbed, looked too hail and hearty to play a convincing invalid.

Neilly stood back as Damon greeted his aunt. She noted that the lady's cane leaning against the bedside table sported a grassy clod of mud on its tip.

"Aunt Isetta, I'm glad to see you looking so well." Damon seated himself on a chair next to the sofa. "I hear it's been eventful here at Rosewood since I left. What's happened?"

Neilly turned to see Arthur, Vincent, and Uncle Cato had followed them into Isetta's bedchamber.

"I think Varina must tell the story," Isetta said. "I saw no one. I'd fallen asleep when I heard Varina scream."

"You tell them, Aunt Varina," Arthur commanded.

"Sit down and shut up, Arthur," Damon said, without looking in his cousin's direction.

Neilly sat down beside Varina, took her hands, and patted them, smiling encouragement. "How did it start, dear?"

"It was only the night before last," Varina began. "Uncle Cato, is that right?"

"Yeas um, Miss Varina. Night a' fore last, it was."

"Yes, after dinner. It was a pleasant evening. So I decided to cut the hips off my roses to dry for tea this winter. Rose-hip tea is good for a bad case of the sniffles, you know."

"Yes, I've heard," Neilly said, still patting Varina's hands. "Go on."

"Uncle Cato brought me a glass of lemonade when I got a little heated with the work and all. It was beginning to get dark, but I had one more bush to do and I decided to finish it."

"It was getting awful dark, Miss Varina," Uncle Cato reminded her.

"Yes, Uncle Cato did tell me to come in," Varina said. "But I was almost finished. Then I heard a howling. Whooooo, like that. It makes me shiver now to think of it." Varina stopped, reliving the moment in her mind. Her icy hands had begun to tremble in Neilly's clasp.

"You were still in the garden when you heard this noise?" Damon asked.

"Yes, but I can tell you, I was ready to run right into the house when I heard that howl," Varina said. "But the sound came from between the house and us."

"Did you see anything?" Damon leaned forward, his elbows resting on his knees, a frown of concentration furrowing his brow.

"Oh, it was awful, Damon." Varina's face sagged, becoming a hollow mask.

"Describe it for me."

"It was tall, taller than Papa. Taller than anything I've ever seen," Varina began, her pale blue eyes wide and dark with fear. "Its head nearly brushed through the Spanish moss. Its whiteness shone in the dark as it came toward us. Then it stopped when it saw us."

"It spoke," Cato said, with a rapid nodding of his head.

"It spoke?" Neilly repeated in spite of herself. This sounded like a prank to her.

"Tell them what it said," Arthur said.

Varina glanced uneasily at her sister. "Shall I tell them, Izzie?"

"Why not? You ran to me with the tale quick enough," Isetta said.

"It wailed. It called Isetta's name. 'Izzie. Izzie.' Like that." Varina's lips had become colorless, and Neilly could feel her pulse racing. Varina believed she'd seen a ghost.

"Then what?" Damon asked.

"It said something like 'The will is wrong. The will is wrong,'" Varina said, almost whimpering.

"You see?" Arthur jumped to his feet. "Clearly it's Grandfather's ghost come about your will, Aunt Isetta. Who else would call you Izzie?"

Damon turned on his cousin. "Where were you while all this was going on?"

"If you must know, Vincent was asleep and I was reading in our rooms."

"I fell asleep playing cards on my bedtable," Isetta said, collected as ever.

"What happened after the ghost spoke?" Neilly asked, holding Varina's hand tight in her own. "Where did the ghost go?"

"It went toward the house, we thought," Varina said. "I thought it might go looking for Izzie, but when we got to the gallery it was gone."

"In the morning I went into the garden to look for footprints," Arthur said, "but I didn't find anything."

"So the ghost could have come from anywhere on the grounds?" Damon said.

"Anywhere," Arthur agreed.

"Did the ghost do or say anything else?" Damon asked.

"No, thank heavens!" Varina said. She turned to Isetta. "I was afraid for you, Sister. What if he had frightened you out of your sleep?"

"I wish it had," Isetta said, reaching for her cane.

Arthur paled. "The ghost never went near Aunt Isetta."

"I don't think there's anything to fear," she said, tapping her chest. "My old ticker is getting stronger. Just seeing Damon and Neilly together makes it feel better than ever. If that old ghost has something to say to me, he'd better say it to my face."

Arthur jumped to his feet again. "You mean you're not even going to think about changing your will after a ghost's warning?"

"Don't be a goose, Arthur." Astonishment and indignation filled Isetta's voice. "Of course I'm not changing the will."

After Arthur had stomped out of the room and Neilly was satisfied that Isetta and Varina were resting she went in search of Damon. She found him in the library.

"What do you think of Varina's ghost story?" Neilly

asked, as soon as she'd closed the door. He'd have his own ideas, she was certain. "This could be bad for Isetta's condition, though she seems to be holding up well."

"But poor Aunt Varina has had quite a shock, too," Damon said, from his chair at the desk. "If I could get hold of that will, I'd rip it up myself. I would have insisted on it if Arthur hadn't been here. I took too much pleasure in seeing him squirm under the thought that he wasn't going to get Rosewood."

"I know," Neilly said, wondering if Damon would ever accept how much the plantation meant to him. "Now there's a ghost to deal with—as well as a thief."

"So it would seem," Damon said, seemingly preoccupied with the account book on the desk.

Arthur walked into the library without knocking and brushed past Neilly. "There you are, Cousin. I'd like for you to meet our guest, Mr. John Minor, art dealer."

"We've met," Damon said, without warmth.

"Mr. Minor." Neilly gave the man a cool nod of her head.

"Miss Lind," Minor acknowledged her. "I'm delighted to see you again."

Neilly couldn't imagine what delighted him. She wasn't in the least pleased to see him. His presence reminded her that she still had something to explain to Damon.

"John is giving me his appraisal of Grandpapa's collection," Arthur explained. "I thought we ought to have a professional look at the things."

Neilly bit her tongue. It was impossible to know if John Minor had inveigled his way into Rosewood, or if Arthur Sitwell had intended to bring the unscrupulous dealer into the house.

"How astute of you, Arthur," Damon said, astonishingly calm about the presence of an art dealer. "By all means, I would be interested in Mr. Minor's evaluation of Rosewood's collection. I hope you haven't been troubled by our ghost, sir."

"No," Minor said with a laugh. "In fact, I think it adds charm to an enchanting place like Rosewood."

"Damned nuisance, if you ask me," Arthur said. "We've already viewed the paintings in the little picture gallery. I'm taking John out into the garden to see the sculptures."

As soon as the men were out of the room, Neilly turned to Damon. "Surely you don't think Arthur's involved in this ghost thing. If anything happened to Isetta now, everything would go to you. That's the last thing he wants."

"I agree, he'd be a fool to be involved," Damon said. "But I'm not sure that would stop him."

Without saying more, Damon took a key from his pocket and unlocked the desk. From a secret drawer he took another key. "By the way, would there happen to be anything else you'd like to tell me, Neilly?"

"Well, yes," she began, wondering if he knew something already. "As a matter of fact, there is. That's why I was looking for you."

"Then come along," he said, leaving the desk and heading for the library door. "We'll talk in the little picture gallery."

The small room under the stairs was warm and stuffy when they entered it. Damon lit the lamp, then went to each painting and drew open its curtain. "What is it you have to tell me?"

"Well, I must admit I don't know the whole truth for certain myself," Neilly said, determined to tell everything, but aware of how damning what she was about to say could be.

"Just say it, Neilly," Damon said.

She studied the cupid painting without seeing it. "I think John Minor is the art dealer who helped my father steal and sell the Ruffins' painting."

Neilly glanced at Damon, ready to endure his anger, but he didn't look a bit surprised.

"I figured as much." He leaned against the wall. "You'd met Minor before because your father had introduced you."

"He called at the house one day to see Papa," Neilly said, her apprehension easing as she talked. "He said he had an appointment and he seemed to be a gentleman, so I allowed him to wait. We visited, but he was vague about his affairs with Papa. When my father came home he was displeased to find Mr. Minor there. He introduced us, then they left the house. I met Minor later in Europe. Again, Papa seemed annoyed that he had made himself known to me."

"Why didn't Minor question your new identity that day when you met him at The Laurels?" Damon asked.

"I don't know," Neilly said, shaking her head. "I've asked myself the same question over and over. The only reason I can think of is that he wanted to protect his own background. He didn't want to be connected with the scandal my father's name might recall."

"That's possible," Damon agreed, but he said no more as he gestured toward the Poussin painting, *Aurora's Seduction of Cephalus.* "Is this piece authentic?"

"You trust me to tell you that?"

A rueful smile tugged at the corners of Damon's wonderful mouth. Neilly caught her breath. She loved to see him smile. But this expression was not the lopsided grin that usually tugged at her heart.

"Let's say I have more trust in you than I have in John Minor," he said.

"Well, that's something at least," Neilly said, miffed once more by his lack of confidence in her.

Unlike the first time they had viewed the work, Damon kept his distance from her. Neilly examined the canvas closely, taking in all the details she could, judging to the best of her ability. With a sense of relief she stood back from the piece.

"I think it's authentic. Does John Minor know it's here?"

"Yes, Arthur has shown it to him," Damon said. "He agreed with you, according to my dear cousin. It is the most valuable item in the collection."

"The thief is sure to attempt to steal it," Neilly speculated aloud. "But this painting isn't well known, like the one Papa stole from the Ruffins. It had been exhibited in Charleston. There were numerous artists who had probably seen the painting, and they all needed to eat. A copy could be commissioned for the right price. But few people have seen this work. You can't forge what you haven't seen."

"But you've seen it," Damon said. "Could you forge it?"

Neilly frowned at him. "I'd need a lot more time with it than I've had to do a credible job."

"I would expect as much." Damon nodded. He closed the curtains over the painting. "But frankly, for Aunt Isetta's sake, I'm more concerned about our ghost at the moment."

"I don't believe in ghosts, let alone one that steals paintings," Neilly said with irritation. "And I wish you'd be as skeptical of this one as you are of me."

"I am, believe me." Neilly caught the dryness in Damon's voice. Unexpectedly, he reached out and tucked a tendril of hair behind her ear. Then he bent to kiss her lightly on the mouth.

The bittersweetness of the kiss sent a shiver down Neilly's spine.

"It'll soon be over, darlin'," he whispered. "I promise. Before you know it, our ghost—and our thief—is going to reveal himself—or herself."

Twenty-one

It was late when Varina settled into an uneasy sleep. The evening had been an unpleasant one, first with a strained meal including Arthur's guest, then with a tense, terse conversation in the music room.

She should feel better that Damon and Neilly had returned together. She'd even seen them holding hands, but something was wrong between them. In the music room, the more Mr. Minor praised Neilly's talent and knowledge of art, the more the girl seemed to shrink and the cooler and angrier Damon seemed to become.

Varina had drained two glasses of warm milk before she began to feel as if she might be able to sleep.

She had just dozed off when the wailing sliced through her slumber. It terminated her sleep with a frightening abruptness that left her wide awake and shaking, too terrified to leave the safety of her bed. In the darkness she managed to shrink down beneath the covers, where she was barely able to breathe. She lay paralyzed, praying she was invisible to the owner of the unholy voice.

Shortly, the wail pierced the night again, a wail just like the one she'd heard in the garden three nights before. This time she could tell that it came from Isetta's room.

"Varina? Somebody, come. Help," Izzie was calling in a thin voice.

The wail came again, and Varina pressed herself deeper into her feather mattress. But she listened. Every ounce of her listened. Even with the covers over her head, she couldn't ignore her sister's cry for help. Fighting her fear, she threw back the counterpane, parted the mosquito netting with trembling hands, and crawled out of bed—more terrified than she'd been in her life. Even the day when she and Isetta were little and she'd gotten lost during the picnic on the bayou, she hadn't been as terrified as she was now. But Izzie needed her.

Knees wobbling, Varina crept to the door between their adjoining rooms. She waited, but she heard nothing more. Maybe it was a false alarm, she prayed. She didn't want to see that ghost again. Maybe Izzie was just dreaming and talking in her sleep, though Varina couldn't recall that Izzie had ever talked in her sleep.

The third wail sliced through Varina. She almost bolted for the protection of her bed, but she heard Izzie call once more. Varina stood her ground. Her sister needed her. Shaking so badly that she could barely grasp the doorknob to turn it, she opened the door and peered into the moonlit room.

The sight of the specter took away her breath in a silent rush. The ghost loomed taller than she remembered, swaying over Izzie's bed, its shadow falling across Izzie's form. With strangely short arms, the towering shade ripped aside the mosquito netting and bent over Izzie.

Isetta pulled herself up in her bed, and reared back. When Izzie spoke Varina heard the strange sound of fear in her sister's voice. "Father? Is that you?"

The ghost wailed affirmation.

Varina stood frozen and speechless, an unwilling witness to the scene but determined to stand by her sister.

"How do I know it is truly you, Father?" Isetta asked, her voice cracking on *truly*.

"I know things no one but I could know," the ghost said. "I know that you wore your mother's brooch the day I died."

Varina covered her mouth to stifle a cry of surprise. She'd almost forgotten that Izzie had worn their mother's cameo.

"So I did," Isetta admitted. "What have you come to say to me, Father?"

"You must change your will back to the way it was or I shall haunt you all the rest of your days." The ghost spoke, an odd, hollow voice like someone talking into a stoneware pitcher. "Rosewood is for Mirabelle's son. It is Arthur Sitwell's legacy. A reward for my obedient daughter."

"I'm trying to do what's best for Rosewood," Isetta said. Despite the defiant words, Varina could see her sister's gray head trembling "You said you wanted Rosewood kept like a showplace. You didn't want to see the collections broken up or the house go to ruin."

The ghost fell silent, as if stumped by Isetta's claim. It lurched away from the bed, then tottered back, leveling a white finger at Izzie.

"I did not ask you to do what you thought best," the ghost argued. "I told you that Rosewood must stay in the Stirling English line. Damon will fritter it away like a Frenchie Creole. Rosewood must go to Arthur Sitwell."

"You were wrong about Damon when you died and you're wrong about him now," Isetta said.

Varina could see her sister better now that the ghost had moved to the foot of the bed. Izzie's face was pale, too pale, even paler than rice powder could make it. Her lips were pressed in a tight dark line. She began to rub her chest.

"I've had a lot of years to think about what you did to us, Father," Izzie continued, her voice growing stronger despite her pallor. "How you controlled our lives for your own benefit. When Rosalie defied you, you pushed her loving son aside. How you ruined my only chance for happiness by forbidding Theo and me to marry."

Varina gasped aloud. She didn't know that Papa had prevented Dr. McGregor and Izzie from marrying.

"There may not be much I can do about what you did

so long ago," Izzie continued, "but I have the power to keep Rosewood from being ruined by your greedy grandson, and I will do it."

"But you promised me, Isetta," the ghost wailed petulantly. "Stirlings never break a promise."

"This Stirling will if it is best for Rosewood and for Damon," Isetta said. She grabbed at her chest. "Oh, God, this hurts. I think I'm having an attack. Oh, the pain! Varina, are you there? Call Neilly."

The ghost gasped and backed away, apparently stunned into silence.

Varina stared at her sister in annoyance. Izzie had gotten so good at this weak heart sham that she could even put a scare into a ghost.

The chiming of the clock on the landing woke Neilly. At least that's what she thought awakened her. But when she thought about it for a moment she realized some other noise had reached her, or maybe it was just her sixth sense, which always warned her when a patient needed her. She reached for her wrapper at the foot of the bed. Quickly she donned it and stepped out into the hall.

The house was dark and silent. Moonlight fell through the window at the end of the hallway and cast shadows along the walls, but nothing stirred. It must have been the clock that had awakened her, Neilly decided. But she'd check on Isetta and Varina anyway. She was already up.

She stole barefoot down the hall toward Isetta's room. She found the door ajar; then she heard the noise—the one that had awakened her.

"Whooooooo—"

Isetta whimpered. Neilly recognized Varina's scream.

Terrified for the ladies' safety, she flung the door open. A huge white figure tottered in front of her; its head nearly touched the ceiling. Hollow black eyes stared down at Neilly from a small head with a lion's mane of gray hair.

"What on earth?" Neilly stared at the thing, unable to comprehend it.

Lurching around, it backed away, toward the gallery door. Varina screamed. "It's Father's ghost. Neilly, it's Father come to take his revenge on Isetta for changing her will."

"Whoooo—" the ghost cried again, raising its shrouded arms. "Stay where you are. My touch is deadly."

Neilly stared at the apparition, paralyzed by disbelief. Then she turned to Isetta, who was clasping her chest with both hands.

"Whooo, Isetta," the ghost wailed again. "Woe to you."

"Miss Isetta, don't believe it," Neilly warned. No telling what the shock of seeing a specter like this might do to someone with a weak heart. "It's a trick of some kind."

"The will must be changed," the ghost cried, nearly out the door now. "Or I shall return."

Anger and outrage gripped Neilly. How dare this creature threaten Miss Isetta and Miss Varina? She dashed across the room after the shrouded spirit.

"Oh, Neilly, don't—" Varina cried.

Neilly grabbed for the fluttering shroud. The ghost teetered away, out the door and onto the gallery. Tattered white cotton flapped just beyond Neilly's fingertips. Doggedly, she stumbled after it.

As she neared the door, she turned to glimpse Isetta sinking back on her pillows.

"I'm here." Varina rushed to her sister's side. "I've got her salts."

Assured of Isetta's safety, Neilly charged after the ghost.

On the gallery the apparition reeled ahead of her, no longer silent or supernatural. It thudded along the cypress boards like any other flesh-and-blood person.

Neilly's bare feet slipped in the dew. She caught herself on the balustrade and regained her balance. The ghost raced ahead and disappeared around the corner. Neilly bolted after it, throwing all her energy into catching the villainous thing.

When she rounded the corner she saw the ghost pass the steps to the garden. She'd expected it to go that way in an attempt to lose her in the hedges. Instead, it scurried down the gallery toward another open door. Neilly fixed all her efforts on gaining on it.

The top half of the ghost swayed strangely from one side to the other. Its shroud trailed out behind it. This time when Neilly reached for it she was successful.

She caught hold of the shroud, planted her feet, and hauled back on it with all her strength.

The ghost screeched, a high-pitched child's scream. The shroud came loose in Neilly's hand. The hair on the ghost's head flipped into the air. The figure under it toppled to the gallery floor. Arms and legs flailed about. A man groaned. A cloud of white powder billowed around them.

Neilly recognized the scent of rice powder. She tossed the shroud aside and circled the struggling apparition on the floor. It began to cry, like a child. "Get off me. Get off me. I hurt my shoulder."

The man's groan came again.

Still puzzled, Neilly stared at the figure writhing in the dark. As it separated before her eyes, she realized she was looking at two people.

"What the hell is going on?" Damon appeared in the doorway. He was clad only in his dark trousers, but he carried his pistol. "I thought I heard a buffalo stampede on the gallery."

Arthur groaned again. "Oh, God, my knees."

"My shoulder hurts," Vincent sobbed.

Neilly could summon little pity for them.

"That was a ghost you heard." She couldn't help grinning up at Damon. "I think we've caught the ghost of Thomas Stirling."

* * *

Damon seized Arthur by the arm and dragged him to his feet. Then he reached for Vincent. The boy yowled, but Damon wasn't much inclined to sympathy.

"I ought to call in the sheriff," he threatened. "Press charges. Frightening two elderly ladies with a Mardi Gras stunt like this."

Arthur mumbled some reply that Damon couldn't understand, nor did he care to.

Cato appeared in the door behind Damon with a lit candle. He was dressed in a dressing gown, and Claude Pugh followed him, pulling the sash tight on his own robe.

"You two escort Mr. Sitwell and his son back to their chamber and keep them there," Damon ordered. He looked around for Neilly just in time to see her scurrying down the gallery toward Isetta's room.

"I must see to my aunt. Don't let them out of your sight. Do you understand? I'll deal with you later, Arthur."

Isetta was lying on her bed with Neilly bent over her when Damon entered. He couldn't see either of their faces. Varina stood at the foot of the bed, her hands tucked in the sleeves of her wrapper.

"Was it really Arthur and Vincent dressed in a costume?" Varina asked, her face pale but her eyes bright and eager to know the truth.

"I'm afraid so," Damon said. "No ghost, nothing spiritual. Only Cousin Arthur and Vincent in rice powder and sheets."

"Oh, I'm so glad to know that," Varina said, relief easing the lines of her face. "Father hasn't returned after all?"

"No, Grandfather is where he belongs in the cemetery." Damon could hear labored breathing coming from the bed. "Is Aunt Isetta's condition serious?"

"I doubt it," Varina said with a remarkable lack of concern.

"I don't like her color." Neilly straightened and looked around toward Damon, her face strained. "I think we'd better send for Dr. McGregor."

"Oh, stop it, Izzie," Varina said, addressing her sister. "This is hardly the time to fake an attack."

"Fake an attack?" Damon looked from Varina to Neilly.

"What are you talking about, Miss Varina?" Neilly asked.

"Not faking," Isetta croaked from the bed. "I feel like an elephant is sitting on my chest."

"Of course you're faking," Varina said. "I think you enjoy the attention you get every time you place your hand over your heart and start to moan."

Damon stared at Aunt Varina in disbelief. "Aunt Isetta wouldn't fake anything as serious as illness."

"Oh, yes, she would, to bring you home to Rosewood," Varina said. "To keep Neilly here until you two could fall in love."

Damon looked to Neilly. She stared back at him openmouthed. He didn't even need to ask whether she was part of the plan.

"Not faking." Isetta gasped this time, her words barely intelligible. She looked toward Damon, her eyes appealing to him for help, her lips bluer than he'd ever seen them, and her hands clawing at Neilly's sleeve. He'd never seen his domineering aunt look so helpless. "Send for Theo," she begged. "Be quick. Before it's too late."

"Her pulse is erratic," Neilly whispered, shaking her head. "I don't think she's faking this time. Send for Dr. McGregor."

During the hour wait for McGregor to arrive, Damon paced in and out of Isetta's room, watching Neilly tending his aunt.

She worked over Isetta tirelessly, preparing her medication, waving the medicated handkerchief beneath her nose, and sponging her brow. Every few minutes she took Isetta's pulse.

Varina, who had fallen silent, burst into tears.

Neilly calmly ordered her out of the sickroom. Damon took Varina into his arms to comfort her, and with Cleo's help he returned his aunt to her own room.

When he entered Isetta's chamber again he found Neilly was the essence of calm, issuing orders in a steady voice to the upstairs maid who had been called to help her. She moved quietly about the room, efficient and collected. Damon realized with relief and admiration how good Neilly was at what she did.

By the time McGregor arrived, Isetta's breathing seemed to have eased and Neilly appeared less anxious about her condition.

But when Cleo showed the doctor in, Damon couldn't keep himself from snapping, "It's about time, McGregor."

"I came as soon as I could, son." McGregor seemed to take no offense. "How serious is it?"

As soon as Isetta heard the doctor's low voice, she opened her eyes. "Theo? Oh, Theo, I'm so glad you're here."

"Rest, my dear," McGregor said, setting down his black bag on the foot of the bed and reaching for his stethoscope.

"I think this attack was serious, doctor," Neilly said, filling McGregor in on what had happened, ghost and all. "She knows the truth now, but I think it was the shock of seeing what she believed at the moment was the ghost of her father."

The calm smile on Theo's face faded. "Thank you, Neilly. You go rest yourself. Do me a favor; take Damon with you."

"I'm staying."

"I need to make my own assessment of her condition."

"Come with me, Damon," Neilly urged, touching his arm. "Give Dr. McGregor some time to examine your aunt. It will only be a few minutes."

Damon finally allowed Neilly to lead him out of the room. When she closed the door behind them they stood in the silent hallway, staring at each other.

"Did you ever think her attacks were faked?" Damon had to know.

"No, but I was puzzled that her physical symptoms didn't always match her complaints."

"Why? Aunt Isetta's always been one to put her cards on the table. Why didn't she just tell me what she wanted instead of going through this elaborate sham?"

"I think that's perfectly obvious," Neilly said. "She and Varina are desperate to have you make Rosewood your home. She knew if she asked you outright, you'd never consider it. Not for a moment. Be honest. Would you?"

"Did you know about this plot to make us fall in love?" Damon asked, bewildered by the pain of his aunts' duplicity. The whole time he'd been terrified by the thought of Isetta's poor health she'd been faking, using his concern to control him. "Was everything arranged? The barbecue? The walk in the garden? Being locked in the cellar together? Would they do that, too?"

"Mercy, the cellar," Neilly echoed, softly. "Oh, Damon, I'm afraid you don't see your aunts the way others do, and they took advantage of your blindness. Isetta knew you'd be here if you thought she needed you, so she and Varina created the need. But they only did it out of love."

Neilly took a deep breath and turned away. "Anyway, their plot didn't work, did it? I mean, they were right. There is a certain attraction between us. After what's happened, we can't deny that. But it's not the same as love, is it?"

It came to the tip of Damon's tongue to refute her conclusion. He had fallen in love with her. She'd become almost as vital to his existence as Rosewood and his aunts. Oh, hell. She'd stolen his heart—if she'd stolen anything—and he wasn't even sure she knew it. But he didn't know how to tell her, not when faced with the realization that it had all been planned. How had they known what would happen in the cellar?

"What about Arthur?" Neilly asked, clearly leading him

away from the subject of his aunts. "What are you going to do about him and Vincent?"

"Oh, damn," Damon said, recalling all that had happened before Isetta's attack. "I almost forgot about Sitwell. I don't much care if he lives or dies, comes or goes, but I have plenty to say to him."

Twenty-two

Theo sat down on the edge of Isetta's bed and steeled himself against the pain of seeing the classic symptoms of a heart attack in his patient: the blue lips, the sheen of perspiration on her face, the gray pallor of her skin.

He forced a confident smile to his lips. "How do you feel, Isetta?"

"Damned awful," she muttered, and reached for his hand, clinging to him like a drowning victim. "My chest aches something fierce. The medicine you prescribed tastes awful, but I think it helped."

"You never complained about the medication before," Theo said. He'd been aware for some time that she hadn't been taking the digitalis he'd prescribed. Her normal heart rate had told him that.

Neilly had already loosened the ribbons at the throat of her nightgown to make Isetta more comfortable. Theo applied his stethoscope to Isetta's chest.

He listened for only a moment, praying to hear the same steady beat he'd heard every other time he'd been called to her side. But this time he heard the unmistakable regularly irregular palpitations of a damaged heart.

In all the weeks that she had complained to him about chest pains, weakness, and shortness of breath, he'd never detected any physical symptoms to confirm her complaints. Shaken, Theo snatched away his stethoscope and frowned. Doctors weren't immune to the fear of death.

"It is serious, isn't it?" Isetta asked. For the first time in his life Theo saw fear in her face. The same fear clutched at his own heart. He'd lots of practice hiding bad news. But this was Isetta and keeping his feelings from her was more difficult.

"It could be serious," Theo hedged. He continued the examination. He looked at the lining of her eyes and touched her forehead to gauge her body temperature. He examined her tongue and peered down her throat, all the time hoping to find some mundane cause for the heart attack he knew she had just suffered.

"Oh, Theo," Isetta said, reaching for his hand again. "It was real this time, wasn't it? For a little while I thought the end had come, and I wasn't going to have a chance to talk to you again. Now I know what a fool I've been."

"Nonsense, don't feel foolish," Theo said, stuffing his stethoscope back into his bag. "Anyone would have been shocked at the sight of a ghost."

"No, that's not what I mean," Isetta protested, waving away his words. "Though I will say Arthur and Vincent did deceive me. I thought it was Papa, and I wish I had faced him sooner. I wish I had stood up to him before this."

Theo patted her hand. "Now, now, donna get yourself upset again, lassie. The past is the past."

"No, that's not good enough," Isetta insisted, struggling to rise from her bed.

Theo quickly slid a pillow behind her. He placed his hands lightly on her shoulders and pressed her back against them. "Lie back and rest, Izzie."

To his relief she obeyed, but she kept talking, as if she hardly had time to spill out the words. "Remember *that day,* Theo, when we went to Papa to ask him for his blessing?"

"This is no the time to talk of such things." Theo's own heart contracted painfully.

He'd tried to dismiss the memory of that day long ago.

Yet how well he remembered passing the lions in the hallway and standing before Thomas Stirling in the drawing
room. He'd decked himself out in his best suit, a fine linen
one he'd had made in New Orleans. He'd had no illusions
about being a rich man then, but he knew his prospects
were good. He would never have asked Isetta to marry him
otherwise. Izzie was not a lady you asked to do without.
But he'd known then she had grit and courage. Or he'd
believed she did, until they'd stood before Thomas Stirling.

Theo did not want to talk about *that day,* and he certainly
did not think Isetta should be discussing it now.

"I can see from your face that you remember," Isetta
said, peering into his eyes.

Theo pulled his hand free of hers and reached for his
doctor's bag. He began to rummage around in it for something to help change the subject. But he could feel the old
resentment stir deep inside him.

Isetta touched his hand. "I let you down that day, Theo,
and myself as well. I sided with Father. I listened to a selfish
man who didn't know how to be happy. A man whose only
joy was controlling everyone around him. How I have regretted it."

"Donna upset yourself, lass," Theo said with a shake of
his head. He wanted to clear the old scene from his head.
"It's no good for you."

"No, these things have to be said," Isetta insisted, grasping his hand again. "I want you to understand, Theo. All
of us girls let Papa rule our lives. He drove Rosalie away
and denied his firstborn grandson. He shackled me to Rosewood with his deathbed wish—and he convinced Varina no
man would want her. And Mirabelle—Papa bought her loyalty with promises of Rosewood for her son. How we all
suffered for what he did."

She settled back against her pillow, clearly exhausted, but
she still clung to Theo with amazing strength.

"Your father made a lot of people suffer, Izzie," Theo

said. "Don't let him reach out from the grave and continue to do it."

"That's what I mean," Isetta agreed, struggling to sit up again, a glow of determination lighting her eyes. "You see, it's too late for Rosalie. Varina will always believe there is no one for her, and that her garden is where she belongs. Mirabelle did Papa's bidding and died as a result. I alone have the chance to change everything."

"No need to change anything today," Theo said. He was beginning to wonder if she'd suffered apoplexy as well as a heart attack—dredging up all this ancient history. He patted her hand. "You need your rest."

"But I can see it all so clearly now," Isetta said. "Arthur's ghost made me see."

Theo was almost afraid to ask. "See what?"

Isetta squeezed his hand, her grip almost painful, and she eyed him with her intent blue gaze. "Will you marry me, Theo?"

Theo blinked at her. After all these years since he had courted Isetta against the wishes of Thomas Stirling, since the old man had practically thrown him out of the house for daring to ask for his daughter's hand—this was the last thing he'd expected Isetta to ask of him.

The old resentment stirred again. How dare she ask now?

"You need to rest, Isetta. This is no time to make those kinds of plans for the future. You've had a shock."

"What better time than now?" Isetta argued, literally wringing his hand. "Don't deny me, Theo. Maybe I don't deserve your love after all I've done, but don't turn away from me. I won't rest until you answer me."

Theo stared at her, hardly believing what she was saying. So many years had passed since the scene with her father, and during those years she had never offered him anything more than friendship.

The old hurt crept into the daylight and Theo frowned at Isetta. He'd had almost left Louisiana plantation country all those years ago, left out of anger, out of humiliation—because he didn't think he could tolerate seeing Izzie again and again without being able to share a future with her. But they'd been friends, and their friendship, if not their romance, had been an abiding one. He'd finally contented himself with professional and sometimes social calls at Rosewood.

Now suddenly Isetta offered more! Now she was asking him to marry her?

Isetta touched his face, bringing him back from those dark memories. She caressed his cheek with a hand he remembered as smooth and slender.

"Tell me, Theo. You know what's in your heart. You don't need time to think, do you? You still love me, don't you? Will you marry me?"

Theo looked into Isetta's light blue eyes. She'd come close to death in the last few hours. He never believed in making decisions in emotional moments. But neither of them were youngsters anymore. They didn't have time for grudges. But they might have a little time together as they'd dreamed of once—if she meant it. He'd be a fool to say no.

Theo took her hand in his, pressed it against his weathered cheek, and took a deep, shaky breath. "I'll marry you, Izzie, if you'll agree to lie down and rest right now."

"Done," Isetta said with a sigh. She fell back against the pillows and smiled a beautiful smile, looking younger than she had in years. He smiled back at her, feeling a little like a lad again himself.

"How long before the wedding?" Isetta asked. "Soon, I hope. No need to wait. Time is short and we must make the most of it."

"We have enough time for you to get on your feet first," Theo said, suddenly brave enough to kiss her cheek. "I donna think it should be any big affair."

"We'll do it quietly, of course," Isetta said, absolutely

radiant now, though still pale. "A big wedding is for the young. But Reverend Blakely will come to the house if we ask him nicely. He loves Mammy Lula's cooking. Then I'll move to Acorn Hill—if you like."

"I'd love to have you at Acorn Hill," Theo said, surprised to find how true those words were.

"You don't have any ghosts there, do you?" Isetta asked, closing her eyes and drifting off into an exhausted sleep.

"Not a one," Theo said, searching his heart for the ugly resentments he'd felt stir earlier, but they were gone.

Arthur, Vincent, Uncle Cato, and Pugh sat gathered in silence and stared expectantly at Damon and Neilly as they entered the Sitwells' sitting room. Even John Minor had joined the group.

Damon dismissed Uncle Cato, John Minor, and Pugh.

"I'm going, too," Vincent said, jumping up from the sofa where he sat next to his father. "I have a headache like my mama gets."

"Sit down," Damon ordered, unwilling to put up with any nonsense. "I want to talk to you and your father."

Vincent's childish smile vanished and he dropped down next to his father.

Arthur had gone white around the mouth. "Is Aunt Isetta going to live?"

"I don't know," Damon said, standing before Arthur. "Dr. McGregor is with her. This appears to be a serious attack. If anything happens to her . . ."

Damon left his sentence unfinished. Arthur looked away.

"Explain this prank of yours to me," Damon demanded. "You thought you'd frighten Isetta into changing her will back in your favor?"

Arthur nodded. "We'd heard all about Mammy Lula seeing Grandfather's ghost up in the cemetery. My mother always said Isetta would do whatever Grandfather told her.

So I thought if she believed Grandfather had come back from the grave, she'd have second thoughts about going against his wishes."

"But why appear to Varina and Uncle Cato in the garden earlier?" Neilly asked.

A good question, Damon thought.

"Because I was afraid to appear to Isetta, at first," Arthur said, wagging his head as if to say Damon should know that. "I was afraid of exciting her too much. But you saw how stubborn she was when Varina told her about the ghost."

"So when she wasn't frightened by your first appearance to Varina, you decided to appear to her yourself?" Damon asked.

"Well, she didn't seem all that sick," Arthur said. "The truth is, Aunt Isetta looked strong enough to outlive us all."

"I don't think she was ever sick," Vincent piped. "She always looked at me like she wanted to box my ears. I liked playing ghost to scare her."

Damon resisted the urge to box Vincent's ears in his aunt's stead.

"Well, she practically challenged the ghost," Arthur said. "You heard her yesterday. She said she'd like to face the ghost herself. So I obliged her."

"That's hardly a justification, Arthur," Damon said.

"You both should be ashamed of yourselves," Neilly scolded.

"I thought playing ghost was fun," Vincent said. "All I had to do was sit on Papa's shoulders, put boot black around my eyes, and wear one of the old powdered wigs we found in the attic."

"I can't believe you risked Isetta's death over this," Damon said, directing his words to Arthur. "Not to mention your own life. If I'd seen you first, I'd have used my pistol."

Vincent scooted closer to his father for protection, but he boldly shook his finger at Damon. "I liked locking you in the cellar, Cousin Damon. You deserved it for embarrassing me in front of the servants. How did you like it in the dark with Miss Cornelia?"

"You locked us in the cellar?" Neilly gasped and stared at the boy.

"Vincent can be excused for being a child, but you, Arthur," Damon said, strangely relieved to know that the culprit hadn't been Varina, or even Isetta. "You should have known better than to do what you did to Aunt Isetta. I ought to turn you both over to the sheriff."

To Damon's satisfaction, Arthur gulped, his eyes wide and his chin thrust forward, as if a whole egg was stuck in his throat. "You wouldn't dare. Think of the scandal."

The door opened. Everyone turned to find Varina standing in the doorway. "Theo says he thinks Isetta is out of danger and she's resting comfortably."

"Oh, thank God," Neilly whispered at Damon's side.

He felt the bleak weight of his fear lift.

Varina walked across the room to stand before Arthur. "So the ghost was you. What I want to know is how you knew about the brooch. How did you know, Arthur? You weren't here."

"But my mama was," Arthur said, with a cocky, pleased-with-himself smile. "I remembered her talking of the cameo that Aunt Isetta wore. It was a blue one of the three muses that Mama had always wanted. I remember how she complained that her sister had worn it during mourning instead of proper mourning jewelry because Grandpapa had asked her to."

"So that's what made Miss Isetta believe in the ghost," Neilly said.

"We've cleared up the ghost story," Damon said, ready now to get to the bottom of the entire mystery. "Arthur, tell us what you did with the artworks you've been taking. The dueling pistols, the Venetian vase, and Varina's jewelry. If you've sold them, you can damn well go buy them back."

For the first time Arthur met Damon's gaze and appeared truly affronted.

"How dare you accuse me, as if I were a common thief," Arthur said, rising from the sofa, righteous indignation in the set of his shoulders. "That's why I pointed them out to you. I wanted you to know I'd discovered your game, Durande. You're taking things that are mine."

"You think I sold them off?" Damon said, nearly unable to believe Arthur's ridiculous accusation.

"How dare you even consider the possibility." Neilly huffed at Damon's side. Her flash of anger on his behalf startled him.

"Well, if it's not you, Cousin Damon, who is it?" Arthur demanded. "Uncle Cato? Cleo? What about the freed carpenter? Elijah? He's constantly in and out of the house. Everyone knows he's desperate for money.

"So, if you have any thoughts about summoning the sheriff, think again, Cousin," Arthur said, pointing a warning finger in Damon's face. "I'll just point out all the valuables that are missing and mention certain investments you've poured money into in Texas. And there was that sudden trip you made to New Orleans. It won't look good."

Damon remained silent.

"I didn't think you'd have much to say to that," Arthur said, suddenly recovered from the cringing, guilty state of a few minutes before. "Come on, Vincent. Let's clean up and apologize to Aunt Isetta as soon as she's well enough to see us. The game isn't up yet."

Damon went straight to the library and poured himself a generous portion of brandy. He sipped on it, never allowing himself to acknowledge his anger. But he itched to call to account the man who was to blame for all this friction. Though that man lay moldering in his grave, Thomas Stirling still ruled Rosewood. The thought galled Damon.

He picked up his snifter and prowled silently into the drawing room, where his grandfather's portrait stared down from the wall. He stared back at the old man's hard face.

"You can't turn a cold shoulder on me this time, Grandfather," Damon said, setting down the candle on the Italian marble mantel. A ridiculous sense of childish victory coursed through him. He had Thomas Stirling cornered at last. "Oh, yes, you will listen to me now, old man."

Thomas Stirling glared resentfully at his grandson.

Damon took a long satisfying drink of the brandy. "I know your ghost doesn't walk Rosewood's halls. It never has. But your spirit haunts this family as surely as your portrait hangs on that wall."

In the pale dawn light Damon paced around the room, surprised at the damp, stale smell hanging in the corners. Aunt Varina and Cleo were meticulous in their cleaning of the drawing room. When Damon turned back to the portrait he saw his grandfather still watching him.

"I could blame my mother," Damon said, "but she was just a frightened girl trying to fill the void your rejection created. I could blame my father and the Durandes, but they only reflected the prejudice you showed them. No better than you and no worse."

Damon took another long swallow of brandy. "No, I blame you, Grandfather. I blame your mean, selfish spirit. It's made a mess of your daughters' lives. You've turned family against family. Your favorite grandson has endangered Aunt Isetta's life. He accuses me of stealing from my own family and I accuse him. Is this what you wanted? Was this your grand plan? To see the Stirlings at each other's throats over Rosewood?"

The portrait's eyes followed Damon as he crossed the room once more. Damon held the gaze, telling himself that his grandfather's regard was only a trick of an artist's brush. Neilly could probably explain the technique to him.

Still, a chill prickled the hair on the back of his neck.

Foolish as it seemed, Damon felt certain someone was in the room with him. Someone was listening.

"You collected everything except your family's love," he continued. "You filled your house with great beauty while your heart was empty. The more you collected, the less you had to give to the people in your life. Maybe that frightened you. Maybe that's why you clung to your daughters. I don't know. But you've caused a lot of pain, old man. I'm not willing to be a party to it any longer."

A dank breeze stirred through the room, despite the fact that the windows were closed. The curtains stirred. The first rays of dawn glowed off Grandfather's silver cup and the elegant scabbard of Andrew Jackson's sword.

"Rosewood belongs to Isetta," Damon continued. "You willed it directly to her for her loving devotion to you. You did know that, didn't you? All the collections in the house are hers to be disposed of as she sees fit. Not by Arthur or anyone else."

Damon swept his hand around the room, taking in all the treasures. "None of these things, not even the house, means anything without harmony. Nothing matters without caring, without love. No matter who gets Rosewood, Grandfather, you failed. What you sought to hold together, you shattered."

Only the ticking of the Lafayette clock on the mantel disturbed the silence. Damon swallowed the last of his brandy. Having said what he'd come to say, he turned and walked out of the room.

Thomas Stirling's silver goblet began to wobble, then totter in a circle. Around and around it lurched, until it fell over on its side, the silver ringing hollow against the wood.

* * *

In the days following Isetta's heart attack, Arthur was as good as his word. To Neilly's astonishment, he and Vincent presented themselves to Miss Isetta—as soon as Dr. McGregor agreed to it—and apologized for their "prank." Then they set about winning themselves back into her good graces, fetching for her, playing cards with her, and reading to her.

Neilly hovered nearby, feeling uneasy with Arthur's new conduct. What was even more astonishing was that Isetta seemed blissfully unaware of their ulterior motives. She accepted her nephew and grand-nephew's attention with amazing forgiveness and good humor.

But Neilly found herself unable to pardon Arthur's reckless behavior. He'd nearly cost the woman her life. Now he wanted to behave as if the midnight escapade had been nothing more than a harmless prank. Neilly could hardly hold her peace.

Varina turned silent and devoted herself to her roses. Damon seemed to turn into himself, spending long hours away from the house, in the fields, at the mill, or around the warehouse. But he appeared at dinner every evening and was unfailingly courteous to Neilly. He appeared for no more late-night meetings on the gallery. Neilly missed his company and longed to know what he was thinking and feeling about Arthur and John Minor.

The atmosphere in the house was strained and grew more tense day by day as the summer solstice came and went. Arthur and Vincent resumed their social life, calling on the neighbors with John Minor in their company. Often they wandered about the house, Minor admiring the artworks while Damon, with the help of Pugh, saw to the running of the plantation.

Dr. McGregor visited Isetta daily, the smile on his face absolutely euphoric. When he and Isetta were together they put their heads close and whispered, giggling like two naughty children with a secret. They seemed so happy in each other's company. Neilly longed for a little piece of their happiness.

One evening, after another unpleasant meal, Damon summoned Neilly to the drawing room. She found him, Isetta,

Varina and Dr. McGregor standing in a circle around two large crates that Elijah was building.

Arthur, Vincent, and John Minor followed her into the drawing room. Pugh and Uncle Cato hovered nearby.

"Here's the inventory," Damon said, shoving the ledger into Neilly's hands. She hadn't seen it since their return from New Orleans because he'd kept it in his desk under lock and key. "If we're going to pack these things away, we're going to make a clear record of the deed."

"Pack things away?" Neilly repeated, not understanding what Damon wanted of her.

"Yes, dear," Isetta said, with a smile of understanding. "But first things first. I have an announcement to make."

Isetta took Dr. McGregor's hand in her own. "Theo and I have kept our secret long enough. I told Damon and Varina about it this morning, but the rest of you should know, too. Theo and I plan to be married at the end of the week."

"You're what?!" Arthur sputtered. "You can't mean it. Marriage at your age, Aunt Isetta?"

"But I think that's wonderful news," Neilly said. Now she understood Isetta's elated distraction. Neilly embraced the older lady and kissed Dr. McGregor's cheek. "I'm so happy for you both."

The doctor slipped an arm around Isetta's waist. "We're looking forward to a long and happy life together."

"But—but what about Rosewood?" Arthur stammered.

"If anything happens to me, Rosewood goes to Theo," Isetta said, explaining the obvious.

"The plantation leaves the family?" Arthur turned on Damon and snarled, "Well, this must please you,"

"It pleases me to see my aunt happy, as it should you," Damon replied calmly. "I'll be going back to Texas in the fall."

Neilly stared at him, but he turned away. So, she was going to be left behind to continue to work off her debt. It would have been nice if he'd told her himself, in private.

"I'll be moving to Acorn Hill," Isetta said. "Damon's convinced me that I should take whatever I want from Rosewood."

Arthur dropped into a fireside chair, as if this additional news was too much for him.

"Whatever you want, Aunt Isetta, take it." Damon moved about the room, stopping before each picture on the wall and examining each porcelain vase on the tables. Neilly noted that his expression had turned unreadable.

"I'm counting on all of you to be witness to the things that we are packing away," Damon continued. "I'm relegating some things to the attic. Perhaps you'll help us assign a value to these things, Mr. Minor."

"At your service, sir," Minor said, stepping forward to get a closer look at the crate. "I'd be pleased to be of any assistance possible."

Damon turned to Neilly. "Note that I'm packing away this vase and this series of small paintings of Venice. I've numbered the crates eleven and twelve."

"I'll wrap each item," Varina volunteered. "Uncle Cato, bring us more straw and some of that cotton wool."

"Yeas, Miss Varina."

Neilly took a pencil from her pocket, perched herself on the edge of the lemon yellow sofa, and began to take notes.

As she worked, she realized that everyone who could possibly be suspected of stealing the treasures of Rosewood was standing in the room, including herself. Damon was up to something, she was certain of it, but she couldn't imagine just what it was.

"Pack this carefully, Aunt Varina," Damon said, taking the sword from its place over the mantel and beneath the portrait of Thomas Stirling. "And Grandfather's cup."

"Oh, no, not Father's cup," Varina protested. "No, it must stay here with his portrait."

"Why?" Damon asked.

"Because it is the Stirling family cup," Isetta said, asserting her authority. "It represents more that just Father. It represents a long line of Stirling men who came to the New World to establish the family here. It must stay."

"Then stay it shall," Damon said, replacing the cup on the hearth. "Does the cup have much value, Mr. Minor?"

"Only to your family," Minor said. "However, the Andrew Jackson sword would be coveted by a number of private collectors, admirers of Old Hickory, not to mention some historical societies."

"I thought so," Damon said.

So they went around the room, Damon selecting pieces to be packed away and John Minor offering ideas about the value of each. Arthur hovered over Aunt Isetta, Varina, and the packing crate, settling each wrapped piece in the box to his satisfaction. Bored and hungry, Vincent wandered off toward the kitchen. Pugh joined Neilly on the sofa, offering her a freshly sharpened pencil and aiding her in locating each item in the listing. He insisted on sitting a little too close for comfort.

The hour grew late. Varina began to yawn. While John Minor discussed a cloisonné vase with Damon, Pugh pulled his watch from his waistcoat pocket and commented on the time.

"Yes, we'll pack the vase away, too," Damon said. He took a key from his pocket and handed it to Elijah. "Aunt Isetta also wants the Poussin painting of *Aurora's Seduction of Cephalus*. Will you bring it here for us? Uncle Cato will help you find it."

Neilly stared at Damon. "You're going to let the Poussin leave the house?"

Damon ignored her question. "In the morning, Miss Neilly, you'll select new furnishings from the boxes in the attic."

"Yes, of course," Neilly said. "First thing."

Damon produced a large padlock from his pocket. "As

soon as the painting is packed, I'm locking this crate. Arthur, witness this."

"I'm witnessing," Arthur said, frowning as if he was being put upon.

"A wise course," Minor said. "Those are very valuable things. Who is going to hold the key?"

"Aunt Isetta," Damon said, handing the key to his aunt.

"Good," Arthur said, "If anything turns up missing, we'll know you had an extra key, Durande."

"We'll know someone had an extra key," Damon said, giving Arthur an enigmatic smile.

In her room, Neilly dressed for bed knowing that she was too restless to fall sleep, even for a little while. Something was about to happen; she could feel it.

Downstairs in the drawing room, a trap was set for Rosewood's thief.

"It couldn't be a better trap if I'd laid it myself," she admitted aloud. "I wonder which the villain will go for, the Poussin or Andrew Jackson's sword?"

Neilly slipped the silk nightgown Damon had given her over her head and closed her eyes as it slid over her body. The slippery fabric whispered over her shoulders, tickled lightly along her ribs, and tantalizingly stroked her thighs almost as lightly and tenderly as Damon's hands.

When the hem dropped around her ankles she opened her eyes and sighed, realizing how much she longed for his touch.

Outside, the evening had turned dark purple and the night creatures were tuning up for their songs as the moon rose over the river. Inside, Neilly was about to go to bed—alone. She'd only slept one night with a man and already she had no desire to sleep alone again. How she longed to lie down beside Damon and sleep, dreaming her own dreams, with him dreaming his.

She wanted to wake to the touch of his hands and the taste of his lips. She wanted to know the texture of his dark curls between her fingers and the weight of his body on hers, in hers, rising with her to a shared pleasure.

Neilly ran her hands down over the smooth silk, over the contours of her own body.

"I am a wanton," she said to herself with a smile, remembering how Damon had laughed at her confession.

She really shouldn't have accepted this gift, she thought. It wasn't the proper sort of thing for a man to give a lady—even if it was to replace a ripped gown. But then, their relationship wasn't the proper sort. She'd watched him bathe, then allowed him to drag her upstairs to a room where she'd pulled off his towel. She'd shamelessly left her ripped nightgown on the floor.

"I wonder what Mrs. Robards thought," she said aloud.

Still smiling to herself, Neilly put on her cotton wrapper, which looked shabby in contrast to the elegant silk gown. Then she wandered through the door and onto the gallery and peeked down the expanse to see that a light fell from the doors to Damon's room. She wondered what was keeping him up so late. Was he having trouble sleeping, too, or was he poring over more ledgers and invoices?

Only yesterday he'd shown her from room to room downstairs, talking of new draperies for the windows and coverings for the chairs and sofas. He'd even talked of taking up the rugs and buying new carpets from New Orleans.

At first she'd hoped his sudden interest in the house meant he was planning to stay at Rosewood.

She'd been disappointed to hear him tell Arthur that he was returning to Texas in the fall, as soon as he was satisfied that Aunt Isetta was settled with Theo. Then he was free to go on with his other interests, his adventures that were more important to him than she was. But then, what had she expected?

A cool breeze drifted along the dark gallery and she hugged herself against the cold. It was about time to go in.

Suddenly the lights went out in Damon's room and he stepped silently out onto the gallery. It took her a moment to realize that he was looking directly at her.

"I had a feeling you might be out here," he said.

Out of habit, she pulled her wrapper closer around her; then, with a small smile, she realized the ridiculousness of her modesty.

"I haven't had the opportunity to ask you—does the gown fit?" he asked, his voice carrying softly down the gallery. In the darkness she couldn't see his face, couldn't see if it still held that hard, grim look that had been there during the evening as they'd packed the crate.

"Perfectly," Neilly said, considering whether to show him, then deciding against it.

He stepped closer, his hard-soled boots surprisingly silent on the gallery floor. His arms were bare to the elbow where he'd rolled up his sleeves and the buttons of his shirt were loosened, revealing his tanned throat, a place vulnerable and sensitive to kisses, she'd discovered. The thought set her belly to fluttering.

"How do your new boots fit?" she asked.

"I'm getting them broken in," he said. "It always takes a while to break in new boots."

He stepped within a few feet of her. "I want to see how well the gown fits."

Neilly hesitated.

Damon sat down on the gallery balustrade, his back against the column. "It's all I ask, darlin'."

The softness in his voice, so unlike the harshness she'd heard during the evening, seduced Neilly. She untied the belt of her wrapper and let it slip from her shoulders. She knew the scoop neck of the silk gown lay smooth across her throat and clung to her breasts, revealing crests that were already betraying her desire for Damon's touch.

The soft fabric draped from her waist down over her hips and lay smooth and silky against her thighs.

"How does it feel?" Damon asked.

In the shadows she still couldn't see his face, but she could feel his gaze caressing her body. He wanted her; she knew it.

She wanted him, despite the knowledge that he was going to be leaving her. But he didn't need to know that. She pulled her wrapper around her and tied the belt snugly. "It's very nice, but a cotton gown would have been adequate."

"Come closer."

"Why? We can talk from here," Neilly said.

"We can," Damon said, "but we could be overheard, too."

"True." Neilly walked to the railing just on the other side of the column against which Damon leaned. "What is it we have to talk about?"

"I keep thinking about our night in the laundry house. Thoughts like that make it damned hard for a man to concentrate."

"I remember the laundry house well," Neilly admitted, her body aware of his nearness, yearning for his touch, but her head firmly in control now. "But under Rosewood's roof, the laundry room seems a world away. I remember all too clearly why I've returned."

"I thought you came back with me to care for Aunt Isetta and Aunt Varina and—to be with me."

"And to repay the debt I owe you," Neilly said aloud, staring out at the garden below. And to discover who is making a fool out of all of us by stealing Rosewood's treasures right out from under our noses and leaving me with the blame, she thought silently.

Damon shrugged. "The debt. Well, lady ghost hunter, I don't think that's of much significance."

"Well, it is to me," Neilly said. "I don't need your pity ~r your charity. I've made an honest living for myself for over three years and I can continue to do it without your help."

"Just like the way you escaped Ruffin without my help?" Damon asked. "You've got too much pride, Neilly."

Neilly huffed. "As I recall, I saved *you* from Charles."

"Oh, the fish heads were a nice touch, darlin'. I could have done without that rescue."

"As far as my pride is concerned," Neilly said, peering around the column at him, "pride is a useful thing."

"Maybe, but not at the moment." He reached out and pulled her to his side, his grip powerful and insistent but not cruel. He held her face in his hands. Neilly could see his eyes glittering in the moonlight. "Taste wine with me tonight, Neilly. It's not far to the cellar."

Mercy, she wanted to stay with him. She wanted to lie in his arms again. She wanted to explore him and offer herself to his quests, but she couldn't. She had a thief to catch.

"Too many problems stand between us," she whispered. "Your suspicions, my debts. Sometimes I think you believe in me, but only a little. That's not enough."

"Then what is enough?" Damon's hand slipped her wrapper and the strap of her gown off her shoulder. He bent to plant a kiss on Neilly's collarbone. Warmth washed through her. For a moment she forgot what they'd been talking about.

He pressed her so close she could feel the bulge of his groin through the sheer silk clinging to her thighs.

"I want to prove to you—oh, what are you doing?"

Damon leaned back against the column, stretched his leg out along the railing and drew Neilly into his lap so she was perched on his thigh. Her slippered feet came off the floor. Damon's hand slid up beneath her gown and stroked the inside of her thighs.

"You don't have anything to prove to me," Damon whispered in her ear. "Just let me hold you, Neilly. Let me make you sigh."

He kissed her on the lips as he pulled up her knee between them, against his chest, and his hand found the hidden petals of her womanhood.

Neilly sucked in a breath. She understood better than she wanted to what he was doing. She thought she should push his hands away, but instead she slipped her arms around his neck and buried her face against his shoulder, shuddering with the pleasure his fingers brought. He explored her slowly, stroking the dew from her until he found the sensitive bud.

He nuzzled her bare shoulder, then whispered into her ear, "I want to taste you, darlin'."

Neilly ached to know the feel of his lips. She slipped her gown lower, exposing her breasts for him. Damon took her in his mouth, doing things as magical and wondrous with his tongue as he was doing with his fingers. She was lost to his kisses and caresses.

When her climax flooded over her she tried to muffle her cry of pleasure against his neck.

He whispered endearments into her ear. Neilly settled deeper in his embrace, weak and sated and utterly astonished at her weakness for his touch.

"Something happens inside me when you give yourself up to me like that," Damon said, stroking her hair. "I don't think either of us can go on like this much longer, so close yet so far from each other."

"What solution can there possibly be?" Neilly murmured against his neck.

"I can think of several," Damon said. "You won't agree to all of them. Hell, I don't know if you'll agree to any of them. But we have a thief to catch first."

"Yes, we do." Mention of the thief banished Neilly's contentment. She pulled out of his embrace. He did not hold her back, but she was aware of him watching her. He said nothing. She smoothed her wrinkled gown down over her bare thighs, unhappy with herself for her weakness, unhappy with him for taking advantage of it. Without even saying good night, she hurried back to her own room and closed the door behind her.

The Fairwinds from where I had glimpsed him once, the Mayne house from my perch at Rosewood, the tree lane... the willow-draped bayou... I wondered if I could ever even return to Rosewood, should it even now...

Twenty-three

The Lafayette clock on the mantel struck one in the morning. Damon settled himself in the shadows next to the gallery door to the drawing room. Through the glass he had a good view of the locked crate inside. At his side in easy reach lay two loaded pistols. He'd tucked his hunting knife into his belt. He hoped the coming confrontation wouldn't turn violent, but he was prepared if it did.

The house had been quiet for some time. He'd prowled the hallway upstairs and down, checking for lights under doors, but each room had been dark. Everyone was abed now. How long he had to wait for the thief to make his appearance depended upon how well the villain had planned his getaway.

An hour slipped by, then two. Damon contented himself with listening to night noises. From the forest the owls hooted to each other. The crickets and tree frogs finally gave up their song around three o'clock. Once in the quiet of the moonlit night Damon thought he heard the eerie cry of a swamp cat, distant, lonely, and threatening. All the sounds were so familiar, so unlike Texas, so much more like home, like Rosewood.

Rustling from the drawing room caught his attention just after the clock struck three-thirty. He stayed low, peering into the room through the lower panel of the glass door.

In the moonlight he saw Neilly, wearing her usual gray

gown now instead of her silk nightgown and bending over the crate.

Damon bit back a curse. Could he have been wrong about her? For a heart-stopping moment he couldn't believe she had fallen into his trap. He was about to step into the room to confront her when he saw her jump, as if startled. She looked back, toward the hallway door. She had not seen him, but whatever noise she heard in the hallway made her duck behind the yellow sofa.

In a flash of understanding, he uttered an oath under his breath this time. He reined in his impatience and waited, praying the next few minutes wouldn't get too complicated. He berated himself for not realizing that Neilly would never be able to resist the lure of catching the thieves.

As he watched, John Minor crept into the drawing room, followed by a shadowy figure. Both men bent over the crate, the shadowy one obviously working on the padlock with a key. They seemed to be having some difficulty. Finally Minor lit a candle he was carrying. Light burst across Claude Pugh's face.

Damon chided himself for not having reached that conclusion before. Pugh had access to everything around the house, especially since he'd moved into the attic after the fire.

Still Damon did not make his move. To confront them too soon would give them room for excuses and denials. He wanted to see them take the goods from the crate and walk out of the house with valuables in their possession. Then they would be thieves without defense. He also wanted them out of the house and away from Neilly, the foolish girl.

Damon peered into the room again. The crate lid was up and the two men hovered over the contents like vultures over a carcass. He could hear the low rumble of their voices, arguing over what to take with them. Obviously they wanted to choose the most valuable items they could carry easily.

The lid of the crate thunked into place. Damon heard it and picked up his pistols to tuck them into his belt. The thieves would be making their getaway soon. He wished he'd enlisted the help of someone else, like Elijah, but when he'd devised this plan he hadn't anticipated two thieves—or Neilly.

Damon peered into the room again, just in time to see Neilly pop up from behind the sofa like a puppet in a jack-in-the-box. She threw herself between the two men and the hall door.

"Stop!" she cried. "Thief! Thief!"

Pugh froze, his back to Damon. But Minor lunged toward Neilly, reacting so swiftly, Damon could hardly believe his eyes. The dark little man slammed Neilly against the wall with the weight of his thick body and clamped a hand over her mouth.

Damon summoned all his will and forced himself to remain still. With luck, the two would decide there was no advantage in harming Neilly and release her. If he made himself known, they might feel threatened.

"What do we do now?" Pugh asked.

"I think Miss Cornelia has played right into our hands," Minor said. "We'll take her out and get rid of her with the Jackson sword and the Poussin painting. The Stirlings will think she's the thief. When everything settles down, and no one suspects us, we'll dig up the sword and painting and leave."

Neilly mumbled a protest against Minor's hand.

"It's a pity you have to leave the house, Claude," Minor went on. "When you and Sitwell are gone I don't how I'll get my hands on the treasures here. There's a fortune sitting in every nook and cranny."

"Let's worry about that later," Pugh said. "I like the idea of taking Miss Cornelia out into the woods."

"Then we'd better get moving."

Minor twisted Neilly's arms behind her back and tied her

with the silk drapery cord while Pugh kept one hand clamped over her mouth. When he was finished Minor shoved her toward the gallery door.

Damon decided it was time to put in his appearance. In one smooth action he rose up outside the gallery doors and pulled them open.

"That's far enough," he said.

Pugh halted, the Andrew Jackson sword in his hands. Minor carried a rolled canvas, probably the Poussin work, under his arm.

"Durande!" Minor released Neilly immediately, pushing her in front of him. "Here's your thief. She brought us the key. Asked me to take the things she unpacked from the crate back to New Orleans for her. We were just about to wake you."

"Damon, that's not so," Neilly cried. "I'm not the thief. I came down to discover who would spring your trap."

"I know, Neilly," Damon said, never taking his eyes from Minor or Pugh. He knew what happened in the next few minutes was going to be critical. "I believe you. Come stand beside me."

The look of relief that spread across Neilly's sweet face almost broke his heart. She had really feared that he would believe Minor. When she stepped near Damon reached out to take her hand, to draw her close to him and out of danger. But Pugh lurched forward, striking swift and fast as a rattler. He seized Neilly by the waist and dragged her away. Suddenly the Andrew Jackson sword glinted in the pale moonlight. With his free hand, Pugh pressed the unsheathed blade to Neilly's throat.

Damon halted.

"Good," Pugh said. "You understand. Come any nearer and I'll hurt the little lady here. You wouldn't want to see her skewered on this sword, would you?"

Damon shook his head. Neilly's eyes were wide with terror.

"Take the sword, Pugh," Damon said. "Take whatever else you want. But let Neilly go."

"Then you'll follow us," Minor said. "No, the lady goes along for insurance."

"If it's insurance you want, take me in her place," Damon offered.

"You really don't like to see my hands on her, do you, Durande?" Pugh laughed with soft evilness. "No, the lady's company will be more fun. More manageable. I think she goes along to make you suffer."

"Why?" Damon asked, playing for time and opportunity, playing for Neilly's life. "Because I didn't like your slightly dishonest bookkeeping?"

"Because being turned out by you gives me a bad name among the planters," Pugh said. "I helped your dotty old aunts when their bookkeeper left. They were so ignorant of what was going on with their money, I could have taken more, but I hoped to make a place for myself. Then you came and expected me to be honest."

"It's a standard I've insisted all our bookkeepers meet," Damon said. "I'm sorry you found it so inconvenient. So, instead of money you started stealing valuables from the house."

"You conclude the obvious," Minor said, moving behind the Louis XIV chair near the fireplace. "Sit down."

Damon hesitated. Pugh twisted Neilly's arm so hard, she whimpered. Damon sat in the chair. Cooperation seemed the lesser of the evils at the moment.

"Pugh's discontent was to my advantage," Minor explained as he tied Damon to the chair with the other silk drapery tieback. "I'd been trying to find someone to supply me with things from Rosewood's collections for years," Minor continued as he tightened the cords on Damon's wrists. "It's a pity my supply line has come to an end."

Helpless and concerned for Neilly, Damon hardly heard Minor's words. Nor did he see the gag coming. Minor's handkerchief cut into Damon's cheek as the art dealer tied the gag into place. "There, that will hold you, Durande."

Only then did Minor light a lamp. Cold terror slithered up the back of Damon's neck.

Minor motioned Pugh and his hostage out the hallway door. Then he followed, throwing the glass kerosene lamp so it shattered across the bottom of the stairs.

Lamp oil splashed across the brick floor. Damon smelled the fumes. Hungry flames followed, licking up the wainscoting of the drawing room. The air warmed and the fire crackled. In the hall the blaze soared into the air, scorching the monkeys in the painted banana tree and the lion guards at the library door.

"That will keep the rest of them distracted for a while," Minor said with a wicked laugh. "They won't know whether to save themselves or their treasures."

When the roaring flames whipped into a spiral and climbed higher Damon knew Pugh, Neilly, and Minor were gone. They'd left the door open so the night air could feed the flames.

Immediately he threw himself and the chair on the floor. His head hit the carpet with a thud. He began to rub his cheek against the musty-smelling rug. The arm of the chair bit into his ribs and his shoulder was wrenched into an unnatural position, but he worked to get the gag out of his mouth. He had to set up the alarm.

Pain shot through Neilly's arm as Pugh dragged her across the lawn away from Rosewood. The crackling of the fire echoed in her ears. The thought of Damon helpless in the chair drove a sob from her throat. The thought of deadly smoke creeping up the stairs to endanger Miss Isetta and Miss Varina brought tears to her eyes.

Pugh twisted her arm once more. "Keep quiet."

"Through here," Minor called to Pugh. He was running

along ahead, carrying a feed sack of Rosewood's treasures and the rolled canvas of the Poussin under his arm. The full moon was bright enough for them to see their way without a lantern. He pointed toward a parting of the trees, then disappeared into the shadows.

Pugh pushed Neilly toward the darkness. She stumbled forward, unsteady on her feet with her hands bound behind her back.

"Keep moving," he warned. Over her shoulder, Neilly glimpsed the sword blade flashing in his hand.

She quickened her step. The lawn and the house disappeared behind them. Pugh and Minor seemed to have a plan, a particular destination in mind. They were headed in the direction of the river. She must do something to alter their plans, something to throw them out of step, to rattle them.

In front of her, Minor stopped. Neilly almost ran into him. "Do you hear anything?" he asked Pugh.

Both listened, faces tight, ears turned in the direction of Rosewood.

"Nothing," Pugh said at last. "We'd hear the bell if they'd discovered the fire yet."

"So far we're clear," Minor said. "Let's keep going."

"I don't see the need to rush," Pugh said, turning his narrow pale gaze on Neilly. He dropped a white hand on her shoulder and stroked down her arm.

Neilly shivered and choked back a cry of protest.

"We don't have time for those kinds of games," Minor said. "We brought her along as insurance, not entertainment. Let's go."

Minor led the way deeper into the undergrowth. Neilly followed close on his heels, keeping as much distance between herself and Pugh as she could. Minor was the closest thing to an ally she had at the moment.

The brush pulled at her skirts and the ground had become soggy, soaking through her velvet slippers. They walked a few more minutes in silence, then they broke free of the trees and were standing on the riverbank. Tied to the muddy bank was a small flat boat.

Neilly gazed out across the Mississippi. Never had the river looked so wide and dangerous.

Minor placed the bag of loot in the boat and turned back to Pugh. "Give me the sword."

"No!" Pugh held the blade straight up in the air, as if saluting someone. Then he swung it downward just beyond Neilly's arm, its swift passage stirring tendrils of her hair.

Neilly stood absolutely still, her blood running cold.

"It's well-balanced," Pugh said. "Feels good in my hand. I'd say Old Hickory knew what he was about."

"Yes, well, be that as it may," Minor said, "let's keep on the move. Help me get the boat launched."

"Get in the boat, missie," Pugh ordered.

Neilly hesitated. Stepping into the boat seemed to be leaving behind any chance she might have of escape. She looked back toward the house.

"I said get in."

"Wait a minute. Maybe there is another way to do this," she said, backing away from the riverbank.

Fury contorted Pugh's face. He grabbed Neilly by the waist before she could escape his grasp and swung her into the boat like he might a bag of meal.

Neilly landed on her shoulder in the stinking bilge water in the boat bottom.

The boat rocked as Pugh climbed in behind her. Minor was still on the bank, about to throw the rope to Pugh before climbing in himself.

"Halt."

Neilly scrambled up from the bottom of the boat to catch sight of the owner of the voice.

Damon emerged from the shadows, a pistol in his hand. He was whole and alive. Other than a smudge of something dark on his cheek, he showed no signs of having been burned alive. He looked cool, collected, and angry. Elijah and Dr. McGregor appeared from right behind him.

"You halt," Pugh threw back. "Drop the pistol."

He seized Neilly by the hair and pressed the sword blade against her throat again. The cold blade bit into her flesh.

Damon froze and lowered the pistol to his side. "Look, you've got what you wanted, Pugh. Let Neilly go."

"Get into the boat, Minor. Let's go."

Minor waded into the water and swung a leg into the boat. The edge of the river current caught the craft and pulled it away from the bank.

Pugh tightened his grip on Neilly's hair, forcing her jaw against his chest and wedging his knuckles under her chin.

Neilly saw her chance. She opened her mouth and chomped with all her might on Pugh's sword hand.

A scream erupted. Pugh tried to pull his hand away, but Neilly squeezed her eyes shut and held fast. She ignored the salty taste of blood in her mouth and the metallic smell of steel. She was fighting for her life.

Pugh let go of her hair and tried to push her head away.

He finally tore his hand from her mouth, swinging his arm wide of the boat. His hand trembled. He lost his grip. The sword fell from his grasp into the river.

In the eternal instant that it took to fall from Pugh's hand into the Mississippi, everyone reached for the keepsake.

Minor, with one leg hooked over the side of the boat, thrust both hands out toward it. Pugh knocked Neilly aside to grab with his uninjured hand. The flat-bottom boat wallowed in the water.

Frantically, Neilly leaned as far away from the men as she could, but her weight wasn't enough to counterbalance the unsteady craft.

The boat flipped over. Neilly saw the gunwale rise above her, but she had no way to duck it. She turned her face away. Solid wood thumped against the back of her head. Red pain burst before her eyes. The water closed around her.

* * *

Caught in the river current, the capsized boat drifted toward the center of the river, sinking slowly as it went. Minor bobbed to the surface, like a cork, only a few feet from the bank.

Damon saw no sign of the other two, Pugh or Neilly. He shoved his pistol into McGregor's hand. "I'm going for Neilly. Elijah, you grab whoever you can."

Damon dived into the muddy water, swimming desperately for the spot where the boat had flipped over. With her hands bound, Neilly had no chance of saving herself. He feared that the current would catch her skirts, taking her downriver or, worse yet, snagging her on submerged debris. The river bottom was a forest of old trees, broken branches, and wrecked boats. Damon had little time to find her.

Despite the moonlight, under the water it was impossible to see anything. Damon could only grope along the bottom, grabbing at the mud and the waterlogged driftwood, allowing the current to tow him along as it would have Neilly. Time and time again he had to resurface for breath before diving once more.

He was barely aware that McGregor had captured Minor and now held the agent at gunpoint, and that Elijah had recovered the sword. Without speaking, Elijah joined Damon in the desperate search.

Once Damon grabbed a piece of fabric. Elation thrilled through him, but the cloth ripped free of the dead tree branch, only a rag in his hand. When he got to the surface with it he couldn't tell if it had belonged to Neilly or someone else.

Frustrated, Damon threw the fabric aside and peered downriver, ignoring the ache in his lungs. The river might have pulled Neilly into its current, but she couldn't have gone that far. Between the two of them they would find her. He would think of no other possibility.

Damon moved farther downriver, ahead of Elijah. This time when he went down his foot struck something soft. He reached for it, seizing an arm, small and delicate—still bound and lifeless.

Neilly was there, her skirts caught in some old rigging from the feel of it, some refuse dumped into the river years ago.

There was no time to think about the fact that she didn't react to his touch. His bursting lungs forgotten, he ripped at the tapes of her skirt, leaving it and her petticoats to the waters. Freed, he clutched her to his side and reached for the surface with a powerful, one-arm stroke.

Elijah helped him lift her onto the bank and pull the bindings from her wrist. They worked as quickly as they could, the necessity for speed and action the only thing keeping Damon calm.

"McGregor?" Damon said.

"I'm here, son." The doctor handed the pistol to Elijah, who took up guard duty. McGregor knelt beside Neilly. "She's been under a long time. Taken in a lot of water."

"I know," Damon said. "Tell me what to do."

"That's a mean bump she's got on her head." McGregor took up Neilly's wrist. "There's not much of a pulse beat, but there is a pulse. Turn her over on her stomach. We've got to get as much of that river water out of her as we can."

They worked over Neilly for a long time. Though they managed to force an amazing amount of water from her lungs, her skin remained pallid and her lips blue. Damon wouldn't give up.

Concentrating all his being into bringing Neilly back, Damon followed McGregor's instructions without questions. She could be saved. He was sure of it. He'd seen other drowning victims revived. And he'd seen others die, white and still as Neilly. He renewed his efforts. She wasn't going to die, not Miss Neilly of Rosewood. He wasn't going to let it happen.

At last Neilly's eyelids fluttered ever so slightly.

"I think she's ours," McGregor said, his voice as quiet as ever, but Damon glanced at the doctor to see the victory in his face. "The pulse is back. She's going to need warmth now, and rest. We need blankets."

Damon hardly heard McGregor. He gathered Neilly into his arms and held her close.

"I'll get some blankets." McGregor got to his feet.

Neilly stirred, a reassuring resistance to Damon's embrace. Her eyes opened slowly. He held her a little tighter.

She whispered something, so hoarse and soft that Damon couldn't understand her at first. "What are you saying?"

"Where's the Poussin?"

Damon cursed. "It's here somewhere. Minor has it, I think. Elijah found the sword. But I don't give a damn about that. You're what's important."

"The house?" Neilly choked, but that didn't stop her from asking her question. "The fire. What about Rosewood?"

"The house is fine," Damon said. "Cato had the fire under control when I left. But the entry hall is going to need repainting. Maybe you could do that."

Neilly said no more, but rested against Damon's chest, her breathing light but wonderfully steady. A tiny hint of pink was seeping back into her skin. Damon closed his eyes, and for the first time in years he truly thanked heaven for a miracle.

"You know, darlin', I think we ought to get married," Damon said, letting the idea he'd contemplated for several days escape for the first time. "You could stay at Rosewood forever and make all the lists you want."

Neilly said nothing. He looked into her face, but her expression was unfathomable.

"I think our marriage would make Aunt Isetta and Aunt

Varina very happy," he added. Mention of his aunts always seemed to sway Neilly's decisions.

Immediately she struggled against him, pushing herself away with amazing strength for a woman just returned from the dead.

"No," she managed to whisper. "As much as I love Isetta and Varina, even love Rosewood and . . . as much as I love you, Damon Durande, I'm not getting married for your aunts' sakes."

In a fit of choking, Neilly sank against him again, her energy obviously gone. Damon sat still, wondering at her words. She'd refused him. Refused marriage. But she'd said she loved him. He'd heard her correctly, hadn't he? She *loved* him.

The coughing subsided. "Damon?" She sounded weak and uncertain.

"Yes, darlin'?"

"I think I'm going to be sick."

Damon could feel the retching begin. He held her over the riverbank and rubbed her back while she choked up more Mississippi water.

Disappointed as he was, he held her tight and stroked the wet hair away from her face. He decided it was a matter of timing. Right after a near drowning probably wasn't the best moment to ask the woman you loved to marry you.

Twenty-four

In the weeks that followed Pugh's betrayal and Minor's theft, Neilly suffered from nightmares. Suffocating blackness closed over her head. She strained against the drapery cord cinched around her wrists. With all her might she kicked at her heavy skirts. But there was no resisting the strength of the current. It roared in her ears and stung her throat. It sucked her away into the cold beyond.

She awoke in the darkness with the sheets damp and tangled around her limbs and the house dark and quiet. Sometimes Varina was there to talk to her, and sometimes Cleo calmed her.

But in the warm, light afternoon hours, Damon filled her dreams, his hands broad and strong, snatching her away from danger. The cold slipped away and he caressed her, warm and glowing to the brink of pleasure.

She awoke safe, alone in her room, feeling just a little disappointed, and a little embarrassed by the intimacy of the images that she didn't dare share with Varina or Cleo.

The first couple of days following the horror in the river were hazy for Neilly, but she remembered Isetta coming in a few times with Dr. McGregor at her side. Her face was stern as always, and her voice imperative.

"Your color is improving, Neilly, dear," Isetta said. "Theo says so, and I can see it myself. Be quick about it, girl. We have something to tell you."

Neilly remembered something else, too. She remembered

that Damon had asked her to marry him on the riverbank, and she'd said no. She had no regrets about the decision, but she was sorry that Damon had made the proposal, because it meant that things couldn't go on as they had before he'd offered. Her employment would no longer be a simple matter of a companion working off a loan and caring for his aunts.

Tempting as his offer was, she wasn't going to marry Damon for the convenience of satisfying his aunts and becoming housekeeper of Rosewood. She loved Isetta and Varina and she'd stay at the plantation forever if circumstances were different. But she'd find another way to take care of her debt.

Damon did visit her, usually with Varina at his side. He said little, allowing Varina to babble on about the garden and Arthur's departure. She'd missed saying farewell to Arthur and Vincent, Varina told her. No loss, Damon commented. The Sitwells had left as soon as the sheriff determined that they'd had nothing to do with the thefts or bringing Minor into the house. The sheriff had also concluded that there was little chance of ever recovering Pugh's body.

Damon had touched her hand and squeezed it reassuringly, and Neilly, in her weakened, emotional state, shed tears of relief.

She wanted to return to her duties as soon as she could, but her strength returned more slowly than she'd expected.

The first day she ventured downstairs—a day sooner than Dr. McGregor had recommended—she found Elijah working on the doorframe of the library. Her knees gave way when she saw the hallway.

The blackened entry walls had been scraped of the charred paper and the brick floor had been swept since the fire. New, unpainted wood molding framed the drawing-room door, but nothing had been done to the walls.

Neilly grabbed the stair rail with both hands and sat down on the steps before she fell. Gone were the delightful birds of the jungle, the exotic flowers, the chattering monkeys and the glowering lions. The loss almost brought tears to her eyes.

Elijah laid down his tools. "You all right, Miss Neilly?"

"Yes," Neilly said, "It's just so sad to see the hallway like this."

"Yeas, miss," Elijah agreed. "But we was lucky, you know. Only scorched the wallpaper. Rosewood is as solid as ever."

"Yes, we were lucky," Neilly said. She'd lived through another crisis. Damon knew she wasn't the thief. "But I miss all the animals."

"I know," Elijah grinned, but not as wide as usual. "Especially those lions. Rosewood won't be the same without the lions at the door."

The front door burst open. A gust of new energy swooped through the hallway. Damon strode in, a smile lighting his face when he saw her. "Neilly, what are you doing down here, sitting on the steps?"

"I was just telling Elijah what a shame it is about the damage in the hallway."

Damon came to stand directly in front of her. "You look well, darlin'."

"I feel all right."

"Well enough to receive a visitor?"

"Who wants to see me?" Neilly asked, old habitual fears rising to the surface.

Damon smiled and leaned close. "I think you're going to like this visitor. Rushed here on a special charter."

"Oh, no," Neilly groaned. She would have turned to run up the stairs if Damon hadn't taken her by the arm and led her to the door. Still, she hung back as she watched a white-haired gentleman slowly march up the steps of Rosewood.

He smiled when he saw Neilly and took off his hat. "Cornelia, my dear," he greeted. "I'm so glad to see you well and safe, in Louisiana of all places."

Neilly forgot her fear and stepped forward to welcome her father's old friend and Charleston attorney. "Mr. Erskine Smith, whatever brings you all the way to Rosewood?"

"Why, you, of course," he said with a charming grin. His Irish blue eyes twinkled. "I have good news for you."

Varina appeared on the other side of Damon. "Invite our guest in, dear. Come in, sir. Come in and rest from your long journey and enjoy a little of Louisiana's hospitality."

As Neilly stepped back so Varina, Rosewood's hostess, could usher Mr. Smith into the house, she realized Varina was blushing like a schoolgirl. Mr. Smith's eyes had brightened with undisguised interest in his hostess. When introductions were made he held Miss Varina's hand a little longer than necessary. Neilly remembered that Mr. Smith was a widower of some years.

When they were settled in the library Mr. Smith got right down to business. He requested to see Elijah Freeman, as well as Cornelia Lind Carpenter.

"You see," Mr. Smith began to explain, once he had spread out his papers on Damon's desk and settled his spectacles on his nose, "there was a reward for the apprehension of one John Minorwitz, a dealer in stolen artwork and such."

"A reward?" Neilly repeated, not quite understanding.

"Yes, the Ruffin family was much embarrassed by the unfortunate affair with . . ." Mr. Smith cleared his throat and looked around the room at Neilly, Varina, Damon, and Elijah.

"That's all right," Neilly said. "There are no secrets here."

To her surprise, Damon came to stand behind her chair. "That's right," he said. "You were saying Charles Ruffin and his family offered a reward—for what?"

"For the apprehension of the others involved in the affair with Neilly's father," Mr. Smith continued. "They knew Dr. Carpenter hadn't acted alone. So they offered a reward for your father's co-conspirators. That was John Minorwitz who left the state about the time you and your family returned from Europe."

"I never knew about any of this," Neilly said. "Why hadn't someone turned him in before no?"

"He hadn't done anything in Louisiana that anyone could prove," Mr. Smith said. "I've already talked to the sheriff. Even if he has, most collectors are too embarrassed to admit to being duped."

I suppose," Neilly said, remembering how carefully the Ruffins had used their power and influence to make certain no one knew about what her father had stolen from them.

"The sheriff says you, Cornelia, and Mr. Elijah Freeman were the ones who apprehended John Minorwitz; therefore you are the recipients of the reward."

Neilly turned to Damon. "Is this so?"

Damon shrugged.

"I didn't do nothing I wouldn't have done anyway," Elijah protested.

"Nevertheless, the money is yours, sir," Mr. Smith said. "I have the bank draft here. You know how to use a bank draft?"

"Yes, sir," Elijah said. "Thank yah, sah."

"Congratulations, Elijah. This is the money you needed, isn't it?" Varina said.

"Yeas, Miss Varina, it was the money I needed," Elijah said. "But I don't need it now."

Neilly, Damon, and Varina exchanged puzzled glances.

"Why? We thought you and Alma—oh dear, did something happen?" Neilly asked.

"Alma done married the blacksmith over at Esterbrooks," Elijah said, his broad shoulders slumping ever so slightly. "Only thing I can do with this money is go away. I was thinking about Texas."

"Lots of work for a good carpenter," Damon said. "I'd

hate to see you go, Elijah, but I'll give you a letter of reference if you want it."

"Yeas, sah, I'd appreciate that," Elijah said, taking the draft. "Thank yah, sah, Mr. Smith."

When Elijah had left the library Mr. Smith turned to Neilly. "Cornelia, here is your bank draft. I understand your father's debt to the Ruffins was paid off."

"Yes, it is now," Neilly said, taking the piece of paper that meant freedom for her.

"It's as simple as that," Mr. Smith said. "I haven't had as pleasant a mission to carry out in some years."

"Well, if that finishes your business, sir," Varina began, "then you must take some refreshment with us. Perhaps you'll have some lemonade on the gallery with me."

"I'd be delighted," Mr. Smith said, taking Varina by the arm she offered.

"You will stay with us a few days, won't you, Mr. Smith?" Varina said. "We so enjoy company at Rosewood."

"Why, I think I might just do that," Mr. Smith said as he closed the door of the library behind him.

"This pays off my debt," Neilly said, holding the paper up for him to see.

"There's nothing to discuss about the debt," Damon said, his tone a little too sharp. He clasped his hands behind his back, refusing to take the piece of paper from her. "Forget about it. Come out to the stable with me and see the new colt. He's come a little late in the year, but he's got good bloodlines."

"No," Neilly said, afraid to spend any more time in Damon's company now that she knew what she must do. "Thank you, but I have things to tend to."

The commotion began upstairs. Damon paid it little heed at first, but it traveled down the stairs and finally came to a halt outside the library door. He could hear Isetta and

Varina arguing over something. He tried to ignore the distraction; he wanted to finish closing out the books for the month. He was also trying to think of some way to tactfully make it clear to Neilly that her debt was not to be an issue between them. Her pride would make the task difficult.

Isetta burst into the library, her lace cap askew and its ribbons aflutter. "Damon, we need you out here, please."

"Aunt Isetta, I'll be there in a few minutes," Damon said. "I'd like to finish this calculation."

"Damon, we need you now," Isetta said. Becoming a married lady had not softened her imperious tone.

Varina burst in behind her sister. "Oh, Damon, Neilly has packed her bags. She's leaving."

"Leaving?" Damon stuck the quill pen back in the inkstand and got to his feet.

Varina and Isetta scattered from his path as he strode out the door; then his aunts fell in behind him. In the hall he found Neilly setting her traveling bonnet on her head.

"I'm signing the bank draft over to you," she said. "It's there on the table. Our debt is settled and I proved I'm not a thief. You're free to go back to Texas."

"Oh, you're not going back to Texas, are you, Damon?" Varina cried.

"I don't feel well," Isetta began, clutching at her chest.

"Oh, Izzie, do stop it," Varina snapped. "I want to hear what Damon and Neilly are going to do."

"I think Neilly and I have some things to discuss before anyone makes any big decisions," Damon said.

Neilly said nothing.

"Talk in the drawing room," Isetta suggested, opening the door. "You won't be disturbed in there."

The fire had done less damage in the drawing room than in the hallway. The lemon-colored sofa and the Oriental carpet were gone, but Thomas Stirling's portrait looked down upon them, and the Lafayette clock ticked the minutes away. Damon glared back at his grandfather for a moment, then decided the task at hand was more important than Grandfather's glower.

"Neilly, I've not handled this well," he began.

"It has been a trying situation," Neilly said. "You were right in the beginning in guessing that I wasn't telling the truth."

"That's beside the point," Damon said. "I realize now that telling a lie and being a liar are two different things. I should have known from the way you cared for Aunt Isetta—I should have known from what happened in the cellar that you were honest. That you were courageous and loyal and loving."

"We don't need to go into this now," Neilly said. "Everything is settled."

"No, it's not," Damon said. "I asked you to marry me, and I admit my timing was bad. I'm asking you again, now. Don't say anything. Stay. Take some time to think about it. I don't understand why you are rushing off."

"Damon, I can't marry a man who doesn't believe in me," Neilly said. She held up her hand to stop him from jumping in with his own defense. "Let me finish. I do think you know me better now, but there's more. I can't marry a man who has chosen to wed because his aunts have been matchmaking."

Damon blinked at her. That was not the response he had expected to hear. "You think I'm doing this because of them?"

The door rattled on its latch; Damon thought he heard someone murmuring. He stepped closer to Neilly. No need for everyone in the house to hear what was meant for Neilly's ears alone. He took both her hands in his. She allowed him.

"You said as much on the riverbank."

"I only thought to persuade you," Damon said. "Aunt Isetta and Aunt Varina mean well, but I've always made my own decisions about my life. You know that."

"I believe you have, until now." Neilly ducked her head.

"Nothing changes that now," Damon said. "It pleases me to think of you as my wife. It pleases me to think of a life shared, here with you at Rosewood. You can't know how much it pleased me when you said you loved me. You did say that."

"I'd just been delivered from drowning," Neilly said with a huff. "I was grateful."

"All right, you're the proud one," Damon said. "Not me. Marry me out of gratitude." Damon leaned close to her ear. "I'll make you love me in time, my little wanton."

"You are so arrogant." Neilly laughed but shook her head. "Why do you wish to marry me? Because I'm courageous, loyal, and loving? Because you need someone to help you with Rosewood? That's not enough, Damon."

He recognized the bait. He knew he had to walk into this ambush unarmed and vulnerable. He had to trust Neilly. "I want you to marry me because I love you."

Neilly's head came up slowly. His heart beat faster with elation. He'd said the right thing. He could see it in her eyes, but she needed more. And she deserved it.

"I love you because of what happens when we're together," Damon said. "Because the sun is brighter when you smile at me. Because the house is more welcoming when you walk through it. Because I'm good, darlin', but when I'm with you I'm better—or at least I like trying to be."

Neilly didn't say anything. She just held his gaze, her blue eyes searching his for confirmation.

"You trust me with your heart?" Neilly asked.

"Yes," Damon said, with all his heart.

"You know I already gave you mine," Neilly said.

"I know," Damon said. "In the cellar, and it scared the living daylights out of me. No one has ever given me anything so precious."

"It's frightening, isn't it? Loving like that," Neilly agreed. "Well then, I think we should marry, don't you?"

"You're saying yes?" Damon said, almost afraid to believe what he'd heard her say.

"Yes, I think so." Neilly smiled. "Definitely yes."

Damon took her by the shoulders and kissed her. "Yes. Right away. Unpack your bags. I don't want to see anyone going anywhere for a long time."

Again muffled whispers reached them from beyond the drawing-room doors.

"We really should deliver your aunts from their misery," Neilly said after the next kiss.

"Let them wait just a little longer," Damon said and captured Neilly's mouth again.

Epilogue

The day of the wedding everything and everyone at Rosewood was in a state.

Varina had decorated each room of the house with glorious roses. Mammy Lula was at her finest. She'd started cooking two days before, baking dishes that would make the neighbors wonder if their imported chefs were worth the trouble. Uncle Cato and Cleo graciously served trays of champagne and food.

The stables were full of the fine horses of the wedding guests, who'd traveled from far and wide. Expectation hung over the crowd. Everyone of them had heard about Dr. McGregor and Miss Isetta Stirling's quiet wedding last month, and most were feeling cheated because they had not been invited. Not a soul in the neighborhood intended to miss the nuptials of Damon Durande and Miss Cornelia Ashley Carpenter—of the Carolinian Ashleys.

The day had dawned bright, clear, and perfect for a late summer wedding, but Varina had discovered something amiss in the redecorated drawing room. She'd gone to fetch her sister. Isetta had to see for herself.

"What is it, Sister?" Isetta asked, following Varina into the room. A new Oriental carpet covered the floorboards and a blue Empire sofa had replaced the yellow one. The gallery doors had been closed to keep guests out—until the wedding supper was served, at least.

In the center of the room, Varina whirled around to confront her sister. "Do you see anything missing?"

"This is no time for games, Varina," Isetta said, folding her hands across her waist. "The room looks perfect, dear, if that's what you want to hear. Now Neilly is almost ready to come down. She looks more beautiful than ever."

"But something important is missing," Varina insisted. She couldn't believe that Isetta hadn't seen it as quickly as she had. "Look at Papa's portrait."

Isetta looked, then frowned. "Where is Papa's silver cup?"

"I don't know," Varina said. "I polished it this morning. When I came in here to arrange the flowers later it was gone."

The color drained from Izzie's face.

"Sit down, Sister," Varina said. "Should I go fetch Theo?"

"No, no." Isetta waved Varina away.

"You were looking for a sign that giving Rosewood to Damon as a wedding gift was the right thing to do," Varina said. "Papa's missing cup must mean something."

"It can't mean anything good," Isetta said.

"Then what should we do?"

"Nothing." Isetta pulled an envelope from her sleeve. She looked up at Thomas Stirling and shook the envelope and its contents at the portrait. "I've already signed the papers over to Damon, Papa. I've signed Rosewood over to your firstborn grandson. If you come after me, you'll find me at Acorn Hill, living happily with my husband. But don't you dare mar this day for Neilly and Damon."

Varina swallowed her gasp. "Oh, Izzie, I think it's bad luck to dare Papa."

"I'm not daring him; I'm just telling him to mind his manners," Isetta said. "Today is Neilly and Damon's day, and I won't have anyone spoil it, not even you, Papa."

Murmurs of delight greeted Neilly as she started down the garden path on Erskine Smith's arm. Guests filled every chair set in the rose garden, and the late arrivals stood crowded along the hedges. Face after face smiled approval at her.

A blush heated her face. The attention was embarrassing. She'd begged Damon for a small wedding, a quiet one like Isetta and Theo's. But Isetta and Damon had started planning the affair, and the next thing she knew their wedding had become the event of the parish social scene. She was thankful for the antique lace veiling her face. When she glanced at Erskine he patted her hand and smiled reassurance at her.

"Your father would be proud, Cornelia," he murmured. "Hold your head up and take joy in this day. Surely you're the prettiest bride these Louisiana folks have seen in a score of years, girl."

Neilly smiled at him and took his advice.

Damon waited for her at the rose arbor. A hint of his lopsided grin played across his lips and made Neilly's heart flutter in that old startling way. In his black frock coat and black Hessian boots he looked calm and confident, if just a little impatient. Theo stood at his side as best man.

Damon looked perfectly at home in his shining black footwear, but Neilly suspected he'd still like her wedding gift. She'd gotten Rene LaBeau to send her a pair of fringed Indian boots from the New Orleans market.

When she reached the arbor where Reverend Blakely awaited her she handed her bouquet of Varina's roses to her matron of honor, Isetta. The ceremony began.

Their vows were exchanged without a snag. Neilly didn't stammer or cry, as she thought she might. Damon said his vows in a loud, clear voice everyone could hear. With a steady hand he slipped the diamond-studded wedding band on her finger.

The hint of a grin on his face turned into the real thing. He lifted her veil, gathered her into his arms, and bent to kiss her before the reverend gave his permission.

The guests laughed and applauded.

Damon's lips moved over hers, firm and demanding, possessive and loving. When he released Neilly she could only stare up at him in wonder. She saw no wounded little boy in the man who stood beside her. She saw a man as willing to give his heart as he was to accept hers.

Then they were swamped by well-wishers.

"It's done now," Varina whispered in triumph, kissing Neilly's cheek.

"So far, so good," Izzie agreed, nearly strangling Neilly in a hearty embrace.

Neilly felt that somehow she'd lost control of the day that was supposed to be hers and Damon's.

Fine champagne flowed—the kind Neilly favored—and guests gathered around to congratulate the bride and groom before taking their places at the banquet table.

At last the chairs at the table were filled and the guests fell silent as Damon rose from his place next to his bride.

He reached for the cup that had been filled with champagne and awaited him on the table. He lifted it into the air. A hush fell over the guests. "I'd like to make a toast to my bride."

Neilly saw Varina's mouth drop open at the sight of the cup. She glanced across at Isetta, who also stared at the silver goblet. Neilly looked at it again and realized that it was Thomas Stirling's silver goblet, the one that always stood beneath the patriarch's portrait in the drawing room.

She glanced at Damon and saw that in the exhilaration of the moment he had not recognized the cup.

"Izzie, did you put it there?" Varina mouthed at her sister.

Isetta, who looked absolutely astonished, shook her head. Uncle Cato passed by. Varina caught his sleeve and asked him about the cup.

Cato shook his head. "It was jis' there when I comes in to fill the waterglasses," Uncle Cato murmured in her ear.

"And, Miss Varina, it was already filled with chilled champagne."

The three women stared across the table at each other. Neilly didn't believe in ghosts, but there seemed only one way the cup could have gotten there: Thomas Stirling.

"It's Papa's blessing," Varina whispered, her relief written on her plump face. She looked across the table once more at Isetta and lifted her own glass. Isetta lifted hers, too.

Damon smiled at his bride, then at the wedding guests. "When Miss Cornelia, or Miss Neilly, came into my life, I had pretty much decided that marriage wasn't for me. I liked fighting Indians in Texas. Plenty of action and excitement. No worries about sugar prices or high water."

The planters and their wives chuckled.

"I wasn't going to have some pretty miss dressing me up in a suit coat and stiff collar and leading me around by the nose."

Neilly blushed. The wedding guests laughed again, especially the men, she noted.

"But she began to lure me with the comforts of home," Damon continued. "Clean sheets and hot water. Good food and warm company. I'm not a soft man, but a little luxury can give a man a new view of his existence."

Some of the guests nodded, mostly the men again.

"Still, I wasn't won over yet," Damon said with a rueful smile in Neilly's direction. "Then, with Neilly's help, I began to rediscover the beauty of Rosewood and, more importantly, to understand the value of the people around me. Life in a fine house began to have an appeal."

"Come on, Durande," someone from the foot of the table called. "There isn't a gentleman here who can look at your beautiful bride and believe you married her to be your housekeeper."

Everyone laughed. Damon, too.

"All right, I'll get to the point," Damon said, good-naturedly. "I married Neilly because she brought me home to family. But more than that, she makes me want to stay."

Varina wiped away a happy tear. Across the table, Izzie was sniffing into her handkerchief.

Damon lifted the silver cup in Neilly's direction. She smiled and held up her glass so they could twine their arms to sip the toast.

"To forever, darlin'," Damon said, sipping at last from his grandfather's cup.

About the Author

Linda Madl lives with her family in Leavenworth, Kansas. BAYOU ROSE is her fifth historical romance. She is currently working on her next Zebra historical romance, which will be published in April 1997. Linda loves hearing from her readers and you may write to her c/o Zebra Books. Please include a self-addressed stamped envelope if you wish a response.

JANELLE TAYLOR

ZEBRA'S BEST-SELLING AUTHOR

DON'T MISS ANY OF HER
EXCEPTIONAL, EXHILARATING, EXCITING

ECSTASY SERIES